*Books by Paul Griner*

COLLECTORS

FOLLOW ME

THE GERMAN WOMAN

*The*

# GERMAN WOMAN

## PAUL GRINER

MARINER BOOKS
HOUGHTON MIFFLIN HARCOURT
BOSTON   NEW YORK

First Mariner Books edition 2010

Copyright © 2009 by Paul Griner

www.hmhbooks.com

*Library of Congress Cataloging-in-Publication Data*
Griner, Paul.
The German woman / Paul Griner.
p. cm.
ISBN 978-0-547-05522-0
1. Man-woman relationships—Fiction. 2. Cinematographers—Fiction.
3. Spies—Fiction. 4. World War, 1914–1918—Fiction.
5. World War, 1939–1945—Fiction. 6. Patriotism—Fiction.
7. Loyalty—Fiction. 8. Historical fiction. I. Title.
PS3557.R5314G47 2009
813'.54—dc22    2008053286
ISBN 978-0-547-33606-0 (pbk.)

*Book design by Brian Moore*

Printed in the United States of America

DOM 10 9 8 7 6 5 4 3 2 1

IN MEMORY OF
*Miriam Griner and Virginia Mahan,*
*deeply loved and greatly missed*


AND FOR
*Kerry, Trevor, and Tristan: the sun, moon,*
*and stars of our little solar system*

If I had to choose between betraying my country and betraying my friend, I hope I should have the guts to betray my country.

—E. M. FORSTER

# ACKNOWLEDGMENTS

My editor, Anjali Singh, helped me discover the real novel inside my manuscript, with a deft touch, smart questions, and excellent suggestions. It's a much better book because of her. Nicole Aragi continues to be an agent without peer, a wonderful reader, friend, and advocate. Chris Kennedy, as always, made early and helpful suggestions, and Anna Klobucka, Chris Fox, Kathryn Griner, Austin Bunn, and Rob Terry helped as the book moved along. My father answered endless medical questions with great care and detail, a further sign of his longtime support. To all, a profound thanks. And to my wife, Anne: without you, this book wouldn't exist, nor would I awake each day feeling the luckiest man on earth.

# PART I

# WILNO, EAST PRUSSIA, JANUARY 5, 1919

JOSEF WAS BEING DIFFICULT; he wanted Kate to stay. After marking his temperature, she let the chart fall against the brass bed frame and tucked her cold fingers under her smock. "There *are* only a few patients here," she said, "but I'm afraid I can't read to you. You're forgetting I have others to care for in isolation."

Josef smiled and patted the bed. "Sit here and tell me about them, *Nurse Zweig.*"

She sighed, her exasperation both mock and real. He was a child, really, and his youthful enthusiasm was infectious, but it was late and she was tired and he, even more than she, needed sleep. She had come only to check on him and to change his bandages. "Father Thomas is on night duty. Perhaps he can read to you."

"Very funny." Josef's breath smoked in the frigid air. "Whistle, perhaps, but not read. Now come closer." She did, because she had to, and he dropped his head. "Do you see?"

In the lamplight his ghastly purple wound looked infected. A shell splinter had pierced his helmet and ripped a furrow across his skull, tearing away skin and muscle and bone, and now the exposed brain pulsed with the beating of his heart.

"Look closely," he said. "You'll see an image of a beautiful nurse. My own personal stigmata! You're all I've been thinking about this evening. And if I could see your brain, I'm sure I'd see an image of me."

She stilled his heavy head with her palm and raised the lamp, scrutinizing the throbbing brain before bending to sniff it. Nothing, save perhaps a faint lingering odor of rancid lamp oil, but no infec-

3

tion; she realized she'd been holding her breath only when she felt herself exhale.

"I've told you." She lowered the lamp to the bedside table. "All I can see is healthy new pink skin and a few words about President Wilson."

Which was the truth, or a version of it. Josef had arrived with his wound dressed in newspaper held in place by a boot string, and some of the reversed newsprint still showed on the uncovered tissue. So far, the wound's only adverse effect had been a series of nighttime seizures, pronounced enough to rattle his bed, and she was glad that they'd stopped, that she no longer had to restrain him, though the raw wound on one so young distressed her. But the dura was slowly regenerating, and soon he would be ready for the insertion of a metal plate.

She changed the bandage on his arm, using a crisp new Austrian army armband in place of the old linens, and scolded him again for his foolishness. Josef and another boy, hearing a shell fly over their trench and explode, had argued over how far away it was. The other boy had said ten meters, Josef thirty, and Josef had decided to pace it off. The second shell came over while he was measuring.

"I was right, though," Josef said, smiling, as Kate pinned the brassard tightly above his biceps. "I'd got to twenty-two before the second one hit. And the greater fool was Krilnik. He stayed behind and was hit by the mortar. I scraped him up with a spoon and buried him in a tin pot."

The brassard's imperial black eagles flinched when Josef clenched his fist. He watched them and said, "Stupid Pole."

"I thought you were a Pole," Kate said.

"Yes, of course. But a Lithuanian Pole."

"Ah, I see. I hadn't realized there was such a difference."

"You needn't play dumb with me," Josef said. "All the world knows there is."

It pained her to think of the future he would inherit, even more to imagine the future he and other young soldiers—creations of the recent past—might construct.

The tin roof vibrated in the buffeting wind, moaning like a violin, and her eye followed the noise down the length of the ward. Rubber hot-water bottles hung from the rafters, and copper pots boiled atop the brick stoves. Once again they had a small supply of coal for the stoves—like the armbands, it was an unexpected gift from an unexplained source—and on a brutally cold night like tonight that would keep the patients alive, but the steam was melting ice that had formed on the ceiling and she would have to push beds aside to keep patients dry.

She was about to go when Josef pinched her sleeve between his bony fingers, not wanting to be left alone. She couldn't blame him; a line of folded-over mattresses and piled clean linens stretched into the darkness beyond the few other patients on the ward, all of whom were sleeping, and the lack of human voices made their presence seem an oddity, but she couldn't stay; she was tired, she had other patients to attend to, she was afraid and didn't want her fear to show.

The approach of Father Thomas spared her the embarrassment of pulling her arm free. Their other orderlies had either deserted or been moved north and west during the past months to staff new British hospitals along the fluctuating front—victors in the recent war, the English now told the German army and its field hospitals what to do—but Father Thomas had argued that his throat wound should keep him behind. Not from fear, Kate knew; it was because he didn't want to abandon them. A hinged metal pipe inserted into a hole cut in his throat, held in place by surgical tape and a small paper disk, its opening covered by a square of sterile muslin; he would have looked ecclesiastical with all that white at his throat even if he hadn't been a priest.

He entered the circle of lamplight, air clicking and whistling through the pipe as he walked, and gestured that he'd watch over Josef and move the beds.

"Thank you," Kate said.

*No,* he signed, *thank you.*

She looked puzzled and he made the sign for a plate, breathing deeply in appreciation, his pipe whistling.

"Ah, yes," she said, understanding. Supper. "The eggs were good, weren't they?" She decided not to tell him that, lacking lard, she'd had to cook them in Vaseline. Their newfound supplies, though bountiful, were a bizarre mixture of the practical and the useless.

As he bent over, his crucifix swung free, nearly striking Josef's chin, and Josef swatted it away. "Don't bless me, Father," he said, "I haven't sinned." He smiled with youthful pleasure at his joke.

*Here, then,* Father Thomas signed, removing his crucifix and giving it to Josef. *Take this.*

"What? Why?"

Kate translated his signs: *Those who feel they're without sin are in the greatest danger of all.*

Josef made a face but slipped the chain around his neck too quickly to be anything but pleased. Father Thomas folded his hand over Josef's, and Kate squeezed Josef's other hand before dropping it and hurrying off, briefly elated by her certainty that Josef would be fine. But her own echoing footsteps down the long empty ward discomfited her.

At least during the war she'd known what to hope for, and her fears, though deep, had been mostly dormant. They'd waited years for peace, and when it had finally come they'd celebrated even in defeat—a last saved bottle of plum brandy—and yet now they were waiting once again, though she couldn't say with any certainty for what.

Even before the Armistice, they'd lived through outbreaks of civil war in Germany, Russia, Poland, and the Ukraine, and in the months since they'd moved their hospital a half a dozen times to either escape from or assist in a series of seemingly never-ending engagements, all at the behest of their new English masters; Germans and Poles versus Russians, Germans against bandits, Germans versus Poles, Poles and Germans versus Russians again, White Russians against Ukrainians. Now the British were standing aside while the White Russians battled the Red ones, both armies appearing in an area that for five hundred years had been Prussian but that, rumor had it, would soon be Polish. President Wilson and his Fourteen Points; she supposed she should be grateful.

But as she made her way to the sterilization room she found herself almost wishing for war. If over time the war's aims had grown obscure, its sides had always been clear, and though it seemed blasphemous to think so, she missed that clarity, that sense of impermeable boundaries. Now, with each switch of engagements, their loyalties grew more tangled, their duties less obvious, their danger greater.

She pushed open the squeaking door, ashamed that she could wish such a thing, but even so wishing it still.

The scalpels and lancets, the saws and clamps and retractors clinked in the boiling water, and Kate stood entranced before the kettle, hypnotized by the chains of tiny rising bubbles, her chest and stomach warm, her sore legs and sorer back freezing. It had been weeks since they'd had sufficient coal to properly sterilize their instruments; that they had it now was troubling.

For days refugees had trudged westward through Wilno, the easternmost outpost of the former German empire, ahead of distant ongoing battles: peasant families and single elderly men and women and stray children, trailing their overloaded carts and toboggans, dumping clothes and dinner plates and leather-bound books, bottles of perfume and spare shoes, occasionally even jewelry; the snowy roads were difficult to pass. No dead infants this time, which was a relief. The civilians were followed by clumps of beaten soldiers and the rare dispirited officer, resplendent in tattered red or blue; then, yesterday, by a few last lame stragglers and the milk carrier's blind nag, spooked and unattended.

Exactly where the fighting was remained unclear; somewhere in the vast east there were disturbances. They had no telephones, their newspapers were dated, they'd received no orders for nearly a month, and the straggling soldiers had been a motley assortment of Poles, Galicians, and Lithuanians, though the refugees—when Kate could get them to talk—had spoken of Russians, both White and Red. Neither she nor Horst nor Father Thomas could make sense of it.

Standing in the hospital doorway, watching the near-silent procession pass—stamping feet, creaking wheels, and an occasional death groan the only sounds in an otherwise unworldly hush—she'd given to the dispirited beggars all they could afford: socks and wraps and aspirin tablets, hoping those would tide them over until they found shelter and food. Of their own dwindling, meager stores of smoked meat and dried beans, they could spare nothing. She doubted it mattered. The people seemed more shadowlike than human, a procession of the soon-to-be dead, and what really scared her was what might follow in their wake, the first sign of which had been a pack of mangy dogs eyeing her as she stood outside the hospital. Had a soldier not shot one, she was certain they all would have attacked.

Then, late this afternoon, just before daylight faded, three ambulances had rumbled into the hospital compound. Though she'd feared they foretold new arrivals for whom there'd be little food and less medicine, Kate had gone to meet them, yet before she was halfway there, the drivers had run to the hospital's truck, climbed in, and taken off. She had no idea who they were or where they'd gone or what had caused their panic, or why, if they were fleeing, they'd fled their own rides. The ambulances themselves were equally mysterious.

One held eggs and the brassards, ink and coal and a few yards of fresh white muslin, which she'd immediately been grateful for and scooped up; the second held stacks of small wooden boxes and, of all things, a piano; and the third a jumbled load of larger crates covered with Cyrillic writing. She couldn't read it and didn't have time to pry the boxes open, as surgery was scheduled and she had wounded to care for, so she'd hurried back to tell Horst of their strange luck, feeling a mixture of joy at their newfound riches and fear that the riches were tainted. Now, warming herself in the sterilization room, knowing that she should look into the crates and boxes, she felt dread. Their contents might be a blessing, but their appearance could only be a curse; someone had almost certainly stolen them, which meant that someone else would just as certainly be searching them out.

She removed the last of the instruments from the water, steaming in the frozen air, and patted them dry on piled muslin beside two sterilized pipes for Father Thomas's throat. The moon was up, fat and low and orange, rising toward swift-moving clouds, the ambulances gleaming beneath it. Beyond them the unplanted fields were deep with snow and dimpled with rifle pits, a skeleton showing in one. Months before she and Horst and the rest of the hospital had arrived, there had been a skirmish in an abrupt, short-lived civil war; in its aftermath the retreating Polish Reds had left behind their dead, and though the local peasants had buried all the others they'd refused to touch this one because of the sacrilegious nature of his death: he'd cut down a roadside cross to make a fire, which had spread to his coat, and, panicked at finding himself on fire, he'd fallen on his own bayonet. The peasants maintained it was a sign from God.

She'd seen too much these past years to credit a selectively vengeful God, but it was no use telling herself she didn't believe in superstitions; others' certainty in them proved stronger than her doubts. As often as she'd started out to the cold cabbage field to bury him, bayonet glinting at his atlas vertebra, she'd always turned back on some pretext or another: instruments to clean, patients to attend to, the necessity of sleep, a fear that the frozen ground would be unyielding. Tonight she turned away once more, grateful for the rare warmth of the ward, not liking to be out on a night when the village was deserted except for his silent watching form; he and the abandoned ambulances would be easier to face in the morning, when the ambulances at least might be of use.

Horst sat leaning over the official army forms, the paper seeming to glow in the lamplight. Kate set his bag of surgical instruments by a pile of red-leather-bound books she'd recovered from beside the refugee track and wrinkled her nose at the rancid air.

"Sorry," he said, and nodded at a bottle on the stove. "Scorched ink. I let it freeze. We'd been so long without it that I forgot, and then I overcooked it. How's our miracle boy?"

"Fine." She laughed, recalling Josef. "Flirtatious."

"Ah, yes. The romance with the nurse. You're the epitome of every boy's dream, beautiful, charming, and uniformed." His blistered lips shone with oil.

She bent over his shoulder and locked her hands across his chest. His blond hair smelled clean, a way it hadn't in weeks. The coal, again. She'd meant to bathe herself but was too tired; she hoped he wouldn't mind. "Was the loose nurse your dream?"

"Never. You forget I'd seen them around my father, which inspired fear, not desire. Too handy with a scalpel and an enema for my tastes."

"And yet you married one."

"The triumph of hope over experience. And as you well know, I innocently fell in love with you long before you were a nurse. By the time you became my loose one, we were already married." He squeezed her hands. "Tomorrow, I'll give Josef the last thing he needs."

"What's that?"

"More newspaper." He tapped the Polish ones beside him, which had also come with the ambulances. "It's the only way to educate him, letting it soak into his brain."

"Horst!" she said, feigning shock.

"And he's a lucky boy. The article he came with was about Wilson. What if it had been a review of some dreary play?" He put the papers aside and stood.

Now was the time, while his mood was still light. She didn't share Horst's stubborn German fidelity to the abstract concept of duty, especially since she wasn't sure to whom they were still to be dutiful; Germany as they'd known it had ceased to exist, the army as well. She breathed deeply and asked—again, though for the first time in a week—if they shouldn't leave.

"We can use the ambulances," she said. "Load the few remaining wounded onto them in the morning and drive west. One of us to each ambulance. You, Father Thomas, and I. We're already packed and ready to move and we have almost nothing here to detain us."

She'd revealed her plan in a rush, faster than she'd intended, trying to counter all possible objections before he even voiced them, as if she might overwhelm his doubts with a tidal wave of words; Horst shuffled the papers together before he spoke, letting the silence—his true answer—build. Then he said, "Kate," and pulled off his glasses.

"We mustn't. At least not yet." He sighed and massaged the bridge of his nose. "We were nearly out of supplies and now we have them. We have to treat them as the gifts they are, not squander them on a trip whose end we can't foresee. And none of our patients would benefit from being moved. Think of the influenza cases. The jolting, the cold air—it would kill them."

His refusal didn't surprise her. Their arrival in Wilno had been horrible, part of an ignominious retreat through the Ukraine before advancing Red armies, crossing the swollen Neman by ferry right after a regiment of cavalry, the deck filthy, wounded laid on the dung; he would not want to leave ignominiously as well. The hospital should be in good working order when he left it, and he would want somcone to turn over command to. Service before self. Still, she pushed on.

"Please, Horst," she said, her voice rising so that even to her it sounded shrill. "Can't we? Those ambulances spook me."

He laughed and squeezed her hand. "Kate! Your mother never told me about gypsy blood. The best English stock, she said. Next you'll be asking to read my palm."

When she didn't laugh, he squeezed again. "Trust me. We'll be fine."

"The refugees," she said, knowing that it was a mistake, but she was desperate.

"Kate." He sat back. "Twice before, we've lived through waves of refugees, and both times it meant nothing. Yes?"

They had, it was true. In late November the refugees fled east, away from an advancing Polish army that proved imaginary, and two weeks later another terrified group swarmed west, ahead of the fast-moving Czech legion. Though that army had proved both real and rapacious, it had also been remote, seven hundred miles away in central Russia at the time and moving east, away from them.

Seeing he hadn't convinced her, he softened his voice. "Three days, that's all. I promise. We owe it to our soldiers who marched north to stay that long."

They had left two weeks before. "They were supposed to be back yesterday."

"Yes." He shrugged. "It's wartime. Better to wait for the soldiers to be sure the way is safe, that no other patients need us. Let's give them three more days. If they haven't returned by then, we'll go. I promise."

He clapped his hands before she could reply and squared the papers on his desk. "Come," he said. "Time for tea and a smoke! Feed that bit of English left in you, yes?"

Water was boiling over a Sterno lamp in a German helmet, and two glass ventouse cups on the table were filled with tea leaves. "Let's enjoy our newfound luxury before bed. The paperwork only multiplies if I attend to it."

The offer of tea, the boiling water, were meant to make her happy, but she was certain it was one more thing they shouldn't have, a poisoned gift. The war had overturned everything: emperors and czars were gone, kingdoms and countries, millions of men; why shouldn't what once was good now be bad? It puzzled her that such things weren't plain to Horst, but she smiled and nodded, having argued and lost.

Still dressed, Horst asked Kate if she was ready for the dark, the game they'd played since their wedding night. Even at their most exhausted, when they moved like somnambulists after hours of surgery following especially bloody battles, one or the other had always teased with this delicious moment of waiting. Tonight, wanting him beside her, Kate wished Horst would forgo it and hurry to bed, but she knew she had to play along; domestic routines were their last remaining anchor.

He cracked the window and turned out the gas lamp and jumped beneath the piled blankets. She drew him close, trying to shake her chill as the windows rattled from distant cannon fire. Explosions flickered across the cloudy southern sky like heat lightning and she felt the pressure from them on the soles of her feet.

"Don't they worry you?" she asked.

"Why should they?" He pulled her tightly to his chest, the scent of tea lingering on his breath. "We've been listening to it for months. It moves, it comes closer, it goes away. We'll be fine."

Rapid pulse, shallow breathing; he didn't seem to believe his assurances either, though she said nothing. What would be the point? They were going to stay. Three days, perhaps their luck would last. She wanted more than luck. Closing her eyes, she prayed for a southern wind, as the warmer air would carry the sound of the guns more clearly, allowing her to identify them, and if she knew whose guns they were, she might know better what was about to befall them.

S HE AWOKE FROM a dream of Father Thomas beating reveille on a tin tray, a dream from a happier past. The dream unsettled her and she lay watching her smoking breath, certain something was wrong, her heart skidding, her limbs paralyzed by a crushing dread, her legs tangled in sweat-dampened sheets. Horst rolled over and began to snore, breaking the spell, making her realize that what had terrified her was the awful, unprecedented silence. Even the roosters were hushed.

She dressed hurriedly. The cannons had stopped. Outside the window a blue mist blurred the land. The thatched roofs of peasant cottages showed blackish green with moss, and the dark church steeple stood out clearly against the first bars of plum-colored light, but the surrounding fields and the roads between them and the stucco roadside shrines might never have existed: roof and steeple and she herself seemed to be floating on a tenuous, shifting blue-white cloud. In the west the moon was still up, though smaller and white now, as if its passage through the dark had drained and diminished it.

Downstairs, she stepped out into the appalling cold. Ghostly figures appeared to hurry toward her from the north, a Jew with his twin side curls, a woman wearing a tall blond wig, but the mist thickened before she could make out their faces; though she waited, the two didn't reappear, and she wondered if she'd imagined them. No one seemed left in the town, and no other refugees had arrived since noon the day before. Who could they be?

Shivering and afraid, she stepped forward uncertainly, hands out like a blind woman's, wanting to touch something to prove she wasn't dreaming, and before she'd gone five paces the clop of horse hooves calmed her. The horses were real; the drumming of their hooves over the frozen road reverberated through her boots, followed by the clink of metal—guns and sabers. The soldiers had come back, and Horst had been right, perhaps they'd have more wounded to care for.

A dozen yards to her left something dark moved, a sentry. *"Feldruf?"* he said in a hoarse voice. The password? She had no idea what it was.

The mist cleared between them; his rifle was pointed at her, and her forehead tingled above her left eye, the spot where she imagined the bullet was aimed. "Berg," she said. "It's me."

He was the son of a Hanoverian cheese merchant for whom he'd kept the books since he was a boy, his father too often taken up with amateur taxidermy to attend to them. "That's why I wear glasses," he'd told her. "I ruined my eyes." She'd learned all that when treating him for trench foot a month before, and now he was about to shoot her.

"Please," she started to say, but before she finished the snorting horses drew closer and he swiveled and repeated his demand more loudly. *"Feldruf?"* he said.

"Berg," she said. "It's all right. They're soldiers. They won't know the password either."

"I know they're soldiers," he said, looking at her briefly before pressing the gunstock to his shoulder. "But whose?"

A small thunderstorm erupted in reply, loud gunshots and muzzle flashes yellowing the mist, followed by the thud of bullets hitting flesh. Berg's dark form crumpled, his gun going off as he fell.

Kate was back in the hospital before a second volley, Horst running toward her, face creased from sleep, holding his medical bag under one arm, working the other into a coat sleeve. The mobile patients had propped themselves up on their elbows; the immobile ones' terrified glances darted from her to the door.

"Here," she said, grabbing the fluoroscope and heaving it toward Horst, "take this to the morgue!"

"What?" He stopped. "What for?"

"Hurry!" she said, wanting him to run, to save himself, but it was too late. Behind her the door burst open and two soldiers strode in carrying a wounded man, their tall hats almost knocking against the door frame, red stars shining on the black fur. They shoved Horst aside and lowered the wounded soldier to a bed.

"Good God!" Horst said, grabbing at one. "What are you doing?"

Kate reached down to tuck Josef's crucifix beneath his gown, wondering if Father Thomas had suspected Red Russians were about, had given away his cross to save himself. The soldiers ignored her and pounded up the stairs to the isolation ward, and Horst was bending over the wounded Russian when an officer came in behind them.

"And who are you?" Horst demanded.

The officer seemed not to hear him. He stood by the nearest bed and raised his boots one at a time, wiping mud from them onto the linens, rubbing them back to an approximation of a shine, finishing just as the soldiers came running down the stairs dragging Father Thomas, his left eye already swollen closed and his breath whistling like a boiling kettle. His pipe had been ripped from his throat and the wound was bleeding and Kate felt unworthy for having doubted him. Her heart beat very fast.

"Wait!" Horst said, speaking first to the officer and then to the privates and then to the officer again when the privates ignored him and dragged Father Thomas out the door. "He's not a soldier, he's a priest!"

He switched from German to Polish and from Polish to French. At the last the officer swiveled toward him. "A priest?" he said, in exquisite French. "Why didn't you say so?"

He called the soldiers back and rested one large, square hand on Father Thomas's shoulder. Tilting his head toward Father Thomas's, he said, "*Prêtre?*"

Father Thomas nodded and the officer unholstered his pistol and pressed it to Father Thomas's temple and fired. Blood sprayed over Kate; her knees buckled and she grabbed Josef's iron bedstead to keep from falling. Other soldiers pushed into the ward and the officer ordered Horst to attend to the wounded Russian before turning to Kate, who felt warm urine streaming down her leg.

"The boy," he said, switching to German and waving his pistol at Josef. "From which army?"

Father Thomas's body lay on the floor, legs twitching, and Kate shifted her glance to her own fingers, white where they gripped the bed. "None," she said.

"What? Louder!" She guessed from his face that he was yelling, but his voice sounded dim.

"None," she said and looked at him, knowing that otherwise he wouldn't trust her. "He's just a boy who got hurt."

"Lying won't save him."

"I'm not lying." Her voice cracked, and she had the odd notion that she herself was very far away, watching the events unfold from a great distance, which allowed her to repeat her protestations in a smoother voice.

He dug his finger under the Austrian brassard. "Then why this?"

She paled, knowing they'd put Josef in danger, as a unit of Austrians was still fighting the Soviets, trying to restore the Russian monarchy. "We pulled them out from one of those ambulances. They didn't come with the boy."

"Yes, those ambulances." He stepped closer to Kate, smelling of sweat and cordite. Behind him, soldiers blocked Horst from moving. "How did you happen to come by them?"

"Yesterday," she said, and shook her head. She told him that the three men driving them had disappeared without saying so much as a word, but even as she recounted the story she realized it sounded thin.

"And these three mysterious wise men. Where have they gone? Were they following another Christmas star?" He smiled, which only deepened her fear.

"I don't know," she said. "They took our truck and left."

"Of course. How convenient. But we've been watching this place for some time. Altogether too many comings and goings."

"We're a field hospital, for God's sake," Kate said. "We send people on when we can."

The officer seemed to consider this before holstering his pistol. He unpocketed a map and opened it over Josef's legs. "And this? Can you explain it?"

"What is it?"

"Do you see these lines?"

Blue chalk chevrons nearly encircled the town. Kate nodded. The map vibrated; Josef was trembling, and she gripped his ankle through the blanket to try and calm him.

"They're the dispositions of nearby Soviet troops. I took it from the first ambulance. What was it doing there? And the third ambulance. Here is a partial list of what it contained." He unfolded and read from another piece of paper: machine guns, mortars, rifle grenades, sheepskin waistcoats, mackintosh capes, ground sheets, cases of rum, tobacco, cocoa, coffee, revolvers, Very light pistols, gloves. He refolded the list and asked, "What would a medical outpost be doing with such things?"

"We're not spies," she said.

A muscle twitched in his cheek. "Why do you protest a charge no one has made? Have you something to hide?"

Kate had no answer, but in any case he seemed not to expect one. How had he known what the ambulance contained? Turning to Horst he said, "Will my soldier be all right?"

Horst spread his bloodied hands above the wounded Russian. "I think so. I didn't have time to clean the wound properly. I'd need to operate for that. A bit of hypochlorous acid would do wonders for him, prevent infection."

"Do you have any?"

"No. But perhaps . . ."

"But perhaps *we* have some?"

Horst shrugged.

The Russian shook his head. "He'll have to take his chances."

He snapped out orders in Russian and soldiers pulled Kate and Horst out of the hospital and ran them across the frozen ground toward the nearest ambulance. Kate slipped but wasn't allowed to fall, the men dragging her forward; first her boot came off and then each of her three socks, and though she felt the skin peeling off the top of her foot she couldn't get her balance to lift it. Behind her the sound of clinking instruments from Horst's bag meant that at least he was going with her.

The ambulances had been rifled, their contents strewn about. Mixed in with the armaments were the remains of the piano, and lying beside them was the milkman's nag, a gaping wound on its exposed belly, its entrails a smoking blue pile. From the hospital a boy's scream was followed by a gunshot. Kate struggled to get loose but a soldier slammed his rifle into her stomach and shoved her into the ambulance and shut the door.

She tried to breathe. The engine started, the ambulance was put in gear, and they moved off, bumping over the frozen mud and rutted ice, Horst reaching out for her as they picked up speed and swerved away.

FEET AND LEGS NUMB, Kate paced the dirt basement, three steps away from the door, three back, trying to drive off the terrible cold. By the coal pile Horst had found a boot. It was wet when she put it on and she hadn't dared ask from what. "No socks," he'd said, and given her two of his own. A hunk of coal stuffed into the curled toe made the boot almost fit.

"Nothing's going to happen," Horst had said. "They let me keep my instruments. Why would they do that if they planned to shoot us?"

"It could have been an accident," she'd said, though now she regretted her earlier doubts and clutched his surgical bag as she walked, wanting to believe him since he was gone. A watch would have made her less frightened. He'd been gone—how long? An hour? Two? Surely not more than three. That might be good—perhaps at that very moment he was convincing some Bolshevik that they were medical personnel, not soldiers or spies—but she feared that the opposite was true, that every minute away made the chance of his return less likely.

Three steps away from the door and the dirty snow that had drifted under it, three back; she couldn't bring herself to go farther, as one corner held a pair of bloody hands.

"Jews," their guard had said before slamming the door. "We wouldn't waste bullets on them."

She and Horst weren't Jews, they wouldn't be cut up, but of course they might still be shot. It was almost to be hoped for; she was far too familiar with the body's fragility, had seen what men and metal could do, to imagine anything but the worst: severed fingers, blinded eyes, submersion in a pit of coals. Her mind focused on this last one and she couldn't shake the image of Horst screaming in pain as his skin charred.

She tried counting as she paced, imagining Horst's return, making herself go farther. Why should cut-off hands bother her? She was a nurse; for years she'd drunk her morning coffee in the cool morgue, ignoring amputated limbs awaiting burial, but those, cotton-wrapped, had been attempts to save lives, not to take them.

She yelled, twice, but no one responded—no other prisoners to encourage her, no guards to order her silence. Was anyone in town even left alive? They'd driven past a line of men in the Jewish cemetery, digging an enormous trench in the snow, and just before their jailers had come for Horst they'd heard a volley of rifle shots.

"My God," Horst had said. "Not the Jews."

"Who else?" Kate said.

"But that makes no sense. Half the Reds are Jews."

True, but nothing now made sense. What were they doing in a slaughterhouse basement, and why had Jews had their hands cut off? Perhaps they'd simply been unlucky, guessing that the Whites were coming and hastily whitewashing crosses on their doors, only to be confronted with furious Reds, who viewed them as traitors. And everyone knew the Red army had one rule for turncoats and captured prisoners: extermination.

Kate had heard of a train near the frontlines at Kiev, in the Ukraine, that had held wounded Whites and their nurses. Four cars had become detached, and as they rolled downhill toward the Bolshevik camp, steadily picking up speed, nurses and prisoners alike had committed suicide, knowing what would befall them. And yet she understood the Reds. If they were captured by Whites, part of their torture before death was to have crosses carved into their chests; the Florence Nightingale was the Whites' joking term for it. But she and Horst weren't even Russian, let alone Whites; surely that would count for something. She stopped and listened, heard nothing, and, to keep her mind from turning inward, her mood from darkening further, she began to pace again, boots shuffling across the uneven dirt, frozen fingers trailing over the rough cold stone.

*　*　*

"Oh, Horst," she said. Even in the dim light his face looked horribly swollen, and his coat was covered with blood.

"What?" He looked down. "Oh, this. The hospital, remember? The wounded Russian. The blood's not mine."

"But your face," she said. Though she knew it must hurt, she found herself running her hands over his skin to be sure it wasn't charred.

"It's all right," he said. "It's not that bad, I think. Nothing broken."

"Forgive me," she said, trying to explain her sudden tears. "This only just started. It's relief, you see? I thought you wouldn't come back."

He comforted her until they heard footsteps approaching, then he pulled back and told her they had to hurry.

"We're to be shot as spies," he said. "I've asked for a priest to confess to."

"But we're not Catholic."

"They don't know that. It might give us a little time. I'm certain they haven't any handy, and they only considered it because I'm a doctor. Do your best to act the part."

The footsteps stopped at the door, the handle turned; someone waited on the other side. For what? At last the door was thrown open and a man stood looking down at them, a backlit, cutout figure in black. She couldn't see his face, but posture and uniform identified him as an officer. Her heart beat so hard it seemed about to escape the narrow confining cage of her ribs; her throat was dry; she wanted to scream.

"Yes," he said in German, and nodded. "I thought so. You two. Come." He summoned her with his hand, and as she started reluctantly up the stairs, she felt her final hope extinguished.

"Quickly," he said, and snapped his fingers. "Or you'll die here."

Horst hung back for a moment, looking at him, while Kate, perceiving a threat, hurried. She felt herself shrinking, floating free from her quivering body, watched herself mount the stairs as if from a vast height, no longer intimately connected with what was about to occur. Would they be shot against the wall or somewhere else in town? Her mind turned over the possibilities as calmly as if she were choosing a picnic spot. Nearer the cemetery, perhaps, so no one would have to transport their bodies, or would they not even be buried, left above ground, food for dogs and ravens? Every day for three months the previous summer, she'd eaten sitting on a stone wall, ignoring the nearby skeletal remains of a horse. How easily one came to accept the death of others, yet it seemed unfair not to know where she would spend eternity. Should she run, scream? Horst's calm presence prevented her from doing so.

She stood blinking in the slanting sunlight, trying not to fall. Early afternoon; Horst had been gone much longer than she'd thought. She couldn't make out what Horst was saying; her ears seemed muffled in gauze. She turned toward their accompanying officer and was stunned to recognize him, his red round cheeks and redder nose. Months before, he'd been a patient, though then as a Polish officer. Pymzyl, Porst, something. She was about to say so when he leaned toward her face and yelled, "Silence!"

Horst, who must have recognized him sooner, nodded at the other soldiers nearby.

"I will bring you to division," the officer said, then turned and limped away.

*Probst.* Yes, that had been it.

One of the soldiers, who was missing an eye, understood German. "We were to shoot them, Dimitry," he said.

"And we will." Probst shoved Horst toward a waiting staff car, a German one, its door painted over with a white royal Polish eagle, the eagle in turn covered with a thin, amateurish Soviet hammer and sickle. "The Germans have been very clever in leaving spies behind. We'll interrogate these two first. Who knows who else is in our midst?"

They were in the car before the soldier could respond, though as they started out, he pulled open a rear door and swung himself in next to Kate and shut the door as they sped away.

They headed into the white abandoned countryside, traveling in near silence, Probst up front with the driver, giving directions in Polish. Black patches of forest broke the white rolling bleakness and twice they passed through deserted towns, their houses, church steeples, and factory chimneys all coated white, as if constructed of snow and ice. The road bisected a field marked with hundreds of small wooden crosses from some forgotten battle, most with their writing obliterated, and then passed a series of telegraph poles papered over with bright yellow posters instructing scavengers to turn in what they found to military authorities and warning them that if they didn't, they'd be shot. Beyond came the response: miles of broken guns, field kitchens, ammunition carts, sleighs, and abandoned rifles that no one had bothered to scavenge. From a shell hole filled with frozen water three hands stuck up, like fins.

Kate studied Probst's profile. Yes, it was really him. He'd come to their hospital with a fellow officer of the newly constituted Polish army, a nearly dissolved bag of salt tucked into one of his wounds and the wound sewed closed, which meant he'd been in a Soviet hospital; the barbaric, painful custom was their preferred method for sterilizing wounds. She'd said nothing about it at the time.

She should have, she thought, watching his still face against the endless white fields; he wouldn't be about to kill them now, though that was foolish, she realized; it would simply be someone else. Still. His fellow officer had been suffering from influenza, so far gone he was cyanotic, hands, lips, and eyes all indigo. His nose had spurted blood, as had his ears, the epistaxis a sure sign of approaching death, and though they'd done what they could to comfort him, he'd had subcutaneous emphysema, air pockets just beneath the skin from ruptured lungs, something she'd never seen before and that caused him unbearable pain. When they rolled him to change his sheets or to wash him, his skin crackled like breaking ice; in the end they'd not moved him at all.

Probst's less painful wounds had been equally peculiar. As she'd scanned his hip and leg with the fluoroscope, marking blue Xs on his skin to show Horst where to cut, she'd picked up the clear impressions of sprockets and dials and shutters, prisms, screws, and springs, from the camera he'd been carrying that had been blown into his leg and down his femur to the knee. No doubt Horst had missed a few, explaining his current limp.

During his recovery he'd told stories to make the other soldiers laugh. The one she remembered best involved a peasant market, where he'd inquired of a fishmonger the price of a carp and then bought it. "This is mine now?" he'd said.

"Yes, Your Honor."

"And I may do whatever I like with it?"

"Certainly, Your Honor."

At which point he'd slapped her across the face with the fish and run off laughing. The officers had all laughed, but Kate doubted his new comrades would find it so funny. *That poor woman,* she'd thought at the time. By now she was perhaps luckily dead.

They drove through miles of black forest, their engine noise echoing from the dense trees, the light almost disappearing, and emerged into a valley, the bright blinding snow piled high on both sides of the car, plumes blowing into the blue sky from tufted crests. Again and again they rose up hills and dropped into valleys, and she had a sense that they weren't really moving, that they were on a stage set, a loop of pretend hills and a fake ribbon of road that might never end. How far were they going? She tried to catch Horst's eye without calling attention to herself, but the car was getting colder, and, shivering, Kate couldn't help bumping against the one-eyed soldier, who glared before pushing her away and saying something in Russian to Probst.

"*Da,*" Probst said, and pointed through the windshield at an upcoming crossroads.

"Here," he said in German as they came to the turn, "and here," he said at the next one, which brought them to an abandoned house and a ruined stone barn, an armored car sitting between them.

The soldier grew agitated. Hands gesticulating, face reddening, he stepped out and asked a series of questions in Russian. Probst ignored him, retrieving a shovel from the trunk. The soldier hectored him with a rising voice, pointing at Kate and Horst, until the engine of the armored car started up, after which the driver came around from behind it and in German asked the one-eyed soldier for a cigarette.

"What?" the soldier said, turning to face him. "But you already have one."

Probst nearly decapitated him with the shovel, holding it sideways like a sword as he swung. For a few seconds the Russian's body didn't seem to react, then he swayed and fell to his knees before tumbling backward with his arms outstretched, his legs tucked beneath him. The driver stepped on his face, pushing his head into the blood-stained snow, flicked his cigarette on him, and moved off.

"Hurry," Probst said, and pulled Kate away from the doorway of the ruined barn, where she'd been staring at a pile of German officers' brass belt buckles, wondering what it meant. They were moving toward the armored car. "We haven't much time."

From inside the armored car he retrieved a fur coat. Kate ignored the dried blood gumming its hem and put it on. They got in and started off, the heavy car clanking as it jerked forward; even at low speeds, it was too loud to talk and excruciatingly hot, but Kate was afraid to take off the coat. Sweating, chilled, she covered her ears with her hands and sat back against the hot metal.

The car stopped and Probst threw open the back door for air. They were near a town that had been shelled, its houses blasted open, tables still set for dinner. What was left of the town seemed to have been taken over by inmates from an asylum. Men in dresses and top hats were pushing walls over; dozens of others tore thatch off roofs, smashed windows and flowerpots and doors with hammers, tied ropes to the beams of houses and yanked them down, and threw chamber pots and kitchen pots and pianos from windows. Smoke and dust rose from every heap. Other men, already drunk, collars open, beltless and barefoot despite the cold, lay on the ground. The sanest-seeming men were carrying chickens under their arms or pushing perambulators filled with wine bottles on the roads out of town. Two were pulling a feather bed in different directions until it ripped and added its contents to the blizzard of feathers in the air.

A Jew had had his stomach slit, his small intestine pulled out through a tiny opening and nailed to a post, and now the Red soldiers stood beating him, making him circle the post, the intestine a thin blue snake slithering out of his stomach as he ran. Above them, three soldiers threw pried-up roof tiles to the pavement below, not caring whether they hit their comrades, and beyond them more Jews' bodies were laid out in a circle like numbers on a clock, faces toward the center, a man in the middle swiveling and urinating into their open mouths. Nothing from the war or from its aftermath prepared Kate for this depravity.

Probst's face darkened. "We'd planned to go around this town.

The German lines are on the other side of it, but I'm afraid we'll have to go through it."

Kate was horrified to find herself cheered by his words; he seemed intent on killing. The armored car clanked over cobbles. Smoke filtered in, and feathers from the ruined bedding, the smell of charred flesh. Probst cocked the machine gun and began shooting at the worst offenders, the terrific rattling noise of the gun and of the spent shells clattering on the corrugated metal floor joining in with the general mayhem of crashing houses and breaking bottles and artillery salvos from the German lines. Bullets ricocheted off cobbles and brick, sank into houses, ripped into bodies; Kate realized she'd been screaming only when her jaw began to hurt.

The urinating soldier looked straight at them, seemingly unaware that they'd been shooting. Plaster dust coated his face, giving him a waxy complexion, and Probst shot him. Then others, as the driver crushed still more against the buildings. All of it was appalling, everything her glance touched, and when she closed her eyes most appalling of all was the eagerness for destruction she'd felt only minutes before.

They stopped beyond the town and got out, blinking in the smoky sunlight. The German artillery had zeroed in, and as the salvos began, the houses disappeared beneath the incoming rounds as if they'd been sucked into the earth, the enormous cones of the shell bursts brown and white when they hit a garden, red when they struck the brick houses. She almost couldn't hear it; had her eardrums been punctured? She wanted the town wiped off the Earth, hoped that no one would ever remember what had happened there.

"That way," Probst said, pointing toward the river. Rivulets of sweat had marked lighter channels through his smoke-blackened face. "The Germans are just beyond it."

"Are you going back?" Horst said. His swollen face was blackened too, as her own must have been; to others they would all look like devils freshly escaped from hell. Her teeth chattered, and she wrapped herself more tightly in the coat, then scooped up a handful of snow and began rubbing her face clean.

"Certainly," Probst said. "Those soldiers were drunk. They won't remember me."

"You saw what they did," Kate said, scrubbing at her skin. "You'll remember."

"Believe me, the Whites have done worse. They were evil, but not all Bolsheviks are. I understand them."

"That they're savages?"

"That they have no hope left save the hope of revenge. What they're doing here, as horrible as it seems, is nothing compared to what's been done to their homes." He looked at her. "By Germans, in some cases."

Horst said, "You'll be killed if you go back. Shooting your own men."

"Perhaps. If we don't go back, the issue is already decided." He held his hands up. "In any case, it's an accident of war. And you see, most of them are dead now anyway, and so will not be able to testify, while I, bravely, have advanced toward the enemy."

He turned to Kate. "If recaptured, you'll be shot. Don't stop to help anyone, no matter how badly wounded they seem."

Horst shook his hand but neither he nor Kate thanked him, and without another word they turned and walked toward the bridge, on the other side of which flapped a German flag.

"Horst," she said, stopping as they came in sight of the ice, red in the slanting light, like a river of frozen blood.

"I know." He pressed his hand to her back and forced her forward. "It's a trick of light, that's all. Hurry. We have to cross."

KATE JOLTED AWAKE as the train slowed near another ruined town—makeshift wooden crosses tilted inside broken rooms, names scrawled on doors, a landscape of the dead—and stopped beside a shattered barn with a row of horse skeletons still tethered to iron rings. Was all of Pomerania destroyed? When their field hospital had first come to the region, four years before, it had been bountifully bucolic; she'd thought they might eventually settle among its hills and lakes and picturesque towns. Now it looked as if it had endured a hundred years of fighting.

Dammvorstadt. She didn't remember it from before the war. The compartment's outside door opened and a blond woman was standing beside the tracks next to her even blonder crippled daughter, who was in her late teens, Kate guessed, only a few years younger than herself. Horst stepped down to help her from her wheelchair.

"If you could just get her to a seat," her mother said, her German inflected with the slightest Polish accent.

Kate stood as Horst began pulling up the girl by her arm; she made noises in her throat like a wounded animal.

"Sorry," Horst said.

The girl blushed as Kate gripped her under her arms and Horst lifted. Even with her useless legs she seemed almost unmarked by the war—glossy hair, smooth skin—a touch of the miraculous that pleased Kate. She wore layers of clothes, at least two dresses and two long coats.

"Sit here," Kate said, sliding the girl to the seat she herself had vacated. "This corner is warm." Which was true; the steam pipes' meager heat seemed least meager there, though it would be many long minutes before the compartment warmed up again now that they'd had the door open.

The mother climbed in once her daughter was settled and sat down next to her. "You're too kind. We're fine, just happy to be going west. Is Berlin home for you?"

"Hamburg," Kate said. "My husband's home."

"Not yours?"

"Yes. Now."

The woman waited but Kate did not go on; there was no point in it. "And you?" Kate asked the girl, shifting the conversation away from herself. "You have relatives in Berlin?"

The girl nodded and fiddled with the scarves at her throat—the top one a beautiful fawn-colored paisley—and Kate wondered if she was another whistler.

Horst had tilted the wheelchair onto its back wheels. "If I can find a porter, perhaps we can get this on board."

"No," her mother said, breath smoking in the frigid air. "We won't need it."

"You have one in Berlin?" Horst said.

"We have relatives. We'll be fine."

Horst looked unsure, but the train whistle decided him.

"All right," he said, and pushed it a foot away over the snow-covered bricks and then climbed back on board. He hadn't shut the door when the train started up again, and people were still pushing their way onto the platform, raising their hands and beginning to run. The train picked up speed quickly, leaving them behind.

"You see," the Polish woman said to her daughter, sighing and sitting back. "We're lucky. We might not have made the train at all."

London in reverse, to Kate; when she and Horst had been forced to flee in the war's opening weeks—Horst as a German national no longer welcome in his adopted country—they'd been given two days to get out before they'd face arrest. At Charing Cross they'd pushed through a hissing crowd to board the last train for the coast, and as it pulled out, Kate had been shocked to see their luggage and that of all the other passengers sitting piled on the platforms, people already starting to go through it; even more shocked to realize that dozens of boys were pelting the carriage with handfuls of potatoes and dung. If they were her countrymen, she didn't recognize them. She and Horst hadn't lived anywhere permanently since then, moving with their field hospital dozens of times; now they were hoping to make Hamburg home.

After the train cleared the station Kate stood. "No," she said, when Horst began to rise. "I'm fine. I want to walk."

The privation of the war years had grown worse after the peace, and it showed in the hollowed faces and mean clothes of the passengers. Even the train had not escaped; leather was gone from the window straps, plush covering from the seats, fine woodwork from around the windows; the compartments were horribly uncomfortable. The truth was she couldn't sit for more than a few minutes without her back hurting.

In the corridor men stood staring out the windows, rocking with the train's motion, one straddling a saddle, perhaps planning to sell it in Berlin; it might have been his last possession. She and Horst were down to her fur coat and his surgical instruments and cigarette case, though at least in Berlin they could visit his bank.

The train rounded a long turn, the rear cars curving smoothly into sight, men on their roofs with their feet dangling over the edge, black cutouts against the blue sky, so thickly clustered they looked like grapes. Were they mad? It seemed impossible they could hold on in the bitter cold. Behind her the corridor door opened and three English officers appeared, laughing and speaking loudly, and though she was curious to hear English—aside from *Hound of the Baskervilles* and a few other English movies shown in the occupied towns of Poland, and Horst's occasional English endearments, she hadn't heard her native language in years—she didn't at the moment want to face the boisterous victors. She turned away, toward the second- and third-class carriages.

Second class was darker and colder, third class almost black. "No light ration," a porter said, seeing her stop to adjust her smock and then fasten her coat more tightly, but it wasn't the lack of light, it was the smells, the stink from cabbage cigars and putrefying flesh. A German soldier had an entire seat to himself, his suppurating leg stretched across it, and though he affected not to notice his lack of company, she was sure he knew what it meant. She wanted to talk to him, to comfort him, but he exuded a fierce isolating pride that she was loath to puncture, and she moved on.

"Please." The porter came up to her again. "You're a nurse. Can you help me?"

"Perhaps."

"This way." He shouldered a way clear. "I have an injured soldier."

*Just one?* she thought, following him through the murmuring crowd. His back was broad, his frame still solid, his posture so erect he might have been in the military. His coat was military too, though his hat and gloves were those of a porter. What had he done throughout the war to stay so healthy? She decided she didn't want to know. People did what they had to to survive; perhaps he'd been entirely honorable.

They passed several musicians clutching violins and oboes, and a troupe of actors still in their gypsy costumes and garish stage makeup. Beyond them was a group of consumptive German soldiers, former prisoners of war, their faces the color of frozen mud.

"Not here," the porter said, and pushed on. When they were clear of the soldiers, he stopped and looked back. "It doesn't seem like it, but they're the lucky ones. The Russian workers released them in a delirium of fellow feeling, but most were shot and killed as they made their way west. Two thousand started out, they said. Only those six survived." Contemplating their journey, he stroked the yellowed ends of his mustache, and she realized she'd been wrong about him, that the recent years *had* marked him; he appeared to have an ancient face grafted onto a much younger man's frame.

At last they came to the soldier, just a boy, really, not much older than Josef had been, his pale open face a mixture of fear and pain, shivering in the cold and reeking of eau de cologne. In the stations, Red Cross volunteers were still spraying the wounded; they knew the Germans were continuing to fight, even if no one else seemed to. If they couldn't bathe them, they could at least mask their odors.

"It's his leg," the porter said.

"Show me."

The porter pulled aside a blanket. The boy's trousers were split over his right thigh, revealing a long but not deep wound; muscle showed, rather than bone. She bent to smell the leg, raised her head, lowered it, sniffed again. "He's fine," she said, straightening.

Relief swept across the man's face. The boy must have been more than just a soldier he was concerned about. His son, perhaps; they had the same Roman nose. "But what about that black material?" he asked. "What's that?"

It was clumped at the edge of the wound, where the skin was nicely pink, and she bent once more to examine its grainy texture. When she stood she was smiling.

"Were you carrying a Dixie?" she asked the boy.

He nodded. "How did you know?"

"Coffee grains," she said to him. To the porter she said, "We had several of these during the war. Shell splinters destroyed the coffee urns, sending shrapnel into the carrier's legs and sides. Coffee grounds too. Don't worry, it's a good thing. They seem to prevent infections.

"He'll be fine. Bathe the wound with clean water, and wrap it with clean linen, if you can find some." She looked around. "No one here, but one of the first-class passengers might have it. You could perhaps trade something."

He laughed. "Yes. We seem to have gone back to a bartering economy. But I don't have much I can trade."

"In any case, it will be all right for a while. Keep that blanket off it. The air can do it some good, and the skin at the edges is pink. It's healing. One thing: don't be surprised if some metal splinters rise to the surface. Don't take them out with your fingers, and don't let him do it, either. That will infect the wound."

Her breath condensed between them. "It's awfully cold here," Kate said.

"It is. You're on half rations of heat up there and we have none."

"You should move him forward. If he's shivering, his wounds won't heal."

"No. He must stay here. But I'll find him another blanket, or a coat."

He glanced at hers, and what he was thinking seemed obvious, but she couldn't give it up. Wouldn't. She had an obligation to Horst and to herself to stay healthy, and the coat was the only thing that kept her from freezing. The boy would be all right if the train proceeded at a reasonable speed. Four hours, perhaps five; in Berlin he'd be able to get warm. Besides, the porter's coat was a rich wool twill. For years the military alone had been given the best fabric; the boy could be wrapped in that.

The porter thanked her and began walking her back, again making room for her with his shoulder. Near the gangrenous soldier the air was so foul that people were now riding with the windows open despite the calamitous cold. She couldn't look at him.

At the doorway, the porter stepped aside. "I have to stop here, I'm afraid. I can't go forward, the engineer won't let me."

"How would he see you?"

"He'll come back. Soon. Once we cross the border into Germany, probably."

"Really?" She wasn't sure she believed him, though he seemed to have an honest face; she'd never heard of an engineer coming back into the train.

Before she had a chance to ask, he said, "May I keep your coat for you?"

Reflexively, her hand went to her throat.

He blushed. "No. I don't want to take it, just to hold it for you. Safekeeping, you see. Because the engineer will confiscate it, I'm afraid."

This she didn't believe, but, not wanting to be impolite, she said, "No, thank you. I'd be too cold without it, and I doubt it would fit him."

The porter touched her arm. "Don't be polite, now," he said. "It won't help you, not with these people."

When she opened the compartment door, she saw the three English officers; one had taken her seat and he smiled at her without standing. Even when Horst stood, his glance left her only briefly. She flushed under his stare.

"Please," Horst said in German, and pointed to his seat.

"Bloody fool," the Englishman said of Horst to another officer. "I was hoping she'd sit on my lap."

The lieutenant laughed and stared too. "Yes. Quite the little fräulein, isn't she? And she smells so pretty."

Horst was looking determinedly out the window at the passing telegraph poles and looping wires, and Kate refused to let them know she spoke English. Doing so might make her feel better, but it would further embarrass Horst and perhaps endanger him. If an argument ensued, they could order him from the train.

The one with a crescent scar on his cheek looked Kate up and down and said, "Rather uncomfortable traveling clothes, I should think."

Because of the English, they'd been ordered to stay in Poland, and because of them they'd been left to die there. Not these specific men, of course, and yet she couldn't help but be angry with what they represented. The war was over, for God's sake, the English had won, they ordered Germans about at will; did simple humanity have to go too?

They chatted on. Kate had always wished they hadn't had to leave London so quickly, that they'd had time to take a few pictures with them: of the Royal Chelsea Hospital ballroom where she and Horst had met, of its grounds where she'd spent hours correcting Horst's pronunciation of the names of surgical instruments, of its chapel where they'd married, of the Surrey downs where she and her brothers had summered. Now in these English voices she heard those places again, missed them acutely—from the officers' accents, they might have been her neighbors—and wondered if she would have been as insufferable if she'd stayed behind; victory brought with it no certainty of wisdom. Her own brothers had worn the uniform; at least one of them was still wearing it. Had he been posted to Germany too? Was he as arrogantly self-assured, as sublimely insensitive? She tried not to judge them harshly until they laughed at Horst, who was shivering in his thin coat. No, she wasn't like them; she prayed that her brother wasn't either.

The train began to slow, and beside her, the Polish woman slid off her rings.

"Here," she said to her daughter, "pull up your coat too. And your skirts."

"Oh, Mother."

"No. You must. Let the braces show."

The daughter did as she was told and the mother pushed her

rings deep into her own pockets. When they were safely hidden, she unlatched her necklace and folded it away as well.

"Is something wrong?" Kate asked. The train had come to a complete stop.

"Fuel," the Polish woman said, incongruously rubbing her fingers together in the sign of money. She slid her unclasped bracelets inside her stockings, showing her white thigh with no more concern than if she were alone with a maid. "They'll be here soon."

"Who?" Horst asked.

"The engineer."

Kate thought of the porter's warning. Had he been telling the truth?

"How can we give him fuel?" Horst asked.

"What have you in that bag?" the woman asked.

"My surgical tools."

"Those would be just what they'd like. From here to Berlin we'll be asked a few times. And there, it might be even worse. I hear the workers' councils have taken over the city government, and that armed sailors run the city like bandits."

One of the English officers stood and opened the corridor door and put his head out. Even through the fur coat Kate felt the blast of cold air. Didn't he know it pained them? Probably not; he'd eaten well, to him a little cold meant nothing, and the air in the compartment was horrid: unwashed bodies, fear, a lingering odor of sickness. He shut the door and asked the lieutenant what was happening.

"I haven't the faintest," he said. "You'll have to ask one of the Huns."

To Kate, in broken French, the captain asked why the train had stopped.

In English, she said, "I haven't the faintest, either."

She didn't know what she'd hoped to provoke—a sense of embarrassment, shame at having been so openly rude—but either way she was disappointed. Without visible emotion he remarked, "For a German, your English is impeccable."

His arrogance spurred her to forget her caution. "I'm English."

His eyes flicked to Horst.

"My husband is German." Then, realizing that it might seem she was abandoning him, she said, "We're German citizens."

"So much the worse for you," the young lieutenant said.

Before she or Horst could reply the corridor door was flung open and the short engineer stood looking them over, face and clothing blackened with soot and rancid with coal smoke. Ignoring the soldiers, he glanced first at the matronly Polish woman and her crippled daughter, then at Kate, then at Horst, who was reaching down to his medical bag.

"What do you have there?" he asked.

"Nothing," Kate said. "Rags. Our last bits of clothing. Old socks."

He looked at her again and said, with no preliminaries, "Your coat, please."

Horst said, "Take my bag instead. It's more valuable. She needs the coat. She'll freeze without it."

"Then let her. I've been freezing in the engine for twelve hours. It's only another four to Berlin. It's fuel," he said, and, like the Pole, rubbed his thumb and finger together in the sign of money.

Kate glanced at the Pole, but the woman refused to meet Kate's eyes. Horst removed his coat and held it out to the engineer.

"Here."

"Sit down," the engineer said. "Or you'll be put off the train. The fur, please. Now."

"It's all right, Horst," Kate said, standing. "It served its purpose."

She handed it over and he put it on, the bloody hem puddling on the floor around his boots because he was so short. Though she wanted to refuse Horst's coat, she would not give the English the benefit of a scene and so put it on.

As the engineer shut the door and moved down the train, Horst glared at the seated Englishmen.

"Horst," Kate said in German, knowing what he was thinking. "Please. We don't want trouble now."

"Yes," the Polish woman said, as if she knew Horst's thoughts too. "But they could have stopped it if they'd wanted, couldn't they?"

*You didn't do anything either,* Kate thought, but she took her own advice and kept quiet. They'd endured enough already, and she

36

couldn't reasonably have expected the Pole to do anything; she had her crippled daughter to attend to. Kate's glance fell on the girl's beautiful paisley scarf and she was glad it hadn't been taken. The poor girl had suffered, she should be left some small measure of beauty in her life; Kate hoped the girl would have the sense to hide it before the door opened again.

As if her thoughts had called it into being, the door opened, and they all turned to look. The porter; was he to steal from them too?

"Madame," he said to Kate and clicked his heels together and bowed his head. "When we stopped, I thought of you."

"I have nothing else to give," she said, her voice flat.

"No, of course. Nor would I ask anything of you." That she might have offended him showed only in a spot of red that appeared high up on each prominent cheekbone.

"Then what?" she said.

He removed his coat and held it out to her. She'd been right, he was military, a German colonel; the Englishmen were looking over his medals and decorations. It was a generous offer—the coat was long, beautifully made, no doubt warm—but she couldn't take it. If the Reds controlled Berlin, as the Polish woman had said, his uniform would put him in danger. Even in the east, reports of men murdering their officers during the November mutinies had reached them, and if he hadn't removed his ribbons and insignia by now he wasn't going to.

"Thank you," she said, "but didn't you say you weren't to come this far forward?"

"Yes," he said, still holding out the coat. "But I'm afraid we'll have a riot in the rear cars if we stop again. They have no heat, no light, and they can't endure further delays. It's my job to prevent that, and so I told the engineer. Now, please, take this."

"That's very kind of you, but I don't need it. I already have my husband's." She held it open by the lapels.

"Then he'll be cold," he said. "That won't do. I'm afraid I have to insist."

This wasn't a polite offer. Though she'd done almost nothing, it was her reassurance he'd sought and that she'd provided; he needed to repay her.

"One moment." She held up a finger. Turning to the English captain, who'd been following their conversation without understanding it, she said, "Do you have a handkerchief?"

"I'm sorry?" He seemed startled by this sudden turn of events.

"A handkerchief? A clean one? It's absolutely necessary. And you too," she said to the lieutenant.

They each produced one from an inside pocket. Linen, large, of excellent quality.

"Here," she said, handing one to the porter as she took his coat. "Put that away for now." She folded the other into a long neat rectangle. "Cover the leg with this, being careful not to touch the wound itself, since your fingers might infect it, and tuck each end under the fabric of his trousers. In Berlin, he'll probably have to walk a bit. When he's resting again, change this one for the one you have in your pocket. And make sure you boil this one before you put it back on."

He bowed again. "Madame. I can't thank you enough."

"That's not true," she said as she handed Horst back his coat and slid on the porter's. "You can't imagine what this means to me."

After the porter had gone, the English captain leaned closer and asked her how long she thought it would be before they reached Berlin. She debated whether to speak, then turned her face to the window, ignoring him as she looked past her own reflection at the endless snowy fields, the occasional lines of people trudging through them. Always westward, paralleling their path but far more slowly. She wouldn't insult him overtly, but she didn't have to respond, the English couldn't make her do that. *Genug*, she thought. *Enough*. For the first time in her life she felt truly German.

## JANUARY 7, 1919

T HE FIRST SIGNS of Berlin were the outlying suburbs, whose houses grew steadily smaller and closer together; as it neared the city center, the train incomprehensibly sped up and its lights went out, its heat off. They passed through a rail yard with a huge collection of Russian train engines—naphtha burning—rusting to the rails, and a few decrepit cattle cars scattered at its edges. A string of farm wagons stood halted at a crossing, piled with coal and guarded by shotgun-carrying boys, and as the train sped through a tunnel, Kate heard scraping sounds and screams. Something darker tumbled through the darkness outside, and she remembered the roof riders, was amazed that no one else seemed to notice or mind, amazed, too, how little it bothered her. Life was growing cheaper by the mile.

Out in the light again they seemed to have been transported to another world: a dense cityscape with the squalid backs of squalid buildings pressed up against the narrow rails: hanging black clothes, tiny, grimy windows, a dark morass of filthy alleys. The train slowed; the passengers grew restless, the buildings meaner. At the last they were simply tin hovels yards from the tracks, their dispirited inhabitants standing in the doorways, watching them pass. The train stopped, paused, jerked forward, and then glided into the Friedrichstrasse Station, the light paling as they slid under the great glass canopy, and despite what they'd just passed through Kate felt herself growing excited—the familiar thrill of a journey's end.

The brakes were still hissing when the Polish woman jumped to her feet and opened the door, and in seconds she was on the platform, holding out her hand to her daughter. To Kate's great surprise, the daughter stood and followed after, walking easily. Seeing Kate stare, the Polish woman said, "Madame, you will need to be quicker now. The war was the men's turn to fight, the peace is ours."

The mother and daughter shouldered their way through the surging platform crowd while Kate watched, appalled and fascinated and a bit envious, thinking they were already prepared for what was coming. She wished she were too; the girl had sacrificed her paisley scarf at the end, no doubt to save something more valuable hidden away.

Hawkers shouted, political speakers declaimed, officers stepped from the train and had their epaulets ripped off by groups of angry sailors. Kate looked for their porter. He was up ahead, his son leaning against him, sailors crowded round him, the English soldiers pushing past.

"Quickly, Horst," she said, and stepped down. She pressed ahead through the raucous crowd and felt him at her back. They had so little that their passage was easy; bobbing a few yards ahead of them was the man with his saddle, which was now riding on his head. Soon they overtook him.

One of the sailors, a red tab like a splash of blood in his hat, pointed to the porter's feet. "Why, those are my boots!"

"That's ridiculous!" the colonel said, and tried to brush by him, shielding his son with his shoulder.

The sailor knocked him down and Kate bent to help him up, but before she could, Horst pulled her back, so forcefully her arm hurt. "Not now," he said. "Not here."

Only then did she see the other sailors watching them, bent forward as if ready to pounce.

"I'm all right," the colonel said, standing and wiping grime from his face. "How foolish of me. Your boots."

He stooped to remove them.

"Put them on me," the sailor said.

The colonel's nostrils flared, but another sailor was holding his son by his jacket, and so the colonel knelt in a puddle before him.

"Here," he said. "Might you know where I could get another pair?"

"You can have mine, if they fit." The man stepped out of his wooden clogs, open at the back; the colonel's feet would be soaked and frozen within minutes. He didn't complain. One of the other sailors squatted and punched him in the face.

Kate did nothing. Horst pulled her away, but over her shoulder she watched the colonel with his bloody face struggle to fit his boots on the sailor, knowing that she'd remember this moment with shame for the rest of her life.

At the station gate Red Cross sisters told the refugees that they could get housing at the criminal courts building, as the courtrooms had been turned into dormitories, and an army band at the end of the platform struck up Wagner's *Lohengrin*. Another Red Cross sister sprayed Kate with lavender eau de cologne as she squeezed through.

Horst said, "It was right not to stop, Kate."

"It was expedient."

"He's alive and so are we. At the moment, none of us can wish for more."

Taxis had disappeared. Instead, lined up outside the station at the high curb were crude beer wagons pulled by stolid bony horses.

"Is this all you have?" Horst asked of an older, stooped man, leaning against the wooden side of the first wagon, wearing the lacquered top hat of a cabman.

"The best we have," he said, and gestured expansively. At first Horst looked about to refuse. Then he laughed.

"Yes. All right." He helped Kate up into the hay spread over the flat back and said, "Just what I've dreamed of for years, taking you down Berlin's most elegant street in a beer wagon. Unter den Linden," he said, and climbed on himself, the hay crackling beneath him as he settled in. Kate slid her hips around until the hay was no longer poking her legs and smiled at Horst, leaned against him.

"Like a ride from my childhood," she said, knowing it would please him.

At every corner people were gaming—dice and cards—while others argued politics. Pacifists hawked pamphlets, yelling that Germany's leaders had lied them into war, and former soldiers tried to drum up support for new units, the *freikorps*, to defend Germany from the Reds. The streets weren't cleaned of trash, no one moved aside to let the elderly pass, and people stepped in front of cars without waiting for lights to change; if the impatient drivers sounded their horns, the pedestrians pounded on their hoods. The air smelled of burned papers and wasting bodies, and the waxy-skinned Berliners, once famous for their curves, were gaunt and thin, with dark rings under their eyes. The few children she saw were older—three or four at the youngest—but even then they were carried by their parents, their bodies misshapen, their heads large, their eyes ulcerated. Berlin was starving; she hadn't been prepared for that; in the east until the last month they'd always had food.

Along the Friedrichstrasse the advertising pillars were covered in competing colors: red posters and the flags of the workers' councils, black and white imperial flags, orange placards with anti-Semitic slogans written in foot-high block letters: THE JEWS — GERMANY'S VAMPIRES and DON'T DIE FOR THE JEW! These last horrified her. In Posen and Silesia, the Jews had been important allies, supporters against Polish land claims, which perhaps explained why the Soviet soldiers had brutalized them. But this meant that the brutalization was a wider phenomenon, the Jews made to pay for the world's tumult. She wondered if it was so everywhere in Berlin or only here in the working-class neighborhoods.

As they moved away from the station, and as the buildings grew more grand, Friedrichstrasse and the side streets were even more crowded, stores and cafés open, people swarming in and out of them; the thin pedestrians stopped at the innumerable street vendors whose display crates sold stockings, cigars, nuts, and umbrellas, indoor fireworks and gingerbread and tinsel left over from Christmas. They also had food—potatoes and turnips, a few scrawny rabbits that looked more like cats, and then, oddly, luxury items like soap and chocolate. Most of the crowd seemed to be just looking. The beer wagon bumped along past them, surprisingly comfortable with its bed of straw.

At Leipziger Strasse, their progress was slowed by a workers' procession, and Horst hopped down to grab a paper. Actors were reciting revolutionary poems, and a woman who must once have been an opera singer stopped at each corner to belt out the "Internationale." Once it passed they began to move more swiftly, and Horst jumped aboard the wagon again and handed Kate the paper.

Socialist, put out by those now in control of Berlin's government, each column a *dictat:* what was allowed, what wasn't, times and places for boot and food distribution, and all ending with the same line: *the least resistance will be punished by death.* She threw the paper aside and pulled the porter's coat more tightly about her, hoping the line was propaganda, not the literal truth.

In the Palace Square, Spartacists and democrats and socialists stood on various corners, haranguing small groups of people. Bright posters showed White Russians murdering unarmed peasants; others urged Berliners not to forget the German prisoners of war in France. Those clustered about the *freikorps* speakers were anti-English, their slogans making Kate shiver: "We shall hate our conquerors with a hatred that will only cease when the day of our revenge comes again." Were they really so desperate for more bloodshed?

The elegant hotels with their liveried doormen and flapping flags began to appear, though with their brass and copper nameplates pried off and paper ones in their places, and, more ominously, with sandbagged machine guns posted outside and bullet holes arcing over their stone window casings. Unter den Linden was closed—street fighting, their driver told them—so they dismounted south of Pariser Platz, near a publishing company that smelled of chlorine, paid the cabman, and began to walk; Horst would find another branch of the bank in a different part of the city. A mock funeral passed, mourning the fallen empire, with the requisite small band playing sentimental military airs, followed by six men in top hats and frock coats carrying manifestoes and poetry instead of wreaths.

One of the mourners handed Kate two postcards, both of which read *Postcards from the Front,* photomontages of the western and eastern fronts, the back of the first a poem made from newspaper clippings, the back of the other a series of poetry meter markings but accompanying no poem. Someone else handed her a crimson leaflet announcing a masked ball that night; the prize for the best costume was a pound of butter and a dozen eggs. *Worth a fortune!* It made sense; the whole city seemed in some way dressed for a costume party—the peculiar clothing, the mock funeral, even the cars and bicycles, whose tires were white or black wood or made of noisy steel springs. She slipped the postcards and the flyer into her pocket.

On the next block was Kubiat's with its famous desserts and pastry. Their display plates, delicate red-rimmed Dresden porcelain, made it seem as if the great enveloping sea of time had missed this small island of the past. Part of her felt guilty that she'd ever cared about such things, remembering how she'd fawned over this pattern in the weeks before her wedding; part of her was transported back to that younger version of herself, a version that hadn't contemplated anything worse than a few broken plates after extraordinary parties; and part of her remembered the first wave of casualties from a failed offensive in the east, during which she'd found bits of the same china tangled in a wounded soldier's intestines and felt revolted at her earlier self.

Now the china held no sting for her; it was simply something beautifully made, hand-painted, lovingly done, from an era when people had time for such things, and she was grateful that such beauty had persisted despite the best efforts of other men to destroy it.

"Kate?"

"Yes?" Horst was leaning toward her, as if he'd said her name several times. "I'm fine. It's just . . . ," she said, and shrugged.

"The food?"

Looking back at the window, she noticed for the first time the neatly displayed open-faced sandwiches. Egg salad, ham salad, liverwurst.

"Yes."

"I have an idea. I'll be back soon."

"What? You're leaving? Where are you going? For how long?"

"Be calm," he said, and took her hand from his arm. "I won't be long. My bank isn't far, but it doesn't make sense for both of us to go to the Ku'damm."

"Where will we meet?"

"Here," he said, walking with her to the corner and pointing out the Hotel Adlon. "The lobby. It's three now. I'll be back by six, no later."

"Horst, it isn't safe."

"It's safer here. The Reds might be in control of the bank. And you're tired, and the subway fare for both of us, well." He shrugged. They had only a few coins left. "But you mustn't worry, even if I'm late. There might be lines, the electricity could go out. I'll be back as soon as possible."

Before she could respond the unsettling *tat-tat-tat* of a machine gun sounded, and she turned to locate it. Those around her didn't react, and when she turned back Horst was already gone, swallowed up by the crowd spilling through the Brandenburg Gate, its massive sculpture of galloping horses casting a foreboding blue-black shadow over them all.

Horst had left her near a soup kitchen and next to a market selling pale cabbage and paltry turnips, which couldn't have been by accident—they hadn't eaten in two days—yet he'd been too proud to go in. She felt a mixture of gratitude and anger that he hoped she would eat and that he might expect her to do what he could not.

Inside, people were drinking the soup from the Iron Cross mugs discarded by the soldiers each time they'd been handed out. Her stomach growled yet she decided to walk off her hunger. West was the Tiergarten, its paths narrowed by piled snow, its heavy trees strung with red banners, its fields swarming with former Russian and French soldiers who stood by shacks with small smoking chimneys, watching her approach. She swerved south toward Potsdamer Platz and its streets of small cheap restaurants, their menus printed on the backs of old war maps and taped to their windows. A few were translated into English. She stopped in front of a restaurant, its windows glowing, frost arcing across the corners, street vendors outside selling cigarettes and soap. A window banner advertised REAL SOUP for sixty *pfennigs* . . . How hungry she was! If only she had a few coins. She took a deep breath and plunged her hands into the coat pockets, meaning to give herself courage, and her fingers struck metal. Could it be? It was. But how? Had the colonel known of the money and left it for her, or had he simply forgotten? She wished Horst were here to share it with her, but even so, astonishingly happy, she decided to go in.

Though without fat, the soup was hot and pleasantly salty, restorative if not nourishing, and she found something almost sensual in once again attending to the senses: her bare fingers wrapped around the warm porcelain, the smells of coffee and of baking bread, steam swirling around her face as she bent to sip the soup, the sense of calm and order that a bustling restaurant gave her.

She let the small roll soak in the broth until it was soft enough to chew, and while she waited, a former soldier came in and played patriotic songs on a harmonium, "Deutschland, Deutschland"; "Die Wacht am Rhein." He played poorly, skipping notes and missing phrases, and during this two older men at the table beside her carried on a heated conversation about dessert wine. The heavier one wanted an expensive bottle of port. "Why not?" he said to his thinner friend. "You've heard the rumors too. Ruinous taxes once we sign the treaty. How else can we pay their outrageous indemnities? Why not spend our money now instead of losing it?"

"But President Wilson—" his companion started to say.

"Wilson! Wilson and the peace! He's going back on his words, they all are. 'A just peace, food for the starving.' Do you see evidence of any of it? Look at this man here," he said, and indicated the soldier who had finished playing and was holding out his cap for donations. The heavy man had a point; the soldier seemed tubercular or typhus-ridden and had a hacking cough, a rash, a sweating face. The man gave him a few pennies and snapped his fingers for the waiter. "A bottle of port for each of us."

The other patrons generally ignored the soldier, eating quietly without meeting his gaze, and Kate, finishing off her soup as he made his way around the dining room, supposed they had become inured to such sights. The soldier looked so abashed that she gave him the fifty *pfennigs* she'd planned to spend on dessert and was happy when her ersatz coffee arrived before the bottles of port at the next table. Sitting next to their bacchanal would depress her.

The drink was hot and black but had neither smell nor taste and was served without a teaspoon to stir in the accompanying dash of molasses. Once again came the *tat-tat-tat* of machine guns, not too far off, and Kate studiously avoided reacting. Too studiously, perhaps. The waiter said, "It's all right. The sailors are probably just firing off their guns over near the palace to make sure people know they still have them.

"You're not pregnant, are you?" he added.

Those around her quieted. She felt herself blushing. "No, why?"

"I could give you milk with the coffee then."

She laughed with relief. "No, but thank you. I didn't expect it. And I'm fine. I've been in Poland. Milk is plentiful there."

"You see," the heavier man said to his companion. "The Poles eat better than us now."

"I'm sorry you didn't come to us before," the waiter said. "We used to serve the best stew in the city. Even six months ago it had real meat."

A church clock struck five thirty, its somber bells sonorous in the frigid air, which seemed to vibrate in the dark. She was going to be late if she walked; she had enough coins left, so she decided to take a tram. The other people waiting for it were oddly dressed, the men especially: military trousers and civilian jackets, civilian trousers and military caps, military greatcoats over overalls. She leaned out and looked down the tracks, then settled back to wait. Others were apparently used to waiting; several began a dice game, hazard or craps, which reminded her of London, where, during her training, she'd twice found dice in a patient's stomach under the fluoroscope. Both times, they'd been lookouts at gambling dens and had swallowed them when the police came.

The tram appeared around the distant corner, bell clanging, car shimmying, the overhead cable sparking. It stopped smoothly before her, the doors swung open, and just as she was about to step forward, men cut in front of her to climb on. Was it just the dark that brought out the worst in people? She waited her turn quietly.

A giant bearded fellow wearing mismatched boots let three nuns in habits get on, but when two older women started forward he held out his arm to block them. "Not you," he said. "Walk."

They turned without protest and Kate started to join them, hoping Horst wouldn't grow too worried.

"You," the man said, his raised voice making Kate shiver. He dropped his arm. "You're all right. You can ride."

No one offered her a seat. The collector pushed through the crowded tram, bypassing the men and charging women varying amounts, and Kate waited for him nervously, wondering what would happen if she didn't have sufficient money. But he simply glanced at her and pushed on.

The bearded man said, "Your coat."

Was he asking her for it? She pulled back. "Pardon me?"

"It's military. High command, from the looks of it. If you have anything military on, you ride for free."

"Oh. Thank you." She noticed for the first time his army tunic.

He spit a mouthful of sunflower seeds on her boots and worked his tongue around his yellow teeth. "He must have thought you were a military nurse."

"I was." She opened the coat, showing her nurse's uniform.

He spit another pile of seeds on her boots and shrugged. "Perhaps. Everyone would like to have been in the military now."

Outside the Adlon with its grand flapping flags another pacifist was hawking his wares; inside, its luxurious lighted lobby was crowded and noisy with well-dressed guests, the raised voices a mixture of French, English, and Italian. The victors' hotel. Horst sat beneath the overhanging leaves of a huge palm potted in a massive brass urn, moving his foot nervously back and forth over the burgundy carpet, looking like an interloper. Until the last months he would have looked as though he owned the place.

He jumped up when he saw her. "Where were you?" His angry tone meant his trip had not been successful. How could it have been? He'd had nothing with which to identify himself even if the bank had been open, and little to trade or barter; on the train, the engineer had eventually claimed his surgical instruments. All they had left now was the porter's coat and Horst's cigarette case.

"Walking," she said, and shrugged. "I'm sorry. I lost track of the time."

"No," he said, his shoulders slumping. "I'm sorry. I was worried, that's all."

If she could get him back toward Potsdamer Platz, she could buy him something to eat and his mood would change; she had enough left for a small meal. He was going to be so happy. She plunged her hand into her pocket and pulled out coins and the flyer for the costume ball. "We could get you something to eat, then have a bit of life."

They'd come to Berlin because the train was headed there; Horst had gone to the bank to get some money. Now they had to do what they could; she hoped he understood.

He smiled, a younger, more spontaneous self. "Yes, let's."

As they climbed the old wooden stairway, they heard a Mozart waltz shift abruptly to a cabaret song, which was itself soon overtaken by an odd assemblage of sounds like metal and wood being struck random blows. The musical battle went back and forth until they reached the top, where a hand-painted yellow sign over the doorway read: ENTERING THE REPUBLIC OF DADA.

Waves of smoke rolled out when the doors opened, smelling like burning stubble, and the bright, large room was low-ceilinged and overly warm after the biting cold, but Kate resisted the urge to remove her coat. There was no one to hold it for her, and even if there had been she wouldn't have trusted she'd ever see it again; some smart Pole ready to take advantage of her. Better to be too hot for an hour than cold for days on end, best of all to be quick.

People crowded in wearing outrageous costumes, bits of pieced-together fabric, an enormously fat John Bull, a tall thin woman with a gigantic raven's head perched on her narrow shoulders, Russian grand dukes who might have been real, country people with their wooden shoes, one man wearing the tall lacquered hat of a cabman. Three bands seemed to duel from a huge makeshift stage, a classical quartet and a more ragged assembly of wind instruments and then a group of people holding trash-can lids and saws. The room swirled with activity, one group of people sitting and listening as the classical musicians played and then standing to dance to the cabaret songs, another, dressed in more traditional costumes, doing the reverse, and a third group moving about the floor in an odd shuffle that looked like nothing so much as shell shock.

Just inside the door, a man dressed in a peculiar assemblage of cardboard pieces grabbed Horst by the sleeve.

"Very professional," he said. "Herr Doktor." To Kate he said, "And you?"

She opened her coat to show her uniform.

"A nurse, good. Stick close then." He pointed out a man wearing a mass of pink feathers. "That man there is a hemorrhoid, and I'm an influenza germ."

"That's rather morbid," Kate said.

He stepped back as if surprised. "You think so? But God created me, you see. A new plague. I'm killing young women mostly, which I need to do."

"And why is that?"

"I should think it obvious." He turned away, and as he disappeared into the heaving crowd called back, "To even out the war's imbalance."

Horst leaned close to make himself heard over the noise. His breath was warm on her ear. "It looks like we've let ourselves in for quite a night."

"Yes," she said. "I only wish we could get something to drink."

"We can," he said, and showed her a few coins.

"Where did you get them?" Five or six marks; it looked a fortune. Why hadn't he shown her when they'd been eating?

He shrugged. "I've talents you've never dreamed of. I wanted to surprise you."

He wasn't going to tell her, but she had a hunch. While still taking in the fantastic costumes—the man across from her wearing an outfit made entirely from corn shucks dyed a deep blue—she asked Horst for a cigarette.

"Yes, certainly," he said, and hurried away after the cigarette girl. She'd been right, then; he'd sold his silver cigarette case to raise money. She wondered if he'd been planning to sell it all along or had only done so upon finding the bank closed. Well, she wouldn't spoil his pleasure by letting him know she realized what he'd done.

The string ensemble was finishing a waltz, but before it did the band next to it—of saws and bamboo poles and trash-can lids—began one of its cacophonous numbers. No one really danced to it, though some women in absurd costumes and yellow- or green-painted faces got up and moved about in odd, rectilinear patterns, while two men took the stage and began reciting poems. Or she supposed they were poems, it was hard to tell; now and then the men would raise their voices, but when they spoke normally their words seemed arranged in meter. Even then they seemed thoroughly angry.

When they finished, the cacophony started again, and Kate asked a woman dressed as a fish what kind of music it was.

"Dada," the woman said, as if Kate should know what that meant.

She nodded her thanks and turned back to the stage, where the cabaret band was now playing. She felt most comfortable with classical music, and the odd assemblage of musicians made no sense, but as she listened to the cabaret tunes she came to find them intriguing and pleasingly unfettered, a contrast with the classical music, which started to feel almost constrained.

Horst returned with two jam jars full of punch and handed her one before turning to the stage, keeping time to the music with a tapping foot.

"I rather like this band," he said at last, and raised his jar in salute. "Here's to the birth of the new!" His voice was loud in her ear, but she leaned in to it and put her palm to his shirt front, he seemed so excited.

Before she could sip her drink a short man in a threadbare tuxedo asked her to dance, and Horst, bowing, took her drink back and let her be led off by the older man. He was so short he barely came up to her breasts, and it was disconcerting to have him staring at them, even more disconcerting that he spoke not a word to her as they swirled around the floor, but in a way his peculiar silence was a pleasant distraction, taking her mind from the difficulty of dancing in boots.

Her attention wandered to the stage, where a man in a red suit was trying to set fire to the curtains. He was tackled, the curtains doused, and then the music and laughter grew louder and another man took the stage and began reading a nonsense poem with his face hidden by a cardboard tube. Kate excused herself from her partner, who was staring now at the stage, and made her way back toward Horst, first getting sidetracked by two Japanese dressed in tennis whites who were playing chess on a table they carried with them, one darting away after each move to pluck cigarette butts from the floor, and then by a man dressed as a carpenter who was balancing wooden planks on his shoulder. He was clearing a path and all other avenues seemed blocked, so Kate followed him to a corner, where a dozen freshly made coffins were stacked.

He shrugged the wood from his shoulder, and Kate asked him if it wasn't a lot of work for a costume.

"It's not a costume," he said, and took a plane from his denim apron and checked its edge with his thumb. "This is my workshop."

It seemed absurd. But the wood, the tools, the line of coffins against the wall; they were all real. "You don't mind a dance here?"

"No," he said, and bent with one eye closed to inspect his work. "I enjoy it, really. My job recently, it's all this." He gestured at the coffins. "I like to think of other things too."

She felt a sharp certainty that the patients they'd left behind in Wilno had been murdered, and she stepped away, back to the music, hoping to find Horst and wanting to leave, but she ran into a group of half a dozen men dressed as officers—and who bore themselves like real officers, backs rigidly straight, uniforms impeccably clean—all blind, traces of their wounds showing behind dark glasses. The next song, a waltz, set them moving, and she turned away so as not to stare, then laughed at herself and watched them.

Shortly it became apparent that they were happy. They were smoking cigarettes and, in one case, a real cigar—whose scent she found indescribably pleasing after the foul cabbage ones—and dancing beautifully whenever the string quartet played, seemingly untroubled by fears of running into others around them, twirling their partners expertly to the three-beat measures of Strauss and Mozart. And why shouldn't they be happy? Even if the war was still on in the east, it was no longer their war; they deserved some joy, a feeling that seemed almost universal in the city after years of privation. She had much to learn from them.

Horst was talking earnestly to an older woman wearing a top hat and little else. Kate caught his eye and took him away. After two dances they sat to rest.

"Oh, Horst," she said, and squeezed his hand. "It seems wicked to enjoy ourselves so much."

"Yes, doesn't it? But you know," he said, "it's almost feverish, the feeling I have. My God, these Berliners, they know how to live."

The music started again and her sense of joy grew. What had restraint and discipline got them? Millions dead, millions of others' lives blighted. *Just live.* She decided to dance to every number, and when Horst grew tired and his legs stiff, she danced with the blind officers, one after the other in a blur.

They laughed, they guided her expertly, they had a young woman smelling of eau de cologne in their arms and if they couldn't see it was perhaps all the better; she could be every woman they'd ever desired. As for herself, she strode among them, enjoying the reversal of roles, the ability to tap another woman on the shoulder—the woman wearing a papier-mâché raven head, the elderly one in the top hat—to choose her partner.

After an hour, hot and out of breath, she decided to sit down again, but the quartet struck the quiet rising opening notes of the Blue Danube waltz—the calls of a distant horn answered by the same notes repeated more loudly on strings, and she remembered how when she'd first heard it she'd danced to it in her own room with only a hairbrush to hold as a partner—and then the glorious swirl of its theme began, and her feet were sliding across the sawdusted floor, circling around the axis of her tall, blind partner again and again; she wanted it not to end. The song flowed on like the river, passing in swirling majesty the rocky outcroppings along the banks near Vienna, rising and falling and rising and falling until it reached the tremulous bars of the pause near the end, where the music seemed about to stop while flowing on more quietly, nearly disappearing and then growing gloriously loud again before its final complete stop left her breathless and thrilled and slightly bereft.

She sat cooling herself by a drafty window, coat thrown open, listening to a man dressed as a palm tree going on about the joys and wonders of the Soviet revolution.

"Food for every person in Russia, every day. And real food. Nothing ersatz."

Two other men stood by, one dressed as a boxer, the other wearing huge spectacles, the rims of which were two small toilet seats. The boxer said, "Just enough bread so no one forgets what it smells like." The second one said, "Yes, and with all the people they've killed, they have plenty for those few left."

"Lies," the palm-tree man said. "Spread by your capitalist brothers."

Suddenly, yet so slowly it seemed she could have reached out and stopped him, the boxer punched the palm tree in the nose, bloodying him. Kate ministered to him, tilting his head back to stop the flow and wiping it dry with one of his green linen fronds.

"Real blood!" the boxer exclaimed, pointing with his padded thumb at spots on her uniform. "Nothing fake about that. Now you're going to win the contest!"

Someone came on stage and held up his arms for quiet, shouting that he had an announcement, and silence radiated out from the stage in waves. When at last it was quiet enough, he said, "Ladies and gentlemen, I'm afraid there's been a mistake. There will be no contest. We haven't a prize to offer."

"Liar!" the boxer said, and pushed toward him. Infuriated, other members of the crowd began to scream and throw things—hats, a shoe, a hammer. The speaker ignored them and began reciting Heine's "Lorelei." Kate left the palm-tree man with his head tilted back and made her way toward Horst as someone broke a chair and threw a leg at the stage and others began to swear at the poem reader. Then a giant man on stilts ducked into the room, his flat level body stretched five or six feet above the floor, an outsize Jew with taped-on side curls and a ridiculous beard, his enormous old coat shiny with wear.

The recitation stopped as the man on stilts made his rounds, swooping and darting, making the crowd ooh and aah as if at fireworks, looming over them all. Greedily, he sank his face into the punch bowl from a height of ten feet in one dizzying lunge, then stood and moved off, picking up giant rag dolls from the corner of the room, two and three at a time, pretending to dance with them and then throwing them into the crowd when he was done.

Closer to Kate, he lifted the hems of women's dresses and stole a wallet from the coat pocket of a passed-out drunk, and people began to whisper as he stood swaying by the stage and holding up his arms. "Be calm," he said. "Everyone, be calm. We do have prizes, just outside. Stay here and I'll bring them back."

He tucked himself in half and ducked through the opposite door, and people waited. One minute, two, three. Kate found herself unbearably excited. What was he going to bring? And when would he return? At last murmurs began; a man went after him and came back, shouting, "He's gone!"

The crowd surged after him. Horst went too, and Kate followed, and just as she reached him she was stopped by a heavy hand on her shoulder.

"Wait, you two!"

It was the boxer, holding a wooden crate. "You see," he said. "I told you. The winners!" Inside was a large ball of butter surrounded by a dozen eggs nestled in straw.

"But why us?"

"Why not?"

Horst took the box from him and held it as if it were a newborn, and Kate covered it with her coat. "So others don't see what's inside it," she said, angling him toward the street, "and so nothing breaks."

It was midnight, church bells were ringing; the few illuminated gas lamps hissed in the snow. An enormous crowd milled on the street and it was almost possible to believe that the people were truly gay, their laughter real; she took Horst's arm, feeling like a giddy child leaving Midnight Mass on Christmas Eve. Even the uncleared pavement appeared in a new light. Perhaps today had been a workmen's holiday, and tomorrow Berlin's traditional order and famed cleanliness would return. She tightened her coat, wanting to believe it.

Horst shouldered a path through the crowd and Kate understood his rudeness; slower, they would have to make their apologies, which might lead to further trouble. Better to anger people and move on than to give them a chance to size them up. Their good fortune might show in their faces.

"Surprising, isn't it?" Horst said once they'd reached the Wilhelmstrasse. "How many people are still out?"

It was. Lights were hit-and-miss and entire sections of the city were dark. She'd have expected that the hunger and cold would drive people indoors, but it was as if a communal sense of expectancy had gripped the crowd; whatever was going to happen they were determined to witness. Up a side street the crowd thinned.

"Look," Horst said. They were in front of Kubiat's again, with its Dresden china.

"Oh, yes," she said. "We were here earlier."

He smiled. "You seemed entranced by it."

"I was. I am." She leaned into his shoulder. "Thank you." She wouldn't ruin the moment by telling him why, what it had reminded her of when she'd first seen it.

"Good," he said. "Let's go in."

"We shouldn't," Kate said. "We don't have much money, and who knows what we'll find in Hamburg?"

"Kate," he said, taking her hand. "We can't put everything off. We've done that long enough. Besides, we'll spend only a small part of our fortune."

They went in and he put the box on the counter. "We haven't money, but we have this," he said, and unwrapped the butter. The waiters clustered around it, staring as if it were the infant Jesus in his crèche. "One-quarter for you, yes?" Horst said. "Some dessert then, and some real coffee? Is it possible?"

Before the waiter answered, shouting arose outside, a blue flare popped open above the street on a parachute, and everyone drifted to the window. The crowd had thickened and was filled now with torches, angry faces and raised voices, and seemed to rock like boat passengers in the swinging, painfully bright light from above. A bedraggled army of supplicants, they were marching toward the granary at the far end of the street, where a mass of soldiers stood with rifles ready. Kate shivered, sensing disaster.

A gray horse burst from the royal stables, coat shiny, leather saddle polished, rider holding aloft a long red banner that whipped behind him, and the crowd roared its approval, but before he reached them a soldier gunned him down. The crowd surged forward, not to help him but to get at the horse; though it was still alive and struggling to stand, they began cutting it with knives, tearing out chunks of flesh.

"Oh, Horst," Kate said.

The soldiers fired again, en masse, and dozens fell. One man held his ruined arm toward the window, the stump flattened and rounded like a mushroom head, and Horst pushed Kate toward the wooden counter just as return fire sounded, an enormous roaring. The soldiers collapsed and the café windows exploded inward.

She didn't know how long she was unconscious but when she

opened her eyes the room was filled with dust and smoke. She struggled up and the air cleared enough for her to see the man with the injured arm lying half in the window, head blown open, Horst lying beside him, seeming to study his empty skull. Horst wasn't moving, and his blood-speckled face looked as though it had been zested.

She must have been screaming; her throat hurt though she heard no sound, deaf in the cannon's percussive aftermath, but at last Horst turned, looking past her, his lips moving. *Kate,* they seemed to be saying, *Kate, where are you?* She crawled toward him over the shattered glass.

K ATE WAS CAREFUL to keep the wash bucket from scraping on the terrazzo stairs so they wouldn't wake their covetous neighbors. Burning shoulders, panting breath, another three steps and she asked her mother-in-law if she could rest.

"Yes, of course," her mother-in-law said, her face a pale blur in the dark. They rested the bucket on a landing and tried unsuccessfully to straighten their fingers. The porter had gone ahead with his load of coal.

"Fruit soup," Mrs. Zweig said, continuing their game of imaginary meals. From the moment they awoke, food was always on their minds, though usually they discussed what they might be able to get that day and how they would cook it. The game was a pleasant respite and made their hauling go more quickly. "You must learn to make that. One of Horst's favorites. A Danish recipe, this one. Sour cream, nutmeg, and fresh raspberries. The height of summer."

"I can just remember them," Kate said, imagining the tart sweetness of raspberries on her tongue, the humid heat when she picked them.

"Or meatballs with bay leaf and peppercorns and caper gravy, and whitefish with apples and onion cream. Though those are really fall dishes."

"It's all right," Kate said. "We can get our seasons out of order." Until then they'd been rigidly adhering to the calendar. "My favorite fall dish is roast lamb with apricot stuffing. I do love it," she said, feeling a rush of happiness at the same time her stomach became even more hollow. "You would too. A bit of parsley and some dark bread crumbs, and the apricots so tender after a night of soaking. Oh, the way the house smells while it's cooking!" She breathed deeply, as if she could detect the aromas now. "And I'd serve it with potato soup. Amorosas, of course, though it's really the other ingredients that give it flavor, leeks and buttermilk and chives."

Her mother-in-law was silent at first, and then said, "If you were in England you could probably have that meal now."

The dig at the English made Kate's throat close. As if she'd read Kate's thoughts, her mother-in-law touched Kate's apron and said, "But I'm glad you're not."

They were still breathing heavily. At last Kate said, "We should be off."

"Yes," Mother said, resting yet. After another minute she stood and they each hefted a side and climbed. Four flights, from the basement to her apartment, then through the hallway and living room to the veranda, where they had to have it all piled up by 6:00 A.M. If their neighbors reported them to the *landswehr,* they would lose their coal and be fined; as it was, the *landswehr* were coming to inspect the basement later in the day, and to help them move and hide it all the porter was taking 10 percent. That would leave them nearly half a ton—almost enough to last the winter, if they were parsimonious. A good trade, really, and possible only because the porter had known the family for so long.

"You will see," Mrs. Zweig had said to Kate. "A good porter means the difference between life and death."

Halfway up they heard him coming down, the rasp of shoes on stair treads filmed with coal dust, and when he turned the corner above them his white tuxedo shirt glowed in the dark stairway. One of Horst's old ones, which the porter was rich enough now not to care if he dirtied. They shuffled aside to let him pass.

"Only one more load for me, I'm afraid," he said.

Kate thought that their bucket grew instantly heavier. Mrs. Zweig must have thought that too.

"What?" she said, leaning forward and struggling to keep her voice quiet. Even so, it echoed between the narrow walls. "You were to help us move it all!"

"I know." He apologized. "I've cut my hand." It was wrapped in a dirty towel.

Though he'd hurt his hand helping them, Kate's first thought was that he was no longer entitled to a full share, yet she said, "You must be careful." She didn't dare touch his hand; her fingers were black with coal dust. "Have you any soap?"

"A bit. Our last cake."

*An entire cake!* If he had that much, he was rich. Kate tried to remember when she'd last seen one. "Wash thoroughly as soon as you're done."

He thanked her and said he would, and they listened to his steps going down. When he reached the bottom the door thunked closed behind him.

They listened until the echoes died out. Then Kate sighed and shifted her grip on the handle. "Shall we?" she said.

"We must." But Mrs. Zweig waited and said, "I never thought it would happen."

"What's that?"

"This. This thievery."

"You're not a thief, Mother. It's your own coal. You must defend each ounce as you would a piece of land."

"Yes, and to keep it, I'm breaking the law. War blinded my son and made me hungry, but peace has made me a criminal."

Kate looked away from the white despair of her mother-in-law's face. What was there to say? Lawlessness and suicide seemed the only two choices now, yet she didn't like to voice the thought, as doing so seemed an admission of failure. Instead, she hefted her side of the bucket and counted the stairs as they rose.

In honor of having successfully moved all the coal, they had a larger fire than normal. Kate stood warming herself by the iron cookstove while she bathed from a bowl.

"We must, occasionally," Mother whispered about the extra coal. "We won't miss a few chunks, and our mood will improve. That's important."

"Mother," Horst said. "Are you talking about me again?"

They sometimes forgot how sharp his hearing had grown since the accident.

"No, Horst," Kate said. "For once she wasn't."

"Then would she be so kind as to share her thoughts?"

"Yes. It's good news. Boiled eggs, for all of us, to go with our dried plums."

"That is good news. Eggs twice in one week. And why are we so lucky?"

"The porter," Mrs. Zweig said. And to Kate, "You see? He's crucial. They were a gift in return for the coal. He didn't have to give us any. The coal was his fee. But he looks out for us."

*Or himself,* Kate thought. And why shouldn't he? The eggs were probably from his brother in the country, where things were plentiful as long as the *hamsterers* didn't find them, and if the gift of a few eggs meant the porter would continue to receive coal or other worthy items in return, his generosity was a good investment. Besides, he'd given them before Mrs. Zweig had bargained for a reduced price, but she let her mother-in-law think as she pleased. Why rob her of her faith in human kindness?

Mrs. Zweig read aloud from a paper she'd found in the entryway. "Two days ago, but still," she said. Wilson was in Rome. "Golden sand shoveled on the streets before him," she said. "He deserves it."

Wilson disgusted Kate. A man who claimed to want peace allowing others to strew sand before him, as if he were a conquering king and they his prostrated vassals. And those poor laborers who had to shovel all that sand for him to tread on and then go back hours later to remove it, most likely without benefit of a meal. She rinsed the rag in the warm water and wrung it dry. "I'll get Marie up, if we're ready."

Marie lay tangled in the sheets, which they'd made of old tablecloths.

"Marie, it's time," she said.

Marie smiled and held up her thin arms to be carried.

"Can you walk this morning?"

Marie shook her head.

"Well then, tomorrow," Kate said, keeping her tone happy. "You'll want to be strong when your mother comes back."

"That's months still."

"Yes. A few." A victim of softening bones, Marie's mother was at a Red Cross sanatorium, a coveted place arranged through other doctors who'd worked with Horst's father. She wasn't scheduled to come home again until summer, but the reports were good. She'd gained five pounds and was no longer considered in danger. "I'll just bring you out."

If the news about her mother was good, Marie's symptoms were not. The pigeon chest, the growing weakness, the teeth so small they looked like buds. As Kate bathed her she tapped Marie's cheek, and the facial muscles spasmed, an alarming sign that the rickets was progressing.

"Marie will come with us today on our outing, Horst," Kate said.

"Again?" Mrs. Zweig said, hovering. "That can't be good for her. It's so cold."

"She needs the vitamin D," Kate said. "She's not getting enough."

"But surely another day won't matter. Or at least a few hours. You should go only with Horst. Then you could get some time to yourself."

"The child needs it," Kate said. But small things were important, as Mrs. Zweig knew, and if they hadn't given up, it was largely thanks to her. She took pride in getting all of them to "dress up," even if it was in the same clothes as always, and in keeping all of their clothes clean, and she wanted Kate to take care of herself.

"Later," Kate said, seeking to be conciliatory, "perhaps I'll walk on my own."

"It will do you good, child," Mrs. Zweig said, and went back to preparing breakfast, feeding paper into the fire to make it flare.

"Mother!" Kate said, surprised. "Not those!"

"Oh, dear," she said. "I'm sorry. I must burn something."

When she saw that they were old letters, Kate laughed with relief. "Oh. I thought they were pages from the medical texts. The yellow paper, you see."

She read to Horst from the medical journals. He was especially interested in eye surgeries, and he wanted to stay up on those.

"For when my eyes are better," he always said. Kate and Mother kept up the fiction, as hope was not a bad thing to lie about having. Horst's doctor agreed. He, too, kept telling Horst to wait. Reduced swelling and pressure, better procedures on the way, who knew what would happen? They might well be able to repair the optic nerve.

"No, not the journals. Never. But your letters from Silesia, I'm afraid," Kate's mother-in-law said.

"That's fine. It's not a time I choose especially to remember."

She had written to Horst's mother while they were in Poland, and when the diseases they were fighting were especially contagious, she'd baked the letters before sending them off. Handling their crisp pages recalled to her the sunken eyes and cyanotic lips of the cholera victims, the lilting babble of typhus sufferers, who moved their heads constantly and for whom champagne was often the best medicine, soothing the sores on their tongues and mouths.

Curiously, it had also been the best of times for them; they'd been stationed in a nobleman's house in western Poland and they'd used the ballroom as a ward, its doors and windows opening onto a court-yard, sunlight streaming in, and there were violoncello concertos on Sundays after Mass. They'd posted regulations—sufficiently ambula-tory patients had to make their own beds, patients who contracted venereal diseases would be tried by summary court—and one eve-ning a week had held a regular scientific meeting during which an officer read a paper and other officers discussed it.

Sent ahead, she'd been the first to arrive at that house and had been scared by the unusual ticking stillness of its vast interior, spooked to hear footsteps upstairs—there were rumors of murders by partisans—then relieved to find out it was only an old servant whose sole job was to go from room to room, over a hundred of them, winding all the clocks.

Horst joked that he'd probably been a young man when he'd started on the first room and that when he reached the last it would mark the end of time. They'd all found it amusing, but now it seemed a dreadful metaphor for what they'd turned the world into: a waste of silver and gold and human ingenuity, an emptiness filled with ruined bodies, most of them young, time ticking away. No, burning such letters was for the better; she'd already burned all the ones that had been waiting for her in Hamburg, though her mother-in-law hadn't wanted her to, letters detailing the deaths of her brothers in the war, of her mother shortly after. All of it could burn, as far as she was concerned; the past was not a time she wished to re-inhabit. She sat Marie in her chair.

"Horst," Mrs. Zweig said, bringing an egg to the table. "This is yours."

Horst felt for his spoon, and then his fingers strayed over the boards. "Salt?"

"I've already done that," his mother said.

"Don't worry, Mother," he said. "I won't be overly generous with it." But he was smiling—a good sign. The first hour of the day usually foretold his day's mood.

"You won't need to be," she said, "because I have been." She turned to Kate. "You're next."

"Oh, no. Let Marie have mine."

"But Kate." Horst put down the spoon. "The egg won't help the rickets, and not having it will only hurt you."

"I don't need the egg. Better to keep it for another day or two, when someone else might. I'm fine," she said. "Besides, I've had one already this week."

"That's not true," Mrs. Zweig said. She took her food journal from its hiding place inside a hollowed-out dictionary where she also stashed the extra food, keeping both from the prying eyes of the *landswehr*. "You see, here," she said, pointing to the week's entry. "You didn't take one earlier either. Come. It must be equitable."

"Yes." Horst pushed his plate away. "If you won't eat yours, I can't eat mine."

There was no sense arguing. Horst was as stubborn as she, and she was hungry. Despite her protestations, she felt relieved.

"Fine," she said, and sat. "If you insist."

From the doorway, Mrs. Zweig called Kate back. "You go ahead, Horst. I'll only keep her a minute."

He paused on the step, raised his hand, then regripped the banister and started down. Over his shoulder, Marie waved to them. Kate hovered, watching, and Mrs. Zweig called her again.

"You must let him go with her. It's good for him."

"I know. But I worry he'll fall."

"Which he knows. He must do some things without being watched."

Kate's face turned warm as she blushed. "You're right. I'm sorry. I shouldn't try to mother him. He doesn't need it."

"No." Mrs. Zweig touched her arm. "Sometimes he does. But it will only work if he allows it."

From her purse, Mrs. Zweig pulled a few hundred marks. "If you pass a butcher's and the lines aren't too long, see if you can find some meat."

Kate put the money in her own bag and said she would.

"And then I want you to take the afternoon to yourself."

"Mother, I can't. Where would I go?"

"Where doesn't matter. You need time away from us."

"I couldn't."

"You must. It's not healthy to have to care so much for us. That and the hospital are all you do."

"He's my husband!"

"And my son. But I can see how he wears on you."

It was true, blindness had changed Horst. During the war Kate had chastised him for his occasional solitary walks because they put him in considerable danger, but now, though she hated to admit it, his constant insistence on solitude was wearying. More than a few times she'd delayed coming home when her shift was done, explaining her late arrival by extra work. She did not want to pity him, as pity was dangerous. Today she was glad they would walk; the cold air and sunshine often drove such gloomy thoughts from her mind in a way that nothing else did, not music, not work, not church, where they only intensified—the dark, the cold, the morbid deep notes of the organ. She found comfort in the open air instead.

As if she'd read Kate's mind, Mrs. Zweig pulled out from behind her a pair of new shoes. Leather, shiny. Kate couldn't imagine what they would have cost, or what she could have sold to buy them. Not the violin—it had been her husband's and was the one thing she wouldn't part with—or the medical texts, and not furniture; they had only two chairs left, and all the spare beds were gone, and the armoires had been the first to go. What, then? She couldn't ask, and Mrs. Zweig wouldn't tell.

She was afraid to touch them. "I don't know what to say."

"Nothing, child. Just try them on."

"Where could you have bought them? No one in the city has shoes."

"I have my connections. Please, hurry," she said, her face excited.

They fit beautifully. Kate turned her foot in the light. And she would be done with those horrible boots from the east.

"But they're extravagant!"

"Enjoy them, child," her mother-in-law said.

"They should be yours."

"No. I'm not out as much as you, and they're your size, not mine."

There was nothing more to say. Kate hugged her silently and turned away.

They steered first for the Hotel Atlantic, their normal route—stumbling or falling was less likely if Horst knew where they were going—the cold wind off the lake numbing their faces. Kate tucked her chin into her coat and wrapped her arms around Marie, and they made their difficult way through the piled snow past the gabled hotel front, where all was quiet at three in the afternoon. Formerly, even at midnight it had been all light and gay. In August 1914, they'd stayed in rooms overlooking the lake, to help get over the shock of their departure from England and while awaiting Horst's medical posting. Then the hotel's shores had been lined with willows and roses, white sails and swans, and peaches had floated in the bottoms of champagne glasses. Now all the swans had been eaten, champagne was reserved for the foreign rich, and peaches were from a past so distant they seemed imaginary.

They turned toward the esplanade and the botanical gardens, past a row of grand houses where roosters crowed from basements, and Horst asked, "Has our route varied? We seem to be near carpenters," he said.

"Sawdust," Kate said. "It's the trees. They're being cut down." The trees in all the parks had already been denuded by the hungry, and now they were being cut down for wood.

"Our fires have been warmer recently," he said.

"Thanks to the parks."

He smiled. "Well, good. It's nice to put them to use. Do we have enough?"

"Some."

"It was stolen," Marie said.

"No," Horst said. "We're just borrowing it. The trees will grow back. By the time you're my age, it will look as though they'd never been gone."

"No, not that," Marie said. "I mean from Aunt Kate. The wood plunderers."

He turned to Kate for clarification.

"The last load I gathered, they took from me. On my way home. It was nothing."

She didn't want Horst to fret; it always made him feel powerless. Marie's next interruption saved Kate from having to. She pointed to a male pigeon with a proud purple chest strutting beside a female over the dirty snow and said, "Look at that!"

Horst turned his head in the right direction and laughed. Kate set her down and let her toddle after them, wanting Marie to strengthen her legs by walking.

"How did you know it was funny?" Kate asked.

"Her tone. She was shrieking with delight."

"Very good," she said, and took his cold face between her hands. "I'll have to watch my step around you, won't I, Horst Zweig?"

"And the wood plunderers," he said. But he smiled to show her he wasn't worried. "My God," he said. "Wood plunderers. What kind of world have we created?"

"One where I can do this in public," she said, and leaned forward and kissed him.

"And to what do I owe that honor?" he said.

"Nothing. I'm just happy."

"Ah," he said. "The shoes."

"That obvious?"

"They sound different. Squeaky. And the smell. I don't recognize it. Leather?"

"I think so." She lifted one. "Your mother is very kind."

"Too kind, perhaps."

"Horst!"

"No. Not those. I'm happy about them. The coal. She needs to be a bit more cold-hearted, really. She can't go giving it away to the porter."

Kate thought of the porter's injured hand. "She's not, Horst. He deserved it. And don't worry. Your mother is fiercer than you think."

\* \* \*

The tram whirred down the street toward them, ringing its bell.

"Shall we ride today?" Horst said.

"I think not."

"Your coat should get us a free ride," Horst said. Then, as if an idea had just come to him, he reached out to touch her arm. "You still have it, yes?"

She let his fingers work over the wool. "I'd rather walk. For Marie."

"But she doesn't walk, you carry her. It's the smell, isn't it?"

"Horst." But it was. Wasting flesh, starving riders, it was too much to endure, although everything else about the ride was more civilized than it had been in Berlin, in Hamburg, even, months before. People were more polite to women, the soldiers and sailors no longer so bold; revolution had not been quite what people had expected.

They circled around the queue, and Marie pointed out a soup kitchen as they passed. "It's the one Kate eats at."

"What's that?" Horst said.

"Marie," Kate said, "you have too much of an imagination." To distract her, she pointed out a series of lurid posters on the wall, which turned out to be anti-Semitic.

"What are those about?" Marie asked. "They look scary."

"Nothing," Kate said. "Foolishness, put up by bitter soldiers."

Over the next blocks Horst fell silent, and Kate guessed he was working out that she did indeed eat at the soup kitchen, that on her frequent night walks after she'd said she wasn't hungry or occasionally when she went out with Marie, this was where she stopped. He would be ashamed, picturing her producing her ration card for coffee and food. The brown, tasteless liquid and the watery bean soup, and the place itself, dirty tables and a dirtier floor, dirty plates and cups and bowls and dirty people. How could they not be? There was no soap, no hot water, and heating was nearly impossible. If they hadn't their extra coal, they would be dirty too.

Yet she wasn't ashamed; she'd come a long way from Berlin. However meager, the soup provided some nourishment, and she couldn't afford to give it up; it made the food at home go that much farther. What would they think if she went in now with new shoes? No matter; she didn't have to. She'd had an egg, and next time she was out she wouldn't wear them.

They turned a corner and Horst stopped abruptly. "Wait," he said. A cab coming from a side street made him hesitate, and he patted his forehead as if trying to remember something until he was sure it had passed, a gesture Kate recognized; it was how he bought himself time.

"Yes," he said at last. "Now we can go."

Closer to the port the neighborhoods grew shabbier, and the nauseating smell of soaking cod leaked from the buildings, even with all their windows shut against the cold. Kate held her nose, depressed by it as always, but grew happier when they heard their first foreign accents among the sailors, English, French, Yiddish, and Spanish. Horst turned his head at each, liking to pick them out, and began sniffing the air. The prostitutes could afford perfume, of course, but it was the cargo from the ships lingering on the various sailors that he was really detecting: coke and ash, manure and straw; one even smelled of licorice.

"You're like a hound," Kate said, which made him laugh.

He sped up now, head down, hands in his pockets; he'd counted the streets and knew the number of steps for each block. He liked to be independent, to fool people into thinking he could see, hated how people yelled at the blind as if they were also deaf, hated even more when they spoke to Kate as if he weren't there. "He should become a piano tuner," one well-meaning neighbor had said. "Many of them are blind." Horst had looked as though he wanted to strike her. At the bar he was always comfortable, enjoying the company of other crippled former soldiers; blind or deaf, missing limbs. The Zokor. Affectionately, he called it the "house of the damned."

It was smoky and raucous, and Kate pushed her way through the crowd, pleased to see von Hoppe sitting on a stool by the billiards table. She could leave Horst safely in his company, and Horst would be happy. They made quite a pair, Horst tall and thin, with his broad straight forehead and narrow nose and his lank blond hair made lanker by poor nutrition, and the squat, stout von Hoppe, whom even hunger hadn't thinned.

"Theodore," she said, and von Hoppe turned and gave a mock bow. "Frau Zweig. How good of you to come."

He appeared to have a sun emblazoned on his face, a perpetual reminder of his luck and his stupidity, as he himself said, making a joke of disaster. During intense shelling two years into the war, von Hoppe had been distracted by six heads that appeared in a crater, unable to tell whether they were six men buried up to their necks or six corpses newly exposed. The latter, he'd decided, as he unscrewed the fuse from a toffee apple that had fallen into his trench, and, finding the powder smoldering, leaned forward to light his cigarette. It had exploded, miraculously not killing him, though blinding him and burning his face.

Horst enjoyed von Hoppe's stories of high jinks in the ranks, which he'd joined despite his aristocratic name, or perhaps because of it. Early in the war there had been stoves in the barns where they were billeted, and one night von Hoppe had rolled against one and caught fire. Though his comrades put him out, the back side of his uniform had been scorched, so he'd had had to wear a greatcoat for weeks, even in summer. In that same barn, fun had been to pour water or cold coffee into the mouths of snorers. It all seemed so innocent, part of a forgotten time, and she thought that for Horst, hearing the tales was like going over imaginary meals was for her: a pathway to an otherwise vanished past.

"Listen," Horst said, tilting his head toward the billiards table. "Did you hear that? In my mind, I can see the balls on the table, and I know from the sound of the striking cue if it's a good shot, whether or not a point will be scored. I can even make out the impacts of the balls against the bumpers. Before long, I might try a game myself."

"It's like being in the trenches," von Hoppe said. "That concentration. Listening to all the clatter and roar of incoming shells, rifle grenades, and mortars, all sensation concentrated on one thing: picking out the sound of one's own approaching death."

Kate thought it gruesome, but it seemed to please Horst, who nodded sagely beside him. "You're sure you're all right here? The lamps don't bother you?"

"No. It's the only place I can stand their smell. Odd, isn't it?"

Inconvenient, too. At home, the garlic odor of the acetylene lamps gave him headaches, so they all had to read by candlelight.

"All right, then," she said. "I'll leave you. We'll be back in a couple of hours." She loosened his muffler so he wouldn't grow overly warm.

He stopped her hand. "No need to," he said, and waved her off. "Nor to come back. I'll make my way home as usual."

He could, though she often feared he wouldn't, and she sometimes imagined him lost or stumbling, robbed, but it was part of his self-imposed therapy.

"Come, Marie," she said. "Now it's our turn for fun."

"Wait!" von Hoppe said, and pulled gift vouchers from his pocket.

"Oh, thank you," Kate said. "You sure you don't want them?" They were from cigarette packs.

"No, no," he said, shaking his head vigorously. "Use them for Marie's book."

"I will." She counted them quickly— a dozen; he must have been collecting them from friends. Now they had nearly enough to buy the picture book. In a month they would. That made her mood going outside all the better, where for a few minutes she would sit on a metal park bench—the wooden ones had disappeared—while Marie played with other girls.

They passed a row of butchers, each with its own policeman stationed outside, and Kate decided not to try her luck just yet. She was tired from holding Marie, the long lines were dispiriting, and it wouldn't do to have to carry whatever she might get throughout the long afternoon. On their way back, then.

She avoided a puddle and looked with great satisfaction again at her new shoes. Foolish, how good they made her feel, but it was true, they did, a bit of brightness in a dull and deadening world. And wasn't that what they were searching for on these endless foraging expeditions, not just food and fuel, warmth and light, but tokens from their own past, buried under the decade's rubble? If not for hope, at least for its possibility?

"How about the market, Aunt Kate?" Marie asked. "I'd like to go there."

"Would you? Good. The market, then."

One of the peculiarities of the ongoing blockade was that in the relentless hunt for food, people brought all their possessions to the market to trade for food and fuel, so it was lush with furniture, carpets and furs, expensive Victrolas and musical instruments, books and bedding and baths. Home, meanwhile, was cold and dark and depressing, a place more often to be avoided than embraced. It was only in such surreptitious markets that one felt at all the vanished sense of abundance; Kate liked at times merely to run her fingers over fabric.

They picked through an impromptu bazaar, established not far from the harbor, stopping randomly at vendors, knowing they wouldn't buy—couldn't—which freed them to pretend. Hats, white gloves, a sterling silver place setting; Marie became entranced with a porcelain doll, rubbing its turquoise eyes with her thumb, hugging it, stroking its pale hair.

"How much?" Kate asked, part of their game.

The woman selling it, hair covered by a faded red shawl, shook her head.

"It's not for sale?" Kate asked.

"For trade. Your shoes." She nodded at Kate's feet.

Kate felt her throat clutch. Those beautiful shoes! What would her mother-in-law say? But the woman had treasures; it would be worth it, and Marie's face was shining.

"Yes, all right," Kate said before allowing herself to think, and heard Marie's breath catch, filled with pleasure. When was the last time the child had been so happy? "But I need something to wear home. Boots, preferably. Have you any?"

Now the woman became animated. The shoes were worth far more than a doll and a pair of discarded boots; Kate was offering a truly amazing deal.

"Here," she said, and held up two matching teacups. "Meissen."

Kate didn't bother to handle them. "Useless as shoes, I'm afraid."

"Or this." The woman reached under the asparagus crate for a bucket of coal.

"The whole thing?" Kate was careful to modulate her voice. It was jet black and lustrous, not the brittle brown lignite they had, and would heat better. Czech anthracite, probably.

The woman's eyes narrowed and she pulled the bucket back. "Half," she said, and quickly added, "And you'll have to provide your own basket."

"I see." Kate breathed deeply, pretending to consider the offer, understanding the woman's sudden reluctance. The last Czech shipments had been stopped as soon as the war ended, and Czech coal was a vanishing commodity; that she had any left at all meant she was a good businesswoman, one it would be worthwhile to know. Even at a loss, trading the shoes might be a smart thing to do. "I don't need the coal," she said at last, "and I don't want the teacups."

The woman's face fell.

"But I'll take them. The coal and the teacups and the doll." Becoming like the Polish woman, Kate thought. "I have other errands to run. I'll be back in about an hour. If you've found some boots in the meantime—size six would be best, but seven will do—we'll trade."

"Thank you, Your Excellency," the woman said, and bowed.

The woman had detected Kate's English roots through her slight accent, which shamed her.

"Come, Marie," she said, and returned the doll to its crate. "We'll be back."

"And can we get the doll?"

"Yes. If everything works out."

The damp tiled tunnel to the harbor smelled of urine and the sea and echoed their excited voices—Marie chattering madly, Kate voluble to cover her doubts. Would her mother-in-law understand or be insulted? Kate hoped for the former but feared the latter, yet Marie was ecstatic, and surely that would count for something.

The blue harbor, flat and cold, was packed with ships but curiously quiet, save for the squeaking of wood rubbing against rubber bumpers; no scurrying dockworkers, no crying gulls, no singing sailors flush with money as they marched off to bars. Instead, armed English marines guarded the entrance to each dock, ensuring that the ongoing blockade was maintained.

"Aunt Kate," Marie said. "Do we have to come here again?"

"Yes, dear." She squeezed her. "It's pleasant to look out on the water."

"I like the lake more."

"Yes, I do too. But we wouldn't want you to forget the sea."

Marie looked puzzled, unable to tell whether Kate was joking. Kate, meanwhile, was balancing as always the need to get exercise against the calories they would consume, though she had even stronger reasons for bringing Marie here.

The barrels of meat were beginning to rot. A month before, a Turkish ship had braved the blockade and charged into port, only to hit a blockade mine and explode; people had rioted over bits of frozen lamb raining down on the docks. The next day, in the paper, there had been a statement by the British admiral in charge.

He'd let the ship go by, he said, as a lesson to the many others who were continually trying to run the blockade and thus putting his own sailors at risk. He had wearied of their attempts and grown more fearful for his men as the efforts to run the blockade grew more bold, and so he had let it happen. Let it be a lesson, he said, and it was; no other ship dared try.

Since then the food stored on the various ships—sent by the Americans, the Dutch, the Swedes, and the Swiss—had remained on board or been stacked on the docks, and Kate refused to allow a single day to pass without the English soldiers and sailors having to see what their government's inhumane policy was doing to the populace. She knew how she and all the women with her on the docks looked, like corpses risen from their coffins. But to no effect, so far; still, if she could shame just one of them into a lifetime of regret she would have accomplished something.

They came upon a young soldier standing by a lone barrel, a briny liquid bubbling up through its broken top. Early in the war, when doing so was still something of a lark, Horst had gone all the way up to the front. A shell hit nearby, sending hot liquid pouring down his back, and he'd been convinced he was hurt badly. Luckily, before he could voice his thoughts, another man told him that a pickle barrel had exploded and that he was awash in brine. He told the story on himself often, before his injury, and it had always been undergirded by a spirit of relief that he hadn't been seriously injured, and yet each time he'd told it, Kate shivered, believing he was tempting fate.

She stopped now in front of the barrel. "What is it?" she asked.

"Pickled pig's feet," he said, seemingly unsurprised by her English. He glanced behind him and then leaned forward. "Would you like some?"

"Please don't joke," Kate said.

"I'd love some," Marie said.

He plunged his hand in and pulled one out and held it, dripping, toward Marie. "Here you go then."

The kindness affected Kate oddly. She noticed many things about him all at once: his health, the pinkish tinge of his nontranslucent skin, his beautiful hair—her own had begun to fall out—the strength and ease of his smooth-jointed movements, which made her see herself suddenly as he must, as she would have when she'd been a nurse in training: weak and slow and unhealthy. He smelled different too, smelled good, a way she'd forgotten people smelled, and because of health, not because he was powdered or perfumed.

Of a sudden she felt neither gratitude nor relief at his kindness, not even joy, but rather anger, a deepening one with profound roots. She recalled the words of her first head nurse, who'd chastised Kate and the other probationary nurses when they'd been shocked by patients with grotesque steam burns: "Remember that you are British women, not emotional Continentals. Keep your heads." But Kate didn't feel British any longer. How could a people so well fed, so well dressed and well shod, so kind individually, be so cruel nationally? She detested the ease of his kindness, the nothing it had cost him. Did he not realize, did those who sent him not realize, that it was luck and nothing else that separated them, that decreed he would be born a hundred miles west and so would live, and not just live but prosper? That her own niece, whose hand she clutched, had had no part in the crime for which she was daily being punished? Worst of all was the thought that except for circumstances, she who had been born English would not have recognized it either.

"Come, Marie," she said, turning away. "We can do without."

She hurried back through the tunnel to find the sun setting over the city skyline, the church steeples black against it, the low sun like a flaming balloon.

"Did I do something wrong, Aunt Kate?"

"Not you," Kate said, shaking her head. "Him. Them."

"But what?"

"It's complicated, dear. But if we'd taken it from him, he'd have power over us. Nothing is worth letting someone have that." It was more important that Marie learn to be right than that she eat. She felt horrible denying her food yet told herself the small amount wouldn't have mattered.

"We're not to go back to the market then?"

"Right now." It was a good thing; it would take her mind off her anger.

Marie at least seemed mollified. Military horses blocked their way, English and therefore beautiful, and she did her best not to look at the riders. One horse dropped a steaming pile of dung on the cobbles, and Kate was shocked to see a man scurry across the street and squat before it, picking out undigested corn kernels and piling them in his hand. When he had several he ate them and then, seeing her, turned away. The appalling thing was that he seemed to do so not from shame but to hide his treasure.

Their shortest way back was past the St. Nikolaikirche, with its massive steeple and more massive cemetery, its constantly tolling bell. They stepped aside to let a moving van pass, and Kate's feet were suddenly damp. She was standing in a puddle, and when she looked down she saw her shoes had split, water flooding in. She felt sick. Cotton, not leather, covered with a layer of varnish; she'd be lucky if they lasted till home; she couldn't trade them now.

"Oh, Marie," she said. "I'm sorry."

"What, Aunt Kate?"

Before she could explain a car backfired in front of them and the horse bolted and the van's wheels hit the curb, rose partway up, and slipped, the frantic horse in its pulling tipping the van on its side. Bodies spilled from the back, wrapped in white grave clothes that seemed to glow in the darkening air.

Another proof that time had slipped backward, plunging them into a medieval world, the curious, terrible afterbirth of the war, where the dead were carted to the cemetery by the dozens as in plague times, and corpses were left to rot unburied, slabs of flesh slipping off the bones like damp brown soap, the bodies exposed to wind and weather as criminals' had been on the gallows, hissing and popping on summer nights as gas escaped them, or trembling and rustling with worms and maggots. Would it never end?

* * *

The walk home was depressing. Only every third streetlight was lit. They used the stairs, afraid of a power outage, and on the way passed Frau Ulm, the porter's wife.

"My husband!" she said, obviously distraught. "You have put him in the hospital!"

"I'm sorry," Kate said, instinctively holding Marie away from her.

"His hand, it's infected! How will we pay for his treatment?"

"We'll help you with it," Kate said, and hurried by, not wanting her to bring up the subject of coal when other neighbors could overhear them. "I'll speak to his doctor myself."

Inside, Horst was already at the door.

"What is it?" he asked. "What's wrong?"

Kate explained about Frau Ulm, and Horst's face clouded over.

"Yes," Kate said. "It's not good." Indeed, it could be deadly; the smallest infections now often were.

"And that's it?" he said. "Nothing else?"

"Yes. Nothing." She didn't want to mention the shoes, the dead, the harbor.

"We didn't get our doll," Marie said.

Kate handed Horst her coat and walked briskly into the room to forestall Marie's description of their outing, saying she wanted to read from the medical journals again. "Where were we? The incision had been made, I think."

"There's something else," Horst said, "something you're not telling me."

"The doll," Marie said. "I already said."

Kate ignored her. "No, Horst. I'm fine. A little tired. Did you try billiards?"

He smiled. "No. Von Hoppe did. One shot, to start with. It was perfect! Three points. He potted the red ball."

"Good. Next time it will be your turn."

"Now," he said, "What's this about the doll?"

"We were going to trade for it. Aunt Kate's new shoes. Then we didn't."

"No?" he said. "And how come?"

"The woman wanted too much," Kate said. "My shoes! Can you imagine?"

"But I thought we were going to," Marie insisted.

"I know, child," Kate said. "But we'll find something for you."

"Not a doll."

"Perhaps not," she said, and petted her hair. "But something."

Mrs. Zweig stood nearby, an expectant look on her face. The meat. Kate took the money from her bag and handed it over. "I wasn't able to get any," she said. "I'm sorry. You must be disappointed."

"No," Mrs. Zweig said. "Even the most crushing disappointments become habit, eventually," and she affected a smile.

Her attempt at consolation made Kate feel worse—it would be better if someone yelled at her. She'd been stupid to wear the shoes out at all; she should have kept them in the apartment, at least then her mother-in-law would never know. And she should never have agreed to trade for them.

"I've just the thing to make us all feel better," Mrs. Zweig said, and bustled off to the kitchen. She came back with a bit of brown bread and marmalade, a mixture of pumpkin, carrot, and apples.

"Mother," Kate said. "Not the Christmas can." Not very good, but it was all they had for the year—a single can, weighing one kilo, given out by the government at Christmas.

"Yes," Mrs. Zweig said. "But it's all right. We'll get more later."

*How?* Kate wondered. *With what?* And did she really look so awful that Mrs. Zweig felt she had to be extravagant? She would eat, to show her spirits had revived.

Mrs. Zweig said, "If we're not going to read, perhaps some music."

Kate flinched. "Oh, not tonight, please."

It was her mother-in-law's constant request, one they rarely gave in to. She seemed not to understand that their musical evenings made Horst feel more keenly the gap between past and present—between blindness and sight—and almost invariably his reaction was the same: angry outbursts about his foolish mother, pouting by her, tears and recriminations and eventual apologies. Kate wanted to avoid the entire predictable sequence.

"First," she said, "I must put Marie to bed. She's had a long day."

She felt duplicitous, using Marie as a shield against the approaching storm, but it was for the best; Horst could refuse politely or argue vehemently without Kate present, and if he and his mother had words, they could do so in private. And Marie *was* tired, worn out by disappointment.

"Come, child." She picked her up from the table. "To bed now, before it gets cold."

She sang the English lullabies Marie preferred, and just as her eyes fluttered closed, Mrs. Zweig shrieked.

"The shoes!" She'd found them on the landing, where Kate had hoped they'd be stolen. Stupidity, she'd been planning to say; she'd forgotten that people had become thieves. A weak excuse, but better than the truth. Too late now. Mother was standing over them at the table, Horst sitting beside her.

"I knew something was wrong," he said. "But Kate refused to tell me."

"Yes," Kate said. "I shouldn't have tried to hide it from you. I'm sorry." She bent and kissed his upturned forehead. "You see so much more than I sometimes realize. And Mother," she said, turning to her. "I should have told you, but I knew you'd be crushed."

"It's all right, child," she said. "Hope and age have made me stupid."

"Don't say that!"

"Oh, but it's true." She sat down and slumped beside them. "I believed him when he said they were kangaroo leather. I wanted to believe him. I knew the zoo had killed all its kangaroos and that people had eaten the meat, so why not tan their hides?"

"It wasn't your regular cobbler?"

"No." She blushed and looked down at the ruined shoes. "He hasn't had leather in four years, and makes shoes only if you bring it to him. This was a street vendor."

Kate said nothing.

"I know." Mother tried to smile. "I should never trust them. You see, I am a fool. Knowing it was too good to be true, I made myself believe. If nothing else, these last years should have taught me not to. But how long can one go without hope?"

Kate was surprised when Horst stood and made his way to the piano. Even more surprised when he beckoned to her.

"I think Mother is right," he said. "We need some music tonight."

She couldn't refuse him, but she knew that, bitter at the day's events, she would play poorly. How could she not?

Horst fingered through the sheet music, talking to himself, "No, no, not this one," as he flipped past Vivaldi. "Too frothy." Could he really tell them by feel? He paused at Mozart, said, "That's better," before moving on to Beethoven. "Yes. Just this."

Why would he choose the poet of darkness? *My God, he'll have us all committing suicide.* But it was pointless to argue; he was holding the music up and smiling.

She sighed and tucked her dress beneath her, sat, spread her fingers, and began to play. The dark ponderous opening notes came out sluggish and dull, and for a few bars she felt herself resisting, but as she went on, Horst's hand on her shoulder, squeezing now and then to encourage her, the music began to calm her, its slowly increasing tempo causing her through its beauty to play it as it deserved. Almost unwillingly, her fingers spread and quickened, her feet on the pedals grew delicate, her shoulders bent forward or back as necessary, and as the ghost of her past came to inhabit her, she marveled that Beethoven's grief-haunted notes should be so powerful, that Horst had intuited their power to soothe.

Nearly done with the first movement, she looked up and found Mrs. Zweig beaming.

"Here," Horst said, "that's wonderful. But it's time for you to stop."

"Oh, Horst, no," she said, bending away from his restraining hand and plunging forcefully ahead into the next notes. "Mother's right. This is just what we need."

"Yes," he said, over the music, "but we haven't heard Mother play in weeks."

Kate stopped and Mrs. Zweig blushed. "But Horst! Kate's so much better."

"You're kind to say so. But really, I want to hear you too. It would please me."

His fingers trailed over the keyboard, the first tinkling notes of his favorite waltz from before the war, the Blue Danube.

Mrs. Zweig came and took her place, Kate standing on one side and Horst the other, and began to play. Too fast at first, and Horst squeezed her shoulder to slow her down. As her tempo evened out, he said, "That's better," and moved his hand like a conductor. "You see? The river's just starting to flow, nothing quick about it at all.

"Kate," he said, and turned toward her, hand still raised.

Behind Mrs. Zweig, so she couldn't see them, yet close enough that Kate's dress brushed against her on each pass, they began to waltz. They hadn't danced since Berlin, but Horst's lead was so steady that she knew he was no more likely to steer her into the table and chairs or crush her bare toes than if he could see. The gritty floor, the cold, Horst's blindness, her own gnawing hunger, the world outside; none of it seemed to matter as she gave herself up to the smoothly elegant three-beat repetition, Horst's warm narrow chest pressed against hers, his strong comforting fingers fanned across her lower back.

"Now," he said. "One request. Close your eyes. So you'll be dancing blind too. You'll see. It's not so bad."

She hesitated, guilty at the memory of the condescendingly benevolent pleasure she'd felt dancing with the blind officers in Berlin, then did as he asked. Indeed it wasn't terrible. At first she seemed to be falling, but after a few seconds of dizziness she began to enjoy it, to anticipate the music with her body and to sense herself twirling in space, her husband's encircling arms binding her to the ring of the dance, the two spinning together as if they were rising into the cold air.

# PART II

# LONDON, JUNE 14, 1944

OGS HOWLED AS the buzz bomb emerged from thick clouds to the south, engine rattling, tail fire turning the night sky a lurid orange. The searchlights found it and yet the buzz bomb flew steadily on, part of what made it so unsettling. Seeking escape, spotlighted planes dove and spun, giving their flight human drama, but the buzz bomb's impersonal straight-line movement seemed somehow more deadly. One antiaircraft gunner got lucky, sending a bit of flaming tail spinning into the night, and it whizzed by overhead just as the bomb's engine noise became deafening, the V-1 so low Claus smelled the paraffin scent of its exhaust. The engine cut, and he blew his whistle and threw himself to the ground, praying it would glide farther.

Pressed against the damp curb, the beating of his own heart audible over the air-raid sirens, he found himself almost missing the swish of dropping bombs and their steady explosive *crump, crump, crump.* At least then you knew what to expect: they either moved toward you or moved away. With the flying bombs, anything could happen. One had caught on a barrage-balloon anchor wire and spun to the ground directly beneath it, and three others at various times had passed over only to turn back and sputter toward him as if searching him out, and the toll from all four had been enormous. From the first he'd been irrationally certain they'd be the death of him. He would never get used to being afraid.

A long two minutes later came the dull thump of a distant explosion, far enough away that the ground didn't tremble. He shivered as he stood—the cold, the damp, some lingering adrenaline—glad that he and his sector had made it through this one, until a man farther down the block yelled.

"Here now," the man said, rising from a puddle and squeegeeing water from his coat with his hands. "What the fuck did you blow your whistle for?"

"Just doing my duty," Claus said, aware that sounded weak.

"Well, how about *you* lie down in the puddle next time, and then we'll talk about duty? Christ." A slurred voice and rocking on his feet; it was not yet eleven and the pubs had been closed for less than half an hour—Claus kept his distance. "You've got to learn where they're going to fall," the man said. "Did you not hear the engine still going?"

The advent of the buzz bombs had put people on edge, and there was no way to tell what this man might do; two wardens at Claus's post had been attacked in the last week for not blowing their whistles, part of the reason he'd been so quick with his. "How about we call it an act of God?" he said.

"Oh, that's a fine idea. Between Him and the Farting Furies, we haven't much of a chance then, have we?" He lit a cigarette, the lighter flashing in the dark, turning into a beacon when he didn't let it go.

The unhappy drunk, angry at the figure of authority; Claus wanted to laugh—it was almost a film cliché. "Put that out!" he said, and when it snapped out Claus turned up Chandos Street, part of his nightly rounds that he usually left until later. Smoke was rising in the service alley behind Winifred's, and flaming balls were darting about the back gardens. As Claus clambered over a low brick wall to get at one, he wondered if this was another of Hitler's secret weapons they'd been warned about.

No stirrup pumps were handy and the sandbags were solid with dog urine, so he chased down the closest flaming ball and snuffed it out with his helmet. He hesitated to shine his flashlight on the smoking mess, unsure what he was about to uncover, then caught a whiff of roasted meat just as he made out a scorched beak. A chicken, then; the falling tail fin must have set it on fire. He shut off the light and had the absurd thought that he should have let it burn longer, to cook; now it was only ruined.

A mad chase to stomp out the other flaming balls before they could ignite the outbuildings, and when he was done, sitting winded on a milk crate next to the last one, he counted a dozen. With the elbow of his coat, he wiped soot from inside his helmet. Winifred would be unhappy, worse than when her shallots and onions had been stolen. Those had been part of a single crop, but the chickens she'd kept for five years, baking and bargaining with their eggs; he decided to go up and see her. A good conversation might still cheer her up.

He never liked her building. Leaning but still livable, deserted by nearly every tenant except for her and her husband, Archie, the hallway echoed like a tomb. If he were to film it, he'd want to capture the sense of claustrophobia the narrow, tilting stairway engendered, though getting the right camera angle would be tricky. He knocked on the door, and inside she turned the radio down, calling out, "It's open."

When she saw him, she put down the knife and plugged in the electric kettle.

"Don't mind the mess, I hope," she said, mounding the chopped cabbage with her palm. "Times I can't sleep, it helps to be busy." She rubbed her damp hand on her apron's faded blue parrots and turned the radio down even more until the piano music almost disappeared.

"Not at all. Good to see it." His helmet clattered on the table. The radio was comforting, and this was one of the few places he could fully relax. "The Granada's reopening. Going back as their organist?" He was sure she'd been mistaken not to find other work after the cinema had been bombed, even a volunteer effort; doing something generally kept the fear and hopelessness at bay, though for him that was starting to thin.

Her lopsided hair trembled as she shook her head. "Too much effort, that."

"How about the shelter?" He unbuttoned his tunic, grateful to be even a bit warmer. June, and yet only a week before he'd been so cold that he'd typed up all his reports while wearing gloves. "They've missed you there."

"That lot? They won't miss me. Always gave me a hard time about the books I was in charge of. If they fiddled one or went over their time limit, I let 'em know about it and they didn't like that, now did they?"

"But Mrs. Bankcroft asked about you especially."

"Mrs. Bankcroft."

From her tone he knew what she thought of Mrs. Bankcroft, who wasn't a favorite of his either, as she'd trained her canary in the peculiar trick of taking bits of sugar from her tongue, but he was not destined to discover why Winifred didn't like her. Having once dismissed Mrs. Bankcroft, she wouldn't bring her up again.

"And Archie?" he asked. Her husband. "Due home soon?"

"That one." She waved the knife. "Too busy winning the war."

"Someone has to."

Joking had been the wrong choice. For two months her son had been missing in action, two months that had accomplished what five years of war had not, thinning her frame and graying her hair, and now her husband's work at the naval ministry no longer interested her; there was only grief for her son. If her picture had been flashed on a screen without words or music, audiences everywhere would instantly recognize it as the face of despair.

"No," she said, eyes filling. "It don't matter much now who fights, does it?"

"Oh, please, Winifred," he said, and patted her hand. "You mustn't."

"Mustn't what?" She sat. "Cry?"

"Give up hope."

"Well, I'm afraid I have."

"But have you heard anything about Harry?"

She looked at the pictures on the wall, Harry and his crew standing in front of their plane. The pictures hadn't been there before, as she considered pictures of the living bad luck, and to see them now was unsettling. "Not directly," she said.

He sat forward. "You've had some communication from him?"

"My leg," she said, and patted her thigh. Before she explained, the water boiled and she made the tea and let it draw.

"He sent me the pain, I'm sure of it. To tell me how he died. His leg was caught, see, when the plane was hit. That's why he couldn't get out."

Claus sat back, disappointed. He'd hoped for good news for her. And for himself, really; Winifred's disintegration was like watching his mother's slow collapse all over again, after he'd been tried and sent to prison. He wanted to reverse that. "We don't know that, Winifred. People saw chutes come out."

"Six. That leaves four more in the plane. And all those six have been accounted for. Four prisoners and two dead."

"But that doesn't mean the six were all of them. It would have been easy to miss some in the middle of combat. Nighttime, wasn't it, when the plane went down?"

"Two months and two days. If his body was turned up, or if he was captured, I'd know." Her pale round face normally had a shiny bland smoothness, but today her red-rimmed eyes looked like peppermints pressed into dough. She moved his helmet aside to make room for a cup and saucer.

"What's this?" she said, holding up her smudged hand. She turned the helmet over and shook her head. "Can't have you wearing it so dirty."

He ought to tell her, but it would only make her sadder. Instead he asked about her husband. "Does Archie know anything?"

"Nothing." She dunked his helmet in a tub of soapy water and began restoring its blue shine. "Not likely to, either. The plane came down over land, not sea."

"That's a good thing," Claus said. "Harry still had a chance then. He didn't drown. And pilots can be hidden by the French for months."

She shook her head and dried his helmet, put it back on the table. The smells of burned margarine and boiled cabbage lingering in the kitchen, dirt ground into the floorboards, her morose insistence on imagining the worst; the strain of her missing son was overwhelming her. She seemed to be giving up, and his efforts to provide the reassurance she so desperately wanted felt feeble, so he picked up the half head of cabbage and sniffed its acidic freshness, trying to turn the conversation elsewhere.

"From your brother?" he said.

She nodded. "Easy enough to get still, but the bread's become dear. We've lost so many freighters carrying wheat."

"That what Archie tells you?" He had supposed he'd grow used to it, this pumping of people for information, even those he was genuinely fond of, like Winifred. Instead, it had grown more and more distasteful, and now it was appalling to stand apart and watch himself in action. So it must be for an actor reciting lines that he despised. Yet he went on with it; he would not be found wanting.

"Says they've stanched the bleeding. The submarines are still attacking merchantmen to starve us out, but he says it won't likely happen, this late in the war."

She leaned closer and lowered her voice, as if they were in public. He tried to be subtle about pulling away from the smell of her unwashed skin.

"Says the naval office wants the Germans to think it is working, though, so they'll keep after merchantmen and not go after the troop transports. Says they're far more vulnerable."

"Must be," Claus said. "Every man we get in Normandy means it's more likely we'll win, I'd imagine."

"And doesn't Archie say the same thing."

The air-raid sirens wailed again, the seventh time that night, but she either didn't hear them or pretended not to as she set out spoons, and he wasn't going to put on his helmet if she didn't react; he settled for turning it nervously by the rim. For a long time she'd tossed a pot on her head whenever the sirens sounded, but she'd given that up now too.

"Important work your husband's doing," Claus said, "fooling the Germans."

"Haven't said the half of it. False figures they broadcast in already broken codes, torpedo boats sent out with fake wooden sides to make the subs think they're merchant ships. It's too hard for me to keep up with, though Archie seems to like it. But what's the use? A few more or less mothers' sons that die either way won't change things."

"For some it will."

"But for others it's already too late. Tea?"

"Thank you." He didn't like tea, but he took it to be sociable. A twist of paper filled with sugar was his contribution; some months, nearly half his ration went to her.

"You shouldn't have," she said as she always did, though without vigor.

"It's doing me no good in my kitchen. The mice get it."

"Well then, thanks," she said, and took her usual two spoonfuls, tonight without blushing. She really was fading.

"You know," he said, and touched her hand. "The weather makes everything seem worse. Sunny day, you might feel better."

Winifred pulled her hand free and dismissed the weather with a backward wave. "Bosh. I haven't been out in ages."

"But you can see the rain, feel it. And the cold."

"Oh, I'd feel the same even if everything was in bloom. All the flowers in the world wouldn't change a thing."

Not true; the weather always made news seem better, or worse. His reports on morale mentioned it, the disquiet the coldest summer on record had caused.

They finished their tea and talked a bit more about the falling prices of eggs and beef, the possibility of even getting pork, and she circled back to Harry. "It wouldn't hurt so much, only he was such a good boy," she said. "And I thought after he'd completed all those missions the one more couldn't be bad. I shouldn't have given him the go-ahead, now should I?"

His own mother had believed that everything bad that happened to him had been her fault too. He took her hand this time. "Winifred. Even if you hadn't, you know he would have gone. That's the type of boy he was." Her eyes glistened at his words and he switched tenses. "Is. The type of boy he is."

But he'd only deepened her gloom, and now it seemed contagious; he had a sudden chill feeling and a mental image of a door opening into a darkened room where a body lay, which he blinked away. He really should tell her about the chickens, but he worried that would push her over the edge, so instead he stood and put on his helmet. "Have to go, I'm afraid. Been inside longer than I should." And nearly longer than he could stand; the sirens and Winifred's small dirty apartment made him claustrophobic, a way he hadn't felt since the first days of the Blitz. Her descent into depression was difficult to endure. For years these visits had been one of his few sources of comfort.

Winifred was already up. "Here." She stuffed a few potatoes into his pack. A bribe, though neither of them would call it that, which he didn't want to take.

Two years earlier, her Swedish tenant had told him that Winifred was up to something. *Always digging in her garden,* Dotty had said. *But only at night. Says it damages the plants less, because they're dormant. Never heard of such a thing myself, though I might believe her if the garden was of some account.* He hadn't put much stock in it—Mrs. Anderson was an unhappy tenant who'd once hung all of Winifred's laundry out on the street because Winifred wouldn't give her a key to the front door—but a few weeks later, making his nightly rounds, Claus had heard metal striking flint and flashed his torch and caught Winifred digging. Flustered, she'd pulled her tattered housecoat more tightly around her and tried the line about not wanting to damage her plants, but when he took the shovel and turned back the earth he found newly interred potatoes.

"Look at that," he'd said, leaning on the shovel. "Lucky you. Potatoes in your garden and you didn't even know it. I should keep digging, if I were you. Might be diamonds next, or gold."

"Oh, please," she said, clasping her hands and shifting from foot to foot in her husband's Wellingtons. "You won't turn me in, will you? They're from my brother in the country, and I only sell them to my tenants to make a little extra money. I don't gouge them, I swear."

"Anything else you should tell me?" he asked, his voice sounding sterner than he felt. It was ridiculous that he should make this mild woman tremble, but part of his duty as warden was to watch for black-market activity. If it was the part he liked least and was least likely to enforce, he couldn't convince her of that; she was terrified of being charged.

"My money's here too," she said, glancing back at the building, "only promise you won't tell. Archie can drink it up fast, otherwise, and I have to keep everything out here so he won't find it."

Claus had fallen quiet, deciding what to do, a silence Winifred mistook as a request for a bribe.

"Here." She'd leaned down and grabbed a handful of potatoes and tried to stuff them in his coat pockets. "Take these."

"I can't," he said and stepped away. A few potatoes dropped to the ground, and in her desperation she slipped on one and stumbled against him.

"No, I insist," she'd said, her voice loud enough he feared she'd wake her tenants. "It's my feeling wardens aren't appreciated enough. It's a way to support you, see?"

He'd taken them, sorry for her desperation, not wanting her to go on, convinced she'd live in fear of being turned in if he didn't. Now the bribe had become habitual, a social ritual that retained only a whiff of its origins but one he still found distasteful. The only way he could think to pay her back was with the sugar; whenever he stopped by, he made sure to leave extra behind on the table. "For Archie," he'd said the first time. "His job is more important than mine." That had seemed to mollify her.

"How about you and Archie go to see your brother up in Norfolk?" he said now. "These bombs are getting worse, and lots of folks are leaving London. Fifteen thousand a day, I heard."

She waved him off. "Archie wouldn't ever."

"You could. He's probably safe at the ministry. But here, well . . ." He left the thought unfinished but she didn't respond. "It might only be for a few weeks, until we overrun the launch sites."

She shook her head. "My time will come whether I go or stay. No sense trying to get away from it. There's Mrs. Caulfield from next block but one what was afraid, and went by train to Reading. The doodlebug hit the bridge when the train was on it and she was as dead as dead can be."

He stood on the back porch, hand on the gummy painted handrail, sensing nothing peculiar. It had rained again, and the smells of damp pavement and ripening trash and turned earth drifted through the chilly air, underlain by the acrid dust from pulverized buildings. A few small AA guns were shooting blocks away, gunners testing their aim, and the surrounding backyards were lit up intermittently by tracer bullets and searchlights, and he closed his eyes in hopes of remembering it exactly in case he was ever to film it, the tiny sunbursts that seemed to erupt inside larger ones whenever the AA guns crackled, the clink of falling antiaircraft shells striking slate roofs and cobbles.

Everything was in order, though that failed to cheer him. As he made his way down the alley behind the tidy backyards with their mounded Anderson shelters he felt furtive, and he was unable to shake off Winifred's corrosive gloom.

At the Mahoneys', an Irish family of ten whose father had been killed at Dunkirk and whose oldest had landed in Normandy the week before, he dropped half a dozen potatoes and several bent tins in the egg basket Mrs. Mahoney kept on the bottom step. Stealing, it would be called if he were caught, as he'd removed the tins from a bombed-out grocer's, though he never thought of it that way. Wartime had blurred formerly clear lines, and he neither sold them nor kept them for himself. To Mrs. Mahoney he now gave baked beans, corned beef, and cherries, the last a luxury they probably hadn't had in months. If she'd saved her flour rations, she could make a pie.

The other needy families about were mostly English, and he preferred giving to the Irish. *Stick to your own,* his mother had always said. *No one else will.* He'd have helped German families too, in honor of her, but they were all locked up; had been for five years. It was only luck that had kept him from being interned for the duration, or so it seemed at the time; now he wasn't so sure.

In the park, he listened behind a sheltering yew hedge. This close to midnight, no one but police should be about, and he was familiar with their routines; still, it wouldn't do to be careless. A chilly wind moving through the yew leaves like water, the steady whine of the all-clear signal, the dim, distant barking of dogs, but no human sounds, no loud footfalls to indicate a stranger's approach. He pulled out his thermometer, unraveled the string, and swung it in a circle over his head, the most dangerous part of his night. How could he ever explain it if someone observed him? Yet it was foolish to be afraid. Who would be watching a warden?

Thirty seconds was long enough to ensure an accurate reading; he covered his flashlight with his fingers and switched it on, reading the mercury by the reddish glow of his skin. Forty-seven, an October chill in June. Even the weather seemed to have gone mad. He dampened his finger and gauged the wind—steady at about five miles an hour from the north-northwest—before rolling the string around the thermometer and slipping it inside his tunic, then heading back to the post. If he made it by midnight, he might still get the best watch.

# JUNE 16

THE VAGUE TINNY NOTES of a gramophone drifted through the walls from another flat. Mr. Morgan's, probably, since Morgan was an auxiliary fireman and sometimes kept peculiar hours, and no one else was likely to be up at 6:00 A.M. Mrs. Dobson, their landlady, complained often about his hours and his soot-stained sheets.

Claus listened, able at last to identify one of Glenn Miller's V-discs, and as the final romantic notes of "Moonlight Cocktail" gave way to the brassy opening tones of "Pistol Packin' Mama," the floorboards creaked in the hallway. Mrs. Dobson perhaps, up to ask Morgan to shut it off, and though he liked the music he wished it weren't being played. He'd been careful to return home quietly himself, and once Mrs. Dobson was up she might come round unannounced.

Even with the door held shut with a sandbag—it was permanently misaligned from bombs earlier in the war—there was always the possibility she could push it open with a tray of tea, saying, *Something special for a special tenant.* He suspected her of snooping, but he might have been only imagining it, though of course he couldn't ignore his suspicions.

The music went on, the floorboards fell silent; he had much to do and little time to do it. He keyed the lid from a cod tin and ate while rereading the just-written letter, careful not to spill any oil, and decided that it was fine except for one small detail. He put the tin aside and added, *Isn't it wonderful about the Allied landings? Five out of every six men is supposed to have survived.* That would alert Madrid to the order of composition; this was letter fifty-six. The embargo on letters to the Continent, in place weeks before the D-day landings, had only just been lifted, and this letter might arrive with ones sent both far earlier and somewhat later, yet its news was more relevant and he wanted Madrid to decipher it first.

His eyelids were heavy, his concentration waning, even his bones felt tired; he wished he could put off the last part of his task but that would only worsen his workload—Lisbon and Oslo were waiting to hear from him too, since he was currently unable to broadcast—so he bent over the table and wrote out on another piece of paper the crucial news: all leaves for American troops in the Hastings area had been canceled and train service there interrupted, indicating the imminence of the long-expected second series of landings near Pas de Calais. This was the real invasion of France, he emphasized, adding Winifred's information on the loss of grain and the naval department's worry over convoys, details on American supplies, and specifics of London bomb damage. Lord Hamilton's unhappy rumblings about ships removed from convoys for resupply of the Normandy troops also went in, a report he'd lucked upon because the speech had been cleared through the MOI, news that would thrill Madrid, and he followed that with scraps of overheard conversations on buses and trams concerning the badges of American and British units now passing through the city. The Americans had large black *A*s on their sleeves; he didn't know what that meant, but he promised to try and find out. He wrote steadily, and though it was dry work and the bone of resentment showed through, weariness was not a reason to quit.

He suggested Madrid discount some of the troop movements because he'd gleaned the intelligence from his fellow warden Herbert after too much stout, Herbert beating Claus repeatedly at darts and not having to pay for a single drink; by the end of the night, Herbert's memory might have been unreliable. Yet Claus thought it wise to include it as the Germans were hungry for news, and it was always better to have too much than too little. The last bits were about the disappearance of the post–Normandy invasion elation with the advent of the V-1s, and a third request for a new radio crystal; without it, he was effectively silenced. A request for money, too. He'd been spending so much on reports and getting gossip that his financial situation was precarious.

Encoding all of this involved a columnar transposition of double substitution, a type of math, really, that in the end to anyone else would look like a meaningless scratch of letters but that demanded great concentration. When he was done, his head throbbed and his neck was stiff and he wanted to break again, but he refused to, as the Glenn Miller interruption had already put him behind schedule.

He ground the antipyrine tablets into fine white powder with the pestle and stirred the powder into water, careful not to let the swirling spoon strike the glass, then strained it through cheesecloth while he gathered a match, a pin, and tape. An organic secret ink from lemon juice would have been far simpler and certainly preferable, but lemons were often hard to come by, and vinegar and ammonia gave off too distinctive a smell, something all Londoners had been asked to look out for in suspicious concentrations. Mrs. Dobson and her sensitive nose would be sure to notice, and the analgesics at least had the advantage of being odorless.

He taped the pin to the matchstick, dipped the pin in the solution, scraped it dry on the glass rim, and at last began writing the encoded material between lines of the letter. The lightest of pressures, the smoothest of motions, since even the tiniest mark raised censors' suspicions. Beginning with the third line he slid a heavy golden ruler under his work, and each time he looked away to dip the stick he memorized his location by inch marks: two, three and a half, six and a quarter; then he always knew where to start again. He'd been at it for ten minutes when he heard the Home Guard tread in his alley and marked his spot at eight inches and stopped.

Without observing the lightening sky or looking at the clock he knew it was six forty, because—foolishly, and against regulations—the local Home Guard unit always ran its patrols at the same time. When they were gone he bent to write again, ignoring his sore fingers until a few minutes later when the Glenn Miller music stopped abruptly, which caused him to look up and listen. He waited; five minutes, six, seven, making sure no one was outside his door listening to him listen, as the last thing he wanted was to be discovered by some overeager Home Guard. The Manchester papers had recently splashed one of the guards across the front page for just such an exploit; he'd discovered a spy in his lair and shot him. That it turned out the man he'd shot was no such thing was of little comfort. At last, certain no one was around, he bent again to his task.

His stomach hollowed and his hands began to tremble. What

had he been doing? And more to the point, where on the page had he been doing it? He had no idea where he'd been writing. He'd pulled the ruler down to his lap when the music stopped, instinctively trying to hide it, and though he stared at the page hoping a visual memory would come to him, none did.

He sat without moving, as if by sheer force of will he could turn time backward, and then began to move swiftly, holding the paper up to the light and shading sections with his hand, looking for the faintest trace of the pin's passage. But he'd been too good; not the slightest mark showed. At last, in despair and disgust, he tore the letter and its encoded news into pieces over the sink, careful not to let a single scrap fall, and when they were small enough to be illegible, he burned them.

Done, he allowed himself the perverse luxury of looking at the clock; he'd wasted two and a half hours. Headache worsening, he drank the rest of the antipyrine solution, certain that his planned-for half-hour of sleep wasn't going to happen. With it he'd function poorly, without it barely at all, but he was too upset to do anything now but toss and turn. He couldn't tackle the letter again, let alone begin the ones to Lisbon and Oslo, since he was too agitated to work cleanly; no, it would be better to do that later, when he was back from his next round of inspections and his hands were calmer, his emotions under control. Better still, of course, not to have to write them, as the strain of doing so was making him old, and with the invasion accomplished it seemed pointless. Yet Bertram insisted.

He decided to bathe early—not caring that it wasn't his scheduled bath day or that the rumbling pipes might wake others—to at least begin his day clean, and in a fit of surliness drew a full bath, ignoring the black line painted low around the tub indicating a properly rationed one.

# JUNE 21

HYDE PARK WASN'T directly on his route, but he made a point of passing Speaker's Corner every few days, as it was a good way to gauge public opinion. This morning the crowd was larger than normal and more vocal; through the damp air, raised voices reached him at a hundred yards. About the V-1s, probably. The Ministry of Information had kept news of them from getting into the papers, but that didn't stop people from talking. Recent rumors had 250,000 Londoners dead, Churchill's daughters among them, both of which were equally incorrect and incorrigible.

It was another damp chilly day, scraps of rain and clouds, though oddly the Bradford pears along the perimeter were blooming for a second time, looking bridal against the gray buildings and grayer sky, so white they were tinged with blue. Pollen filmed the pathways, the air smelled of pine pitch, and even the birds seemed confused; only a few were singing throughout the park, as if afraid of what their songs might conjure up. The year without summer, people were already calling it: the explosions, the unusual cold, and the endless rain; nature seemed not to know what to do in the face of a disintegrating world.

He slogged closer through puddles and realized he'd mistaken the day's topic. Evidently someone had been arguing about the French, saying they were weak and of little service during the invasion; the speaker—French himself, from his accent, and fitted out with the requisite black beret—brought up 1914 and the Miracle of the Marne, when the all-but-beaten French had stiffened and stopped the Huns. "Where were the British then?" he asked. Younger, he might have shouted; now, older and stooped, it seemed all he could do to make himself heard.

A nurse in a white cap and scarlet cape stepped forward. Her face wasn't visible, only the unusually healthy shine of her hair, but she had a strong voice.

"Smartly, on the sidelines," she said. "And the French themselves would have been better off losing that battle."

"What?" said the man on the soapbox. Aghast, he wobbled and looked in danger of falling. "Lose the Marne and let the Germans roll into Paris?"

"Yes. Then all of that wouldn't have happened." She gestured to the wiped-out buildings stretching down Oxford Street beyond the Marble Arch, the crumbling trenches that had been dug before it in the grass. "Hitler wouldn't have happened."

"You disgrace the memory of the heroes of the Marne," the man said.

"Heroes of the Marne?" She wasn't at all flustered by his anger. "They're nothing more than dead fools, and the victory of 1918 was a senseless one. It served only to make the French suffer more a generation later. Those deaths brought this life," she said. "What kind of life will this war bring?"

A few in the crowd called for her to quiet down, and one stout woman, speaking in strongly accented English, threatened her with a furled umbrella. Claus slid between her and several others, the lot of them smelling of damp wool, and pulled the nurse away with him. "There have to be easier ways to commit suicide," he said quietly, leaning close to make sure she heard him as they walked. He caught a whiff of her perfume—real perfume, blackberries and vanilla—which he didn't know but liked, and instantly was on guard: Myra had been the last person he'd responded to as a woman rather than as someone who might help or harm him, and that had been a terrible mistake.

"I wasn't in danger," she said. "Those French weren't going to fight."

"I was a bit more worried about some of the English," he said.

"Ah, but I'm a woman."

"I'm not sure that would have mattered, had it gone on longer." He looked back. A few of the crowd were still eyeing them though none had followed, a good thing for him as well as for her: it would be difficult explaining what he was doing sheltering a woman with antiwar sentiments. He released her arm, but she walked beside him as they passed the looming bulk of the Marble Arch, near enough that their elbows bumped. "You want to be careful," he said. "You'll end up martyred like Edith Cavell."

"Please. No more propaganda." She looked at him directly for the first time.

He stopped, flustered by her pretty but pained face. "She *was* shot by a German firing squad," he said.

"Yes, I know the story. I'm a nurse too."

He turned away, determined not to stare, and started off again. "I wouldn't have guessed. Given that you seemed intent on starting a riot, I thought the outfit might be for a party."

"Sarcasm," she said. "The refuge of the defeated. You brought her up, not I. Yes, she was a nurse, but she wasn't a martyr, any more than soldiers were. Are. Spies know the risks. She understood that if she was caught, the penalty for helping English soldiers escape Belgium would be death, which means she's not quite the victim the English like to believe."

"You certainly know your German propaganda."

"Just because I'm English doesn't mean I approve of everything they do. And you?"

"Me?"

Her glance flicked over him, her deep green eyes marvelously clear. "Despite the uniform, you're American, not English. Do you approve of civilian bombing?"

"In the abstract . . ."

She stopped and another gust of perfume drifted over him. He knew he'd touched a nerve because even in the midst of being shouted down she'd shown no physical signs of fear or anger; now her cheeks reddened as if they'd been slapped. It gave him an obscure pleasure to have discomposed her when an angry crowd hadn't.

"There's nothing abstract about it," she said. "It's done nothing to shorten the war, only provoked a general misery."

She started off again, a bit stiffly as if arthritic, the color cooling in her cheeks, like a woman who'd just come in from a brisk chilly walk. He had the odd wish that she was returning to an apartment they shared. Dangerous to succumb to loneliness—the more profound it was, the more potentially disastrous—and yet it had come to him so quickly he found himself nearly defenseless before it. He had to make a conscious effort to enter his usual mode of attention: half fastened on what was happening, half fastened on himself, checking and rechecking to be sure he wasn't giving too much away; he resented how easily this habit came to him. The strength of his desire not to give in to it, this once, surprised him.

"So," he said. "Do you really believe all that you said? That we'd have been better off if Germany had won at the Marne? That France—and England—would not now be at war if we'd let the Germans win the first time?"

"Certainly."

"And you blame England for this, then?" he said, waving at a ruined apartment building with two names and an address chalked on the remaining brick wall.

"No. I blame England for Hitler."

"We didn't vote him in."

"'They,'" she corrected. "You're not English, remember? And in any case, the Germans wouldn't have either if they hadn't been starved. I saw it. Berlin 1919, the signs were all there. A few fools were blaming the Jews as soon as the treaty was signed. The rational ones wanted no part of it until we starved them."

She had full lips and beautiful teeth, and he forced himself to look away, lest he be obvious. "Ah, the innocent Germans," he said.

She sighed, making a visible effort to control herself. "Look. We were innocent before the last war, but not before this one. Let's not pretend otherwise. The Germans themselves thought the first war a grand thing, at least at the beginning. Have you read Mann?" She quoted from memory. "'We knew that world of peace, that can-can culture, horrible world, which now no longer is, or no longer will be, after the great storm passed by. Did it not crawl with spiritual vermin as with worms?' The war was to be the end of disgust, of the boredom and lassitude that were sapping their culture's strength. Please. None of us should be so foolish now. Slaughter isn't virtuous."

"Well," he said, stubbornly returning to his point. "Perhaps we wouldn't be worrying about slaughter if the Germans hadn't been foolish enough to elect Hitler."

"Hitler is evil. No rational being would argue that. But rational Germans supported him because they starved under the republic, thanks to the French and the Poles and the English. Even the English soldiers were appalled by what the postwar blockade did. This bombing is atrocious, but it was the English who brought war to civilians, not the Germans. How many have died here from the bombing this time around? Forty thousand? Fifty? Every one of those deaths is unjustified, but eight hundred thousand Germans died during the last war from starvation."

"Terrible. But didn't their kaiser have some responsibility for that?"

"Of course. But what responsibility did he have for continuing the blockade a year after he'd abdicated and the war had ended? Another half million died then. After, not during, and every one of them due to the blockade. The English wanted to ensure that the Germans would sign any peace agreement, no matter how brutal, if only to end their starvation, and you Americans didn't stop them. You'll notice too that the kaiser did none of the suffering, whiling away his time in a Dutch castle."

He let the comment about Americans go; his lineage was too complicated to explain. But he wanted to sting her too. "You seem to have escaped the suffering," he said.

Her face changed. "You're quite wrong there. I survived, but I never escaped."

For the next block they were silent. He'd have to let her go soon if he couldn't prolong their conversation.

"So you don't think anything in the war is justified?" he said at last. "You think it's wrong to kill Nazis?"

"That's the problem, isn't it? To kill Nazis you must kill Germans too. That the war is justified doesn't justify everything in it. Civilian slaughter. That's the sticking point."

The rain had brought out the faded, painted ads on the sides of brick buildings below Oxford Street: Teller Pianos, Prince Powders, the Barbee Company, remnants of the not-too-distant past. Beyond the last they had a sudden vista of low mounded ruins and cleared lots, as if a madman had got loose with a bulldozer and knocked down six blocks' worth of buildings for a better view. Claus contemplated it silently as they walked, the exposure of a deeper past, foundations of the earliest churches, buried walls and Roman baths, ancient wells. They were moving backward in time; soon they'd all be carrying clubs.

She'd been watching him. "You see," she said. "It bothers you too. Can you tell me that if you knew where a single bomb was going to land, you wouldn't do everything in your power to stop it?"

"I would. But I can't. None of us can." He could, he might, but he certainly couldn't tell her that. Still, it was an odd coincidence that she brought it up just then.

At Orchard Street they waited for traffic to thin, and he studied their reflection in a chemist's window by force of habit. No one seemed to be watching them, none of the women, a few of them tarts, nor the lone man, a thin small fellow with orange freckles, bad skin, and a prominent Adam's apple like a partially swallowed brick. His clothes looked too big for him. They'd overtaken him on Oxford Street and he was still with them, but he seemed besotted by the tarts. Claus himself looked like a schoolboy with his hands stuffed in his pockets, so he took them out, but then he didn't know what to do with them and stuffed them back in again. The whole thing was like a Fritz Lang scene, his trademark camera angles from inside store windows: the silent, surging crowd, and the two of them the odd note in the composition. The audience would understand their connection immediately, on an emotional level; he wondered if she did.

"You're a very fine speaker," he said, "though I don't think you quite fit the country's mood. And I wonder. At this point, do you really think the Germans even remember what the English did in the last war?"

"History has a long memory," she said. "When I was in France, and the English began bombing French towns, the local French gossip was that the British were systematically destroying all the towns through which Joan of Arc had marched. And that was five hundred years ago."

The orange-freckled boy peeled off, following a tart.

"France?" Claus said. "It couldn't have been easy getting out of there."

"It wasn't."

"And yet you did. Somehow, I'm not surprised." She didn't respond, which *was* a surprise. More surprising still was how much he wanted her to, but nothing he said seemed to reach her; it was like talking to an egg. "You know, this is all rather ridiculous. Arguing when we don't even know each other. Perhaps I should introduce myself. Charles Murphy." He gave a mock bow, which caused the corners of her mouth to turn up. Not quite a smile, but a start.

"Charmed, I'm sure."

Abruptly, he decided to try another tack. "For what it's worth, I understand."

"Yes? Understand what?"

"Everybody lost someone—or something—in the last war. Myself included." And he had: his citizenship, his parents, and, for nearly a decade, his freedom.

She stood straighter, her manner suddenly chillier. "It wasn't the war," she said, "it was in the peace that followed that I lost something. An English peace."

"So you've said. But you know, you really should be careful. You'll get yourself arrested if you anger the wrong people with your anti-English sentiments."

"Feelings you yourself must hold or harbor. Otherwise, you'd arrest me. You're in uniform, after all."

"Not police."

"Military should be enough to do the trick."

"Mock military, I'm afraid. I only look official. Ministry of Information."

"Ah, that explains it then," she said, striding a bit more quickly.

"Explains what?"

"Why you're so poorly informed."

He laughed for what seemed like the first time in months. "Please," he said, moving to keep up with her long rapid strides. "Could I know your name?"

"Planning to turn me in after all, are you?"

"No. Hoping to get to know you."

"Tell me," she said, ignoring his last words. "Why is an American working for the Ministry of Information?"

"Oh, it's not unusual. Most of my colleagues are foreign. French, Poles, Russians, Serbs. We're quite a mixed lot. Filmmakers tend to be."

She turned up the underside of her forearm and looked at her watch. "Intriguing. Films during wartime. Important work, no doubt. But I was asking about you, not them."

He felt his ears redden at the subtle rebuke. "It's a long story."

"And an interesting one, I'm sure," she said over the diesel rattling of an oncoming maroon double-decker. From Glasgow, one of the dozens brought in to replace the destroyed London buses; the V-1s seemed to have a special affinity for their depots.

As it passed she smiled, which pleased him, since it robbed her words of their sting and was the first sign that she might actually be enjoying his company, but before he could respond she went on. "Which I really would like to hear, though I'm afraid I don't have time to, today." She tapped her watch and strode into the street. "I'm past due."

He couldn't think of a suitable reply in time to stop her, and hurrying after her would seem ridiculous, yet he felt terrible watching her go, almost bereft. She was a nurse, but beyond that he knew nothing. How on earth would he ever see her again?

On the far curb she turned to face him. "Kate Zweig," she called out. Another bus was coming, and he was going to ask which hospital she worked at, but by the time it passed she'd disappeared down the dark narrow entrance to the tube.

# JUNE 23

**M**AX STARED AT Claus's palm. "Been writing on yourself again?"

A series of faded blue marks. Claus remembered the chemist's window, jamming his hands in his pockets; he hadn't looked at them in the intervening two days. When would he have had the time? Work, endless shifts as a warden, a long series of letters, daydreams of Kate Zweig.

"You're blushing!" Max said. Claus blushed harder. "What's this about, then?"

"An uncapped pen in my pocket."

"Really? And why were you fondling it?"

He changed the subject but Max wouldn't let go and finally Claus laughed—the toll he had to pay to move on—and Max tapped the script with his folded glasses. "I agreed to three lines for the film," he said. "You've only taken care of two."

A terrible sign, the joking, the sudden switch; Max's moves were predictable, and this combination usually meant rejection. Claus began to sweat.

Max's instructions had been simple: A refugee making her way back to her village near war's end, passing through Allied lines into an indeterminate zone, perhaps even beyond the front. The scenario was to be dramatic. After various travails, all her choices, she would return home successfully, would triumph. *The Refugee's Return.* The request had come down from very high up, Max had told him. "They want something to show in recently liberated France. A rush job. My suspicion is they'll forget about it as soon as we turn something in. Don't spend a lot of time on it."

But Claus had, and it was not something he was willing to let go. "Which one am I missing?" He moved a beaker from a chair and sat. Before the war, the MOI building had housed London University's biology department, Max's office a lab, and it seemed permanently to tremble on the brink of reversion; swarms of beakers and test tubes, racks of Bunsen burners, stacked slides on a counter. Especially unsettling were the pale bloated jarred specimens floating in formaldehyde on shelves behind Max's head.

"The second part," Max said. "There's no drama here, no spectacle. It's what they're going to want. These people have lived through years of privation and dread."

Claus was certain that the film wouldn't have any value if the French found it sensational or sentimental. "They've had enough spectacle," he said. "And trying to guess what they want is a mistake. Griffith did that in *Hearts of the World* and regretted the film the rest of his life."

"Yes, and he gave people what was good for them in *Isn't Life Wonderful* and no one watched it."

"Max, these people need to figure out how to lead normal lives again."

"They'll never lead normal lives. Not after what they've been through." Max drummed his fingers on the desk and sat back. "They need to forget their past, not be reminded of it. They want to be amused and entertained."

Claus couldn't afford to seem dismissive; without Max's backing, the project had no chance. He knew his idea was good if not yet fully formed, he just had to convince Max of that, get Max to support him while he finished it, and keep Max from ruining it as he did. It was better to let Max take the lead, so he ducked his head and pretended he was listening to the raised voices from down the hall; the Polish section. Why did they always seem to be yelling? The scent of his sweat was overpowering.

At last Max put his glasses on and bent over the pages so closely that the glasses seemed a prop. "It's propaganda, Charles, but it doesn't have to be dull. This scene with the dress. What's that about?"

One of the first scenes to come to Claus, it featured a woman standing outside two stores in a recently liberated French town—so recently that the Germanized store names hadn't been returned to their original French—her head swiveling from one display window to the other. In the first, newly abundant food supplies were piled on slanting tables: cheeses and meats, plump pears and ripe tomatoes, glossy onions and swollen peppers; the other store featured a single beautiful silk dress with large white flowers on a bright background. Which would she choose? To Claus it was obvious. No one could resist a bit of color after five years of war. Max had blue-penciled it and written *What about the café?* in the margin.

"Did you show the scene to Alina?" Claus asked.

Max's wife, a Polish refugee he'd married a year into the war; Claus owed the scene's genesis to her. At a recent party she'd seemed drunk—red eyes and slurred speech—but had only been horribly sad. The Germans had killed her brothers and the Russians her father, and the party had fallen on one brother's birthday. She'd worn what looked like a brand-new dress—peacock blue with a plunging neckline—stored, obviously, and brought out for the occasion. Alina would have chosen the new dress.

"No need to," Max said. "I was sure it was boring."

"It's not boring. She's presented with a choice. It's the second turning point, the scene that sets up the entire third act."

"That's not a choice that matters. In my version, the café's customers are cowardly or brave, and she chooses which side she'll join, but your version has a woman wondering about food or a dress. Who wouldn't pick the food? She's hungry."

"And she'll be hungry the next day too. But she wants something that shows the horror of the lean years is over."

Max's original brief had been that higher-ups were thinking of a film about the difficulties that those living in formerly occupied lands faced when they reentered a life of freedom and personal choice. "It's distasteful, really," he'd said when he'd first brought it up. "They want us to mint coins from people's suffering."

But Claus had been hoping to make a real film since the beginning of his time at the MOI, and scenes had sprung instantly to mind, bits of action, visuals as precise as a Modotti or a Lang, and he'd pushed for the film. "It won't be using their suffering, it will help them move beyond it."

Eventually, after much pleading, Claus had gotten Max to agree to his suggestion of a refugee, the barest outline of her story, perhaps because of Alina. And perhaps Max didn't like what Claus thought would occur. But Claus's enthusiasm for the film was tied up with his hopes for it. If in America he was infamous and untouchable, here he'd been known, if at all, as a maker of industrial films. Still would be if the war hadn't come, though until now none of the documentaries he'd made for the MOI—about germs, about the need to save scrap metal, about the lives of ordinary working people during the war, for which he'd leaned heavily on Winifred's experiences—had any but local value, and he was looking forward to something more at last. Sooner or later the world would have had enough of destruction, and he wanted a film that would give him work once that happened. He paused, trying to figure out how to convey all of that without giving himself away.

Max said, "Just put the café scene in. It's what the film needs."

It was a horrible, over-the-top scene, featuring boisterous Frenchmen conversing in a café until two German officers arrived, at which point several men placed their watches face-up on the table, determined to stay not a second longer than the required fifteen minutes, while others bent their craven heads to cheap wine. Max had left a synopsis of this scene on Claus's desk the week before with a note asking him to consider it, but it was completely contrary to Claus's conception of the film. If the war was in many ways noble, at its margins it could yet be wrong, and if Claus could contribute anything, it would be that small note of reason.

During the last war, hundreds of anti-German films had been screened in the United States. Worst of all was *To Hell with the Kaiser*, in which German soldiers gleefully bayoneted ten-year-old children or smashed housefuls of French porcelain. A final scene showed dozens of German soldiers carrying something in their bloused shirts, running and laughing and jostling one another for the privilege of being the first to dump their take—French eyeballs—into a bathtub. Claus wanted nothing of the sort. He was half German, for God's sake. There shouldn't be any Germans in this film at all.

"But this scene with her looking at the dress is crucial," he said. "It grows out of the first reversal, at the end of act one. The luggage."

"How?"

"Metaphorically. Luggage, clothes." He flipped back to the luggage scene, where in the margin he found *Good* written in red pencil in a tiny, feminine hand. "Someone liked it."

"Alina," Max said.

"You don't?"

"That's the thing," Max said. He swiveled in his creaking chair and removed his glasses. "Actually, I do."

Claus felt the first glimmer of hope, but quickly squashed it. Max could approve of dozens of scenes and still turn the project down; his likes were only part of the process.

This scene featured a man standing on the platform between two uncoupled train cars; a woman on the one that was moving away implored him to jump. Glancing at the battered, rope-bound suit-cases beside him, he hesitated, reluctant to give them up. She called out again and at last he was ready to leap—too late; the gulf between the cars had grown too wide. It had a nice metaphoric specificity, Claus thought, dramatizing the past's fateful lure.

"But trains will be impossible for us to get," Max said, switching tactics. "They're too busy supplying the invasion. We won't have a chance to film it."

Claus wouldn't fall for that. Film people were always saying things were impossible. When he'd made *Spirit of '76*, before the last war, one producer had argued that he'd never be able to shoot the winter scenes. "Washington crossing the Delaware. How are you going to do *that?*"

It had proved arduous but mechanically simple. Three men held the tripod legs on an ice floe and a fourth tended a fire beneath the camera to keep the camera oil from freezing. The wind, the blowing snow; he'd had to breathe on the lens every few seconds, and two cameramen had suffered frostbite while he himself had contracted pneumonia, but the scene worked. Coupling and uncoupling a train on a siding would be easy.

"Getting the trains shouldn't be hard," Claus said. "We won't need them for more than an hour or two. They're stuck in the yards all the time."

"Still, this second act." Max waved his hand over the script. "It feels thin. The real problem is your heroine. Jeanne. We don't know enough about her yet, haven't seen her make enough choices."

Claus squeezed his fingers together because closing his eyes and moving his lips in silent prayer would look foolish. *Please,* he thought. His fingers began to tingle.

"And how does the dress scene fit in with this?" Max said. "How does she even get to the town?"

"Car. Horse cart. On foot."

"A journey, back through modes of transport, and therefore back in time."

"Exactly."

Max swiveled in his creaking chair again, pencil at his lips. "And the third act?" Max said. "It's hardly as subtle as the rest of this."

In it, the townspeople emerge from the basements and barns they've been sheltering in, see the newly stocked food store, and rush inside. Understandable, given their long years of privation, but also ultimately self-destructive, as a stray bomb then hits the food store, killing many. Jeanne, who enters the dress shop, is safe.

"The bombing is accidental," Max said. "Which isn't satisfying, emotionally or dramatically. The bomb could as easily hit one store as the other."

Claus saw that Max was right, but he was certain that the scene had to stay, altered somehow but unchanged in its essentials. "Yes," he said. "It has to be better. Work with me. We can get it right."

"And the specific scenes themselves?"

The crucial moment. Claus was ready for it. He looked at Max steadily. "I'll have them soon."

"You need them now. *I* need them, to have a clearer idea of where the film is going, its final arc. That's not clear yet. You can't sum it up for me in a single line, can you?"

Claus shook his head.

"I don't see how I can approve it without knowing those things."

Claus felt all his enthusiasm draining away. In an outer office a teakettle began to boil just as the air-raid sirens started. He could use that, he thought, perking up again, the conflation of war and domesticity, the very problem his heroine faced. Images began to fill his head, Jeanne in a kitchen moving a boiling kettle off the fire, realizing as it stopped whistling that the air-raid sirens were sounding. For the first time he had a face for Jeanne: Kate Zweig's.

Max was studying him. He shook a cigarette free from a pack

and offered it to Claus, who declined, and Max lit his cigarette and closed his eyes and inhaled deeply. Though Claus welcomed the scent of smoke—the former labs still smelled of formaldehyde, and the stagnant air sometimes gave Claus headaches—the closed eyes were a bad sign. It was Max's signature move before he turned something down. "What worries me is that you've got only three weeks. If Bracken is to approve this, we have to complete the script by then." He opened his eyes and touched a date circled on the calendar, July 14. "War's coming to an end sometime, and our funds will dry up first. Three weeks," he repeated. "That's when they've said our requests are due."

"What if it takes longer?"

Max shrugged and blew out a stream of smoke, watched it drift to the cloud hovering under the ceiling. Claus laughed at the gesture's theatricality and Max smiled, which meant that he was signing off on the idea. It was a stunning reversal. Had he intuited Claus's excitement, his belief in the film's possibilities? Claus felt a sudden elation and tried to keep from showing it.

"Here," Max said, sitting forward. He flipped the script and scribbled notes on the back page. "The way you've got it now, with the stores next to each other, cutting from a camera in one store to a camera in the next, that won't work."

"The close-ups and cutbacks clarify her emotions and move the plot along."

"Yes, but if you have the stores on opposite sides of the street, with her standing between them, the metaphoric choice will be clearer."

Claus visualized the scene instantly. "Yes," he said, standing and gathering up the script. "And if the grocer's camera is mounted high, the food will seem to press down on her. Then we'd shoot from inside the dress shop at a low angle, making her eyes go up to the dress. Very good." He was set now, he had it; he wanted to go before Max made him lose his train of thought.

"One last thing, Charles," he said.

"Yes?" He made himself linger.

"You want audiences to feel, not think."

"No," he said, backing out the door. "I want to make them feel *and* think."

"Well, think about this," Max called after him, loud enough for Claus to hear over his echoing footsteps. "The woman's name is too plain. Change it from Jeanne."

Claus finished his notes about camera angles and crosscuts and added a few details to the suitcase scene: stickers from various colonial ports on the suitcases, the man checking the African carvings he'd stuffed inside, which he was reluctant to give up because they were valuable. Then he sat back. He wanted to do more—Max's objections were legitimate—but it seemed impossible; the MOI building's heat, his closing eyes, the mistakes he kept making on the typewriter. The buzz bombs were coming over more heavily after dark, killing people in their beds and depriving survivors of sleep, and he'd spent the previous three nights at the post, napping for an hour, wondering if any of the explosions were anywhere near Kate Zweig. Myra, the post leader, hadn't slept at all.

His vision began to blur and images from his past came to mind: his father, and his father's store. It made sense, he thought, lazily watching them unfold, wartime and its confusion, though these scenes were from a war's beginning rather than its end and their sweep was toward disaster, not triumph.

Red letters arcing across a store window spelled out KRAUT AND FRANKFURTERS, then the window was smashed as a crowd roared its approval, and a man's pale face hovered inside. His father. When the United States had gone to war against Germany in 1917, a competing storeowner had put all his German items in the street and invited townspeople to burn them. Food, fabric, books. He'd given out free paint and asked the assembled mob to paint over his window signs: KRAUT, HAMBURGERS, FRANKFURTERS. When they were done he stood on the porch and looked at Claus's father's store. "Well, Declan? How about you?"

Claus's father had said, "Most of the customers that have made you rich are German. Our wives are. What's changed about that?"

"The war. It changes everything."

"It changes nothing, William. Unless you let it."

In the morning his storefront window had been shattered. He restored the window, prudently not repainting any German words on the glass, but that hadn't stopped people from smashing it two more times or a mob from coming to his house at three in the morning weeks later, demanding that he sign up for thousands of dollars in war bonds. Bobbing torches in the dark, confused shouting, trashcan lids banging together.

Declan had tried to find out who was outside and someone had yelled, "The Americanization Committee! You have to open up. It's the law!"

It wasn't the law, but Declan had recognized William's voice among the others, and both times after his store had been damaged, William's boys had helped clean it up. He came out and two men pulled his arms behind him and bound them with rope; another punched him in the stomach. On his knees, he couldn't protect himself, and several men began battering his face. Claus could almost feel the blows as he imagined it.

"Hold on there, now!" William had said. "You're going too far!"

Eventually William had freed him and convinced the others to wait outside while he cleaned Declan up, telling Hettie that she should stay upstairs.

"The crowd might not take kindly to a German accent right now."

"They can take kindly to a frying pan if they try to come in," she'd said.

William had ignored her and tried to get Declan to buy bonds.

"I already bought seven hundred dollars' worth," Declan had said, wiping his bloody face with a damp blue rag. "More than anyone else in the summer drive. I'm not buying a single cent."

"But you have to! They'll burn the house!"

"Not now. Not after that. Not ever."

William had argued for over an hour, putting the mob off again and again, finally telling them something that made them cheer and disperse, and when Declan's name appeared on the fall bond-drive list for a thousand dollars, Declan was sure William had paid it himself, guilty over his role in the affair and his own continued success. He was still selling frankfurters and hamburgers and kraut, though under the names of hot dogs, liberty sandwiches, and liberty cabbage, while Declan's store had gone out of business. To the end

Declan had put out free German pretzels, something that incensed the townspeople. Even his wife urged him to stop. *You're not even German!* But he wouldn't listen.

Claus was still unsure if his father had been courageous or foolish, especially with a son in jail on charges of treason, but that the scene had come to him so vividly meant something for his current project. Generally he didn't linger on his personal history—it made him bitter—but his mind had turned to it of its own accord, so he wrote the scene out longhand and added notes to himself on how he might use it, then closed the file and stood, thinking that a bit of fresh air might revive him.

His footsteps sounded loud in the deserted hallway. At Max's door he cleared his throat. "Fancy a bite to eat or a cuppa?" Whenever he wanted to be ingratiating, he dropped in Anglicisms, hoping they didn't sound as false as they felt.

Max shook his head without raising it. "Sorry. Production schedules. Bracken wants them tomorrow and I'm behind." He began to whistle, to show he wasn't angry at Claus's part in the delay.

"Sorry to hear that," Claus said. He was. He felt a piercing desire for human contact, as he often did after writing. It wouldn't come from Max, so there was no sense lingering. "Another time then," he said.

Outside it was warm and windy, a welcome change from the long cold spell. Dust in the blue sky, but no smoke; at least the buzz bombs didn't often start fires. Still, the air around the massive, derelict wing of the British Museum smelled charred, a remnant of the Blitz, and he relegated it to the back of his mind through an old trick, imagining that someday he might film it.

## JUNE 25

THE STREETS WEREN'T as crowded as he'd expected and as the warm windy air usually conjured, but even so there was an early-evening bustle once he left behind the residential squares of Bloomsbury, with their converted front-yard vegetable gardens and their window-box tomatoes. At Oxford Street a policeman was lowering the traffic-light shutters with a long pole, a difficult job made more difficult by the wind, and on the far side a queue of women waited patiently outside a shoe shop, a few glancing nervously skyward, where hundreds of yards up a trio of barrage balloons nosed into the wind, pink and silver in the fading blue light, quivering like trout in a stream.

A chalked sign said that several dozen pairs of shoes remained and that the store would stay open until all shoppers had had their chance or the shoes were gone, but from the look of the line it would be the latter. They'd do better with Herbert, Claus's fellow warden who was able to get almost any kind of shoes, though boots were a dicier proposition. To cut down on pilfering, the government shipped left and right ones separately, and sometimes when you got one you had to wait months for its mate. An unmatched left one stood stiffly in Claus's closet.

London had turned surly again, and most of the people he passed, Soho-bound, grim, and quiet, seemed off for a quick bite before heading to the shelters. Though he wanted company he tended to avoid Soho, not because it was a bit seedy and a lot damaged but because so many other MOI writers clogged its cheap restaurants and grubby pubs. He preferred the military clubs around Charing

Cross and Piccadilly Circus. *Your own kind,* Max had once said. *Americans.*

It wasn't the Americans that attracted Claus, it was the military news he could gather and the chance to be around strangers. If he had to lie about his past, and Bertram insisted on it, better to do so with people he didn't know. Best of all would be to do it with the one interesting stranger he'd met recently, but finding Kate Zweig was next to impossible. Too many nurses in too many hospitals; he'd raise suspicions trying to track her down.

He contemplated going home, but what would he do there other than sleep or endure the agonizing routine of composing letters? Besides, Berlin might get suspicious if he wrote at unscheduled times; the Germans loved routine. His mother had made it easy to understand what the Germans wanted. *From order, all good things flow.* Was he betraying her memory? No. She'd have wanted him to do it, seeing what Germany had become.

Outside the Whitehall Theatre, a slender woman apologized for bumping into him and then asked for a light in a thick Continental accent. Not a prostitute; the skirt pressed against her legs was good and her hair its natural chestnut color, and she hadn't propositioned him. *Want some love, dearie?* Yet she cupped his hand with hers and leaned toward his lighter, her touch lingering.

"If you've a few spare petrol coupons, we could have both of us a good time."

He hesitated, blushing—he didn't like being so badly wrong—and she smiled encouragingly, taking his hesitation for an invitation; he couldn't look her in the eye when he spoke again. "Sorry." He nodded at the ballroom behind her, Cupid's Arrow. "I'm to meet someone at the club."

Her mild, inoffensive face grew angry and, angry, was suddenly ugly, the nose too long, the brown eyes too small and close together. "This I will just bet," she said, and blew smoke at him. A dozen yards farther on she turned to watch him, arms crossed, standing near a pile of orange peels outside a milk bar.

Now he was committed to Cupid's Arrow, a frequent destination though not one he'd been thinking of tonight, and he foresaw his entire evening: he'd pick out a likely hostess, lonely and hanging back in the corner, and dance twice with her before chatting her up, laying his accent on thick. She'd tell him that she liked Americans, and that she'd danced with a lot of them recently, and from there, getting information would be simple. *I have a buddy in the Third Army. He said he'd danced with the prettiest girl here at the end of May. That must be you.*

She'd laugh, nod. The Third Army had been on leave just before the invasion and now was nowhere to be seen. Normandy, then; the Germans would already know, but confirming their knowledge made each of his lies more believable. He pulled the door open, not easy to do against the wind, and went in.

He grabbed a beer and a sandwich before moving to the dance floor. The beer was warm and surprisingly good, the sandwich nearly inedible: austerity bread, watercress, and clumped, oily fish that passed for herring; he ate while looking over the program, hoping to be distracted. The Skyliners were up in an hour and until then Paula Schreffrette was spinning records, Vera Lynn and not Bing Crosby, as would be the case in the American clubs.

He had found his taste changing over the past decade; now he preferred the subtler, less-brassy English sound to the all-out assault of an American band, and he felt himself relax as he ate and drank. At the click of billiard balls he closed his eyes to listen and heard also the *tick tock tick* of table tennis from the side rooms and the echoing voices from the tiled showers, but he was jolted back to full consciousness by a rousing female laugh from the dance floor. It came again, twice, and after finishing his beer, he went to investigate.

Two hostesses were dancing together by the bandstand, a relaxed slow shuffle, while a few others spun around the dull floor with dull civilians, but most milled by the entrances, awaiting a larger crowd. At a nearby table were two women, the younger, blond and stolid, leaning forward in her chair and listening intently to the other, who was in her late forties and well dressed. His pulse quickened at her black hair, which reminded him of Kate Zweig's, down to the one gray stripe at the temple.

As the stolid girl tilted her head back and laughed uproariously, holding her hand in front of her mouth so that the laughter looked forced but sounded genuine, the second woman reached for her drink, and he was stunned to see that it *was* Kate. He crossed immediately to stand before her and only when she looked up expectantly, composed but smiling, did he realize what he'd done.

"Hello," she said.

Claus took her offered hand, feeling himself blush, and said hello.

"This is an unexpected pleasure," Kate said. She waited, but when he didn't respond, she added, "My name is Kate. Remember?"

"Yes, of course." His face grew hotter. "Kate Zweig. And I'm Charles Murphy."

"Oh, good." She took her hand back but continued to tease. "You haven't changed your name either."

Now he felt himself burning. There was nothing to do but turn and smile at the younger woman. "And you are?"

"Greta Andrus." She spoke with an unmistakable German accent.

Kate touched Greta's shoulder. "A probationary nurse. She's not had fun in ages, so I made her come out with me." She leaned forward and, just above a whisper but recklessly nonetheless, spoke to Greta in German. "*Er ist der, von dem ich Ihnen erzählte.*" He's the one I told you about.

Claus's scalp prickled. He couldn't let on that he understood, though he was pleased she'd mentioned him; it was awkward being in public with German speakers. People were denounced for less. Kate looked up. "Won't you dance with her?"

"Of course." He held his hand out to Greta. "May I?"

"Please," she said. "This, I would to enjoy."

He led her onto the floor. Judging by her awkward carriage and heavy frame he would have guessed she'd be ungraceful, but she was a surprisingly fluid dancer, responding to his slightest touch. Still, he didn't hold her close—her perfume was almost acrid—and it was all he could do to keep himself from looking over her shoulder at Kate.

Paula Schreffrette played with the pearls at her throat as she sorted records for her next song. Remembering his manners but also gathering information, he asked, "And where are you from?" after they'd spun silently around the room.

"London. St. Pancras Hospital."

"Yes. Of course. And before that?"

"Guernsey. Nanny for a family."

"And you never got home. Where was that?"

She glanced over at Kate for guidance, but he spun her away. "Leipzig," she said, reluctantly.

"I'm sorry," he said. "I shouldn't pry. It probably makes you unhappy."

She said nothing.

"I'm from abroad too, and I know what it's like to be an exile. Haven't been back since '31." Not allowed back, though he didn't tell her that.

He talked a bit more but her answers were monosyllabic and they lapsed into silence for the rest of the number, sitting just as a raucous group of American officers burst through the front door. Unusual here, as they tended to stick to the clubs farther down Piccadilly or over in Charing Cross.

"Oh, good," Greta said. "Americans."

"Do you like them?"

"Yes. They're more friendly than the English. I do hope they sit near us."

Kate smiled over her glass. "Don't worry," she said, and touched his knee. "I'll talk to you, even if you disguise your nationality."

"You're American?" Greta said.

"Yes," Kate said. "And a filmmaker."

"Oh!" Greta looked at him again. "I would not have guessed this."

Kate laughed.

"And what films have you made?"

"None you'd know of, probably. *The Beer Bottlers of Manchester* wasn't much of a hit outside of trade groups, but I did help write *Intolerance*." In response to her blank face, he said, "D. W. Griffith? *Birth of a Nation*?"

"Oh, yes." She brightened. "I know that. It was silent though."

"Yes, *Intolerance* too, but I still had to write some of the scenes." He regretted instantly the note of insecurity behind his boasting.

Two Americans approached, the shorter and younger asking Greta to dance.

"Yes!" she said, and stood. "I'd love to."

Claus was about to ask Kate to dance when the major, ignoring Claus, asked first.

"Thank you." She smiled with what looked like genuine pleasure. "But I'm going to sit this one out. Been on my feet all day."

"Another one, then?" he said.

"Yes. I'd like that."

He nodded, his black, brilliantined hair flashing in the light, and walked away.

Kate waited until he was out of hearing. "You see," she said. "I'm all yours."

"For now," Claus said. "But he'll be back. And you should be happy."

"Why is that?"

"You still have admirers."

"Do I appear too old for them?"

"No, I . . ." He stopped, realizing how he'd sounded. He'd simply meant that it was a compliment that the major had come to her first. He would have himself, though now he couldn't say so. Why was he being so awkward? "I didn't mean it that way."

"I'm sure. But to tell you the truth, I never wanted admirers at my age." She put her glass down. "I wanted to be old and married."

She smiled, to remove the taint of self-pity, but they fell silent, Claus unsure how to begin again, Kate blowing blue smoke rings over her drink and watching waiters bring food to other tables.

"How long did you live in France?"

"A few years."

"Caught there when the war started?"

"No, I went there after it had begun."

"From London?" He couldn't keep the surprise from his voice.

"Hamburg." She stubbed out her cigarette. "You needn't be confused. I was married to a German doctor and we lived in Hamburg."

"And from Hamburg to France? How did that happen?"

"My husband's family was Alsatian. Both parents. His father had moved to Hamburg to practice medicine. Through them I had a kind of international citizenship, and by 1939 I preferred France to Hamburg."

He studied her elegant fingers, which were wrapped around a

jam jar. She still wore a silver wedding ring. "And your husband?" he said. "Did he go with you?"

She didn't answer, her eyes were on Paula Schreffrette and her flaming red hair as she spun a record between her fingers to catch the light. Then Kate pulled out another cigarette and waited for Claus to produce a lighter.

"A nasty habit," she said, when he had. "I picked it up after the last war, quit, and started again in France."

"Nerves?"

"Hunger. It makes one forget." She sat back. "But to answer your question, no. I had to leave him behind."

She'd taken a while to answer, and he thought it best not to push along those lines just yet. "And eventually you came back," he said.

"Not entirely by choice. A few of us from a Parisian hospital were having a party and one of the doctors, drunk, decided to dye his dog the colors of the French flag. It got loose on the street, and since there had been a lot of recent anti-German propaganda appearing at the BBC's urging, it infuriated the Germans.

"They demanded names of everyone at the party. Along with my other problems, it meant it was time for me to go. Of course, there was some choice in my coming back, and that part was easy. Hitler, the Nazis."

"Hitler and the Nazis were there for many years."

"So we've discussed, I believe." With her pinkie and thumb she picked a bit of tobacco off her tongue, then quickly changed the subject. "You have a tattoo!" she said.

Claus's pant leg had ridden up, showing the red and blue *Spirit of '76* just above his right ankle. She leaned down to study it. "The only people with tattoos I knew as a child were criminals or in the navy," she said. "Which were you, navy?"

"Yes." Not true, but he wasn't about to tell her that. It surprised him that lying to her felt wrong. He'd grown so used to it over the years. He dropped his leg so his pants covered the tattoo, not wanting her to see how crudely it was done. "A long time ago."

She raised an eyebrow, but he turned his glance to Greta. "She looks happy."

Kate watched her twirling around the room. "You've no idea how good this is for her," she said. "Only a few of the other nurses will even speak to her, and only one has brought her out. To a gramophone record concert: Bach, Beethoven, Chopin. Each record was introduced by a master of ceremonies and followed by polite applause. Very highbrow, as you can imagine, and therefore very dull, the women in matching hats and gloves and she not even able to buy stockings, so of course they snubbed her."

"Her situation's improved," he said, and nodded at her legs. "Stockings."

"Yes." She laughed. "Much better." Then she turned serious. "But I think people don't understand how hard it is for Greta. She's afraid to be in public."

"Her accent?" He thought of his mother. "People will get past that. She should speak up for herself."

"Ah," Kate said. She was looking closely at Claus now. "Be brave, in other words, and tough it out." She moved her drink aside and sat forward. "Tell me," she said. "Do you read the obituaries?"

"Not as a habit, no."

"I do. Always have. It's a marvelous way to learn about whatever area you're living in. And in France, they're no less informative. For instance, if Germans take hostages in a town and say they'll be released if the murderer of a German soldier is turned in, and those hostages are shot, their obituaries read, 'Who died on Friday . . .' No mention of them being executed."

"Murdered, you mean. Convenient for the Germans, not to have it broadcast."

"Precisely. But of course it's not as simple as cowardice. If you're an editor and offend the Germans, it might not be you they imprison or select as the next hostage, it might be your wife or son. So tell me, if each time you put a few words down on paper, you had to worry they might lead to your wife's death, or your child's, would you be so quick to speak out?"

He shrugged. "I don't know. I don't have either."

"Come," she said, her voice scolding, a teacher faced with a willfully obtuse child. "Use your imagination. If this is collaboration, is it really a form you can abhor?"

How had this happened? He wanted to get back to the easy banter of a few minutes before. "All right," he said. "Perhaps there are levels."

"Ah, levels." She finished her drink and sat back. "You see, already it has become tricky, and at last you have some doubts. But I'll bet that no matter where you draw your line, I would have crossed it."

"I doubt it."

"I don't. In fact I'm sure of it. And I wasn't alone. Everyone collaborates."

"Really." It was not a question.

"Yes. Really. Buying something in a French store when the Germans provide supplies is collaboration. Obeying a German police officer at a stoplight is collaboration. Even shooting a German and dying for it is a form of collaboration. When someone else scripts the play, controls the scenery, the hiring, and the lighting, everything you do is controlled by them, even the desire to strike out at them. It's a type of movie you seem never to have been part of."

The air was suddenly stifling, the music too loud. "Besame Mucho." *Not likely.* He spoke up to make himself heard, curiously determined not to appear weak. "That's rather simple, isn't it? To declare Jean Moulin and Pétain one and the same?"

"They're not the same, but both are reacting to the same situation, one forced upon them."

"Which they're not obliged to accept."

"Please. One can't pretend the Germans aren't there."

"No. But one can fight against them."

"Yes. But tell me, if you were a nurse in a hospital, do you do more for the French by running down a stray German when out for a drive, or by letting one flirt with you who will then procure necessary drugs, drugs that you can give to French patients?"

"Flirt? And what about kiss?"

"What about it?"

"So, everything is acceptable? A few days ago you were arguing that even in a just war, not everything was justifiable."

"On a governmental scale, certainly. But on a human scale nothing is out of bounds, not if you mean to help the wounded, or the sick, or the old."

"You forgot the young."

"No. Not for a moment. Never." Her cheeks were burning; he hadn't realized how angry she'd grown. Why was he being so stupid? He hadn't meant to antagonize her, but it had been years since he'd really talked with anyone this passionately; all his other conversations were designed to elicit information. And really, he was saying these things because he wanted her attention. Anger was better than indifference.

She stood and caught the eye of the American major, who was smoking and leaning against the wooden wainscoting. As he made his way toward them between the mass of dancing couples, she leaned over the table to make sure Claus heard her.

"You know, I hope as devoutly as you—perhaps more devoutly, since I've seen what the occupation is doing—that the Germans lose. But in the meantime, thousands of Frenchmen must try to survive. Heroism doesn't consist solely of shooting soldiers. It's a different type of courage to survive a disaster you had no part in bringing about."

It was foolish to argue. He wondered what had caused him to. The V-1s, his impotence in the face of ongoing destruction, but neither was Kate's fault. After a few excruciating minutes of watching her dance with the major—a bit too closely—he stood and cut in on Greta, and when the song ended he intercepted Kate and the major before they made their way back to the table.

"May I?" He took her hand and led her back to the floor, where he purposely kept his conversation neutral, alluding to his time as a warden, his apartment near Charing Cross. She didn't respond. As soon as the dance was over he asked Greta to dance once more, then Kate once again when they were done.

"So you're a warden," Kate finally said on their second outing.
"Yes."
"Tell me, what's the strangest thing you've seen on duty?"
"The strangest?" He thought. "Burning chickens, perhaps."
She held herself away, back from his shoulder. "How gruesome."
"Yes. But you asked."
"So I did. And what's the most beautiful thing you've seen?"
"That's an unusual question."

"A very wise woman once told me to look for beauty in the midst of disaster, a means of survival. My mother-in-law."

The marriage again; he decided not to touch it. "A burning paper warehouse, probably. Enormous sheets of flaming paper sailing into the night, floating above buildings on fire-created winds like burning magic carpets and then, all at once, darkening to cinders and embers and cascading to the streets below like flocks of glowing birds."

"That *is* beautiful. I would have liked to see it."

Over her shoulder, he saw Greta making her way back to the table.

"Looks like your charge is about done."

"I was so glad you asked her," Kate said. "She's been dying to dance."

"Well, I haven't."

"Oh." She pulled back and looked at him. "A duty rather than a pleasure?"

"No." He pressed his hand to the small of her back, bringing her closer and inhaling her blackberry perfume. "Not at all. I simply meant that, before tonight, it wasn't something I was sitting at home wishing I could do."

"Well, I was. A way to soothe the tensions of work. You can't imagine how difficult it was to dance in France. Outlawed, unless you went to clubs with German officers, so you had to go to private homes, but the trick was you had to be invited."

He squeezed her hand, feeling hot and happy.

"I'm sure you were, often."

"Not enough to save me."

"And what does that mean?"

She leaned closer. "I'll tell you later. Another part of my French troubles."

Through two more dances they remained on the floor. After the third one he said, "May I ask you something? Do you always dance with your eyes closed?"

"Yes," she said and rested her warm head against his shoulder. "Old habit."

\*   \*   \*

Kate was dancing with the major again, Greta glassy-eyed and hic-cupping. One of her garters popped, and her stocking twirled down her leg like a corkscrew. She fumbled with Kate's bag and knocked it to the floor and sat blinking at it until the song finished. Kate made her way back through the applauding crowd, and Claus stood to meet her.

"Shall we?" he said.

"Dance?"

"Go." He nodded at Greta. "I think she's had enough excitement for one night."

Kate gathered both their bags. "Trying to cram in a year's worth. Never a good idea, but understandable. You know, normally she's quite tough. Earlier this year, one of the other nurses hid in a dark room draped in a white sheet, trying to scare her, and Greta conked her on the head with an oxygen bottle and knocked her out. Caused quite a bit of trouble, I can tell you. Dark rumors of Nazi spies un-dermining our health care."

"Yes," he said. "They show up in the strangest places."

It was always disorienting to emerge from lit clubs into full dark with the blackout in effect. They clustered on the sidewalk, letting their eyes adjust, Greta bumping first against Claus's shoulder and then Kate's, a stone pushed by an invisible current. The AA had started up with a distant crackle of explosions, and the outside air was noticeably cooler than the fevered atmosphere of the club, which spilled out onto the street suddenly when the door opened behind them and a group of sailors, boisterously drunk, tumbled into them.

"Fuck," one said. "Dropped my peanuts."

"Let 'em go," another said. "We'll get some after we shag."

Kate stepped aside to let them pass just as two MPs strolled by in their white helmets and gloves; Claus was glad for female company, as they never stopped men with women, knowledge he'd used more than once.

"Where do you live?" Claus asked Greta. "Nearby? We'll walk you home."

"No. I want to have a cab."

"Please," Claus said, taking her elbow. "It would be best for us to walk you. You'll feel better in the morning if you get a bit of air."

"No," she said, and pushed him away. "I'll be fine."

The snowdrops had stopped to listen. Claus turned to Kate and sensed her shrug. "All right," he said. "Stay here."

A few others were hailing cabs, but his American voice got one quicker, the London cabbies knowing the accent usually meant money. This one, though, sounded unhappy to have to cart a drunk.

"It's all right," Claus told him. "She's a nurse, not a commando." To make sure she got safely home, he overtipped. They watched the cab drive off and Kate shifted aside, treading on the spilled peanuts. "She misses home," she said. "Your questions, evidently."

"I didn't intend to depress her."

"No, I'm sure. It happens with her relatively easily, I'm afraid. Often at night I find her listening to the BBC accounts of where we've bombed that day, and if it's anywhere near home, she's desolate."

"And I'm sorry about earlier," Claus said. "I'm not usually so quick to fight, or so obtuse. Can I make it up to you?"

He waited during the long intake of her breath as she rocked back and forth, deciding, the peanut shells cracking beneath her shoes. When she said, "Yes, all right, walk me home," his chest filled.

She took his arm. "You don't mind, do you?" From the sound of her voice she was looking ahead, rather than at him. "It's just that I hate the dark."

"A bad childhood experience?" Claus asked.

She was silent longer than he'd expected, and he worried he'd touched a raw nerve. "Didn't mean to pry."

She shifted her arm in his. "No. It's all right. I have had a few bad experiences in the dark, but unfortunately, they've all been as an adult. I didn't want to bore you."

"Bore away," he said, and then, worried she might mistake his joke, squeezed her arm. "Really, you couldn't. I'd like to know."

She told him a bit about Hamburg after the last war, how little electricity and light they'd had, how her husband, Horst, had played the piano for them in the dark, which was usually a fine thing, a way of making them all happy, but came at last to seem futile.

"How so?"

"Well, probably because it felt so heavily metaphoric. Art against the darkness." She laughed. "Sometimes that seemed too much to bear, but I suppose that was only on the days we hadn't much to eat."

"And your husband?" Claus asked, unable to wait. "What happened to him?"

The light wedge of her face dipped and he had his answer even before she spoke. "He died." Her chin rose again. "Only a few years ago, it seems, though it's been closer to ten."

"I'm sorry." He felt heat leave his body like water flowing from a balloon. Leaving him behind must have meant leaving his grave. To escape his guilt, he asked if she liked her hospital.

"Oh, yes. It's a wonderful place. Well supplied, which is nice. It's been years since I worked in one of those. Though it's rather busy now, with the invasion casualties and the flying bombs. And it seems we get only the worst cases."

"Unpleasant."

"Strangely, no. The more intractable a patient is, the more involved you become."

"If I get injured, I'll do my best to be difficult," he said.

She turned her head toward him and he wished he could make out her face, to see if she was smiling. That beautiful mouth. He leaned toward her but she walked on, hurrying ahead to pass a telephone box whose door was shaking, the dark forms inside writhing.

After a long, embarrassed pause she said, "The only lines outside buildings in Paris are Germans at brothels. And do you know the most peculiar part of it? The prostitutes are labeled 'heavy workers' and receive the same rations as factory hands."

Near a cinema, its side doors blown off, bits of disembodied music floated into the warm air, the last bars of "God Save the King." They faded out and the ALERT slide flashed on the screen, and the patrons put on their steel helmets.

"Home's not far," Kate said. "Let's go."

He imagined she did not like to be out when the buzz bombs were dropping; the unavoidable conviction that danger could hunt you out more easily in the open.

"Different than Paris, isn't it?" he said. "You probably wish you'd stayed."

"You know, I hate the fog, creeping in through all the windows.

I'd forgotten that. I like that restaurants can charge only five shillings per meal and that I don't need coupons, but the English can be so cold. No sense of life, of living. They're incredibly efficient, and resolute, but they seem to have no passions, though perhaps it's just the war sharpening their qualities, both good and bad."

"It's not bred in the bone," Claus said. "You've changed. Perhaps they will."

"That would be nice. And after all, being able to walk like this *is* better. The Parisian nights were so empty between curfews and blackouts that it seemed medieval."

"It's dark here too. Some stars are visible for the first time in five hundred years."

"But without the violence. Murder, beatings, shootings."

"Of Germans?"

"Sometimes. Sometimes of collaborators, sometimes of innocent civilians, sometimes of people who were anti-German before the war. No one's safe from it, and no one's allowed out after eleven."

"Wearying, I imagine." He found himself explaining his film, the scene where the woman is suddenly confronted with a choice between food and clothes.

"My," she said, "that's difficult."

"You don't find it realistic?"

"No," she said, and laughed. "I do. After years of privation, who wouldn't want something a bit better, some reminder of what once was, of what one once was?"

"Perhaps you can come when we're filming, give pointers to the actress."

"Only I've never acted."

"Here now, love," a woman said. "We all have." A prostitute, who shined her flashlight over Kate's ankles.

When they didn't stop, she said, "Got one, have you?" though it wasn't clear to which of them. Kate's arm stiffened in his.

"Quite a lot of them, aren't there?" he said.

"Yes, how the fallen are mighty."

He laughed and they continued down the dark ravine of Piccadilly toward Green Park, the invisible taxis passing noisily, the black, beleaguered buildings looming above them. Up and down the street, cigarette lighters flashed like lightning and the pedestrians' blue torches jiggled like swarms of summer fireflies, stopping only to inspect someone. He was happy not to be among them.

"It's changed a lot since I was a girl. The duke of Wellington still had a great house here then. Gardens too. And the prostitutes would never have been out by day."

"Do you miss it?"

"Some. It's surprising. I remember walks here with my father as a young girl, on the way to his hospital."

They passed a boisterous crowd of Scotch Guard band members, lugging their instruments back from an evening concert, then came within smelling distance of the Hyde Park piggery; the sudden odor of spring in the country, manure and mud, scents he'd always liked. The pigs grunted.

"Not Americans, I hope," Claus said.

Kate caught the reference to soldiers and their public sex and laughed.

The great ring of antiaircraft guns in the park began firing their rockets, and the concussion of the blasts made it seem they were bouncing into the air, causing Kate and Claus to hurry; the noise and the falling shells, the blinding flashes, the rank noxious scent of burning rubber. She gripped his arm as they ran.

Nearer Curzon Street they slowed to a walk and began to talk again, Kate pointing out neighborhood landmarks, her butcher's, smaller than the others and often more poorly supplied but whom she frequented because he didn't cheat immigrants, the street baths, the clock over the druggist's that hadn't lost a minute in years despite all the bombs, but their conversation stuttered to a stop as twin doodlebugs approached. Their engine notes grew louder and progressively more cranky, and bolts of fear surged through him—like many, he had an irrational belief in the safety of his own district, an equally irrational sense of increased danger in strange ones—and they found themselves crouching and holding their breath by the stairs to her building when one engine cut completely.

"I can't see it," Claus said, and Kate put her finger to her lips and shook her head, as if talking might lead it to them, her eyes wide in her pale face.

It passed over them with a peculiar rustling sound, like a huge bird flapping ungainly wings, but even so the explosion a few blocks away caught them both off-guard and knocked him onto her. "Are you all right?" Kate asked, as if she'd been the one to fall on him, squeezing his shoulders and face like someone checking for wounds. Before he could answer she kissed him and before he could even think they were upstairs in her darkened rooms yanking off each other's clothes.

After, she got up and pushed aside the blackout curtains. The moon had risen late and Claus tilted his watch into a sliver of white light.

"I suppose you're about to say you have to go," Kate said.

*Is that the English way?* Claus realized that his joke might be taken as an insult, implying that she slept with many, and didn't say it. "Sorry. I'm not in any hurry to leave. No work tomorrow. If you want me to go, you'll have to tell me."

She reached to squeeze his hand. "Stay," she said. "Please."

"I'd love to." When he rolled over, he laughed and drew his fingers across her thigh a few inches above the knee, where apparently dark skin gave way to light.

"You're lucky," she said. "At least I can afford the cream. 'Stockingless Cream, by Cyclax, so he'll never know,'" she said, quoting the ad, "or Elizabeth Arden Fin 200. The latter is harder to get, but far superior. Some girls I work with use gravy or cold cocoa."

She patted his calf, the *Spirit of '76* tattoo. "The difference between me and you is that mine runs in the rain."

He didn't want to talk about that yet and said, "How come Greta had stockings tonight and you didn't?"

"Gave her mine. I wanted her first night out to be memorable. Poor thing. I'll bet right now that if she's not passed out, she's remembering it far better than she'd like."

"Do you want to go check on her? Cure her hangover?"

"Yes, but I won't. I want more to stay here. Wicked, aren't I? But the older I get, the more I find that indulging myself now and then isn't a bad thing."

He shifted around so his head was near hers and they lay quietly on the hot, wrinkled sheets, listening to the sounds of the city drift through the open window. Claus ran his thumb over a needlework clamshell on the pillowcase.

"My industrious past," she said, and rested her hand on it.

He thought he might have slept. Kate touched his face, lightly, and closed her eyes. After a few minutes, her fingers twitched and she murmured something in German, *Trost*, he thought, but he didn't respond, and then her hand dropped away and she was sleeping profoundly.

He leaned over and whispered in her ear, to be sure. Her name, twice, which elicited only a flutter of her eyelids, and then, hardly believing it even as he said it, his own. *Claus.*

# JUNE 26

BERTRAM DIDN'T PUT DOWN the newspaper when Claus came in. "Bloody Irish." He shook his head. "Couldn't trust them at the end of the last war either. As ungrateful as the Indians. Look at this." He tapped an article. "Blowing up power plants in Belfast. Bad enough that we have to deal with the renewed destruction of London by the Germans. Now this in our rear."

Claus never felt more Irish than when Bertram attacked them. "Perhaps that's just it," he said. "They're hoping you'll deal with them once the war's over."

"Not bloody likely, if they keep this up. If that's what they want, they should help us."

"They tried, for several hundred years. And especially during the last war."

"Listen to you. You're not even Irish."

"Half," Claus said. Normally they didn't talk politics, but at times like these Claus couldn't hold his tongue. "Which isn't how you framed it when you first contacted me."

Bertram put the paper aside and glanced ostentatiously at the cuckoo clock.

"You're late."

In a previous existence, Bertram must have been one of the lesser gods of time. "Sorry." To forestall further complaints, Claus held out his hand. "I do have a reason."

"Haven't you always?"

Claus didn't want to talk about hurrying home from Kate's to change before coming here—doing so seemed a type of betrayal, though earlier in the war she'd have been a godsend, someone he could use in letters and broadcasts to Germany, a woman with torn loyalties — but he couldn't avoid her completely. Bertram was bound to find out about her. "A damsel in distress."

He sat down, crossed his ankles, and told Bertram about Kate's argument with the Hyde Park speaker, her claim that the French would have been better off losing the last war, leaving aside the intervening days and the fact that he'd slept with her the night before.

"Interesting. And you stopped to listen? This morning? You look good. Younger. The rest of London is exhausted and you look like you've had a month's rest. Remarkable."

Claus didn't pause long, as Bertram might begin to suspect him, and he decided to ignore the second part of his comments. "I stopped to save her. The crowd was getting ugly. I thought a few of the Frenchmen might rough her up, though she seemed convinced that the French, gentlemen to the end, would do nothing of the sort."

Bertram snorted. "She was right about that, though perhaps for the wrong reasons. The French wouldn't fight from a deep-seated inferiority complex. Deserved, I might add. The Almighty in His infinite wisdom didn't see fit to make Frenchmen in our image." He sat behind the desk. "Let's get on, shall we? I have other appointments."

The backfiring-engine sound of a buzz bomb came briefly through the window and Bertram said, "Don't worry, it's the first ten years that are the hardest."

A line from the Blitz. "I should think after the Guards' chapel, buzz bombs wouldn't be a topic of humor," Claus said.

Bertram paled. "The Guards' chapel was exaggerated."

"Please. I saw it."

"The bomb itself?" Bertram seemed surprised.

"The aftermath." Most of London had made a pilgrimage to the site, scene of a Sunday-morning massacre. The walls were standing, a portico, but aside from the bishop — presiding from the protected altar — nearly everyone else, all holding open their purple hymnals and singing dutifully during the morning Mass, had been crushed by the collapsing roof. Children and their parents, some of the army's best officers.

"Well, many of the tales you've heard are exaggerated. I'd think you'd have realized that by now. My God, your job is propaganda."

"This isn't propaganda, Bertram. The destruction is real."

"Yes, but the deaths aren't. Eight hundred, the latest rumor was. If you've seen the chapel, you know it held no more than two."

"No more than two," Claus said, but did not go on; saying it once was sufficient comment on Bertram's callousness. "Can I pass along the figure of eight hundred dead?"

"Certainly. Give the Germans the higher count. Another mark in your favor."

"How about the bombs themselves?"

"What about them?"

Claus uncrossed his ankles and leaned forward. "My suggestion to move the landing points?" Madrid and Hamburg were asking for information about where the bombs were landing, and Claus had proposed giving them incorrect coordinates, saying they were landing a bit north of where they actually were so the Germans would correct south. Soon, they'd be landing in the country. If that wasn't possible, he'd suggested he ask about upcoming targets, so they could move people. The night before, lying awake next to Kate, catching a whiff of her blackberry-scented skin while listening to the bombs buzz across the sky, he'd felt a greater urgency. Not just because of her, of course, it was Winifred and millions of other Londoners, but suddenly it had become more personal.

Bertram moved to the window, its panes crosshatched with tape. A bus passed by with few passengers on the roof, common these days. Only a month earlier it would have been jammed despite the cold, people's arms thrust between the crowd to grab a railing, but London's human tide was ebbing again.

A caravan of American jeeps followed the bus. Bertram counted them and turned back. "Fourteen," he said. "Present company excluded, I fear you Americans are going to be insufferable in the years to come."

So now he was American. When Bertram needed Claus to do something, he was German or Irish. Bertram had recruited Claus—if a form of blackmail could be counted as recruitment—by telling him that if his Irish ancestry was suspect, his German lineage was more so, and he'd made it clear that the only way Claus could avoid being deported to Canada or interned for the war's duration was to work for them. The master manipulator. Though that wasn't quite fair; Claus had allowed himself to be manipulated. Part of him wanted to be useful and prove that he was loyal.

"Americans insufferable?" he said. "How?"

"Saint-Mihiel and Château-Thierry in the last war, and now Normandy." Bertram opened both his hands. "You'll have won the war again, you see, just like the last one. Of course, that again disregards the years we fought before you were even in."

"And what has that to do with my suggestion?"

"Nothing. Trying to avoid it." He turned to the window again and clasped his hands behind his back. "On the issue of redirecting the bombs, you should know that high command agrees with you. As do I. We brought it up at a cabinet meeting."

Claus kept his voice neutral; if he appeared eager, Bertram would grow suspicious. "Then we can do it?"

Bertram opened his hands behind his back. "No. The cabinet didn't like the idea."

"Politicians."

Bertram glanced at him; Claus's voice had been surprisingly bitter. "Yes, you have much to complain of them, American ones, at least." He straightened the photographs on his wall, Churchill above the king. "But Churchill doesn't like the idea, and not because of politics. He won't play God."

"But why not? We do all the time, determining what information to give the Germans. Besides, the war is nearly over. What better time to do it?"

"Normandy isn't a sure thing, even now. Could be another Dunkirk, if the Germans release the mechanized units from around Calais."

He sat and swiveled the chair to straighten his bad left leg. "I understand your desire. But to be fair to the politicians, how would you like to explain to one of your Sussex constituents that you'd allowed her mother or child to be killed instead of an office worker in Westminster or a widower in Southwark?"

"It's common sense. Bombs in the country are far less likely to hit anyone. In the city it's a certainty."

"Less likely, more." Bertram waved his hand back and forth as if turning pages. "Neither is certain. If the bombs fall on a farm and destroy a husband and wife, their family won't think it kind, or fair. Nor would you, I suspect." He sat back. "You know, you're not choosing where the bombs land, you're only reporting locations and times, information the Germans might also get from other sources."

"Then let them. Let someone else transmit the information." He had a movie to make, a life to begin to inhabit.

"The German army hasn't broken down under tremendous pressure. What makes you think German intelligence has? They're crippled, not killed. They have to hear from you, and your information has to be accurate. You know that."

He did, that was the rub. Yet he was tired of it. More than 90 percent of what he told them was true; 95 percent, probably. But it was that 5 percent that mattered, information that they got only from him. That the real invasion hadn't happened yet, that Normandy was just a feint, that Calais with its working port was the true target. And as long as they believed him, they'd hold their mechanized armies in reserve, and the Normandy invasion would have a better chance. But would a few more bits of misinformation really be so bad?

Bertram had said no to changing the landing coordinates; Claus had been prepared for that. What surprised him was the depth of his disappointment. For Winifred, Myra, even Herbert. Their physical selves, but also their mental ones. The constant sirens were literally driving people mad; a woman on his block had been taken away screaming in the middle of the night because she'd snapped. Really, though, it was Kate that bothered him, the danger to her. Why pretend otherwise? He sat forward.

"You support my idea?"

"My support is immaterial," Bertram said.

"Not to me. I could quit. Or what if I went ahead and did it anyway?"

"In either case you'd be interned as a danger to the war effort."

"You couldn't speak on my behalf?"

"It wouldn't matter."

He pried at Bertram's doubts again. "You don't think we should do this?"

"You mustn't twist my words. To make myself absolutely clear, you may not jigger the landing results." He shrugged. "And it wouldn't be of much use to try. Even if we allowed it, you couldn't misdirect them. Too many people know where the bombs are falling."

"But it's not published information. The Germans don't have it. We're squelching every bit of it. The papers only say that they're hitting southern England."

"So far." Bertram pulled a map of Croydon from a drawer. Dozens of crosses marked where bombs had hit in the past weeks, decimating the borough. "This is from the *Croydon Times*. The censor canceled it, but eventually they'll have to let one pass."

Claus looked it over. "Eventually, yes. But even then the map won't say when the bombs hit, so the Germans won't get much of anything from it. I can't possibly give them times and locations for all their bombs, just enough to influence them."

"True again. And yet, if they have other sources, they'll quickly point out your mistakes, and then the Germans will begin to suspect you. You must always keep your eye on that. Nothing else matters."

Claus dismissed the notion. "Other sources? Another spy? You must know them all by now. The ones I've given you, the ones those men have." Germany always alerted him to impending arrivals, and each time he turned over a new name, Claus knew he'd sealed the man's fate. A few would transmit from various safe houses, especially if they had English contacts they were supposed to meet. Most would hang.

Bertram steepled his fingers. "Tell me about Julius Silber."

"Who?"

"Exactly." From his bookshelf, he selected a slim green book. "Julius Silber. Very few know of him. We certainly didn't. A senior postal inspector during the last war, almost from the beginning." Bertram peered at Claus over his glasses, as if trying to determine how much more he should say. "He'd come here from Germany specifically to spy. Very successful. Made it undetected through the entire war and then went home. We'd never have known if he hadn't written about himself." He set the book down, spine along the desk edge. "Cost several people their jobs. But the point is that we knew nothing about him—didn't even suspect that he existed. I don't doubt that twenty years from now we'll have our own Julius Silber to deal with. And I don't want to help him out in any way, which letting you change the locations might do."

Bertram plucked a pear from his desk and turned it in his hand, giving Claus one of his rare smiles, which were always disconcerting; his teeth were so small they seemed nonexistent, his mouth mostly red gums, as if he'd just eaten an especially bloody meal. Claus was saved from contemplating it further by the clock striking and the cuckoo shooting out, launched into its hourly frenzy. Inside its chirping beak was a miniature camera; the Abwehr had sent it to Claus and he'd turned it over immediately, explaining to his German handlers that it must have been intercepted by the censors.

Bertram put the pear down and it occurred to Claus that he'd never seen Bertram eat anything, never observed him doing anything remotely human; even his breathing was unnoticeable, even the pipe on his desk, bowl always full, was never burning. He seemed to have effaced anything not having to do with his realm, the shadow war against Germany.

"We'll have those launch pads soon enough," Bertram said. "Or such is our hope. In the meantime you might as well tell the Germans the truth. Morale's so bad it's even reached the papers. The censors thought it would be worse to deny it. Correctly, probably. And if you give it to the Germans a day or two before it hits the papers, so much the better for you.

"Speaking of which," he said, and pulled a piece of crisp paper from another of his innumerable files, "we need you to send this. Operation Leopard."

Unnecessarily, Claus smoothed the page before beginning to read, a habit to buy himself time. Troop deployments, altered train schedules, operational code names. "Pas de Calais," he said, when he was done. "So the invasion is to happen at last. And how did I come across it?" He folded it and slipped it into his jacket pocket.

"Of course it isn't real," Bertram said. "But you've several options for how you found out." He flipped open the blue folder on his blotter. "Tottingham, Mrs. Honeywell. Perhaps Madame Blavatsky."

Claus thought them over. "Not Honeywell. She wouldn't be able to put all this together. The Air Ministry wouldn't have it all."

"Tottingham could."

"Yes."

"You don't sound convinced."

"I'm not. As a builder, he has access to many of the bases there, but I don't know that he'd gather all these pieces on his rounds. He's good at telling us what's happened, not what's about to. I think Madame Blavatsky is best."

"Distraught wives?" Bertram ran his fingers down the folder. "Yes, that should work. You see?" he said, and smiled. "That's why we can't afford to lose you."

Claus had created Madame Blavatsky, a fortuneteller who lived outside of Hastings, between an American army base and a British aerodrome, and from whom officers' wives routinely sought good news about their husbands' upcoming operations. She made up her face with an ace of spades, wore acorn earrings, and had one large expense—black-market fabric, to make her multicolored capes. Necessary, Claus had explained, to have her clients believe her, and the Germans were happy to pay.

"You might have her arrested soon," Claus said.

"Yes. When Madrid and Berlin get this, they'll press for more details. Exact dates. The train schedules will give them an approximate time, but they'll want perfection. And if she's arrested, it could be a reason the operation doesn't come off."

"Certainly. The Americans would want to stall for at least a couple of weeks after that, which would buy us more time."

Bertram made a note on the file. "I'll slip an item into the paper next week, sufficiently vague but with her name prominently displayed. Send it off immediately, and say that Winifred's husband has confirmed the shipping details."

"Some," Claus said. "But we shouldn't go too heavily down that road."

"No? Too much, you think? All right. We'll keep it mostly Madame Blavatsky."

The truth was Claus felt squeamish taking advantage of Winifred's present condition, even though she'd never know it. Using people, however blind to it they were, felt suddenly less acceptable. It had been years since he'd had such qualms; it was almost as if the war were beginning again for him under different circumstances.

Bertram seemed to intuit his mood. "Cheer up. Your wireless will be back in service."

Claus turned his eyes back to Bertram's instantly. Not looking at him would be read as dissimulation; he knew Bertram well enough for that. "Did my German finally come?"

"Yes. And with him your vacuum tube. Captured just north of Reading."

"Recently?"

Bertram looked at his notes. "Not quite sure on that score. In any event, you'll be able to use your radio again."

The radio. Claus had never liked it, had been glad it was broken. Before the war, in Hamburg, his mother's cousin had invited Claus home after agreeing to buy an industrial film. Once there, he'd offered Claus the radio.

"Whatever for, Robert?"

Pink and pudgy, Robert had shrugged. "Who knows? It might come in handy in the next few years. The English government has never been especially kind to you. The Americans either. You've said so yourself. And what happened to you broke your mother's heart. Her last letters to me were filled with nothing else."

True, though Claus hadn't fallen for the sentiment; the real issue was that Robert, a former socialist, admired the Nazis. Claus had demurred but mentioned the offer to his boss at Taylor Films, who'd evidently told a friend in military intelligence. A week later Claus was summoned to an office in Jermyn Street, where a government official told him that on his next trip to Germany he was to accept the radio. It hadn't been a request; Claus's immigration status was cloudy. Claus had kept the handsome Saba model in storage for years, along with its codebook. At their first meeting, Bertram had told him to begin using it.

Now, Claus said, "They must be desperate, dropping someone in after the invasion."

"The endgame is precisely when one is most likely to take risks, and is therefore most dangerous."

"You admit it's the end."

"The beginning of the end. But the end itself may take a long time," Bertram said, and slipped into his usual Latin pedantry. "*Nil actum reputa si quid superest agendum.* 'Don't consider that anything has been done if anything remains undone.'" As if casually, he added, "Trust no one you meet. No one."

He stared at Claus so intently, Claus wondered if Bertram knew more about he and Kate than he'd told. Then Bertram stood and opened a metal box.

"So," Claus said. "Money." He liked to get this part of their meeting over with as quickly as possible; it was humiliating to have to account for every penny he spent. "I need double the normal amount today."

"*A fronte praecipitium, a tergo lupi,*" Bertram said as he fiddled with the money.

"My feeling exactly."

Bertram smiled. "Ah, so now you're a Latin scholar, are you?"

Claus translated. "'A precipice in front, wolves behind.'"

Bertram stopped counting, small fat thumb motionless on a pile of pound notes, but he mastered himself sufficiently not to look up. "You know Latin?"

"You've used that one before."

Bertram went back to his counting. "Unlike me to repeat myself. Weary, I suppose."

"Aren't we all?" Claus pulled a sheaf of notes from his breast pocket.

"What's this?" Bertram took a quick look. "Rent, tube rides, toothpowder. No. I don't want them." He folded the receipts and gave them back.

"But I always give them to you."

"Not today. Not to me at least." He opened the door. "To Miss Smithers. I'm afraid I do have other meetings and this one has already run over."

Claus understood; the Latin had been a mistake. There was ever something of the scholarship boy about Bertram—the Union Jack bow ties, the heavily thumbed copy of *Debrett's* left casually on his desk, the frequent mentions of his Boodle's membership—and since Bertram was never quite sure of his position, he was quick to quash those who challenged it. Showing Claus the door was a way of showing him his place.

*This is the man I work for,* Claus thought. It didn't improve his mood.

Madge was just outside the office, but even standing still she managed to look the bustling blonde.

"Been listening at keyholes?" he asked.

She put one manicured hand on her narrow waist. "Should I have been?"

"You didn't miss anything. You've wonderful color, by the way."

"Tar beach."

Madge moved beside Claus with her careful stride, putting one foot directly in front of the other as if walking an invisible chalked line. Through an open window came the sound of Vera Lynn singing on the radio. "One simply has to visit it in this dreadful weather. It would be a sin not to snatch any sunshine when it comes. Besides, we're so god-awful busy that if I don't take my lunch, Bertram won't give it me."

"You look years younger."

"In other words I looked older before."

"You see," he said. "I can't win."

Flirting required an effort, and he wished he could be more like her; her professional insouciance seemed to both recognize and dismiss the importance of her work. *I do it well, but somehow I can't take it all that seriously.* It had been months since he'd thought of this work with anything but dread, and even now, his mood lighter, it was hard to muster sufficient enthusiasm to banter.

She held up a green file. "Air Ministry," she said. "Care to walk me? We lie out on our lunches. The roof's quite a spot, filled with beautiful girls."

"Sorry," Claus said, "not today."

She sighed. "It's never a good day, is it?"

Feigned sadness. They weren't allowed to see one another outside of the office and even if they met accidentally they were to ignore one another.

"So," she said. "If you're not falling for me, who's the lucky gal?"

"No one, I'm afraid." He thought happily of Kate and sat beside

Madge's desk. "I only want to get paid. Bertram said I was to give you a list of my expenses."

"Ah, the usual. It seems I'm only good for money."

He didn't touch the obvious line. "Listen, I'm sorry to rush you, but I have to be at the MOI soon."

"My, you're in a mood." Her voice turned brisk and chilly. She yanked open the top desk drawer, scissors and pens rattling against metal. "Old piss and vinegar must have been particularly sour today."

Guiltily, he touched her arm. "Are there days he isn't?"

"Not round us. Perhaps at home he's secretly nice to the help."

"Does he have help? Who on earth would stay with him?"

Softening, she gave a quick half smile. "He must have, mustn't he? The big cheese?"

# JUNE 28

THE POST WAS NEARLY fully inhabited again. A few wardens were talking quietly over a pile of abandoned playing cards, the fine-boned Rosalyn shaking her head, Williams sullenly silent, Herbert, with his blue breast-pocket square, bent over a map of London, since in the aftermath of the V-1s, the invasion of Normandy and the euphoria it had generated had been nearly forgotten. Londoners once again were worried about their own survival, and with good reason: thousands had died already from the buzz bombs.

"When is Monty going to get on with it?" Rosalyn said. Monty was bottled up on the east flank, supposed to head for Calais, where most of the buzz bombs were being launched. It was the same everywhere; people were discussing the bombs and not the invasion. That too would go into his report, along with Rosalyn's weary resignation. Only six months on the job, she was normally so vital it seemed at times that her very cells would burst into flame.

After the Blitz ended, in May of '41, the wardens had gone home when the all-clear sounded around midnight, but these past weeks they were back to sleeping on post, as if the war were beginning all over again. It was depressing. They no longer played darts or cards while talking about their own plans for after the war, or how England would change; instead, they were on about the damage and the bombs, speculating about how long London—themselves, really—could stand it. Long-term odds weren't good, especially from Herbert, who before the war had been a bookie in Prague. "Six months and we're through," he'd first said. Recently, as the bombs came with greater frequency and deadlier accuracy, he'd dropped it to four. It was extraordinary how Claus's short time with Kate—a few hours of wakefulness, if he totted it up—had changed his perspective. For the first time in months, years perhaps, he felt apart from the gloom.

In the kitchen a green bowl with three brown eggs was sitting on the counter.

"Have one, if you'd like," Myra said.

"Oh, hello," Claus said. "Didn't see you." He was surprised she'd spoken to him. They'd dated a few times just as the war began and then quarreled violently, and since then she'd been cool to him at every turn. Cold, even. Deserved, since he'd started the quarrel on the slimmest of pretexts, but sometimes her manner still irritated him; one more thing he wasn't allowed to explain. After the war, he kept telling himself, though with the advent of the buzz bombs that day seemed to be receding farther into the future.

"Sorry, didn't meant to startle you," Myra said. "I'm being quiet. It's late. But you really should have one."

How many mornings he'd wanted eggs. They were becoming easier to find, food more plentiful as the V-1s continued and London emptied out once again.

"No, thank you." He knocked them together with his finger. "I'm too tired." He was. He'd spent an unfruitful day at the MOI. The script wasn't coming along, and Max, who had tried not to push, nonetheless had made it clear that the deadline was fast approaching.

"I'm going up to take my watch," Claus said. He was glad it was the first one; after, he'd at least have the possibility of uninterrupted sleep. But before he left he felt he had to say something more. "I didn't go down in the shelters tonight." Myra didn't respond and he went on. "Somehow I couldn't face it. The shelterers are all scared again, and it's worse now. You've seen it. When the bloody PM's office said last month that the Battle of London was done, they believed it. First they were elated, and now they're depressed."

And they were angry, at the lies put out by the Ministry of Information about Londoners' fantastic morale despite the V-1s. The truth was that the citizens were exhausted. He hadn't wanted to face that either. Even his time with Kate couldn't affect that.

Myra set her book down between the ring of keys for the post's houses and a glass of milk, the milk, like the eggs, a novelty. Had survivors of the plague marveled at the small good things the general disaster had brought them? he wondered.

"I know," she said. "The old women and their canaries, the offers to fetch a cup of tea. It's strangely wearing, isn't it, now that we're being bombed again. And the accordions can drive you barmy. Of course, there are the amusing bits too," she said. "Day before yesterday, in Croydon, a man was after his wife to come down to the shelter because the sirens had started.

"She called down and told him to wait, saying that she had to find her dentures.

"'Listen, you,' he said. 'Hitler's dropping bombs, not sandwiches.'"

He smiled, but it didn't assuage his guilt. He should have stopped by the shelter to see Mrs. Bankcroft. She'd have been playing something from the Andrews Sisters, softly so as not to wake others, expecting him to check in, but she'd have wanted him to put the gambling adolescents either in the lavatory or out on the streets, and he hadn't had the endurance for that. He failed to see the harm in cards, and if he ordered the kids to the lavatory they'd only gamble there, while out on the street they'd be in danger from debris and bombs. Mrs. Bankcroft and he had fought a subtle combat over the gambling for four years, and he was tired of it.

Myra seemed to know what he was thinking. She put her hand on his forearm, the first time she'd touched him in months.

"It's all right, Claus."

The use of his real name shocked him; even Kate didn't know it. He'd told her in a moment of weakness years before. Myra smiled, unusual, as it showed the gap between her front teeth—seemingly aligned with the part in the middle of her shoulder-length hair—of which he knew she was ashamed.

"This has all of us on edge. It's horrible, really. Everyone thought it was over."

"Yes," he said. "I wish we'd been right."

Keeping his eyes open required effort. He paced, he flapped his arms, pressed his nails into the skin of his palms. Eventually he dropped into a kind of semi-trance, letting images float to the surface. The strongest was of their first incident, when he and Myra had dug out an old woman together. Before the bombs hit they'd been chasing children back into the shelters, children lured outside by the peculiarly attractive sound of shrapnel falling through trees, a kind of savage whistling, and who were trying to pick up the shrapnel from the pavement though it was still hot enough to burn.

Near the blue incident flag a group of teenage girls on roller skates were bumping around the blown-about bricks and plaster, their faces and smocks black. A bomb had hit behind the skating rink, its blast wave forcing soot down the chimneys, and beyond that the back of a house had collapsed, trapping three women. Claus and Myra hung their coats and gas masks on a door that stood up from a mass of masonry and wood and began to dig, tossing aside rubble by hand at first, then filling wicker baskets when they realized they had a long way to go.

Every ten minutes either Myra or Claus shouted for the buried people to give their locations; at first all three women replied but after half an hour they were down to one, a Mrs. Timothy. Soon it grew dark and began to rain and the dusty ruins turned grimy. They'd each wanted a cigarette but had no way to light it; stupid, really—there were fires all around, as the Germans were dropping incendiaries—but neither of them had a match, so they complained about it as they dug. Mrs. Timothy heard their voices and talked back, and they realized it was a good thing to keep her entertained or, if not entertained, alert, so they chatted with her. At one point she'd said, "The stunning call of the wild goose," and they thought she was becoming delirious until they realized that another of the diggers had just blown his nose. Their laughter was revitalizing.

Each time a plane went over, someone shouted, "Lights," and they doused their torches, which was maddening. Claus continued to dig with his hands—the shovel worthless amid all the broken timbers—and Myra took away basket after basket of debris. Her fingertips were bleeding and he asked if she shouldn't take a break but she shook her head no and kept going; neither of them wanted to quit when they seemed so close. They uncovered a severed forearm with a still-working watch, and Claus wrapped it in a bit of blanket and handed the package to Myra, who took it without a word. Behind her through the blown-open roof came shell flashes against the dark clouds, the insistently probing searchlights, a glowing sky when the incendiaries hit their marks.

After two hours a chunk of plaster had fallen away and Mrs. Timothy had said, "Right here, dear," and the feeling of dull excitement he'd been laboring under exploded into a belief in their work's nobility. It was right and good and useful, three things that had seemed hard to come by those days. While digging they'd uncovered a Bullet Talcum Powder tin under her bed, and they gave it to her, which cheered her immensely. All her treasures were in there: ration books, a marriage certificate, her children's christening papers; she'd held up each in turn and said that she was sure she'd be all right. "Won't anything stop me from eating now."

They were thrilled. It took another hour to free her legs, Claus having to wriggle under jammed but creaking timbers to insert a jack, getting a mouthful of dust for his trouble, but she was fine when they pulled her out, still chatting madly. They put her on a stretcher and she died before they got her to the ambulance.

He and Myra had started to date, and a month later Myra had introduced him to Madge—an old school chum—at a pub. Madge hadn't been able to hide a flash of recognition.

"Know one another?" Myra had said.

"No," they both had said, too quickly. "He looks like my old beau," Madge had added, only making it worse.

Later, in her apartment, sponging off the black line she'd drawn up the back of her calf to mimic stockings, Myra had questioned him about it, and he'd turned her questions into an argument, berating her for being nosy. Bertram had told him that if his cover was ever blown he'd be arrested and interned for the duration, and he'd had a sudden intuition that any kind of intimacy could be disastrous.

After their quarrel, he and Myra hadn't seen each other again socially. Madge had found out about it and seemed to take a perverse pleasure in alluding to the pickle she'd put him in, but Claus had always felt guilty. He'd often wondered if it would have been different if Mrs. Timothy had died right away, before they tried to dig her out, if their first incident hadn't been so cruelly misleading. But over time he'd come to see that he hadn't been misled, he'd misled himself. The work was necessary, not noble, and he'd been wrong to think otherwise. It was simply a matter of surviving and of helping others to do the same, and if his survival meant cutting emotions from his life, so be it. Yet he couldn't imagine being so cruel to Kate. Had he grown smarter with time, or simply more tired?

With fifteen minutes left on his watch, a flight of three buzz bombs appeared, their tail fires heading directly toward him. One veered east, one dropped south of the river, but the third one flew over, its engine cutting out no more than a couple of miles away, and the dull sound of its impact was followed by a second but much larger explosion. Gas. He checked his watch when the night sky glowed orange. Crews would already be mobilizing to find survivors and remove the dead; at least it wasn't in their sector. The phone rang down below and five minutes later Herbert came up to relieve him, smelling of musky cologne, his jaw cracking as he yawned.

"You all right?" Claus asked. Herbert had been beaten badly by a disgruntled Londoner for not blowing his whistle at one of the first buzz bombs—both eyes were still blackened—or such was his story; Claus wondered if it hadn't been one of his black-market deals gone wrong.

"Fine. Fucking cold, though. Jesus." Herbert waved his arms. "A little bit of summer would be nice. In my country this is not June. Czechs like heat!" He rubbed his stubbled face and made a burbling sound with his lips. "Not sleepy. Two to one I stay awake."

Claus didn't believe him but in any case it didn't matter. He opened the door and shouldered aside the first blackout curtain, knowing from experience that even if Herbert fell asleep, any nearby explosion would wake him.

Downstairs Myra stood with her hand on the phone, as if expecting it to ring. She was wearing a white sweater now and kept her back to him, a seeming return to her regular coolness, but when she continued to stand unmoving as he approached he gathered something horrible had happened. She'd stood just so after a nearby bomb had blown out a window, after which he'd spent an hour with tweezers picking glass shards from her skin and hair, and again when her own house had been hit, killing her father. Both of those events, which had happened before they'd begun dating, seemed from another lifetime.

She half turned when he drew up beside her, her sweater giving off the odor of mothballs. "A pensioners' home," she said.

"How badly?"

"Disastrous, apparently. A direct hit. Its gas exploded."

The glowing sky. About 12:45. "Where?"

"Regent Street, north of Oxford."

He knew he was tired when the thought *Tony spot for a pensioners' home* popped into his head. "Do they need me?"

"No. They have enough." Her left eyelid blinked uncontrollably and he had to restrain himself from reaching to still it. "And besides, we can't spare you." She looked at him for the first time. "Others have been spotted over the coast. We're in for a long night, I'm told."

He had a premonition that he was about to die, which faded as quickly as it had come, and he said, about the home, "That's awful." What else was there to say? Another appalling loss. He felt guilty at his relief that the incident hadn't happened in their sector. The torn and crushed elderly bodies with their anklet nametags, the hopelessness of the Heavy Rescue crews, the awful fact that almost no one would be there praying for individual miracles; he didn't want to see any of it.

"I hope they all died in the explosion," he said.

"I'm sorry?" Myra turned so sharply she knocked the keys from the desk, and he guessed the extent of her surprise when she didn't kneel to pick them up.

"I was thinking that to die in the fire would have been worse. And that perhaps it's for the best, after all."

"For the best?"

He waved his hands. "They probably had no relatives."

"That's horrible."

"I'm not saying it right," he said, and fell silent.

"Yes, even so," Myra said, "it's always better to live."

"Yes. Of course."

He retrieved the keys for her and in the next room sat on the cot that Herbert had vacated. The blankets were still warm, which was strangely comforting, so he quickly removed his flashlight from around his neck and his webbed belt from around his waist, lay down, and covered himself as best he could, pulling the blanket up around his chin and slanting his tin hat over his eyes. He didn't care that his boots stuck out or that the blanket smelled faintly of disinfectant, and in the quiet darkness, as he sought to still his racing mind with thoughts of Kate, he nearly believed that he was safe.

# JULY 2

H E WOKE IN AN unfamiliar room to the tail fire from another buzz bomb pinking the walls, reminding him of childhood Septembers, his bedroom glowing gold in the reflected light of overloaded hay wagons trundling past; their Pennsylvania house had been yards from the road. Until he saw Kate lying face-down, a strand of hair drifting in and out of her open mouth as she breathed, he thought he was back at the post. He wanted to brush the hair aside but was afraid that would wake her and instead stood up in a single motion and slipped his pants on, holding the belt buckle so it wouldn't clink.

His shoes were warming in a block of sunlight on the wood floor, and the scent of strawberries drifted up from the street, where a vendor had parked his cart, chocking the wheel with a loose cobble. Claus wished he could go down and get some, but Kate's landlady didn't know he was there; he'd snuck up and knocked on her door after midnight, taking a chance that she'd be home, hoping she'd let him in. Mrs. Dobson didn't even let him have food in his rooms after nine at night, and if a single woman ever slept over he'd be asked to leave. At the corner a young girl, no more than four or five, was putting broad cabbage leaves in the neighborhood pig bin.

The strawberry vendor looked up, his tin hat flashing in the sun. Claus stepped away from the window, afraid of being spied on, and then told himself he was being foolish. Who would have followed him here? Angered by the need for continual caution, he carried his stiff shoes into the other room.

Books covered every flat surface: tables, chairs, bare spaces on the floor; they were leather-bound, mostly, and expensive. He moved on with his investigation, from habit and curiosity, at the moment not disliking himself for it. Floral prints from newspapers hung on the walls, making the place look comfortably lived in; his own rooms decidedly did not.

At the sink he drew himself a glass of tepid water. Propped on the counter was a silver-framed picture of a young girl in her christening gown, gap-toothed and curly-haired. Had Kate had a child? Twice now they'd spent frenzied nights making love, but they hadn't really talked. He heard a noise behind him and turned.

Kate stood in the doorway in a thin floral cotton robe, hair messy, face puffed with sleep, the skin around her mouth lined, which he hadn't noticed previously; the only place she showed her age. He put the picture back, guessing that she might not want to talk about it, and glanced around the apartment to avoid an awkward stare. He wondered if she wanted him to leave.

"I'm afraid it's rather a mess," she said. "I wasn't expecting company."

Next to a bowl of lemons, a plastic toy gun lay on the counter. He held it up with a quizzical look.

"Sentimental value," she said, and laughed. "The first decree the Germans passed after occupying Paris was that all Parisians were prohibited from owning guns. Residents, regardless of nationality, had to turn them in. I bought two from a toy store. One to keep, and one to give them."

"Protest," he said.

This time her laugh was bitter. "Yes. For all the good it did."

"And these?" He pinched a lemon. "Pancakes?"

"Hoping to get some if you stay?" she said.

He felt himself blushing but was relieved when she came and drew herself a glass of water too. She drank slowly, set the glass in the sink, and picked up the picture.

"My niece," she said. "Marie." She splayed her fingers over the girl's face and fell silent.

"You're maternal."

"I tried to be. It was horrible, after the last war, watching her waste away. The blockade."

"Did she make it?"

"Yes," Kate said. "She's alive still, in Hamburg." She seemed suddenly sadder. He wanted to kiss her but wasn't sure she wanted to kiss him—whether she was silent now from regret or discomfort or simply because she didn't talk much in the morning. He knew so little about her.

She rested her head against his shoulder, her hair smelling of smoke and perfume, which made him crave a cigarette. She tilted her face up and kissed him, slowly, and he felt himself stiffening against her but she pulled back.

"A smoke first." She produced a pack from her bathrobe pocket.

"Isn't it better to light up after?" he said.

She laughed and he took the cigarette.

"American," he said.

"The benefits of my position. Yanks like to think they're getting extra care."

"Ah, so you deceive them."

"No. But a little casual flirting goes a long way."

"Is that what last night was?" He liked seeing her smile. "What about your landlady?" he said. "Will she be up to check on you if you don't stir?"

"Oh, no. Saturday and Sunday are our Sodom and Gomorrah days. Anyone who lives through the bombing deserves whatever fun they can arrange. Plus bomb nights. At the first warning she's off to the neighborhood shelter, though she insists we live by the regulations. If we won't vacate the building it's our hard luck, but we have to leave the front door open and unlocked so anyone seeking shelter can come in."

She tipped soap out of a small shell on the sink and gave it to him for an ashtray.

"In prison," he said, "I had to use a matchbox for one."

She grew still. He hadn't meant to say it but was happy that he had; he wanted for a change to be honest about his life, as she had been about hers. The endless lying had become second nature, but with Kate it chafed unbearably. He went on. "You were right about my tattoo. Though it wasn't a crime, really, what I was in for."

She raised an eyebrow.

"No. Really. Or rather, not a crime you'd recognize as such."

"Tell me."

He blew out a mouthful of air. "The history of my misfortunes, eh? Okay."

Before he started, the mechanical rant of a buzz bomb interrupted, seeming to burrow through the blue morning sky directly toward them. They both stood stiffly, and as it passed over the engine cut and they waited. Two seconds, three, four; the waiting seemed interminable before the noise of its explosion came, close enough to blow the curtains in and to make her doors creak, and they both shifted on their feet.

"So," she said, as if they hadn't been interrupted, and as if the interruption weren't possibly fatal, an enforced calm in the face of danger he was finding increasingly hard to maintain. "What landed you in jail?"

"A movie."

"It must have been quite a film." She sat, demurely flipping the robe closed over her crossed knees. "Would I have seen it?"

He sat next to her. "No one did. It was suppressed."

"Ah. A blue movie."

"Far worse. Political. Or so they said. And anti-English."

It was a story he hadn't told for a while. In the late twenties and early thirties, over his shame but still nursing his anger, he'd told it often, usually to appropriately outraged listeners at socialist meetings in Birmingham and Leeds and Dublin, and once to a smaller but angrier crowd in Hamburg, told it so often that it had become rote. But over the past several years, because of his cover, he hadn't been able to tell it at all, and now it was difficult to remember exactly what he'd felt versus what he'd come to think he was supposed to have felt. Where to start?

"I was working with D. W. Griffith, on *Intolerance*."

"You must have been just a boy."

"Nineteen. Film was a young man's game then, which helped. Griffith was close to forty and he was ancient. *Intolerance* was a financial disaster, but it convinced me I could make a movie myself, and I wrote a script about the Revolutionary War."

"Ah, the Colonial troubles, you mean."

"Yes. Well, by the time I finished it, in 1917, it was called treason in the United States."

"Was it any good?"

No one had ever asked him that. "Yes," he said. "I think it was."

"Good for you, no false modesty. Your time here hasn't completely ruined you."

"The judge in my case felt differently. The Americans and the British were fighting together against the Germans then, and it wasn't sufficiently pro-English to suit him. There's a scene in the film in which the British, defeated at Saratoga and afraid of losing New York City, set fire to prison ships docked on the Hudson. It's based on a real atrocity, but it especially incensed the judge. And my name didn't help. 'Murphy?' The judge's contempt was obvious, worse when he found out I was half German. How could I have received a fair trial?"

"You're German?"

"My mother's side."

"*Sprechen sie Deutsch?*" she asked.

"*Ja.*" He hesitated, then took the plunge. "*Mein richtiger Name ist Claus.*"

She surprised him by laughing. "You've changed your name! So many secrets. It must be terrible." She leaned forward and put her hands on his knees. "What else are you hiding from me? Have you been there? Do you have relatives there?"

"Yes and yes. Between the wars, a few times. German industrial films."

"And your relatives?"

"Oh, distant cousins." He had to be careful. A discussion of Robert might lead to Bertram. "I'll tell you about them later."

"Yes," she said. "You must. But first, prison. Claus." She smiled and sat back to listen.

"I hadn't seen the anti-German hatred rising to the surface in the run-up to the war, too immersed in the movie, and nearly everything I did for it came back to haunt me. Worst of all was a publicity stunt, spreading rumors that our female lead had been killed in a St. Louis auto accident, and then, just before shooting began, buying newspaper ads around the country announcing that she was alive and well and working for me. The film was already notorious at release, and among the crowds were government agents. Since we'd declared war against the Germans just weeks before, I was immediately charged with treason.

"It took the jury an hour to convict me. The whole thing was preposterous. During the trial, the papers said I refused to eat anything but German food, and at one point some teenage boys bombarded me with rotten cabbages. The judge admonished them but didn't make them leave. At my sentencing, he held up one of the movie posters. 'To accuse the British of something like this, at a time when they need all our help.' He gave me an extra five years because of it."

"And how did you end up here?"

"Exile. When I got out, the naturalization laws had changed. England and Germany were my choices."

"You're not American?"

"Legally, no. My parents met in London, working for the same family. When my mother announced she was married and pregnant, she lost her job. As soon as I was born, they emigrated."

"So, born in London, raised in America, then tried for treason because of an anti-British film?"

"Yes. The courts have little sense of irony."

"And your parents? Were they forced to leave America too?"

"They might as well have been. Pennsylvania had a huge German population, which grew very skittish as the war went on. They had a store that went bankrupt, and with me in jail, they both aged very quickly. They died before I was released."

"Oh, Claus. I'm so sorry. And that you should end up in England after that."

"So I've often thought."

"And here you are, sleeping with an Englishwoman."

He laughed. "Yes, well. It's a bit better than my first fifteen years here."

"Perhaps it was for the good," she said, and stood. "Jail, I mean. Not for your parents, obviously, but it kept you out of the service and you're better off that way. Joining would have been unnecessary. The war will come to an end without you. Or me, for that matter." She bent to kiss him and cradled his warm forehead against her chest.

Back in bed he picked up a heavy leather book from the stack on the bedside table. It fell open to a page marked by a slightly charred German cigarette card, a picture of Bobby Box fleeing his own drawing.

"Oh, I'm glad you found that!" she said with evident pleasure, and turned it in her hands. "Marie's. She was going to fill up a Stefan Mart book with them. Do you know them?"

He hadn't heard of them.

"Great fun. Marie had most of them. The book was ruined much later."

She took the card and went to sit by the window, where she lit a cigarette. "When I left, I gathered everything I could. I don't know why I took what I did." She gestured at the room. "Most of this is from my mother's house. My brothers died in the last war, my father too. And she died before I came back. The last of the line, I'm afraid. But some of this I'd shipped far earlier, from Germany." She flipped the card. "I wish I had the entire book this came from. It was the only picture book we could afford, after the war. We bought it with vouchers from cigarette packs."

"And these?" he said, pulling out a journal, its pomegranate-colored leather spine dry and cracked. "Did these get shipped early on too?"

"Yes." She smiled. "But they're private."

"Sure they are," Claus said, and opened a page and began to read aloud: "'In 1915, outside Danzig. A house with a hundred and twenty clocks.'"

When he looked over at her, expecting a smile, her anger surprised him.

"Kate," he said, and snapped the journal closed. "I'm sorry. I only want to find out about an earlier you."

"I can tell you all you need to know," she said, taking the journal and slipping it under a pile of books.

He ran a thumb down the book spines, thinking that his social skills had grown dull; he should have known not to presume. "Trollope," he said. "Quite a collection." She didn't respond, and when her face turned scarlet, he said, "I'm sorry. Did I say something wrong?"

"Time for full confessions, I guess. It seems to be a day for them." She stubbed out her cigarette. "They're stolen."

"*Stolen* stolen?"

"Not pinched, if that's what you mean. I found most of them blown into the streets after raids; picking them up didn't seem like stealing. Especially since they were about to get ruined by the firemen's hoses. Do you think me horrid?"

He laughed, unsurprised; civilization's thin veneer. He'd been guilty of peeling it back too, and that she told him at all meant she forgave him the misstep with her journal. His turn. "I have a collection of pipes. My two favorites are real Turkish meerschaum, which I discovered beneath an uprooted tree, the site of some former alehouse, probably. Those aren't stolen at all. But the others I've found in the streets." He'd gathered them throughout the city, labeling where he'd found each one: Bethnal Green, the Guards' chapel, Madame Tussaud's. "I'm almost done collecting them. I have nearly a boxful. Once it's full, I think I'll stop."

"Do you smoke a pipe?"

"Never. And I doubt I'll start." Bertram did, and he couldn't imagine wanting to be like him. "But the first two just seemed to lead to the rest. A slippery slope, I guess."

"Yes. At the time I started with the books, I felt I was doing a service, performing a rescue. It's only in retrospect that it seems otherwise."

The state of his life, though of course he couldn't say so.

"You see this," she said, holding open a copy of Trollope's *The Warden*. The name Mildred Jones was inscribed on the inside cover. "She might be dead, for all I know, which makes me something of a grave robber."

"No," he said. "It's a bit more complex than that."

"Yes, everything is. At the club last week, when I got so angry at you, about collaborating? A bit of guilt, I suppose. Something along the same lines. I left Hamburg in the late thirties and moved to Strasbourg, then Paris. It was fairly easy to find work, even without papers; the French were convinced war was coming and that it would last for years again, that they'd have a shortage of nurses. And once France fell, the Germans at first seemed not to mind my presence.

"But my comments about helping a German general weren't hypothetical. The commander of the Île-de-France region was ambushed as he sat admiring tame swans on the Seine. He needed two surgeons; one was French, the other German. I served as the interpreter. Luckily, they saved him. Two French hostages were shot because he'd been wounded, but dozens more would have been killed had he died. Still, the anger in certain quarters was immense. He'd been involved in reprisals and was a notorious womanizer, and many French would have preferred him to die.

"The following day, the German surgeon stopped by, bringing some chocolate, as relieved as I that the massacre had been averted. I gave the chocolate bar to a neighbor who'd been kind to me. The next I saw her, her head had been shaved and she'd been doused with Mercurochrome."

Claus stopped her. "Wait," he said. "Why?" The scene sprang full-blown into his mind. "And where were you when you saw her?"

"I'd just come out of my apartment, and she was sitting on the curb, sobbing. Evidently someone had seen the officer enter our building, and the chocolate had been found in her apartment. The assumption was that she'd traded sexual favors for the candy. *Collaboration horizontale*. A true scarlet woman.

"I knew it wouldn't be long before my turn came. I was with the Germans often, after all, and the Germans were growing suspicious of me too. Unlike the French, they cared that I was of English birth. My service in the last war only carried me so far. With the invasion in the offing, they began questioning me ever more closely about my loyalties, and since others with similar backgrounds were being interned, once the contretemps with the dyed dog flared, I decided to flee.

"I had contacts in the resistance, had passed on secrets learned from German patients and from loose talk in the hospital cafeterias, since all in it were assumed to be German. It was surprisingly easy, in the end."

She fell quiet and he reached to turn the radio on, but she stopped him.

"No," she said. "Let's leave it off."

"You don't like music?"

"It's not that. This is extraordinary, to be in the same room with you and not feel alone."

Confused, he said, "Why would you?"

"My last years with Horst, he became a recluse. Sometimes for days he refused to talk to anyone—his mother, me—and sometimes he'd rant against doctors or retell the same stories, usually after a few beers. Romantic recitations of his youthful triumphs, or fond memories of his father. Touching at first, but they became pitiful when he repeated them so often that I could anticipate his inflections near the climax. In the end I was loneliest when in the same room with him, least lonely when alone. I'd turn on the radio with him so as not to feel it. So."

He settled for quietly holding her hand until his stomach growled.

Then, as if to pull back from the emotional door she'd opened, she said, "Hungry? I can burn you some toast."

"Not much of a cook?"

She shrugged. "After the first war, my mother-in-law and I used to pass hours describing imaginary meals, down to what spices we'd use, but it's been a long time since I've been in the habit of cooking for more than one."

"Yes," he said. "It's a bit hard to be inspired when it's just you you're cooking for, isn't it?"

Her breasts bounced as she stood and slipped her robe on. "How about those pancakes you were begging for earlier? I can make you those."

"Begging?" He playfully tapped her bottom. "I did nothing of the sort."

"Begging," she said, walking away from him. "It was most craven."

She returned carrying a white enamel tray, the pancakes, lemon juice.

He tasted one and made a sour face. "I have to say, this is one of those English customs I've never grown used to, lemon juice and pancakes. Do you have any syrup?"

"Sunday," she said, lifting his arm to slide in next to him. She kissed his throat. "The complaint department is closed."

They dozed for a while in the afternoon heat and now in the cooler dark Claus felt better rested than he had in weeks. They left the lights off, the windows open, and for the moment London seemed far removed from war: the clop of horse hooves as the strawberry vendor hitched up his wagon and left, the steady burr of traffic, a honking bus, a stray ambulance bell, the air-raid sirens mercifully silent.

Jack Payne's orchestra finished off one of Sousa's lighter pieces on a neighbor's radio that was playing ridiculously loud, and after a few ads came a series of exhortations from the MOI, one of its ponderous campaigns urging people to save money and metal.

"My God," Kate said, her eyes still closed. "You work for an organization that pumps out that? How can you stand it?"

"Another department, luckily."

"How did you ever end up in there?"

"The MOI? Simple. I was making industrial films. The switch was natural."

"They weren't suspicious of your background? A dangerous felon and all that."

"Once the war started, and they decided I wasn't a danger, they needed people too much to be suspicious."

He stroked her hair in the ensuing quiet and before long she was snoring again, which was just as well; his MOI history was too tortured to go into.

In September of 1939, five days after England declared war on Germany, he'd been arrested, along with every other nominal German in England, and at first held with a group in Brixton prison. Though the German internees were segregated from the regular prison population in their cells, during the limited free time they mixed together, and since most of the interned Germans were Jewish communists, dozens were beaten up by jailed British fascists or by the few real Nazis. During one fight, three of the Jews were stabbed to death.

Eventually the internees were transferred to the muddy mess of Kempton Park Racecourse, cheap canvas tents in the sodden infield with neither mattresses nor blankets, so that they slept—all six thousand of them—in three inches of cold brown water. Once a day they were fed outside, rain or shine, and twice a day they stood in line for water that tasted powerfully of chlorine. The bathroom was an unsheltered slit trench at one end, as far away from the tents as possible, where men and women squatted side by side on the muddy, crumbling rim, trying desperately not to slip backward and fall in. To keep himself busy, to move, to stay warm, he'd volunteered to spread chloride of lime on it every half-hour, and like all the other volunteers was easily spotted in the crowd because the front of his clothes was stained white.

Safe in the racecourse from a wider prison population, the internees were still depressed—all had been separated from their spouses and children and were driven nearly mad by the total news blackout. They couldn't get mail or read newspapers and no one had a radio, so everything was rumor: they were to be interned for the duration, to be shipped to Canada or Australia, to be sent to Sweden and shoved across the border into occupied Denmark, and a feeling of general despair soon erupted, amid which several internees committed suicide, hanging themselves beneath the grandstands.

At the hearing on his status the board classified him as B, a bit disappointing because he'd thought he'd be a natural C—released with complete freedom—but, worried that if he complained they'd reclassify him an A—permanent internment—he hadn't argued. The few restrictions he could live with: no trips within three miles of the coast, no visits to military installations, no travel outside the country. Where would he go? A week later, thirty of them were released early on a hot Tuesday morning; alone of the group, he was steered aside by a guard and shoved into the back of a bakery van and taken to meet Bertram. The mild friendly tone of Bertram's "Do sit down" didn't disguise the peremptory nature of the command, or that he wanted something and expected to get it. That Claus smelled of freshly baked bread put him, he felt, at a further disadvantage.

"You have a German radio," Bertram said, picking up the topmost sheet from a thin file as if reading it, though he seemed to already know its contents. Claus's time in prison would have been in there, his deportation from America.

He was about to object but Bertram held up a hand. "You do only because we told you to. Is that it?"

"Yes. I didn't want to take it."

"No," Bertram said. "But it's good that you did. It might keep you out of prison."

Claus didn't respond and Bertram said, "Helping us wouldn't be bad. You may not like us, but we're not rounding up Jews and herding them away."

"Just Germans. Or anyone who has German blood. Which is going to get tricky."

"How so?"

"Soon the royal family will be in trouble."

Sitting beneath his portrait of the king, Bertram ignored the jab. Instead he leaned forward and slid a telegram over the desk. "The Germans, yes. Look at what they're doing." It was from Charles Bernstein, a German American Hollywood producer from the 'teens. Claus had worked with him on *Intolerance*. In the telegram he asked for money to help flee Germany, the nine dollars needed to process his passport application. He sounded not just desperate but afraid.

Claus studied the back of its yellowed form, as if more might be written there. "And what's happened to him since?"

Bertram shrugged. "I wish I knew. But he's a Jew, so I can imagine." He shut the file and stood. "And I can tell you that if you don't help us you're likely to spend the war—however long it lasts—in some kind of confinement. Brixton, perhaps."

"Where Jews are also being murdered."

"A few."

"A few? And is that acceptable?"

In the end Claus asked for a week to decide; Bertram gave him one day. He left certain he wouldn't return. He didn't trust Bertram, and Bertram certainly didn't trust him; working for Bertram would be an endless series of compromises, at the end of which he was likely to be cast aside. If jail was still being offered, better to choose it than to give Bertram that power, which he seemed likely to flourish at the slightest provocation. There was something moist about him.

But when he'd gotten back to his apartment, he'd found his landlord moving his things out onto the street.

The landlord's wife had been apologetic. "I'm sorry, Mr. Murphy," she'd said, "but my 'usband wouldn't 'ave you. Part German and all."

Her red-faced husband, with his brick-shaped head, stood at the top of the stairs, arms crossed over his narrow chest, refusing to discuss it. From behind Claus came murmuring and he turned to see a small crowd and a man in a morning suit walking off with a side table.

"But that's mine!" he said, and tried to go after him.

"Not no more," a heavyset member of the crowd said, and along with the thin pimply youth beside him made his shoulders rigid so Claus couldn't get through without having to knock them down. He'd had a vision of himself in prison, enduring an endless series of such tests, and knew he couldn't face it. Ashamed of his own cravenness, he'd gone back to Bertram, who'd found him the apartment in Charing Cross and arranged for Claus to become a warden; the work would make him less suspicious to others and allow him greater access to sources.

Then in May of 1940, after the Germans invaded France, Bertram had arranged his position at the MOI, working on films. Exciting, initially. His first script concerned the Home Guard, a short film meant to prepare them for the likely German invasion, and it was a real joy to tinker with the writing, to fix others' words so they weren't wooden, so the part-time soldiers faced believable dilemmas; a boy appears in the town crossroads, bloody and mute, the Home Guard gathers around him. Who wouldn't? But might it not be a ruse, allowing the Germans to sneak past those guarding the post office and capture the center of another town? It had been a thrill to be part of it again.

And further work for the MOI meant that he got to blunder about the countryside, scouting locations for films. On each trip he picked up bits of information for the Germans, sent on by coded letters, first to his cousin Robert, then to an Abwehr handler. Less often, he transmitted by radio. The English were seeking out forbidden transmitters and he had to keep his broadcasts short, vary their timing; it wouldn't do to be caught by his own side.

That entire first summer his information was mostly about English readiness, which he'd been instructed to magnify. His version of the Home Guard was more fully staffed and better equipped than the real one, drilling with modern rifles rather than mops, though he was careful to add that this was only in certain areas he could be sure about; others might not be the same. The Germans, foolishly quick to believe him, instructed him to develop agents in other parts of Britain so that all of their reports would be so accurate, and he'd complied, making up most of his contacts. A matron in a Brighton naval hospital, who, like him, had German ancestry; a disaffected

Irish supply sergeant billeted in Edinburgh; though there were a few, like Winifred, who were based on real people.

Bertram had encouraged him. *"Mus uni non fidit antro,"* he said, and Claus, instinctively certain that he shouldn't reveal everything about his past, hadn't let on that he knew Latin.

"No knowledge of Latin?" Bertram had said. "More's the pity. An American education. 'A mouse does not rely on just one hole.' Apt, you see."

That July, all his earlier doubts about working with Bertram had returned when the *Arandora Star* sank. It had been filled with German refugees, many of them interned with Claus at Brixton or Kempton Park, who'd been judged for various reasons to be enemies of the state. Single men, mostly; but for the accident of a Nazi cousin and his gift of a radio, Claus would probably have been on the ship himself. Bound for Canada, and overloaded with 2,500 refugees, it had been sunk by a U-boat seventy-five miles off the coast of Ireland.

"That, yes," Bertram had said, pushing aside the paper Claus laid on his desk. "Accidents of war."

"An accident?" Most of the people Claus had been interned with had been scared, a few angry, nearly all had despised Hitler, had given up everything to flee to England for precisely that reason; it was intolerable that Bertram should be so dismissive. He couldn't help recalling the suicides, their gray, cold bodies—he'd been detailed to cut several of them down—and he grew so angry even his shins tensed. "It wasn't an accident, it was sheer stupidity, and if you're going to be that bloody callous about it, I'd prefer to resign."

"Don't be stupid, man," Bertram said. "That would put you on the next ship."

Claus didn't doubt he meant it. He'd continued to work, though admittedly with less enthusiasm, telling himself that the war would soon end, or that his role in it would, that he needed to hang on only a while longer. Over time, keeping track of all of the imaginary spies and their jobs and the information they'd passed on had grown overwhelming, especially as D-day approached and he'd worked desperately to fool the Germans into believing that he'd discovered where the landings would take place: Calais. Bertram had given him freedom on that.

*Where do* you *think they're likely to land?*
*Calais.*
*Tell them. You'll be doing what you should, making an educated guess.*

Bertram must have known the truth. Claus had been the perfect decoy, believing his own misinformation.

As if their conversation had never stopped, Kate rolled over and said drowsily, "Tell me about prison. What it was like."

He found it easier to discuss in the dark, the images that sprang to mind, like the beginning of a film. "Radio earphones were attached to our beds, we played baseball and basketball. We didn't go to our cells directly from work."

"Work?"

"Sewing, that was my first job. Or a kind of sewing. And on Sundays, we were out of the cellblocks all day—in the yard, reading in the library, or in winter playing dominoes or chess in the old hospital. We had movies twice a week."

She lit a cigarette. "It doesn't sound so bad."

"It wasn't," he said. "Not all of it."

But it was hard to explain. His uniform with the wide striped pants and jacket; the blue cloth shirt and cap and the square on it, red, blue, or black depending on the number of infractions he'd committed that week; the petty rules that were ridiculously easy to break, often unintentionally—if his top button was unbuttoned, if he forgot to return his fork separate from his tray, if he wrote a third letter in a span of seven days. And the dispiriting food, cold because he had to walk from the steam tables where it was served outside and across the yard to the dining area, rain, sunshine, or snow, the cockroaches he picked out with one hand while he ate, the phenomenal heat of the nights since the ventilation for their entire block was controlled by a single prisoner, Beasley, short and short-legged and with tattooed fingers, who had an irrational fear of breezes; the joy he'd first taken in the Thursday-night scrub-downs since it was a break in the routine until that, too, became part of the deadening sameness. And the emotional cost of his endless fury at the injustice of being imprisoned for making what he was convinced was a patriotic film, it was best not to discuss that; he always felt as though he was whining.

Absently, she ran her hand over the *Spirit of '76* tattoo. "So why did you get it?"

"Youthful bravado. To show that I didn't repent. And I don't. But now I prefer to think of it as a reminder of another prisoner. William Simon. He's the one that did it, a jailhouse artist."

"And what happened to him?"

"Tuberculosis. He'd been in a local jail in Oklahoma and the sheriff didn't want to pay his medical bills. One day a gust of wind blew over an oil lamp in his cell, starting a fire, so the sheriff charged him with malicious destruction and shipped him out to die in the federal prison, as a way to save money. Your government at work for you."

"And yet here you are, making films for one."

"Just so. Perhaps you shouldn't trust me."

"Don't worry, I don't." She leaned forward and stubbed out her cigarette, drank from a glass of water by the bed. "Not this early, at least. That requires hope, which I've found to be a rather expensive commodity. I prefer endurance."

"Like the German Jews," he said.

She shook her head. "No. Not like them. They won't be left even that."

"Yes," he said. "I could see what they were in for, even when I was last there in '36. In any case, perhaps that's why I'm where I am now. The choices were obvious."

"Stark, rather. They were only obvious if you could get out." She stroked his chest, fingers damp from the glass she'd been gripping, and said, "It's good you told me. We shouldn't have secrets from the start."

"Yes," he said, meaning it. Hadn't he told her most of the truth? Not even Myra or Winifred or Max knew about his prison time. They knew he'd been an exile, but not a prisoner. His rationalizing made him uncomfortable, so he stood and went to the window, telling himself that though it was a good thing to talk, he still had to be safe.

Kate left for the bathroom. Downstairs someone seemed to move in the dark, ducking behind a rail screening a basement entrance. He watched, waiting. Five minutes, ten; he'd been imagining it, then, no one was there, no one cared what he was doing, it was only a shadow shifted by the warm sea-smelling wind through the trees.

# JULY 7

**B**LOCKS BEFORE THE ORPHANAGE the yellow diversion notices were up, and even this far from the epicenter the blast wave had done its work. Windowless buildings, trees stripped of their greenery, drifts of broken roof slates; London was growing shabby again. A return to the time of the Blitz in a way, though there were differences: fewer fires, if greater blast damage, and a wider swath of misery. Claus felt a peculiar dissonance having his own life headed down a different path, and he wondered if it wasn't the same for Kate, something he didn't dare ask, fearing it would wake her from a spell or reopen old wounds. Horst, mostly; her final years with him had been brutal.

Yet for all the past sadness, their times together, dependent on the whims of scheduling and destruction, were generally spontaneous and immensely pleasurable. They were trying to cram years into days, and there wasn't time for all of it. In St. James's, Kate had pointed out the Floris Perfumery, where on shopping trips with her mother, their change had been returned on a silver platter after it had been washed and ironed; some evenings Claus and Kate ambled alongside the dried Serpentine or the full Thames, and once on impulse they'd decided to attend a piano recital in the emptied National Gallery, where the month's single painting was a triumphant Watteau. They'd skipped it when they'd seen the long snaking line to view the art and ended up having peppermint ice cream at an American milk bar instead; feeding each other, smiling, they declared the ice cream better than art.

They were happiest in her apartment, where he and Kate spent hours stretched on her bed, making love or reading aloud to each other from her dubious library, their legs twined, or her head resting on his stomach, and they'd begun to cook, taking advantage of emptying London to find ingredients that only a month or two before had been impossibly scarce: chives, lamb, once even pork. From Winifred he accepted extra potatoes, letting her think he was going to sell them, and they'd peeled them together in companionable silence, Kate making potato pancakes that were burned and salty. They'd laughed about it and tumbled into bed. After, lying next to him, Kate said it was wonderful to *want* to cook again. Another evening, he stopped by just in time for carrots steamed in beer that tasted remarkably like his mother's.

The more time they spent together the more Kate switched back and forth from German to English, which he found erotic in bed but problematic in public, and Claus had slipped in his transmissions to Germany; twice in the past week his handler had asked if he was ill—his hand was sketchy and he'd missed a scheduled broadcast—and once he put in the distress signal by accident, though his handler either hadn't noticed or didn't comment. It unnerved him, but he refused to curtail his time with her, no matter how tired he became.

One outing, to an American jazz concert at the Royal Chelsea Hospital, had been a rare misstep. Her father had practiced surgery there, and Claus had thought the concert, a surprise for her, would evoke pleasant memories. It hadn't. Horst had trained there too, it turned out, and the younger Kate had spent hours walking the grounds with her German husband, drilling him on the English names of surgical instruments in preparation for exams, memories she didn't like being reminded of.

"I can't go back to what I was," she'd said. "That's always been the case. After Horst died, I couldn't inhabit my old life in Germany or my previous one in England, so I tried to make a new one in France. That didn't work, so history washed me up here once again. I won't go forward pretending that the past hasn't happened, but I don't want to dwell on it either."

Coming away from the Royal Chelsea, she'd told him about Horst's final years. She hadn't realized how depressed he'd become. He'd survived the blockade's starvation, the euphoria of its lifting, the hyperinflation that followed, the street battles between right and left during the long years of the twenties, but the Nazi rise to power in the early thirties had defeated him. He believed the anti-Jewish and anti-foreign rallies were a sign of impending war, a war he didn't want to live through, not in his helpless condition, and he'd killed himself by drinking a cocktail of mothballs and ammonia, though unfortunately he hadn't been able to drink enough of it to die swiftly.

His mother, not wanting to admit the truth, had ignored the burns to his throat, mouth, and chest, and had treated him as if he had an ulcer, giving milk and lime water, and toward the end even a nutrient enema. But the bleeding from his stomach; his fever; his severely tender upper abdomen—all indicated a perforated stomach, Kate said, and everything Mrs. Zweig did only increased his pain and danger.

Mrs. Zweig's funeral followed Horst's by a month, and with Marie busily married and the despised Hitler in power, Kate had had little reason to remain behind. So, France, until France too had become untenable.

All of this had come out in bits and pieces on a long walk, and even now he wasn't sure he had it properly ordered, as he never felt he could ask too much, nor did it help that she described some of it in German as her German was a dialect he had trouble understanding at times. Still, switching to German made sense. Putting it in another language was a way to put it in another life.

A foray to Brompton Cemetery, which on the surface might have seemed depressing, had been happier. Kate's father was buried there, and at one point her brothers had been too, and they'd visited to clear the grave of two decades' growth. All three brothers had joined up during the war's first days; one died in training, one his first day in battle, and one, Reginald, her favorite, during the war's last days. Her father had been an ardent militarist, her mother against the war from the start, and when her last son had been killed she'd determined never to let them rest by their father's side. Shortly after the war she'd had her sons' graves moved to Bristol, where she was from, and left her husband behind. Kate had yet to see their graves, but to keep the cemetery visit from becoming morose, she'd brought with her blue builder's chalk and wax paper in addition to shears and hand trowels, and after they finished their grave clearing, each of them had chosen a favorite stone and made a rubbing. Claus gave his to Kate.

He'd discovered that her collarbones and the undersides of her forearms were inordinately sensitive, and that she didn't like to have them touched in the same manner or with the same pressure from one time to the next, while she'd found that using her lips and tongue on the small of his back and reaching around front to grip him made his entire body shiver. The closer he came to the orphanage, the more impossible it seemed to feel such joy.

Feral cats wound like smoke through the mounded debris—London was filled with them, bombed out or left behind—and the air was clotted with the usual acrid postbombing dust; the standard mixture of broken slates and shattered glass was being swept from the streets and scraped into bins. At least the rain had let up. Toward Portland Street, where the smells of crushed leaves and powdered brick were thicker, Claus followed the crowd past a taxi crammed full of loaves of bread from a damaged bakery and past a couple holding suitcases who were being let into a sagging building, given a few minutes to recover what they could before the dust ruined everything. Beyond that, the Salvage crew and gas-company men were gathered near the blue incident flag. When he stopped by what looked like a perfectly good armchair on the curb, a redheaded Salvage woman in her green tweed suit detached herself from the group.

"Mind you don't sit in it," she said. "Glass splinters. It'll tear your clothes to pieces if you do."

Most of the bodies would already have been recovered, for which Claus was glad. Sometimes after an incident they were lined up by the dozens, and the small tarps covering children were the worst. Often it was impossible for parents to identify them—the aging process of dust and gore, their torn, unrecognizable bodies, a final reluctance to admit the truth.

Up the street a road mender was already working on the damp, shiny pavement, and chatting women stood clustered in doorways in their winter coats, all of them stopping now and then to take a look, but there was nothing to see beyond the milk float with its tinkling glass bottles. The orphanage had simply disappeared. In its place was a block of mounds of burned rubble, none higher than a dozen feet, and the very air smelled charred. Farther up, an elderly man was moving sooty bricks from a stack in the rear of a building to the front, using a wheelbarrow with a warped wooden wheel. Claus stopped him.

"Awful, isn't it, targeting an orphanage?" Claus said.

The man loosened his grip from around the worn wooden handles and flexed his blackened fingers. "Not bloody likely they were aiming for this." He ran a thumb under a suspender held together by red twine. "Three blocks that way they're after." He pointed over Claus's shoulder. "And if it's 'it, we'll all go up. I know. I worked there."

A munitions factory; Claus hadn't known about it. He looked casually over his shoulder to mark the spot as the man began tossing bricks on the pile, one with each hand, alternating. Of course it might not have been what they were aiming for. Berlin had told him that he was required only to find out locations and times of the landings; he couldn't know what they were truly after and so couldn't judge their effectiveness, but an orphanage? What would be the point? Morale busting, perhaps. He wanted no part of such a plan.

He had an approximate time for its landing, but he needed an exact one. If he was accurate, they could be too. No more slaughtered children. He again tried to convince himself that it was better he hadn't changed the coordinates of any V-1 landings in his reports, that he had to follow Bertram's dictates.

"Are there any clocks?" he asked.

The man tossed the brick from his right hand and stopped, still holding one in his left. "Sorry?"

"Clocks. I work at the Ministry of Information." He pointed to his uniform as if the man might not have seen it. "We're asked to find clocks from each incident."

"What the bloody 'ell for?"

Claus shook his head, equally dubious. "Beats me. The higher-ups think it will help them with planning, I guess."

The man dropped the brick in his left hand and reached for two more. "No. No clocks."

He seemed angry, and Claus decided not to push him; someone else might know the exact time. Twenty yards farther on a man about

Claus's age was squatting over roof tiles. Claus approached him as he squared one pile and scrabbled over to the next one.

"Excuse me, sir," Claus said. "Did you work here?"

He looked up at Claus from under his hat. Unlike in Claus's neighborhood, where blast survivors were a uniform terra cotta color, this man was ocher colored. Yellow bricks, a different-colored dust, which gave his face a faintly Asian cast. On his nose were crescent-shaped imprints where glasses had rested.

"Used to," he said, and bent again to his task. "Nothing left to do now."

Familiar with the despair of shock, Claus squatted too. "That's not quite true," he said, keeping his tone light. "Those roof tiles can be used to repair houses."

The man tilted his head up. "Perhaps you're right."

"Listen," Claus said. "You're busy. I won't take much of your time. But I work at the MOI and we need to know. Are there any clocks from the blast, ones that might show the exact time it occurred?"

The man stood and turned to point, his slender hands a sign that he wasn't used to such physical labor. The back of his pants had been blown off. He had the front of his pants, the waist, the belt, but everything in the back was gone save the pockets, still attached at the waistband. Claus, reeling, wondered whether anyone had spoken to him about it yet, if he didn't feel the draft.

"Back there, I think," he said. "That corner, if there are any." Two timbers stuck up in a V shape from the largest pile of rubble. "That's where the offices were, and it seems a bit better off than the rest of this. If any survived, they'd be there."

He squatted again and began arranging another pile of slates.

"Sir," Claus said. "Can I take you anywhere? To some relatives? You look as though you could use a rest."

"No. I'm fine." The roof tiles clicked like dominoes under his restless hands. "This was home, you see. It'll take me a while, but I think I can get it in order."

"You lived at the orphanage?"

"The wife and I. Yes." He bit his lower lip and turned to look at the rubble. "She's in there still, I believe. Eventually we'll find her."

Which explained his apparent calm. Before the war Claus would have guessed wartime grief would be noisy, but the exact opposite had proven true: those who found others alive that they'd presumed dead were loud in their relief, but most mourners mourned silently.

He felt evil questioning the man in such a state, even if the information he gathered for the Germans was meant in the end to fool them, so after telling the Salvage woman about him and getting him a blanket, Claus dusted off his hands and left, wishing he could be away from it, done with the entire business.

# JULY 9

OR THREE HOURS he worked on the script, barely moving from his seat, writing the dialogue quickly but struggling with camera locations and angles. He'd have to use tracking shots, moving closer and away, to keep the passages of dialogue between sitting characters from seeming static. His forearms stuck to the table in the unusually humid night air—made worse by his closed windows—and he peeled them one at a time from the wood, leaving pear-shaped smears on the grain. For some reason Jeanne's companion still didn't sound right, and when he switched to the typewriter, Claus left some of his lines blank, to be filled in later. He had less than a week until Max's final deadline and he didn't think he'd make it; even if he did, there was no guarantee Max would approve.

Jeanne was going to pass through a city that had been bombed—Rouen, perhaps—trapped there both when she fled the outbreak of the war and when she returned, so that memories of one journey blended with the reality of the other. And her memories would be Kate's of Hamburg. Kate had told Claus about her visit in '43, but only after a few glasses of scotch. He wondered how his mother's cousin Robert was—would ask later in the evening when he broadcast, as he usually did, part of his cover this feigned, ongoing concern—but from Kate's description of Hamburg's devastation, of the Altona district specifically, Claus doubted Robert had survived. His mother wouldn't have liked what Germany had become, but she wouldn't have liked her family destroyed either.

Kate had returned to Hamburg in late September, two months after its horrific firebombing, and it was almost impossible for her to believe what had happened. Four days' searching had turned up Marie, which she knew to be incredible luck, given that fifty or sixty thousand had died in a single night.

Marie had heard the sirens, but after five straight days of bombing she'd been too tired to go down to their shelter. Yet the bombs kept coming closer, and at last through her apartment windows she saw the firestorm burning toward her, swallowing building after building and street after street, so she'd grabbed her son, Rory, and run downstairs and boarded a northbound tram. Marie, Rory, and all the other passengers were pushed to its hot back—the side closest to the fire—by the enormous, hurricane-force winds rushing into it.

Behind them, burning people staggered after the tram or were sucked into the melting asphalt. A horse galloped past, ablaze from head to foot, and one girl who'd been wrapped in soaked sheets was pulled from the tram by the winds and hurled into the center of the firestorm like a whirling torch. When the tram slid into a bomb crater, Marie and Rory stumbled into a building burned in a previous raid, which turned out to be their salvation; the walls were so hot that jars of stewed prunes steamed and exploded, and in other nearby basements people were dying of the poison gases, but the cracked foundation let Marie and Rory breathe in cool sewer air in great gulps and live. Yet the firestorm grew stronger, its winds screeching and droning, howling and roaring, and at last it pulled the shelter door off its hinges as if it were something hunting for them and plucked Rory from her arms. She stood and sprinted after him, but a line of burning uprooted poplars flew past and knocked her down, and just before her eyes closed she saw other children soaring past like flaming angels.

The next day, only the shells of buildings stood, their bricks glowing, their window frames empty. The pavement burned the soles of Marie's feet through her shoes. The worst part was the silence; the night before she'd thought she'd go deaf, and now it seemed she had. She passed a tram in the middle of the street, its metal wheels melted to the melted tracks, corpses swollen inside, and a group of thirty people huddled together in one basement as if sleeping, their tomato-colored skin a sign of carbon monoxide poisoning.

Closer to the city center, shrunken bodies were clustered in dried-out fountains or on the road, naked except for their shoes, their hair and features burned off, their faces as smooth as miniature tailors' dummies. One woman went about removing their shoes, and another woman gathered chunks of charred humans in a pram. The very small children, like Rory, looked different from the other dead, blackened, curved, no bigger than eels. There were a dozen of them altogether. Marie collected them in a single zinc washtub and buried them under a small brick cairn, ignoring her blistered palms.

Somehow Marie survived even that. Kate found her living in a garden shed outside the city, subsisting on tulip bulbs and grubs. Though it was September, the lilacs and chestnuts were in bloom again, their internal clocks thrown off by the fire, and Kate had said that it was remarkable to see the snowy flurries of the chestnut blossoms and to smell the lilacs' roseate perfume in the midst of that smoking wasteland.

When Claus had said he was surprised the city had still been smoking, Kate had given a short laugh. "They're Germans, after all," she'd said. "Already prepared for winter and storing coke and coal in their basements. I imagine it's burning still."

At last he put the script aside and stood—having worked on it so long he'd come to the recognizable point where everything seemed horrible—stretching his sore back and numb legs, listening to the building's rhythms. Water in the pipes, someone singing, pacing from Mr. Morgan's—all as it should be. He turned the radio on and let it warm up, staring at the pulsing yellow dial, then clicked the Gramophone/Radio switch, common to all Sabas but that on his turned the radio into a transmitter. After pushing a screw on the bottom, he maneuvered the tuning dial counterclockwise and pressed a recessed Bakelite panel twice to release the secret drawer, withdrew the miniature telegraph key, and began tapping out messages about weather and wind to alert Hamburg to his presence. A few more messages about troop dispositions to let Bremen and Bordeaux triangulate him and then he fell silent, to throw off any nearby radio-locating teams, since Bertram had told him to broadcast on a higher frequency for now. A change from the usual procedure, which meant Claus had to be on longer.

"We're getting reports of radio locators in your area," he'd said, "concentrating on the lower frequencies after dark." Broadcasting was much easier than writing the letters but also far more dangerous, yet Bertram insisted he do it from home as he always had. "We don't know if they can fix you to within yards or miles, and if they take your bearings and you've moved, well, your cover's blown." So from home it had to be. That Mr. Dobson had been an amateur radio enthusiast meant the building had an antenna, and that his room was on the top floor meant his signal was usually unimpeded. Both were important, as every extra minute he spent broadcasting increased the danger of discovery, which pleased Bertram: he wanted Claus to live as close as possible to the way a real spy did. "Makes you sharper," he said. "More believable."

When Robert had first demonstrated the set for him, his glee that it might in some uncertain but longed-for future help defeat the evil British had been off-putting. Claus had no love of the Brits, but any war was bound to be disastrous, and when he was called on by the British to use the set, he resented immediately that it tethered him to a position he hated. Twice he'd had laughably theatrical dreams about it, in both of which he was broadcasting, one hand resting on the table, the other on the key, when his fingers began to grow roots. He'd tried to pull his hands away but the roots had spread quickly, binding his hands to the table, the table to the floor.

Yet recently, under Kate's influence, he was beginning to see most things German a bit differently, and he now regarded the radio's simple design as marvelous. Even after closely examining it, an observer would never suspect its dual purpose, and Claus hadn't the slightest qualm that Mrs. Dobson's fastidious cleaning might unlock the radio's secret. It was close to impossible to do even when you knew it, and if Mrs. Dobson lived with the radio for her entire life, she'd still never guess.

But this fondness for things German was disconcerting. He'd long since given up thinking of those he was in contact with as people, made easier because at the war's start Robert had been replaced by an agent code-named Wind, yet when Kate played Marlene Dietrich records in German—in which she sounded vastly different than in her heavily accented English versions—or called him *"meine kleine Kartoffel,"* her "little potato," before drifting off to sleep, he found parts of his suppressed Germanic past creeping back into him, and he wasn't sure what to do about it. He awoke often to acute memories of his mother's cooking, and he found himself wondering about Wind's real identity; if he had family in Hamburg, if they'd survived.

Now he repeated his first signal, the metal warming under his finger, and took care to keep his fist recognizable, though whoever was decoding for Wind seemed a plug—asked twice that Claus repeat certain sections, probably missing a dot here and a dash there as he switched from sending to receiving—and Claus did his best to rein in his impatience; that kind of amateur mistake could be deadly. He transmitted again, still without flourish, and when he sat back his shoulders ached and his neck was stiff but he was pleased: he'd been very fast, sending out over fifty words a minute. The air-raid sirens were sounding, a good thing as it meant fewer would be listening to their radios and be upset that their reception was thrown off by his transmissions, and Mr. Morgan's regular bath started up as he began to receive, the rattling pipes covering the radio's low clicking.

Questions about landing coordinates of V-1s, about Calais, about aircraft and parachute factories, about convoys and submarine escorts; he deciphered as he listened, answered what he could, wanting to alter the landing coordinates but afraid to do so, then sent back the most important information he had, a series of dots and dashes that, elongated and translated, meant: *Dover and Folkestone marshaling areas conspicuously empty.* They were, though of course they never had been swarming with real tanks or assault divisions, yet the Germans believed otherwise. Plywood tanks and barracks had been used to fool German reconnaissance flights, and all his broadcasts and letters had supported this, and it was the information they asked for again and again. *Like Brighton and Portsmouth before the feint,* he tapped out. *Believe Leopard a go, Calais landings imminent.* He signaled a break to let them decipher and sat with his hand on the exposed drawer in case he needed to shove it home, thinking of the merciless bombing of Calais.

Bertram had instructed Claus to tell the Germans Calais was due for massive raids. *It's been happening, and it's coming anyway, and they believe it, and they need to believe it more. Our deception needs to hold up longer. We're actually flying more sorties against Calais than against Normandy.*

*They'll be ready for the planes then,* Claus had said. *Antiaircraft. Fighters.*

*They'll be ready anyway, and their air force is quite seriously degraded. The RAF knows what it's in for. They think it important.*

He heard a noise outside his door, Mrs. Dobson on her usual rounds probably, and he quietly slid the key into the drawer, the drawer into the radio, then sat until her steps went away down the hall, when he reversed the process and dialed a bit higher in the 7 MHz range to throw off tracking devices. Once Wind found him again he transmitted the White City damage report from memory—*Factories hit, many workers idle, parachute production precipitously off*—wondering why Bertram had become so obsessed with the possibility of someone following him. He'd insisted that Claus go out to White City for his "reconnaissance," even though Bertram had fed him the numbers, and though it had seemed a waste of time Claus hadn't asked him why; it would have been as useless as talking back to the radio. On certain things, Bertram worked in one direction only.

*The Germans are sending people now, I'm sure of it.*

*But you caught that one.*

*There are others. It must be a firsthand account.*

He was about to give the parachute-factory coordinates when the front doorbell rang. He hadn't made it this far by being sloppy, so he broke off the transmission, put the key away, shoved the drawer closed, and turned the switch from Gramophone to Radio. Steps approached his door, followed by a quick, quiet knock.

He buried the paper from which he'd been transmitting among the pages of script spread across his table and opened the door to Kate.

"Oh, I'm so glad you're here," she said, stepping in and hugging him. That perfume again.

He tried to compose his face, as the trick was to look as if she'd caught him in the middle of something, just not in the middle of something he shouldn't have been doing. Unable to stop himself, he said, "How did you get in?"

"The front door was open. I waited but no one came. I'm sorry," she said, catching his tone. "Should I not have come?"

"No. Of course you should." He pulled her farther into the room, looked down the hallway, and shut the door. "It just surprised me. I was thinking about you, and it was as if I'd conjured you up. We'll have to be quiet." His voice was just above a whisper. "My landlady."

"I know," she said, whispering too. "But I had to see you. I was out for a walk with Sylvie and something dreadful happened."

"The Russian nurse? Is she all right?"

"Yes. No." She sat on the edge of his couch and looked around. "My," she said. "Homey."

The rooms had always seemed fine to him, but he saw them now through her eyes, barren rather than spare, a place that didn't look like a home. His spying of course, and yet something more, a desire that if someone stumbled across him, he'd give no offense, go unnoticed; a habit he'd picked up in prison. It came as a shock to realize how much his past still controlled him.

She touched his arm. "When our shift ended Sylvie asked me to walk with her, and I agreed.

"We passed a beggar. A woman with three children, barely out of her teens herself, it looked. So poor. Laddered stockings, filthy clothes. I was reaching into my bag for some coins when Sylvie put her hand on my arm and whispered, 'Don't.' So I passed her by, pretending to have been looking for cigarettes." She paused and took a breath, lowered her voice once again. "When we were a bit further on, I asked Sylvie if she knew her, if the woman was running some type of scam. Drinking with the money she raised, perhaps. She laughed! 'God, no,' she said. 'But I could tell from looking at her she was a Jew. If you give her money, she'd only breed.'"

"How horrible," Claus said.

"There was something about it that made it seem worse. It was so, I don't know," she said, raising a spread-fingered hand.

Claus supplied the word. "Casual."

"Yes, that's it!" she said, and touched him. "Perfect." She seemed inordinately pleased that he understood her. "That threw me. That she'd have assumed I'd agree with her. What kind of person does she take me for?"

"Bigots think everyone is bigoted."

"I hope you're right." She shuddered, as if any other possibility was appalling, then brightened when he whispered a few words to her in German. "I forgot to tell you. You have an admirer. Greta."

"Greta?"

"Yes. She saw you in White City. Picked you out right away, and was very pleased to have done so."

"What was she doing there?" Claus asked, careful to keep his question from sounding urgent. Greta was German after all.

"Some of our nurses might be moving to the area. Casualty overflows from Normandy. She was checking out a converted warehouse."

"Well, if she saw the same things I did, she'll know that any such move is unlikely. A few direct V-1 hits."

"Anyone killed?"

"No. Lots of buildings gone, but luckily no one was in them."

"I haven't seen the area in ages; since 1908, I think. The great Franco-British Exhibition. Father loved it."

"Never been to the dog track?"

She laughed. "My family would have been appalled."

"We'll have to go," he said.

"I knew there was a reason I loved you," she said, and took his face between her warm hands and kissed him.

There was a knock on the door, much louder than Kate's; Mrs. Dobson must have heard them. "Mr. Murphy?" she said, and knocked again, which gave him the time he needed. He ushered Kate into his closet and picked up a few pages of his script to have something in his hand when he opened the door.

"I'm sorry to disturb you, Mr. Murphy," she said, and smiled, showing her yellowed front teeth. Her small blue eyes had almost disappeared. "But it's rather an extraordinary situation. No tea this evening, I'm afraid. The gas has gone out."

He didn't believe her. The false smile and the pipes still knocking as the last of Mr. Morgan's bath drained away, her face a mixture of anger and disappointment, but of course he couldn't say so. He opened the door wider and let her in.

She strode past him to the middle of the room, where she turned her head from side to side, then moved closer to the closet.

"Are you alone?" she said. "I thought I heard voices." She reminded her tenants from time to time that they'd agreed never to have female visitors in their rooms, as she ran a respectable establishment. Mr. Ivory, who'd ignored the strictures in the first months of Claus's tenancy, had been forced to leave the very same day Mrs. Dobson found out.

"The wireless," he said, which he'd been smart enough to switch on as he moved toward the door. He turned it off now so she wouldn't notice that it was still warming up. "And I've been practicing my lines aloud." He waved the script at her.

"You do the female parts convincingly," she said, her gravelly voice dropping in register, and, breathing deeply, she looked at the closet with her lined cheeks glowing, as if refraining from opening it was making her feverish. She couldn't declare her distrust—on the small chance that she was wrong she'd never recover her dignity—and as long as Kate was quiet he was safe.

He thought, not for the first time, that she'd missed her calling: a born schoolmistress, meant to intimidate students into acquiescence, and if he ever needed such a character in a film he'd be sure to cast her. He felt a peculiar mounting pressure in his chest, which he at last identified as pleasure. In the situation, in knowing that his landlady suspected him, in teasing her by not hurrying her along. Kate understood what was necessary, but of course she might grow disoriented in the dark and stumble backward or simply have to shift or sneeze, and he had a wild fantasy of what would happen if he was thrown out. London was emptying, he could always move into Winifred's building, or Kate's; the apartment below hers was vacant. *I knew there was a reason I loved you.* He'd be re-inhabiting a younger, less fearful self.

But merely flirting with a costly decision was good enough for now. He turned Mrs. Dobson's bluff back on her.

"Come," he said, taking her elbow. "We can't go without tea, can we? It won't feel right. Let's duck around the corner and see if they still have gas."

They did. "Must have come back on quickly," Mrs. Dobson said, and they hadn't been seated five minutes when Kate strolled past the window. How smart of her to let him know she was safely out. He was free to go, but he liked Mrs. Dobson and felt guilty at having provoked her, so he bent toward her over the polished marble tabletop and asked about her sister in Folkestone, which was always good for a quarter of an hour. So many failings! From there they moved on to the potato soup she was making with Winifred's black-market potatoes, though to be fair she didn't know their origin, and when she was done he paid and brought her back to his rooms on the pretense of asking if a new stain on the ceiling might be a leak. She'd want to come upstairs again but be at a loss for how to do so, and he decided to make it up to her. Kate's perfume was immediately noticeable.

Mrs. Dobson turned to him and cocked one eyebrow.

"So where is this stain?" she said, and he had to keep himself from laughing. She knew she'd been right but was furiously unable to prove it.

The stain turned out to be nothing, and Mrs. Dobson left after reminding him that he was not to eat food in his rooms after nine o'clock—a direct reference to house rules, with all that implied—and when he shut the door behind her, listening for her retreating footsteps that did not come immediately, the quiet felt weighted without Kate, the rooms smaller. They'd come briefly to life in her presence, and now seemed more thoroughly empty than ever.

He looked for clues to her visit, some scrap to hold in his memory, but found none, really, or certainly none that Mrs. Dobson was likely to have spotted, though the piece of paper with his encoded message seemed to be sticking out from his script more than he remembered. He pulled it free. Numbers and letters, which he could read as an account of destroyed buildings and delayed manufacturing, but which would have been meaningless to Kate. Still, he'd grown sloppy, and he felt foolish for having even allowed the possibility of being found out. Without a moment's hesitation he burned it.

# JULY 14

CLAUS HANDED KATE a fifth of scotch when she opened her door.

"My!" She took the green bottle. "You must think me a lush."

"Just wanted to show that I have connections too."

She laughed. "You're so transparent. *Mein kleines Fenster,*" she said, which meant "my little window." "You must have been a rotten liar as a child."

"I was." He told her about a time at age three he'd broken a piece of a neighbor's fencing and let a pig out and had run home to tell his father that he'd done nothing.

Two nights before, he and Kate had gone to see *The Uninvited,* which so scared Kate that she'd asked Claus to sleep on the outside toward the door, and he'd woken alone and shown up at the hospital to surprise her, only to have his mood punctured by the sight of an American major handing Kate a bottle.

"Oh," she'd said, and flushed. "Thank you."

"No," he said, bowing his highly coiffed head toward her. "Thank *you.*"

He'd nodded at Claus, then gone on his way, smelling of lime aftershave.

"Who was that?" Claus had asked, unable to keep the curiosity from his voice. The major's shoulder patch indicated he was with the Big Red One, most of whom were in Normandy, and those left behind would have been fairly senior—planning and intelligence.

"A patient."

"Who gave you scotch?"

"It was a rather delicate matter."

"Wasn't he the major from the dance club?"

"Yes." She seemed to be holding her breath. Then she sighed, put out a hand, and said, "He was embarrassed by his condition and wanted to go to someone he knew. So he came by the hospital and asked for me. I lanced a boil for him. Must have been infinitely more comfortable when it was gone."

"Where?"

"On his buttocks."

"Scotch for a pimple on his ass?"

"It wasn't just a pimple. Rather larger, I'd say. More like a root vegetable."

Their joint, spontaneous laughter broke the tension and caused an elderly woman in black to look at them disapprovingly, but he'd had a lingering case of jealousy, and the scotch was the only way he could think to expunge it. Herbert's bargain was fierce—two extra night shifts that Claus would have to cover—but seemed worth it.

Now she put the bottle on her counter and they went down the stairs and out into the bright sunshine where she linked her arm in his. Soon they were near the Green Park tube entrance.

"There," Kate said, nodding at a group of elderly Home Guard drilling in mismatched uniforms in the park, their rifles resting sloppily on their shoulders. They marched back and forth between deep trenches that had been dug earlier in the war and now were grown over with lush grass, the long uncut blades bending in the warm wind. "That's you in twenty years, if the war lasts that long."

She was forgiving him his jealousy. "And here's you, then," he said of a dowdy Salvage woman striding toward them with a red face. "Angry I've forgotten the steak and kidney pie."

She tugged his arm, pulling him closer. "Oh, we'll be a fine couple, won't we?"

It was a moment of intense pleasure for him, that she could anticipate a shared future. Max had a draft of his script, and Claus was off on an outing with a woman he loved. He raised her clasped hand to his mouth and kissed her fingers.

"And now," he said, "I'm going to fully corrupt you."

"Promises, promises."

"Oh, I will. By the end of the afternoon, you'll be a committed gambler."

His mood darkened in the overcrowded station. It smelled as always of sweat and piss, but what bothered him were the hundreds of people who seemed to have moved their entire lives there—beds, coat hooks, kitchens; his usual tube stations were too small for these tableaux. The people had marked out their areas with chalk and hanging blankets, and some even had plants and Victrolas. Two small boys were peeling carrots and chattering about German planes—one claimed to have seen a new type—but worse were the people sleeping in an unused side tunnel, ranked one after the other in two parallel rows with a narrow passage between them; unmoving in the near dark, extending to the edge of vision, they looked like lumps of coal ready to be shoveled into a furnace, like bodies lined up after an explosion waiting to be ferried away. Prime candidates for living entombment. He felt a coward for not redirecting the bombs.

The train clattered into the station and as soon as they boarded and headed out, his chest seemed to expand; it was a pleasure to appear in public with Kate, to have a public life for the first time in years, to have people look at them approvingly. She seemed to enjoy it too, leaning back and rocking against his arms as the train curved around corners and braked, metal squealing, at stations.

At White City, the tube lights were out—people talking in subdued voices about the explosion above ground that had made the entire station tremble, the roof crack—and the lit flares were smoky. They hurried up the stairs, coughing, eyes watering; Kate moved ahead as Claus helped a pregnant woman, and she turned back to look at him from the top. He blinked, the bright light stinging his smoke-sore eyes, Kate like a cutout of a woman, reaching back with the light shining around her, while brassy music from an elderly band played loudly to welcome all visitors.

Topside, remembering Bertram's certainty that new German agents were about, he grabbed Kate and ducked around the corner of the tube entrance, out of the flow of the crowd and the sight of anyone on the stairs, then bent to retie both shoes. He took his time, recuffing his pants, wiping his eyes, making sure they hadn't been followed. Someone lingering below would have seen them dart around the corner and would have hurried after them, but no one came.

"Come," he said, and took Kate's hand. "Let's go."

White City's blocks of whitewashed buildings dazzled in the sun. Warehouses, factories, huge hangars that had temporary walls; here and there remnants of its earlier incarnation as an exhibition hall and Olympic venue showed—the stadium, under whose enormous shadow they passed on the way to the entrance; and the disused swimming and bicycling pavilions; the turreted, crenellated domes of the French colonial displays.

"Are those the film buildings?" Kate said, nodding at several large brick warehouses whose damage was obviously recent. Police stood guard outside them.

"No. War work," he said, and lowered his voice. "Parachutes are made there, though we're not supposed to know that."

"And how do you, then?" she said, and ran a finger along his jaw. "Secret contacts?"

He smiled. "Drunks at the track." Which was true. He'd picked up several tidbits on his most recent trip, amazed by how quickly bettors would talk while watching races.

Most of the people in the crowd pushing through the turnstiles were older, and many of them appeared out of work. It was a weekday, and almost everyone that mattered was at work for the war; he found it liberating not to be. A few patrons smelled of beer, though there was a contingent of American naval officers, uniforms pressed and shoes polished, whose healthy youth and relative prosperity drew numerous looks. The infield was inhabited by thousands of standing gulls, all facing west into the wind. He stared out at them, remembering his internment in Brompton, and Kate touched his arm as if she knew what he were thinking.

"Okay?"

"Yes." He smiled. "Bit different from when you remember it?"

"My God, yes." She laughed. "We were here for part of the Olympics—I remember the marathon runners staggering toward the finish, and officials helping a British runner across—but never came to the dog track, even though royalty did. My father pointed that out once and my mother refused to relent. 'They'll return to their senses soon enough,' she said."

It pleased him to show her a part of England she didn't know, to make it hers through him. The first race was about to begin so he walked her to the rail and pointed out the box the mechanical rabbit would break from. The dogs with their colorful blankets pounded past, the number-seven dog, white with a white blanket, seeming to have the numeral painted on his fur, stretching at the last for the victory.

"Quite a dog," a bearded man next to them said, and dropped his tickets. "Wish I'd bet on her."

They had fifteen minutes before the next race, and Claus bought a program.

"Here," he said, pointing to one dog's line: *21-6-1 3-8 S 38 80 3 6 4 2 1-1/2 6.25 A Late speed insd.* He moved his finger beneath the line as he explained it. "That means the dog's last race was the first on June twenty-first; it was three-eighths of a mile on a slow track, with the winning time of thirty-eight seconds flat. He weighed eighty pounds, broke from the three hole slowly in sixth place, moved to fourth, was second coming out of the turn, and finished first, half a length in front. Odds were six and a quarter to one at post time in a class-A race, the highest, and he won with late speed on the inside."

"And this next race?" she said. "Also three-eighths and also an A?"

"Yes."

"Let's bet on him then."

"But we haven't read the other lines."

"True. And it's also true that he's won at this distance and class before. Why go against him?"

"All right," he said, turning toward the barred betting windows where men were leaning against the narrow counters. "It's your future."

"On the contrary," she said. "You're paying for everything. I distinctly heard you say so."

"Yes." He had to raise his voice now, to make sure it reached her over the intervening crowd. "But if we lose it all, we won't have any left for supper."

He won by three lengths. For a long time they stood at the rail, elbows touching, as they watched the handlers herd the dogs. At last Claus turned to Kate.

"Well?" he said. "I'm waiting for you to gloat."

"Not an English trait, I'm afraid. Or German."

Their luck held for two more races, then deserted them for three. Claus said it was time to go with a new system and studied the program for trends.

"Look at you," Kate said. "Like a schoolboy trying to figure out his maths. The tip of your tongue between your lips."

He felt himself blushing but she laughed, touched his chin. "Don't feel bad," she said. "It's adorable." She excused herself and went to the bathroom, and when she returned Claus was talking to an older man and taking notes on the program.

After he moved away, Kate asked who he was.

"Nobody," Claus said. "Just someone who claimed to have inside information on the dogs. Which ones have been off their feed, which not sleeping."

"And what did he say?" Kate asked. "Show me."

It wasn't dogs they'd been discussing, it was a V-1 strike on a dog barn. The information was useless except for the date and time, two minutes past noon on the previous Wednesday. The man had been sure because he'd just sat down to his lunch.

Claus fanned the program out for Kate. Was he showing her the code on purpose? What on earth for? Years of wariness, the fear of being imprisoned. He wouldn't have believed it of himself, yet he was, and it was too late to stop.

She looked at the figures scribbled on the blue paper and spent a few minutes trying to puzzle them out. A basic code, the first the Germans had taught him.

"Wait," she said. "That's not the dog line, is it?"

He felt enormous relief, a bit of guilt; Bertram had him paranoid. She wouldn't have asked if she were covering something up; she had nothing to hide. "No," he said at last. "It's about the damages to the sound stages. Max wanted me to find out."

"And why didn't you just say so?"

"Didn't want you to think I was mixing business with pleasure."

"But you were."

"Yes. Forgive me?"

She tilted her head to the side and made him wait, teasing. "Only if you give me the winner in the next race."

He unfolded the program. Laughing Lackey was running. "Bet against him," he said. "He's a terrible dog."

"But look." She tapped his line. "He's won six of seven races, and finished second in the other." She smiled, taking evident pride in being so quick to catch on.

"Yes, and it's time to bet against him. Too long a winning streak."

The sailor next to them muttered, "Balleynennan Moon," and then moved away.

"Balleynennan Moon?" Kate asked.

Claus said, "He won forty races out of forty-eight last year, and finished second seven times. All set to clip the record for consecutive victories when Laughing Lackey beat him."

"Ah, and you liked the Irish name, no doubt. All right," she said. "But remember, I won't forgive you if you're wrong. Here," she said, and bent toward the program. "Let's pick our winners."

In the end they decided to go with a long shot. They'd nearly broken even for the day, so a loss would be relatively painless, and if they won it would put them far ahead. There were two to choose from, one moving up a class after winning one of three races against weaker competition, another that seemed to do well only on Fridays.

"Let's choose her," Kate said of the former.

"But she has almost no chance," Claus said. "At least in Redbolt's case it's a Friday."

"Yes. That's the point. He might get some late money, but *no one's* going to bet on Cursed Woman."

"See? You *have* been corrupted."

"Shh," she said, and tapped his shoulder. "Go put the bet in before we lose our chance."

The dogs broke cleanly, Redbolt moving better than Claus and Kate had expected, running third on the rail as they hit the turn, just out of second to Laughing Lackey's first, a good spot, Claus thought, not in front where he'd tire from setting the pace and not last with too much ground to make up and not too far out so that he'd stumble in the turn. A late-speed dog, he was within striking distance. Cursed Woman he couldn't make out; he'd put money on them both. As they curled around the infield with its low boxwood he could still see the dogs, and Redbolt seemed to fade, though it was hard to tell because even with his distinctive yellow and black blanket there were other dogs in the race with black or yellow and when they were next to each other it could also have been the four. Down the stretch Laughing Lackey seemed to surge forward in response to the yelling crowd packing the rail, and then, as if he had hit a wire, to drop back all at once, and every other dog rumbled up and passed him in the sudden silence, kicking up clods of dirt that made him turn his head and run an off route. In the end Laughing Lackey finished second to last, Redbolt just in front of him, but Kate was jumping up and down and laughing and tugging at Claus's arm.

"She did it," she said, and pointed to where Cursed Woman was loping out ahead of the others as the handlers made their way onto the track in their blue boilersuits to round up the dogs. "How much did we win?" she said, and they both peered at the scoreboard, waiting for the results to be official, the amounts to be posted. Claus tore Cursed Woman's line from the program and folded it into his pocket during the interval. Twenty-seven pounds, in the end.

"My God," Kate said, linking her arm through his as they shouldered through the disappointed crowd to retrieve their money, trying not to show their happiness. "We'll be able to order everything on the menu wherever we go. I haven't been this rich in *ages*."

On the subway, Kate's head bumped against Claus's shoulder through the long dark tunnels. The smoky flares in the White City subway had made their eyes tired, and it was if they were coming home after a long night out in the cold. They were headed to Soho, with its cinemas and numerous small Italian restaurants that still had potable red wine, and near Piccadilly she stirred and said, "What's that?"

He'd unfolded a piece of paper on his knee. It looked like newsprint.

"Our lucky numbers, from the track," he said, looking up at her. "Cursed Woman's line. Want it?" He held it out.

"You keep it," she said. "You have more need of luck." She was sitting up now. "It was a lovely outing." He smelled cloves on her as she moved.

"It was, wasn't it?" He patted her hand. "But I think you really liked it because your parents would never have approved."

"'Thou shalt not' has its own charm, but it's not that, or rather not *just* that. Outings like that make me feel less estranged."

"From what?"

"From England, from myself. I've come to realize these past weeks that the world for me exists as a patchwork of different shades of foreignness. Even England. When I go back to things I've been to before, places I loved, I feel . . . an outsider. I find I'm neither English nor German. Sounds dramatic, I know, but almost nothing is as I remember it, which of course makes me feel odd, but the few things that *are* are worse—then I feel separated from the girl I was nearly thirty years ago, and for some reason that temporal estrangement is worst of all."

He knew exactly what she was speaking of. He'd filmed *The Spirit of '76* in New York, but when he'd passed through the city on his way out of the country, his nostalgia was for a time he'd lost and a person he'd been, not for a place. They fell silent again, and to cheer Kate up, to lift his own spirits, he suggested a movie before dinner.

"Let's," he said. "We'll make a late night of it. Movie first, dinner, then a club. We'll spend as much of our winnings as we can."

"Oh, Claus," she said, and, leaning toward him, kissed his ear. "You wicked, wicked man."

They decided on a double bill of William Wyler documentaries, *The Memphis Belle*, about a bomber crew, and *The Fighting Lady*, about life onboard an aircraft carrier, as even if they watched both of them they'd get out early enough to find a table somewhere. The week before, they'd gone to Lewis Milestone's *The Purple Heart* and had left halfway through, finding it jingoistic, a huge comedown from his earlier antiwar classic *All Quiet on the Western Front*, and they worried the same thing might happen to Wyler, but both *Wuthering Heights* and *Mrs. Miniver* were great films and Claus thought he might use some of Wyler's framing devices for his own film if they were good.

They arrived just as the newsreel was about to start, the usher leading them to their row with her flashlight, sweeping it across a line of shoes to indicate that their seats were farther along, and Claus let Kate go first, tipped the usher, and slid across murmuring apologies, just in time for "God Save the King."

He began humming before he even sat from long years of habit and Kate squeezed his arm. He turned to her. She was neither humming nor singing; he didn't have to either, and he stopped, feeling oddly conspicuous, but no one had noticed and she squeezed again before removing her hand. The newsreel made Claus wish they'd arrived later. Hamburg again—fleets of bombers, their bomb bays opening, bombs dropping out and wobbling toward their targets; far below, buildings and railroad tracks and bridges disappearing beneath sequential clouds of smoke and debris. He pulled his handkerchief from his jacket pocket and nudged Kate's wrist, but she shook her head, surprisingly dry-eyed, and he turned back to watch Hamburg's ongoing destruction. From the shape of the harbor and the river, he recognized the Altona district. Completely burned out, Kate had said. There seemed no way Robert could have survived *that*.

Kate shifted beside him and he realized he'd missed the movie's opening scenes, but soon he was swept up in the drama of a bomber crew about to fly its twenty-fifth and final mission, with all of its original crew still intact. Very rare; it hadn't taken a single serious hit on any of its flights, and, as the film progressed, it became clear just how lucky they'd been. The Wilhelmshaven raid, where 50 percent of the bombers had suffered serious damage and 20 percent hadn't returned; Hamm, nearly as bad; Antwerp; Lorient; Kiel; and nineteen others, too numerous to list. The scenes of damaged planes struggling toward the landing field only to crash and burn were heartbreaking.

The crew would all be able to return to America if they survived, and if the film had none of the deep-focus artistry of Wyler's earlier films or the technical innovations like his receding-mirror shot, it was nonetheless rife with drama and laced with his signature diagonal compositions, and Claus found himself enjoying it far more than he'd expected. Kate seemed to also, as did the rest of the crowd—there was an excited buzzing as Kate and Claus made their way to the overheated lobby during intermission, stuffy with its red and gold brocade and golden classical lamps, most of which were dim.

He had just ordered tea when he turned at his name and found Max and the beaming Alina. His face flushed; Max had asked him if he wanted to see the film and Claus had turned him down, complaining of extra warden duties, but now Max shook his hand and made their introductions without seeming the least put out.

Clearly, from his face, Claus could tell he hadn't yet read the script, so there was no point in asking about it, and Claus shifted gears quickly, beginning to talk about *The Memphis Belle*'s long sweeping shots, the way the camera moved in unsteadily, when Kate said, "Oh, you. Every movie is a competition!"

Alina laughed. "Him too? It's *awful*. Max has to beg me to go, and then I spend all night hearing about what was wrong with it. The camera angles are bad, or the dialogue is clichéd, and the pacing and scene selection, *ach*." She put her braceleted wrist to her forehead in a parody of bad acting. "So poor!"

Kate touched her bare arm. "Your accent is so familiar. And so welcome," she added when Alina's face fell. "Where in Poland are you from?"

"L'viv."

"I lived there for a while during and after the last war. As a nurse."

"Ah, very beautiful."

"Yes, it was. Your poor country." She turned to Max. "Claus has been working for you today, scouting damages."

Max looked puzzled. "The sound stages," Claus said quickly. "Out at White City. But what do you think of the film?" he said.

"You first," Max said.

"Well done, the structure a bit plain, but a riveting narrative."

"And free of that boosterish mentality you find so troubling in most war documentaries," Max said. He smiled.

"Blessedly so," Claus said. Wryly, he added, "Must be Wyler's German roots."

Max showed his molars when he laughed.

The tea came. Claus paid for it while Alina and Kate chatted and Max made his way to the bar. Kate said something about dinner and Claus pinched her elbow.

Max returned and picked up that Claus didn't want to join them even as Alina was saying, "We would like this very much."

"Here now," he said, putting away his billfold. "Can we do it another night?"

Alina looked crestfallen and Claus was about to give in when Max said, "Maybe next weekend? There's a new Hitchcock coming out. We can make it an evening."

* * *

"I like her," Kate said, eyes trailing after Alina's departing back. "I knew so many Poles in the last war. And I'd have liked to have dinner with them. He seemed nice, and she seemed lonely. I know what that's like."

"Me too."

She looked at him. "You wouldn't have turned them down if you did."

"It's just that I don't like to mix my private and work lives."

"You did earlier."

He made a face. "That was different. And I apologized for it."

"Were you worried about me?" Kate said. "Your little German woman? Didn't want them to think you'd hooked up with the enemy and jeopardize your job?"

"Actually, I *was* worried, but that you'd tell them something about my past."

Her teacup stopped halfway to her mouth. "Claus, please. I'm not a fool."

"Of course not. But something might slip." He shrugged. "An accident."

"I can't believe you'd think that. In fact, I don't. I think you're ashamed of me."

"Kate, please."

"No. Really. Why can't you let them know about your past? Prison?"

Her voice was loud enough that an elderly couple at the next table turned their heads; Claus wanted her to speak more quietly but guessed that telling her so would only anger her. He began flipping the spoon under his hand against the marble tabletop.

"It's not as if you murdered someone," she said. "Your government imprisoned you on ridiculous charges! I should think you'd want Max to know that."

"It's not won me many points with people in the past. I didn't tell him at first, and then there didn't seem to be a proper time, and then it became too late."

She stirred her tea and wiped the spoon clean on the rim and shook her head. There were people around so when she spoke she used his other name. "Charles. You've got to stop hiding it. You'll end up bitter and alone."

"You didn't tell Alina that you'd been in Poland for four years."

"Why would I? We'd only just met, and it would only have made her sad. But you've known Max forever. And what would he care about your time in prison? It wasn't as if he arranged it."

"But I've been waiting for this chance to make a film for years. And I'm not sure it would ever have come had he known."

The waiter was hovering, no doubt sensing that a fighting couple wasn't likely to order more, and Claus suggested that since people were waiting for a table they should leave. He took her arm.

They decided not to stay for the second film. Mistakenly, Claus had thought that the cool evening air would cool her temperature. She began again, pulling away from him when he pulled her close, though she didn't drop his hand. "Claus, I'm serious. You must."

"And why must I? I could lose my job."

"Max? He's not the type. He's a filmmaker, for God's sake. He's not rigid."

"You can't know that. You just met him. You never know," he said.

"No, you don't. You never know until you risk it."

"And by then it could be too late."

"Oh, really? And what other deep dark secrets are you hiding that make you so afraid of him? Your Hamburg connections?"

"He knows I have relatives there. We don't discuss it."

"Ah, the private life again."

He shrugged.

"But you don't *have* a private life. You've said so yourself. Work and warden duties. Between them you have no time left over for other things."

"All the more reason not to share what little time I get with you."

She was unconvinced. "And why did you lie to me at the track?"

"Lie to you? About what?"

"The sound stages. Max didn't know what I was talking about."

He started to say something, stopped. "No. You're right, he didn't. It was . . ." He felt himself blushing. "I can't tell you."

"You can't tell me?" She stopped, and his footsteps echoed back to him until he stopped too. Dry leaves blew past her as if she'd created her own wind. "I know that your real name is German, that you spent time in jail for treason, things you say that you've told no one else."

"I haven't."

"And there's something else you can't tell me? You're married? You're ill? You're not American at all?"

"God, no."

"Then what? What could be so bad?"

How could he explain years of wariness? Some of it would make sense to her, but not all of it, not without revealing everything, and he wasn't ready for that. "Nothing. It's not important."

"It is to me."

"Why?"

"Why? You have to ask? The first man I've been close to in more than a decade and you have to ask?"

She started walking again, rapidly, and he stumbled over a loose cobble trying to keep up with her. "Wait," he said, "wait," and he pulled her around to face him.

She was breathing fast, her nostrils dilating.

"Wait."

He dropped his head, ostensibly to catch his breath. No one was nearby, but he couldn't bring himself to say what he wanted. It was impossible. He was going to lie. He'd already doubted her and he could feel the lie unspooling on his tongue, candy cooling in water. He'd grown so smooth at it over the years, but he couldn't say it out loud. He whispered. "I've been asked to keep an eye on Max, that's all."

"By whom?"

"Someone higher up in the ministry."

"They don't trust him?"

"No."

"Why?"

"I don't know."

She pulled back to look at him. "And you're willing to do that to a friend?"

"No, don't you see, that's just it! I don't want to."

"So you're trying to stay away from him?"

"Yes." He smiled. He felt horrible lying to her, but he was glad she understood. He tried to take her hand but she pulled back.

"Why don't you just tell him that he's not trusted?"

"What?"

"Afraid you'll lose your position?"

"No. I . . . No." Now that he'd told the lie, it was too late to come out from under it. Why hadn't he told her? If he did now, it would seem another lie, told to wipe out the previous one.

"What, then? He's a friend. Haven't you learned anything from all you've been through? Haven't you learned that if you don't trust your friends, you'll have nothing?"

"Yes, of course. But if I tell him, he might do something foolish."

"Ah, I see. You're *protecting* him."

It sounded as if she were talking about a disease. "Don't say that, Kate."

"I won't. But do me one favor? If someone ever comes to you about me, don't *protect* me. Ever."

He sighed. He was losing her. And he understood perfectly why. He saw no other choice.

"I have other jobs."

"Other jobs? What does that mean?"

He shrugged. "Things I do. I can't really say."

She laughed. "Please." She started to walk off.

"No, Kate, I do."

"Yes. Of course. And what are they?"

"I . . . find out things."

"Things?" But she'd stopped again. She was listening. "Like about Max? How *important.*"

"I hear things, like about the parachutes, and pass them on."

"To Max?"

"No. God, no. Far above him. Max hasn't the faintest idea. That's why I don't spend time with him. Why I can't."

"And why are you telling me this? So I won't be angry with you?"

"Yes, no. Yes." He stopped and took a breath. What was he trying to say? "I want you to know everything."

"Everything?"

Now he laughed. "Well, as much of everything as I can tell."

"And how much is that?"

"I don't know," he said, and he didn't. "I've already said too much."

"Then don't."

"Kate." He put his hand out to still her anger.

"No. I don't mean it that way. I mean don't. You needn't prove anything to me. I believe you."

"You do?"

She stepped closer and touched his face. "Yes. I knew you were lying before. I believe you're not, now."

He felt his shoulders go slack. "Oh, Kate. There's so much. I have a radio."

She touched his lips. "Shh. Wait until you're sure what you should tell me."

It was extraordinary. The more she quieted him, the more he wanted to tell her. But she was right, he could wait until he was certain that he should. Bertram would be appalled. The thought made his lungs expand like a bellows. He breathed in the crisp air, the odd, autumnal scent of decaying leaves, Kate's perfume, then she took his hand as if she'd never dropped it and they walked on.

# JULY 17

BEFORE THE WAR Claus had often detoured by Selfridges to take in its famous Christmas displays, but now the ground-floor windows were bricked up and the store gloomy despite its inventive light wells; on each floor only every third lamp was lit, and the alluring brightness of the perfume counters, still clustered near the entryway, was dimmed by lack of stock.

During a break from filming *Spirit of '76,* he'd spent two hours in Macy's with Dorothy Gish as she sampled dozens of perfumes, refreshing her nose every so often with a handful of coffee beans, but she could have made her way through Selfridges' entire supply in minutes. Set amid displays of colored stones and commemorative plaques, the few bottles for sale looked rather forlorn; the old standby Lily of the Valley and a handful of others, Houbigant Wisteria, Du Barry Comtessa, Richard Hudnut Violet Sec, and Evening in Paris with its cobalt blue oval bottle, of which Myra was especially fond, though it had been years since he'd smelled its woodsy scent on her. Last was a diamond-shaped Acqua di Parma that he would have thought illegal.

The saleswoman, a tall, matronly blonde, seemed to have read his mind. She stepped forward and said, "It's one of our last bottles from before the war. Interested?"

"No, but thank you." None of the perfumes was Kate's, a German scent made by Hoffman. A half dozen bottles stood ranked in her armoire, shipped back to England before the war with her furniture.

"That book," he said, tapping the glass above a Moroccan-leather-bound copy of Trollope's *The Warden*. He could begin her new collection. "How much is that?"

He took the stairs to the fourth floor, where the store restaurant had been moved after the Palm Court burned in the Blitz. Surprised to find himself out of breath, he stood with his hands on his hips looking up at the ceiling and its tracery of water damage. Beneath the light well, the tables in the center of the restaurant glowed as if on stage, and Claus instinctively asked for one away from them. "And from the windows too," he added. The maitre d', his lapels shiny with wear, nodded almost imperceptibly and steered him to a round one between the two sources of light.

He had an hour and a half until his meeting with the punctilious Bertram, and ten minutes before Max's arrival. Claus liked Selfridges because it had the benefit of a large officer class from which he often picked up information, though Max had been the one who'd chosen it for their lunch, saying he preferred its good service and poor but plentiful food to the real eggs and undiluted milk they would find in a smaller, local establishment. It was also one of the few places that the bombing had actually improved; the restaurant now had one of the best views in London—almost to the Thames—and an outing there always seemed a bit of a celebration: genuine crystal, heavy silver flatware. "Powdered eggs are a small price to pay in return," Max had said.

But Claus suspected Max insisted on meeting here because of his wife, and because of Selfridges' connection to his personal film history. To honor Alina and the dishonorable dismembering of Poland by the Soviet Union and Germany, Max made it his business to speak to the manager monthly to ask Selfridges to take down their Soviet flag from among those flying on the roof, one for each of Britain's current allies.

"But you know they won't," Claus had once said. "Our stalwart Eastern friends."

"Yes. But they know I'll be there, every week. They'll get tired before I do, and when it does come down, I'll be there to say, 'I told you so.'"

And of course each visit recalled the high point of his prewar film career, his work on *Love on Wheels,* an early romantic talkie about a department-store manager and a concert pianist, much of which had been filmed here. Claus understood Max's attraction to earlier successes. He harbored an obscure fondness for the inside secrets of Griffith's working style, which fortunately Max loved to hear about: that before cameras were sophisticated enough to have closing irises Griffith had developed fade-outs by slowly raising the lid of a cigar box in front of a camera, and that he'd made other shots look soft-focus by shooting through gauze, details Claus liked telling him because in doing so he could re-inhabit small parts of his past. If he'd been right to withhold other things from Max, from nearly everyone, and not just because Bertram wouldn't allow it, he was right not to do so with Kate. Still, he'd woken in the night to sheets damp with sweat, wondering if he'd said too much to her. Better not to dwell on it, he decided, obsessively spinning his fork. He'd already taken the plunge.

When the waiter arrived, Claus ordered for both of them—an uninspiring lunch of stewed prunes and pea soup, since they didn't have much else left—and made two requests of the waiter: that he hold off serving until Max arrived and that he, Claus, not his companion, receive the bill, then he smoothed the *Times* flat on the tablecloth, skipping past the first-page birth and death announcements to the war news on page three. He hoped he'd find enough to keep his mind off the upcoming meeting, as he couldn't pretend not to be nervous. Max always chose such luncheons for momentous decisions.

A French Vichy official had been gunned down in Paris—by French terrorists, the Nazis said; a brave Dane disguised as a dockworker had blown up three ships refitting in Copenhagen harbor; rich Hungarian Jews had taken a special train from Budapest to Lisbon while leaving behind one family member as hostage. The German papers were saying that the flying bombs were only a beginning, to be followed by other, more destructive weapons, and that every means of self-defense was justified and sanctified by God. *What our side says,* he thought. He turned to an article about a bomber shot down over occupied France that had crash-landed in a Normandy cornfield behind German lines. Captured, the bomber's crew members were taken to a local chateau and served brandy, champagne, and black bread and butter by a German noncom. To top it off, he made them a pot of real coffee.

> As the advancing English army began lobbing mortars into the chateau, the captives and the chateau's sixty Germans were sent outside to a slit trench, where the Germans, passing back and forth in their duties, kept saying, "Excuse, please, British soldiers." Eventually the Germans pushed the mortar groups back, and the English, let inside again, were happy to discover the commandant affixing a white flag to the chateau wall. He sent out a local Frenchman to find a British patrol and then asked the captives to intervene for him and his men. "The guerre is nicht bon," he said. They surrendered, and all sixty were flown back to England in a bomber piloted by the crew of six.

It was the kind of story that Max would not only like but see something in; Claus tore it out, thinking that if Max still held reservations about his most recent version of *The Bells of Liberation,* giving this to him right away might incline him to be more kindly. Making up for not having supper with him and Alina would be trickier.

A loud, friendly American colonel one table over was talking about Saint-Lô and American chances. "I'm telling you!" He pounded the table hard enough to make forks jump. "We'll break through any day now."

A lieutenant colonel put his hand on the colonel's arm to quiet him, and, with only minutes left until Max arrived, Claus flipped through his copy of the script to make notes on his chosen sound effects. Beethoven in the last two scenes, the background noises inside the food store, the silence inside the tailor's. They were meant as counterpoints, though the dress store's silence was also in direct contrast to the film's loud beginning. The movement pleased him, noise to silence giving way at last to music; it underscored his heroine's journey nicely.

Max emerged from an elevator. Claus was always surprised he took them. Half had been put out of commission by bombing, and, afraid of power outages, Claus never rode one himself, but then Max could be a bit showy about displaying nerve. The result, Claus suspected, of having been rejected for the army because of bad eyes.

"About this," Max said, and took the script from his briefcase before Claus had a chance to hand over his news clipping or even say hello. He seemed angry. "Let's get to it, shall we?" He flipped to a place marked with a small Polish flag while the waiter arrived with their soups. "This bit about the time bomb. Did what happened in Naples suggest that?"

Claus wanted to apologize for the dinner slight but sensed it wasn't the time. Nor for handing over the news clipping. He shrugged. Everyone knew about Naples, it was front-page news. The Germans had pulled out overnight, seeming to spare the city, but had planted time bombs in many public buildings, none of which had been found before exploding. The massive one in the central post office had killed hundreds.

"Really what made me think of it was your suggestion that the stores be across from each other. If the food store had a time bomb, the explosion wouldn't destroy a building across the street. And if the explosion is filmed from a low angle, like the scene where she's shown choosing the dress, the flying debris will be more dramatic."

"And the repeated camera angles would metaphorically tie the scenes together."

"Hadn't thought of that."

"Yes, you had. You just wanted me to feel good about it," Max said.

Claus bowed his head.

"Mock obeisance," Max said. "You're laying it on thick." He put his glasses on and flipped farther back. "That's quite strong, actually, but other parts still concern me." A good sign. Max was often theatrical but he had no poker face; if he hadn't liked the script he'd have complimented it right away as a prelude to rejection. Claus had known it was good, had hoped it was; Max's mock-stern exterior banished his doubts. He felt a surge of elation, which he promptly tamped down. Until Max said yes, it wasn't a go.

"The third act," Max said. "Furious at the bombing, the townspeople destroy anything German in response, then go after the 'horizontal collaborators,' one of whom is the dress-shop owner?"

"Yes."

"Here, where Marie—I like the new name—finds the storeowner being dragged away as she comes out of the dressing room and then witnesses her hair being cut off, her body being doused in Mercurochrome, I like that. But after, when she shelters the woman crying on the curb with an umbrella, how about having the townspeople rally around her then, bring her some food from the wreckage?"

"No. That's not believable. They're not going to forgive her so quickly. Better if they simply go about their business."

"Okay," Max said. "And of course, some of them will still be venal, grabbing food supplies from the rubble as they clear it. But the horizontal collaborator," he said. "Who is she? We need to know more about her for that image to have any resonance."

"That's easy enough to write. I've already thought of several scenes. A German officer comes into her shop with a chocolate bar that he puts down while sorting through fabric. He orders a dress to be ready in two days; they're about to pull out and he wants something to bring back to his wife. That's the dress we see in the window at the end. She'd made it, but the German had already gone, and now she needs to sell it in order to survive. He hadn't paid for it, after all."

"And the chocolate bar? How does that play out?"

"Neighbors see him go in with it, then one finds the chocolate on her counter after the German leaves. They interpret it as something else. And all of those scenes could be interspersed with the ones of Marie making her way back to the village."

"I like the parallel action."

"Other early scenes might be of the townspeople begging her for clothes, which she has access to because of her closeness to the Germans, while a later one would show her trembling as she watches the townspeople shouting and marching by after the Germans have gone."

"All right," Max said. He shut the script. "But why do you call for silence as she's choosing the dress?"

"To play off the noise at the very beginning, and the noises all the way through—the bombs dropping, the train, the boat—her world is made up of noise."

Max looked unconvinced. In the window a fleet of bombers appeared. Claus watched them cross the pane, then played his trump.

"Surely you understand the dramatic possibilities of silence. Think of the beginning of *Love on Wheels*. There's almost five minutes of silence there, as the store manager tries to impress the pianist while both look for seats on the crowded bus. That can't all have been a hangover from the silent films."

"Of course it wasn't. It was crucial. Love is often silent at first. It's gesture, a glance, the touching of hair or a hand. We wanted to show that."

Claus sat back. He'd been certain that line would work; Max was a sucker for talking about the film, but it also led directly into what he wanted to say.

"My point exactly. It's the same here. Remember, the picture starts with that buzz bomb blowing up a building, followed by a gas explosion. And those noises continue throughout the film. This is a moment she's reasserting some power over that world. An inner silence, a moment of choice, made clear by the silent screen."

Max bowed his head as if conquered. "All right," he said. "One last thing. You've got Beethoven music in the background where she holds the umbrella open over the shorn, Mercurochromed woman. A sort of reconciliation of cultures too. But why don't you make it so that either she or some little urchin is playing a record on a gramophone left outside in the rain? You could have the woman choose the record."

Claus didn't want to point out that that would be both obvious and sentimental. It had gone so well. He said, "That could work. Let me think it over."

Max laughed. "I can see by your face you already have. Yes, well." He shrugged. "It's your film. Do what you can. But remember." He tapped the table with his forefinger, loud enough that the Americans looked over. "We've already missed the last day for requests. I can't hold it more than another two days."

"You're approving it?"

"Haven't decided." Max closed the script up in his briefcase again. "Tell me about the final scene."

He hadn't said no. That was the important thing. "A fade-out from the two women with the music continuing to play, then cutting to the townspeople, recognizable now, dressed in whatever ragged finery they've discovered, clearing away the rubble. That, too, would be an image of reconciliation — the townspeople coming alive, as the woman choosing the dress metaphorically suggests."

"Yes. And it's a nice echo of the mob scene. Which is very well done, by the way. Visceral. The villagers descending on her store at night, the shouting voices, the torches."

A tribute to his parents, even if very few people other than him would know that. He would tell Kate, of course, and he wanted to tell Max. What would it matter this late in the war? Max didn't even know his real name.

"I should tell you about that scene," he said, and leaned forward.

The American colonel next to them raised his voice again just then. "By July twenty-first, we'll be out of Saint-Lô. With Operation Goodwood, I guaran-god-damn-tee it," he said.

When he quieted down, Max turned his glance back to Claus. "Yes?" he said. "That scene?"

But the moment had passed. Bertram had found Claus this job. Was he running Max too? No, that would be impossible, but it was the kind of paranoia Bertram inspired, the kind he liked to inspire. Claus felt lucky to have one person it hadn't touched.

"Kate," he said, needing to say something.

"Yes. What about her?"

"She's helped me a lot on this, given me some good ideas. I was wondering if we could use her on the film."

"As the refugee?"

"No, of course not." He couldn't hesitate to turn that down; he suspected Max was hoping Alina would get the role. Her accent would be wrong, but they might be able to finesse that. "No. An unofficial adviser, that kind of thing."

"Research, eh?" He smiled. "Well, I'll see what the budget can take."

"And the other night, at the theater?"

Max held up his hand. "You don't have to explain."

"But I want to."

"Don't. She's new, you look happy." He laughed. "Believe me, I understand. Not the time you want to spend with an old married couple."

Claus paid the bill and Max said, "I think you've got the arc down here, all three acts. But sum it up for me in a single sentence that I can take to Bracken."

Claus paused, enjoying the moment. He'd prepared for this. "Simple. This isn't a film about a woman going back to anything, really; it's a film about a woman who can't go back but won't go forward as if the past hadn't happened."

"Articulate today. What's gotten into you?"

On their way out Max stopped into the clergy department and bought half a dozen collars. "To keep it open," he said, nodding at the otherwise empty counter. He slipped his change into one of the War Comforts Fund boxes. "My small war effort."

Really the collars were for his wife, who would hand them on to struggling Polish priests, refugees without churches, but Max would never admit it. Nor would Claus admit that that was why he'd bought the lunch.

Outside the sun was still high and very warm. They stood blinking in the light.

"Back to the MOI?" Max said. "Or off on one of your walks?"

Claus studied his watch, as if deciding. "Yes, I think so." Whenever he was off to see Bertram, he said he needed a walk to sort things out.

"Was Griffith a walker?" Max said.

"No. He preferred being driven. A purple Mercedes, of all things."

"Not likely either of us will get one of those. Remember," he said before turning away. "It has to be done in two days. No extension. I can't stretch the deadline any farther. Take time off from the *Fishermen*. I'll make our excuses. The need not to disturb the workers at their work." He waved over his shoulder and left.

The peculiar weather, warm air and sunshine after days of chilly rain. The hundreds hurrying back to work after lunch seemed either to glory in the change or to not trust it; some wore raincoats, while others were in shirtsleeves and sleeveless dresses. Claus, carrying his coat and growing hotter as he walked, fell somewhere in the middle.

Daffodils bordered the Victoria Embankment walkways, spent and hanging but buttery in the sunlight, blooming a second time in the unusual warmth. The rest of the gardens looked ragged despite the middle-aged female volunteers weeding the flowerbeds and trimming the shrubs. Elderly women watched from the remaining benches, a lucky few wearing flowered hats with exuberant roses or dangling cherries—old Victorian styles, since new hats were so hard to come by—the others with practical handmade tricorn newspaper affairs covering their gray hair.

Near Cleopatra's Needle he came across a cluster of hatless internees, women in blue overalls picking up trash, red-faced from the sun and their exertions. This late in the war they couldn't harm anyone, and that they were still interned angered him. A heavy-limbed one straightened and said in the Bavarian dialect of his mother, *"Die Sonne ist heiß!"* and a bolt of sadness shot through him. He wanted to talk to her, to agree that the sun was hot; instead, he put his shoes up on a bench one at a time to retie them.

The heat on his temple and neck, the green-tinted summer light; in this weather his mother would have been painting her springerle cookies red, white, and blue in honor of the Fourth of July for her husband to sell in the shop; the scents of anise and almond. Baked three weeks ahead of time to season properly, his mother checking nervously until they were puffed on the top but not browned; after letting them cool on a rack, she layered them in wax paper with slices of apple to keep them soft and then tucked them in the cookie tin.

He waited but the woman didn't speak again; she'd not seemed to notice him but she was paying particular attention now to cigarette butts and condoms clustered in the grass—both of which she picked up and pocketed with a birdlike movement of her hands, for resale, perhaps, or because she could use them in prison—and she seemed to be ignoring him on purpose; he slapped his cuffs clean and hurried on, certain he could use this scene too: women picking up trash, dragooned into the great war effort, average people caught up in something they'd had no part in bringing about. Somewhere on his heroine's journey through France she would pass them.

The air-raid sirens started as a redheaded girl cycled past near Kingsway, the long rising and falling notes of an alert. People looked up and froze as if they'd seen Medusa. Claus joined them but saw nothing; not a cloud, not a plane, not a single flying dagger. Then the all-clear sounded and his feet became unstuck from the pavement and he walked on, sympathizing with Londoners angry at the wardens; the bloody fools running the sirens couldn't get their messages straight. Several people had turned for the tube entrance, hunting safety, but the press of humanity in such confined places nauseated him. He'd pulled bodies from Bethnal Green after the panic had crushed hundreds, and he could never forget the trampled woman and her daughter in identical pink suits in a side tunnel, the cloth quite obviously from old curtains, the mother's hands locked over her daughter's eyes.

A cluster of giggling Girl Scouts passed in their green uniforms, lifting his mood again, and near Bush House a French colonel stepped out from a florist and handed an older woman with a caged rabbit a bouquet of flowers. In a slim pewter vase behind him were carnations dyed black, yellow, and red—the Belgian national colors, out because of a holiday—and Claus thought of pinning them to his lapel, knowing they'd irk Bertram.

Bertram's displeasure, so easily accomplished, would please him no end, and, his mood lifting even more, he entered the florist shop with its damp cool air and said, "These are just the thing."

The clerk tied string around the bundle and handed it over without reply.

He understood; he was not a regular customer, she might never see him again, she was tired. It showed in her face, her listless movements, the slump of her shoulders. They were all tired. He smiled at the clerk before turning away, hoping to communicate some of his happiness.

Two steps from the shop the colonel knocked the woman and her caged rabbit to the pavement. Shocking, but Claus didn't have time to think what it meant before a swift-moving shadow blocked the light and a wall of air smelling of earth blew him backward.

# JULY 21

"OUR CUP OF COFFEE against my dessert," an unfamiliar voice said, his words followed by a peculiar clicking. At last Claus identified the sound as tumbling dice. Evidently he said something.

"What's that?" a woman said.

He opened his eyes and his mild headache exploded into throbbing pain. It was a nurse, leaning over him, her cap a bright light. He shut his eyelids again but the pain didn't lessen and he felt like vomiting.

"Kate?"

"That's it," the woman said. "Go back to sleep. We're not ready for you yet."

He was in a hospital then. On the inside of his eyelids, a dark double image of the nurse pulsed; he wished she would remain stationary. He shifted in the bed, though it nearly made him ill to do so, wondering why he was there. Soon he smelled soap and heard the whisper of clothes rubbing together as someone stood beside him. "Kate?" he said again.

"Sorry," she said. "Not me you're looking for, love."

"Oh, yes," he said, and blinked his eyes partially open; that way they didn't feel as if pencils were stabbing into them. Another nurse. "I must have been dreaming."

"Let me look at you." She turned his head. "Good. Your pupils have gone down."

He couldn't make out her face (it was as if he was looking through glasses smeared with Vaseline), but it wasn't Kate; the voice too deep and the body—both of them, since there appeared to be two of her—too round. He remembered the first nurse, and something about an odd dream.

Her cool fingers gripped his wrist, his own skin felt hot. Had he been burned? "Was I in an accident?" he asked.

She waited until she was done counting before answering. "Yes," she said, and wrote something on a chart. The pencil scratched loudly.

He watched both of her put the two charts down. "Was I in an accident?" he said.

She nodded. The movement made him nauseated, so he closed his eyes before going on. "Was I in an accident?"

The springs on the next bed creaked. "Mate, she already told you you were." An Australian accent. "Give it a rest."

"Yes," she said. "Don't worry. You're fine. It was a flying bomb."

"Was I . . ." Before he finished, the man in the next bed shifted again. "What happened?"

"You'll be all right," the nurse said. "A concussion, probably, and a few glass cuts, but it looks like nothing was broken. Lucky, really." She patted his arm, and her shoes squeaked away over the terrazzo floor. He moved his uncomfortable arms and legs back and forth over the hot sheets, trying to find a cooler resting place.

Someone farther down the ward was moaning.

"Stop that!" a nurse's curt voice said. Then the nurse was beside him, taking his pulse again. Why wouldn't they leave him alone? "Was I in an accident?"

She cut her eyes to the next bed but evidently the man was sleeping. He must have slept too. The light was different, fading; earlier it had been bright. Behind the smells of bleach and sweat was a new one of institutional food; mealtime must have come and gone. From the lingering greasy odor, he hadn't missed much. Still, what was happening to him? "Was I in an accident?" he repeated.

"Yes, a flying bomb. You won't remember it probably. Quite an incident, really. Hit a church just behind Aldwych. Went right down into the crypt and started a fire. The old coffins. People buried for a hundred years and then they get cremated. It took a dozen fire appliances and two fire brigades an entire day to put them out."

"A day? I've slept that long?"

"I wouldn't really call it sleep, but you've been out for four."

He couldn't recall any of it, yet the lightness of her tone meant she was trying to divert his attention. Not from his own wounds, as they seemed mostly superficial, but from the carnage caused by the bomb. Deflections and jokes indicated something serious.

He closed his eyes to make it seem that he was sleeping, though he doubted he could fool her. Kate had told him of trying to take one patient's pulse and getting none, only to look up and see the man smiling; somehow he'd learned how to stop blood flow to his arm. Then a memory startled him: a wall of air sending him flying. He gripped the sheets to keep from falling and only when he was certain that he wasn't did he relax his fingers. The nurse was there. Still, or again?

He reached out for her hand. "How many died?"

"I don't know."

He squeezed, hard enough that her face changed. He hadn't meant that and relaxed his grip. "Please."

She looked down the ward, then leaned toward him, close enough that he made out the soft blond hairs on her cheek.

"Officially, near a hundred." Her voice was just above a whisper. "But I've heard rumors that it might be as many as three or four."

He released her hand and shut his eyes. "Thank you." It calmed him to know the scope of the disaster. What he imagined was always worse.

He'd slept and his skin felt sticky; he hoped it would soon be time for a bath. Someone was sitting beside the bed. Bent head, dark hair, his part a deep white furrow so straight it looked surveyed; at the very end it took a jagged turn. He spun his hat by the brim, the gesture Claus knew him by.

"Max," he said.

Max lifted his head and smiled.

"The script."

Max let go of the hat with one hand, showing his pale pink palm, before putting it back. "Oh, the script," he said. "You mustn't worry about that."

Claus slept again. Now the ward was hot and dark and smelled of disinfectant and, faintly, of burned flesh; the man to his left, probably, a new patient with a screen around his bed. No chair. Had he dreamed Max? On the other side was the Australian, a bluff fellow who gambled with a partner in the bed beyond, whom Claus had yet to see as lifting his head hurt, though he was used now to their wagers. Every meal had been parceled up and the coffee was evidently quite good. It went for more than just about anything, though spoons seemed hard to come by.

Twice he'd started books on the bedside table but the print was cruelly small and deciphering it gave him a headache. Gambling was out—he couldn't concentrate and the rattling dice irritated him—so his only entertainment was trying to discern patterns in the vaulted ceiling's cracked plaster or lying very still and listening to the various steps coming down the ward and guessing who they might belong to, male or female, nurse or doctor, visitor or ambulatory patient. Now there were two sets, one of an orderly mopping the central passageway and that of a woman with a purposeful stride. He made out her dark shoeprints on the recently polished floor and was surprised when she stopped before him.

"Myra!"

"Charles. We worried you'd died in the blast." She stood at the end of his bed, purse clutched in both gloved hands, pearls glowing at her throat.

He tried to make a joke. "That why you got dressed for a funeral?"

"No." She shook her head, the smallest of motions, the cherries on her hat clicking together. "Bad news, I'm afraid."

He resisted the urge to sit up. From the level of sorrow in her face, he tried to gauge whom it concerned. "Someone from the post?"

"No. Well, not that. I mean, that isn't what I came to tell you—in fact, I didn't come to tell you anything, rather to see you, though Herbert *was* hurt."

"Badly?"

She shrugged. "In his mind, certainly. A blast loosened his teeth. He'll have to get them all pulled now, poor fellow."

Herbert was unduly proud of his large, even teeth but Myra had never liked him, and it was an accomplishment for her to extend him sympathy. She was wearing her perfume again. It seemed overly strong and, peculiarly, to be growing stronger. At least she wasn't standing directly beside him; he didn't think his nose could take it. He closed his eyes and tried to think of something else.

She cleared her throat. "But I should tell you this. Madge."

"No." His eyes blinked open and he tried to sit up.

"Yes, I'm afraid so."

The bright smile, the endless mock-cynical humor. Bertram's office would never again run so smoothly. He lifted a hand and let it fall back on the bed. "I'm sorry," he said.

"We all were. To have come this far. It seems at times that there will be no one left for the peace."

"What happened?"

She breathed deeply. "Just after your Aldwych bomb hit, a dozen WAAFs leaned out a window to see where the noise came from. They were all sucked out by the blast wave. Those and the girls sunning on the roof. Madge was among them."

That explained why she was wearing the perfume. She was probably on her way back from the service. She didn't stay long after that.

The breeze blew up, carrying with it the lilac scent of linden trees after a rain, and then he heard Kate's voice.

"You'll not get healthy, Major Walford, betting away your supper."

"Who says I'm going to lose?"

"You've not eaten an entire meal in three days. Planning on better luck?"

She was at his bedside. He did not want to give away the extent of his happiness. "Is this your hospital?"

"It is now, I'm afraid. The Middlesex was hit rather badly. I'm not supposed to be here—I'm in surgery—but once I saw your name on the roster I had to come up. Are you all right? Are they taking good care of you?"

"I think so," he said.

"You don't know?"

"I'm never sure what day it is, or if I'm dreaming."

"The concussion. You'll be fine in a day or so, as long as you don't move much. And you're lucky it wasn't the last war. We'd be pumping you full of caffeine."

Something about her looked a bit odd. He stared until he had it. "Where's your cap?" Without it she seemed half dressed. All of the other nurses wore them.

She put her hand to the back of her hair just above her high, starched collar, where normally it would have rested. "A bit of excitement. A bomb blew in some windows and I lost it."

"But you're all right?"

"Yes. We all were luckier than you." She smiled at him. "Though perhaps not."

"I'm sorry?" he said.

"I saw your visitor earlier. Another conquest?"

Behind her joking tone he detected doubt, a twinge of jealousy. He felt an odd mixture of emotions, happiness to hear it, sorrow for Madge. "My superior."

"At the ministry?"

"Wardens' post."

"Gets to boss you around, does she?"

"Yes. Though she doesn't take advantage of the privilege very often. I'm afraid she had some rather bad news. A mutual friend died."

"Oh, Charles." She touched his hand. "I'm sorry."

"Nurse?" It was the Australian in the next bed. "I'm in a bit of pain. Do you think you could do something for me?"

"Certainly," she said. "In a minute I'll send your nurse down, or the doctor."

Normally the nurses would have been behind a central desk with the beds around them, but because of the recent spate of bombings Claus and the others were in a long, windowed corridor. All the glass had blast netting.

Claus knew he couldn't take her hand, and his frustration seemed disproportionate. He made an effort to overcome it. "You have to go?"

"Yes. I'll be back to check on you after eight. I'm off then."

"That would be good." He didn't look forward to the dark.

She squeezed his arm and he watched her quick efficient steps, the pale bottoms of her shoes. As if time had warped, another woman came through the doors just after she'd left, older, gray-haired, stooped, but otherwise about the same size, carrying a package wrapped in brown paper. Her steps down the ward were so slow she might have been Death herself, weary of her rounds.

She passed his bed and disappeared behind the screened bed beside him for several minutes, and when she came out she no longer had the package; he watched her make her slow way back down the ward. She was halfway to the door when he grew excited. How long had her entire trip taken? An hour? More, perhaps; perhaps for some of it he'd slept. Now he didn't take his eyes off her, believing that if he watched her all the way without blinking Kate would come through the doors again right after she left, the mirror image of her first appearance, but it was no use. The older woman took so long he couldn't help blinking. When she finally disappeared and Kate didn't return he felt foolish.

Because he'd been listening for her returning step so acutely—it was already nine thirty and she hadn't yet arrived—he seemed to hear the buzz bomb before anyone else. Far off, but making its steady implacable way toward them, its engine note just audible under the wail of the sirens. Then it stopped. The Australian started coughing and Claus thought he might miss the sound of the explosion, but it came, dimly, along with a faint puff of air that rippled the yellowing curtains across the ward.

"Did you hear that?" Claus asked.

"Wasn't for us, mate. Might as well relax. They'll be falling short tonight."

Claus put his arms under the covers to grip the damp sheets unobserved. The man to his left made a muffled noise behind his screen. Had he heard it too? How much worse to be immobilized. Then another one started, this one much closer, its cranky clanking like someone beating on pipe with a hammer, and Claus forgot about anyone else. He worked his shoulders from side to side, trying to dig to safety through his own bed.

Its tail fire brightened the room, trapping him in the open like a deer that had been dogged and jacklighted. Sweating, nauseated, with a nearly uncontrollable urge to go to the bathroom, all he could think of was escape. Then Kate's soothing voice said, "Lie back," and her cool hand was on his wrist.

"Please," she said. "It will help. You're straining to hear them. It's perfectly normal for concussion patients."

"Help what?"

"Relax you."

"I don't need to relax."

She touched his shoulder instead of arguing. "Just trust me."

Once he was lying flat she asked him to close his mouth. "Don't worry," she said, and smiled. "I'll let you talk again soon.

"There. That's right. Now concentrate on deeper breaths. Good."

After a minute or two she said, softly, "Now, let go of the sheets."

He hadn't known his hands were clenched, and the sudden embarrassed awareness made him breathe quickly once more. "No," she said. "That's all right. Now you've let go you can close your mouth again."

He did. The sweat in his hair began to dry. Soon his muscles were looser and his lungs seemed to get enough air.

"There." She let go of his wrist and patted his hand. "Your pulse has dropped back to normal. You see? I do know what I'm about. You just need to trust me.

"Now," she said, "I must be off. Other patients to attend to."

He started to sit up again and she pushed him back down. "Please."

When he was flat he said, "You'll be back?"

"As soon as I can."

"You were supposed to be here earlier." He sounded petulant, and the Australian was watching him, but he didn't care; his panic was rising again.

"I know. I'm sorry. We had some dreadful cases."

"I thought you weren't hit." A shiny burn mark showed on her forearm.

"I wasn't."

"Then what's that?" He pointed at the burn.

"I went back in, after some of my patients." She shrugged. "Unsuccessfully, I might add. So you see, I have to go."

She squeezed his hand tightly before letting go.

"Don't be long."

All night he lay awake, listening to sirens and bombs and his snoring and moaning and farting ward mates. One bomb landed nearby. Some time after dawn he slept, only to be woken by another bang; whether real or remembered he couldn't tell. He sat up, planning to leave, and found that his head wasn't too bad and that the rocking motion in his stomach stilled when he did. If he didn't move too quickly he'd be all right.

Beneath his sweaty feet, the floor was cool and slippery. He slid forward until he reached the screen, where he paused, as the smell of burned flesh was still strong, then breathed deeply and made himself step forward. His fears proved worse than reality: a mass of gauze enveloped the man's hands and his swollen-looking head, hiding his injuries. A clothes package was at his feet. He had the pants on before Kate was suddenly beside him.

"What are you doing?"

"Independence Day."

"I'm sorry?"

"July Fourth. Our Independence Day. An American holiday. My favorite." Fishing, freshly made doughnuts, the high school fields where he and his friends gathered for fireworks, his first kiss. As a child he'd loved it, but now it seemed so long ago, from a different life, as if it were something he'd read about.

"Really? Well, you've missed the date, I'm afraid. Weeks ago. And this seems to be the first time you've wanted to be an American."

"Nationalities do change, given the circumstances. You should know about that."

"Perhaps I do." She seemed taken aback by his sharp tone, and he knew his anger was irrational. "But nonetheless you mustn't go. I'll call the doctor if you don't get back into bed."

He regretted the jab but bile was rising in his throat and if he stayed he was likely to get sick. "Call him. I'll be gone before he arrives."

"But you're not fit to leave."

"I'll decide that."

"Please," Kate said. "Is this about your friend? It's not as if you could have prevented the death."

"No. But I might prevent others."

"How? You're in no shape to work as a warden."

He ignored her and kept dressing, though his fingers seemed stupid, slow and clumsy with the buttons.

When he didn't answer she said, "Wait a few minutes. I can walk you home."

"I'm fine." He finished tightening the belt and bent to lace the shoes and lurched with dizziness, grabbing the bed to keep from falling.

"You see," she said, propping him up.

"Yes. I do. Tying shoes isn't smart."

She sighed. "All right, then. I'll do it for you." She knelt and began on the right one. "Is that tight enough?"

"Yes," he said, quietly, feeling like a little boy. "Thank you."

"You're welcome. But who will do this for you over the next few days?"

"No one," he said. "I'll just shuffle around barefoot."

"Charles," she said, and looked up at him. "Your anger is a sign of your concussion. All the more reason you shouldn't leave."

"All the more reason I should." He forced a smile. "Otherwise you'll not want to see me again."

The hallway was bright and smelled of witch hazel. Kate looked tired, the lines around her eyes more pronounced. He let her guide him as she chatted. "What a mess the day's been. At the start, we didn't have any running water, just a basin of cold water, and all the casualties showed up covered with dust and pierced with glass splinters.

"After each dressing, we washed our hands in it, and by the end of the day, when the same water had been used more than fifty times, it was thick as soup.

"When I finished, I was going to check on you, but I didn't want to wake you. Then I fell asleep and someone roused me when they needed the bed, and after that I worked more. Now I'm nearly set to go home. I just have to tell another nurse that I'm going to walk with you instead. Can't you wait five minutes?"

Sirens were going and bombs coming over. "I've seen your five minutes." Still, he made an effort. "Can you swear it will only be five?"

"I can't swear, Claus. Sylvie might need more time to finish her paperwork."

"That's fine. But I can't wait. I need to be at work."

"You're in no state for that."

"Then I have to be home."

"You won't be any safer there, Claus." She breathed deeply. "This is perfectly normal after a bomb. Don't you see? Won't you be smart enough to stay?"

"Please, Kate. We've discussed it."

"I give advice and you ignore it? Is that your idea of a discussion?"

A passing gray-haired doctor glanced at them. "Is everything all right, Nurse?"

"Fine, Doctor," she said, though a blush rose up her neck the longer he watched.

"Good." Light flashed off his glasses when he turned his gaze on Claus. He looked at him for a few seconds before moving on.

"See," Claus said, making his unsteady way toward the door after he'd passed. "You're causing trouble for me."

Her sigh sounded exasperated, but she held her tongue. "Sorry, I didn't mean to snap. It's just that I'm worried about you. Will you call?"

"Yes. I promise. I'll even stop by, if you'd like."

"I would." She looked around, making sure no one was within hearing distance, and touched his arm. "*Mein wenig Deutsch.*" Her little German.

"How long are you off?"

"Today? Not very, I'm afraid. Until four. And you should sleep."

"Taking back your invitation?" Before she could respond, he squeezed her arm. "I'm kidding. Tomorrow then. How's two o'clock?"

"Good. I'll be ready."

"Tea?" he said.

"I was thinking more of pancakes."

"But it's a weekday."

"I know." She leaned in to kiss him. Her lips were soft, damp. "But I don't care. Don't you see? There's no sense following rules now."

That made him smile. He returned her kiss and felt himself growing dizzy, so he broke it off and turned away, pushing the iron bar on the door and stepping outside, where the air cooled his forehead. He was so glad to be out that even the air-raid sirens didn't bother him, though his headache began to worsen. Walking might cure it, which was just as well; there were no taxis around. He paused at the top of the stairs and didn't look down, afraid he'd get dizzier. Instead he gripped the rail and took the steps as quickly as he could so he wouldn't look like an invalid.

THREE BLOCKS FROM the hospital he heard a V-1 and crouched on the sidewalk, staring up at its red nose cone. A young woman passed, holding a child by the hand, and both observed him neutrally, looking down, which shamed him; better if they had seemed angry or appalled. He felt his face flush and he waited until he could no longer see her green dress before standing. A minute later the ground shook from the explosion and he felt relieved; it had been close enough to fear.

He wasn't far from the MOI, and though Max had told him not to worry about the missed deadline, he wasn't sure what that meant; he wanted to find out. At Whitfield Street he turned north. Halfway down the block a pipe-smoking man stood on the ruins beyond the police rope in violation of posted orders, looking down into the exposed basements of Tottenham Court. Claus recognized the ruined building as the Mercury Theatre that in '41 had been bombed and burned, then collapsed. For some reason a statue of Sisyphus had once stood outside, and during the fire the flames had made a spectacle of his struggling form, blowing nearer and away, illuminating him and throwing him into shadow.

Claus called out but the man didn't respond, so he ducked under the rope and clambered over the wood and bricks, pausing when dizzy. The man didn't bother turning at his noisy approach; he was looking at flowers. "Ragwort, lily of the valley, and lilac," he said when Claus came up beside him, aiming his brown pipe stem at each bloom. The splash of pink growing near one charred wall was rosebay willow herb. "London hasn't seen that since the great fire of 1666. It likes burned-out ground. And that," he said, obviously having saved the best for last, "is mimosa." A small blue-green bush, it looked like overgrown rosemary. "Brought back from China a hundred and fifty years ago and never seen in the wild. Only in the Natural History Museum. The bombing in '41 must have sent up seeds. Won't bloom until winter." The pipe stem clicked against his yellow teeth.

The flowers infuriated Claus, nature taking advantage of brutality for its own ends. Had the man left, Claus would have uprooted them, but he was too obviously taken with the view, so Claus climbed down and dusted off his pants and kept going north, determined now to see where the bomb had landed. It would be all right. By the time he got there the first awful moments of silence, when dust was settling on everything, would be over.

He had only to follow the crowd. Even this far into the war the disaster tourists were out, though others came from the practical desire to help or to reaffirm their luck; he knew because he often felt that himself. His first clue that the bomb had landed nearby was the cucumbery sweetness of flowering limes. A brick garden wall had been knocked down, and the limes' glossy green foliage and white flowers lay tumbled into the street, already withered. Claus skirted them, his stomach heavy, to find the road ahead bright and busy: people darting to and fro and hoses snaking over the rubble and a few undamaged vehicles moving about the wet pavement. A bus lay on its side, dust-coated passengers still in their seats, and two houses were on fire. Worse was the rancid dust that clogged the air, making it almost foggy. They were breathing ashes; it might have been Pompeii.

So it would have been at the Aldwych, only then he was one of the figures on the ground, like the man stretched over rubble, arms above his head as if killed diving for safety, or the laid-out dead. For the first time, he wondered why they were always placed face-up, something he himself had done dozens of times. What did they care that their faces should be turned to the sky? It was to assure the living that they too would be handled with respect. How gullible we were, to think that such a thing should matter.

Hatless, as the recently bombed-out often were, men were beginning to pile the debris street side to make passage easier, and one woman wearing full-length gloves and a sleeveless dress had so many leaves and twigs in her hair she looked costumed for some peculiar stage drama. Dozens of terrace houses had been blown up, their brick walls pulverized, and hundreds of other houses had had their roofs torn off or their windows shattered; he passed one with its lone standing kitchen wall covered with jam. Beyond that, other houses were missing roof tiles, and with the rain their owners were going to return to sodden ruins, though on some, workers in boilersuits were already climbing about, tossing down damaged tiles and laying out canvas. Behind the acrid smell of pulverized houses was the more acrid smell of the explosives.

"Gas," a man in blue overalls said, and Claus caught its rank scent. "No matches." But no one put out his cigarette.

An American in a dark blue air force uniform said, "Why doesn't somebody get a shovel, for God's sake?" People were digging in the rubble with small trowels and handsaws.

Claus didn't want to call attention to himself and no one else responded.

"Jesus," the American said. "I'll do it myself."

He went off. It was possible he'd find one—the main ruin had been a department store—but doing so was useless. Though the wreckage looked easily moved, everyone there had seen enough blasts to know that just below its pebbly surface it was nearly impossible to shift in volume. Broken rafters, skewed joists, destroyed furniture, collapsed stairways; whatever was to be moved was to be moved by hand. And with the gas, anyone trapped underground was probably already dead. Better that way, more peaceful, though again no one would say so.

"And the dead?" Claus asked a WVF worker beside a radio blown intact into the street, hands on the shoulders of a tiny elderly woman whose legs and lips trembled and whose gray hair kept falling over her face; her flowered smock was absurdly childish.

"Eleven off, so far," the WVF woman said, "but there'll be more. The bus landed on a queue. And in those houses we'll find dozens." She took out a comb and began ministering to the woman, who stolidly withstood the grooming. Each stroke uncovered black hair, the dark strands turning the woman younger. Dust, not age, had grayed her, though from her face Claus would never have guessed it, and eventually she was transformed into a child. It took a few seconds for his shock to pass.

"When did it hit?" he said at last.

"Six eleven."

"Are you certain?" It was time to redirect the bombs, Bertram could go to hell. Madge, Kate's hospital; the V-1s were coming too close, though altering the coordinates without the exact time would be useless. They might confuse it with another launching.

She pointed the grimy comb at the clock. "See?"

It stood outside a news vendor's, which still had its plate-glass window even though its interior was demolished, but the impact could have blown the clock hands forward or back; he'd have to ask someone else who'd been there. The girl's eyes were dull, she'd survived the blast but wouldn't be able to tell him anything, so he repeated the time to himself, then borrowed paper and a pencil from the woman and wrote down the figures, worried he'd forget them. His postconcussion memory was still dicey.

"Wait," the WVF woman said when he turned away. "Were you to meet someone? Someone we should look for?"

He continued on as if he hadn't heard her. "Sir," he said. "Can you help me?" Reckless to be so brazen, but he didn't care.

The man smiled. Blood clotted the side of his face. "Need directions?"

"No. But thank you. I was wondering, do you know what time the bomb hit?"

"It wasn't a bomb."

"I'm sorry?"

He winked. The blood around his eye made his eyelid stick. "It was a gas main. Exploded. The damnedest thing."

"Right. Could you tell me when? Exactly?"

The man looked him over. He had to be an official to give out the gas-main line, and Claus didn't want to raise his suspicions, especially since without his uniform he lacked official cover. Claus breathed deeply, genuinely afraid. "It's my wife, you see. She came down to get a paper, and . . ."

"Haven't seen her since?"

"No."

"Six ten, I believe. Where was she coming from?"

"Over there." Claus pointed over his shoulder. What was the name of the street with the lime trees? Starcross Place? "Starcross Terrace," he said. He started to move away. "Thank you. She was here about six. If she didn't stop to talk, she'll be all right. Excuse me, I have to look."

From behind the overturned bus Claus saw the bloodied man watching him, then signal to two others, and Claus turned and shouldered through a group of women, back toward Hampstead Road, fighting the visceral urge to run. If it had been dark he would have been safe mingling with the crowd or sheltering in a doorway, but with the summer light he couldn't lose them and running would only increase their suspicions. Above him people leaned out of windows, two men in shirtsleeves, a young blond woman in a green apron, a pale child. Did they know he was being followed? He didn't want to get shot in the back. He took the paper from his pocket as footsteps pounded toward him over the wet streets and swallowed it, sharp as glass going down his throat.

"You there, stop! I'd like a word with you!"

Claus kept walking, as if he hadn't a clue they might be talking to him, though he began to hurry despite himself and his renewed dizziness. How stupid to be arrested for wanting to help people. Why now, when thousands of other times over the past few years he'd been out for information that ostensibly aided the Germans?

# JULY 23

**L**IGHT CAME BEFORE the warder's whistle, but Claus had been
awake for hours. Bruised arms and hips—the detectives had
beaten him professionally, avoiding his head and face—yet what
disturbed him most was his cellmate's incessant pacing. Six steps,
a scraping of his laceless shoes as he pivoted at the wall, six more
steps back to the door, all accompanied by a relentless low mumble.
From the bottom bunk, Claus had a good view of red-rimmed ankles, rubbed raw by the shoes' stiff leather, and of too short flannel
pants stopping halfway down fat white calves.

His cellmate paused as, farther down the block, another cell door
squeaked open, followed by passing footsteps and muffled voices.
Kitchen workers; breakfast would probably be served soon. Despite
everything, Claus was hungry.

The sounds of passage died out and the pacing began again.
Claus wanted him to knock it off but decided not to fight. Instead he
faced the cinder-block wall and pulled his damp, sour blanket over
his head, drifting into a kind of milky sleep. His Schuylkill cellmate,
Larry Baxter, had been a muttering pacer, going on about revenge.
Against his wife, against the warden, against Earl Yarborough, their
block bully.

For a while at Schuylkill, Claus had been a thread waxer. He was
given a grapefruit sized ball of blue wax and spools of thread, which
day after day he pushed through the wax and re-bobbined while sitting in a square, mustard-colored room with windows on two sides
and the guard standing along the blank front wall near the wood
stove. His fingers were coated with wax, his hair, it got in his eyes;

eating was difficult because of his slippery fingers and the nauseating smell. For diversion, inmates bet on which raindrop would slide down the glass first or held cockroach races on their worktables. Summertime, greenhead flies flew through the tilted-in windows, and the prisoners argued over whether they should stifle in the heat or be tormented by the merciless greenheads, whose bites were enormously painful, the arguments circular and repetitive and totally pointless. Yarborough decided, and Yarborough always chose flies in the morning and heat in the afternoons.

One prisoner delivered bobbins of waxed thread to leatherworkers in another building, a prized duty because you got to move about, and for a long time it was Baxter's, but then he'd done something to anger Yarborough and lost it. Ever afterward Yarborough delighted in hounding him, Baxter in planning his revenge. During one especially hot July morning, flies crawling over the sticky worktables, the air so humid Claus felt he could lean against it, Baxter looped a length of waxed thread around a fat, drowsy fly to keep as a kind of pet, anchoring the leash with a chunk of wax. Every now and then the fly flew awkward buzzing loops over Baxter's head only to land beside him again, making everyone laugh. The guard, woken by the break in routine, looked baffled, causing even more laughter, and for an hour Baxter was a hero for getting revenge on their tormentors. Yarborough's face grew darker and darker.

At last Yarborough threw his neighbor's ball of wax at the sleeping guard and in the ensuing struggle—Yarborough stepping away from his workbench so the guard could strike Merkle with his cosh—Yarborough grabbed the fly leash. When the guard fell asleep again, Yarborough held his blue ball of wax over Baxter's fly. "I'm going to kill it, Baxter, you watch."

Yarborough wasn't going to kill it, that was obvious, he had power over Baxter only while he kept the fly alive, and Claus wondered why Baxter didn't simply capture another. Instead, he whined, begged, and offered cigarettes, an embarrassing display that only increased Yarborough's power. Then, surprisingly, Yarborough flattened the fly, revealing that it wasn't the power to make Baxter beg Yarborough had been after—or rather, not just that—but to show Baxter that nothing he did or said could ever influence him. Why enslave someone when you could crush him? Claus had always thought it his most important prison lesson.

His reverie ended when the warder's whistle blew. As if on cue a beam of red sunlight splashed against the far wall, and his cellmate stood on the edge of Claus's bed to look out the window. Claus pushed his cellmate's feet off the thin mattress without a word.

"Oof, I am sorry," his cellmate said. "Rude of me." His English was good but heavily accented. Claus suspected instantly that he'd been put in the cell for a reason.

"I'm used to being by myself, and to watch the sun rise over the surrounding fields." He smiled at Claus. "But I have to stand on the bed to see."

"Day to start a new habit," Claus said, and sat up.

The man laughed. "This is funny!" His thick glasses magnified his eyes, which darted back and forth so quickly they seemed to be trembling.

In the other cells men were getting up and shuffling about in response to the whistle; running water, calling to each other. A few cells down one even yodeled.

"Shut up, you stupid fuck," a guard said, and banged the door with his baton.

Claus said, "So, you've not had a cellmate before?"

"No. By myself, always."

That seemed true. Trousers as short as a schoolboy's, coat sleeves so long the coat might have been his father's; he'd been kept in isolation. You traded only in the showers.

"For how long?" Claus asked.

"More than a month now. Almost forty days."

Claus calculated. Forty days before, a spy had come over to deliver the crystal for his radio. Bertram had passed it on after the man was caught.

"And when did you lose the shoelaces?"

The man looked down at his feet. "Yesterday afternoon. Peculiar. They gave me other things back, but took my laces and belt. When they gave them to me, I thought, *Kaput!* They are seeing their mistake and letting me go!"

That explained his pacing. Before parole hearings, Claus's nerves were almost tangible, a heavy stomach, sleeplessness, but he was also fatalistic, so when parole was denied—as it always was, treason being to parole boards unpardonable—his scalding bitterness lasted only a day or two. Then he'd sink back into routine, knowing that hope was necessary in small doses but dangerous in large ones, though calibrating it properly was often impossible. Raw ankles and a sleepless night; this man had hopes of freedom.

"Knew I was coming," Claus said, and pointed out his own shoes, also laceless. "Didn't want us going after each other."

The man was clueless not to know it was unusual to suddenly get a cellmate after a long stretch of isolation. Did he not realize he was in danger? Someone was hoping one or the other would do something stupid, and doubtless the cell was bugged. The barred, high window, the metal bunks, the scraped floor and solid walls, the light overhead; that seemed the most likely place.

"What are you here for?" the man said.

"Asking too many questions."

He paused, as if trying to decide whether or not Claus was warning him off, then snorted. "It's an inhospitable country."

There was no sense avoiding it; Claus might as well know. "And you?"

The man shrugged. "I tried to explain who I was, and they wouldn't listen."

Before he could finish, the breakfast bugle blew and Claus stood reflexively.

"No," the man said, and tapped him on the shoulder. "Not for us, I think. Always to me they bring the breakfast. Unless for you it's different."

Just as well. As at Schuylkill, the food would probably be cold, and if he was going to eat cold food he preferred to stay put. He rolled back onto his bunk to wait.

"You see," the man said, sitting next to Claus without being asked. Claus ignored it, sensing it wasn't a challenge. "They don't want me to talk to anyone, except now to you. A spy, they say. You they must not to trust either."

Thick and clumsy, with thinning curly hair, ineligible for military service because of flat feet and vibrating eyes, his name was Dieter

Einschuffen; he came from Dortmund and was the source of the persistent garlicky smell Claus had thought peculiar to the cell. Before the war he'd been a photographer's assistant, though his most recent job had been as an inspector at an Alsatian tool-and-die factory, overseeing hundreds of Frenchmen.

"They don't bother me," he said of his eyes, "but the military, they worry I don't shoot straight. Though that's just good. I couldn't stand Hitler and the Nazis from the start. In the army, what would I have done? Here!" he said, apropos of nothing. "I've got news clippings about myself."

A wallet full, about his supposed resistance activities, including grainy pictures.

Claus wouldn't reveal that he understood German. "What do they say?"

"They're about explosions in the factory. I set them off."

Claus handed them back. No real resistance member would carry such a cache of documents, since at the first inspection he'd have been caught and killed. An incredibly naïve amateur spy then.

"And here, see?" He thumbed through the clippings to a more recent one. "How do you say this? *Zeitung?*"

Tempted, Claus didn't answer.

Dieter snapped his fingers and supplied the word for himself. "Newspaper. That's it. Now I'm in the English newspapers."

Accounts of his arrest and internment. "Where did you get these?" Claus said.

"The guards. Some of them are almost friendly."

A death sentence. He seemed not to realize that if the English had planned to turn him, they'd never have announced his capture.

There was a rattling at the door, the lock turned, and the door swung back on old, noisy hinges. Two guards carrying trays stood in the hallway.

"'Ave we got a feast for you!" one said, and they put the trays on the ground.

Claus stood, holding up his unbelted pants. "Spam and eggs. It figures."

"Yes? How so?"

"It's Sunday," Claus said, as if that explained it.

"Sunday?" Dieter said.

"Seems like the world over, Sunday in prison means Spam and eggs."

Claus retreated to his bed and had already started cutting the rubbery slab when he realized Dieter was still watching him.

"You have been to the prison before?"

"A long time ago. A mistake."

"So it would seem to be often. But before this, I never would have believed it."

He tucked his napkin into his collar as if he were in a restaurant and broke his bread carefully into four pieces, eating each after several bites of Spam. Claus had been done for minutes when Dieter took his napkin from his collar and cleaned his lips and placed his silverware neatly by the plate.

"Are you not going to eat that?" He pointed at Claus's bread.

"Not now," Claus said, and put it on the windowsill.

Dinner, at four thirty, would consist of tea and a couple of crackers, and Claus hated sleeping hungry. "For after dark," he said, in explanation. Dieter seemed not to understand. He looked longingly at the bread, his skin such a peculiar texture that a thumb pressed to Dieter's forearm might leave an impression. A fat man deprived of food; Claus disregarded a pang of guilt and turned to the wall, hoping to sleep again. It didn't work; Dieter's garlicky presence, his huffing breath as he pressed his ear to the door, listening to other prisoners released for their exercise.

Claus imagined the yard, as effectively regimented as every other aspect of prison life: the newer prisoners throwing balls to one another, older ones walking around its perimeter, the oldest of all merely leaning against the wall and talking. That had been him at the last, and how ecstatic he'd been when his sentence was finally done, even though release meant exile.

He'd welcomed it. What did he have to go home to, both parents dead, their store bankrupted, and their home sold to pay legal bills? On the train ride to New York, he'd been certain the woman sitting across from him knew he'd been in prison, though his clothes didn't give him away; unlike most prisoners, only too happy to accept the government's shiny blue ex-prisoner suit and square-toed black shoes, he'd had his own clothes to wear. Still, he felt he'd given off some kind of inescapable scent and he'd fiercely avoided her glances.

The guards arrived now, sloppy and rude, taking back trays and slamming the door closed. Dieter seemed shocked and it felt cruel to have lured this quiet, inoffensive man here, totally unnecessary. Had Dieter really expected to affect the war, to wander the English countryside without being captured? It would be like Bertram to argue such a thing was justified.

Early in 1942 sixty-one Dutch agents were executed in Holland; they'd been caught because the Germans had broken their cipher. For weeks the Germans had signaled a need for more agents, more guns, and more ammunition, all the while waiting at every drop to capture them. Bertram had told Claus about the operation to show how cunning the Germans were, Claus first thought, but as time passed and rumors percolated about the captured network, Claus decided his purposes were more devious. Such a disaster could hardly be kept secret, and Claus believed he'd been told as a way to divert his attention from an entire other Dutch network that a select few at the MOI knew about, larger, more entrenched in key Dutch cities, which had not lost a single agent. Could it be that Bertram or others had sacrificed dozens of agents so that the Germans would think they'd destroyed the Dutch underground while at the same time being fooled into believing that the invasion of Europe would come in the Netherlands? Most of the captured spies had carried fake invasion documents.

Dieter stood with his back to the window, holding his book open in the day's last light as the walls faded from pink to pearly gray. Claus took care not to read the title; the less he knew about Dieter, the better. He startled Claus by clapping the book shut.

"No light left," Dieter said, and dropped the book on his bunk. He began to pace again, Claus making sure he didn't hesitate by the windowsill and grab the bread. Eventually the evening whistle blew, the guards made their rounds, and other prisoners sang cheap sentimental war songs. The choruses spread out in rings, and when those died out a few foreigners began loudly repeating phrases in English.

"'What time is the train?'"

"'There are the shoes. One is red, the other black.'"

At last the night whistle sounded and the guards called, "Shut up, you!," and rapped on the doors with their batons until everyone did. Then the tapping began, quick and short. Dieter stopped at the sound of it.

"Do you hear that?" he said. "Tell me, please, what's it mean?"

"How should I know?"

"Because you said you've been here before."

"Not here."

"No." Dieter shrugged. "I thought it perhaps was universal. Every night it is the same thing, this tapping. I wish someone to explain it to me." He sighed. "You think I'm a spy then too. This is for you won't talk. The English are hard to convince."

"I'm not English," Claus said, and rolled upright on his bunk. The cell grew unbearably silent once Dieter stopped his pacing. In a few minutes Claus had it. "Math problems," he said.

"Math?"

"To keep their minds sharp. Here's one. How many bananas can a camel carry? She has three thousand bananas but can carry only one thousand at a time, and she must eat one banana for every mile she travels." After an interval, the tapping started up again.

"The answer," he said. After another break came a longer series, slower and repeated. "Two trains and a fly."

"Two trains and a fly?"

"You don't know that one? Everyone does. Two trains, one hundred fifty miles apart, traveling toward each other, one at ninety miles an hour, the other at sixty. The fly flies from one train to the other until they collide. How far does the fly fly?"

Dieter stood in the dark with his head tilted forward on his fat neck, as if trying to see the answer on the floor. From down the corridor, steps came toward them. Claus knew they were for him. All day he'd been successful, not a word of German, not a mistake that would link them together, but nonetheless his stomach knotted, his armpits began to sweat, his chest filled with the belief that they were coming not to release him but to hang Dieter. He opened his mouth to speak—in German—then closed it and stood.

"Can you tell me the code?" Dieter said. "To the tapping?"

Did he genuinely not know, were the Germans so desperate now that they weren't training their spies in the most basic of techniques, or was this a trick to get Claus to reveal his own training? The former, Claus decided, but even so he shook his head in the dark. The cell door swung open and a blinding light shone in.

"You then," he said to Claus and tossed in a belt. "Put that on and come along."

Claus held the belt in his palm.

"Goodbye," Dieter said. In German, he added, *"Freund."*

*Friend?* Claus paused, unable to bring himself to reply.

"Come on then," the guard said. "Don't be all day about it."

Claus reached up to the windowsill and took the bread and put it in Dieter's open hand and then turned sideways to slide by him, not wanting to touch him as he passed.

# JULY 24

"GOT YOURSELF ARRESTED, did you?" Bertram said before the door had even clicked shut behind him. The new secretary had ushered Claus in without a word and he'd been careful not to catch her name or refer to Madge, grateful she'd said nothing; half-meant condolences would only anger him.

"Good touch that, eating the paper. Made you seem a real spy."

Claus flushed, embarrassed and angry. It had been instinct, born of years in prison, where the smallest contraband could lead to isolation and loss of privileges, and he'd realized only as he did so that it made him look guilty. He waited a few seconds before responding. The cuckoo clock seemed unnaturally loud, its pinecone weights trembling. What seemed worst of all was that he'd noted how the detectives beat him and the kinds of questions they'd asked so he'd be able to tell his handlers. Bertram had trained him too well. "Did you think that was on purpose?" he said when his breathing was calm. "It got me beaten."

Bertram gestured with his hand.

"Yes," Claus said. "I'm sure it's nothing if you've never gone through it."

Bertram raised his eyebrows. "Were you scared?"

"You're damn straight I was. And am. They freed me, but they might well not the next time. And you're a liar if you say you wouldn't have been."

Bertram opened a whiskey and poured himself one, Claus as well, without asking. "One of the many things from the Colonies I can't do without," he said. As near to an apology as he would get, Claus realized.

Bertram studied him. "You haven't asked about redirecting the bombs," he said.

Startled, Claus shrugged to buy himself time. "Why would I? I already know your answer."

"That's never stopped you before."

Claus sat down but didn't pick up the glass, and Bertram shifted topics once again. "*Canis timidus vehementius latrat quam mordet.* 'A timid dog barks more violently than it bites.' The London police aren't much to worry about, truthfully, though I'm sure they made it uncomfortable for you. Shouldn't have, of course, but then these days the police aren't really attracting the best people." He re-stoppered the bottle and raised his glass in salute, sniffed the shimmering liquid. "They made quite a deal about Dieter, and you, until I let them know who you were, but they've not arrested a single spy on their own."

Bertram shook his head. "A fool, Einschuffen. Managed to get himself captured by a railroad porter. Asked what station he was at, in heavily accented English, in the middle of the countryside. The detectives only had to fetch him, though I've no doubt one or two will get a medal. But it's not as if even then they had to work. He had pyramidon powder on him and his papers were obvious forgeries and his ration book hadn't been used for a month. German chocolate in one pocket, matches from a Munich barbershop in another. Saved us a good deal of trouble.

"He should have had one or the other—the German clothes and chocolate, indicating that he was escaping in a hurry, or the pyramidon powder and the forged ration book, to show he meant to fool the Germans into believing he planned to spy. Not both.

"Though all in all, it actually works in your favor. You can tell your Abwehr contacts they're not up to snuff. Put them in a bind. They'll believe you that much more."

"I'm to tell them I shared a cell with him?"

"You're to tell them many things. More about Calais, for one. And about plans for an invasion near Marseille. But that you shared a cell with Einschuffen? Yes. Standard police procedure. Put two suspected spies in the same cell and hope that at least one gives himself away. You said nothing and were released."

"And what will happen to him?" Claus said, though he knew.

Bertram looked out the crosshatched window. "He was hung, of course."

"*Was* hung?" Claus had barely had time to return to his apartment and sleep.

"No point in putting it off. It was to be his fate anyway. Not even the Germans would credit that all their spies made it safely. And the public does have to be reassured."

"The public?"

Bertram bowed his head. "I know. Still, it must be done."

"Yet you paused before telling me."

"Not from moral doubts, I assure you."

"Then what?"

"You didn't tell him what his fate was going to be, I take it?"

"You can hardly expect me to have been the bearer of that news."

"No, I couldn't." Bertram sighed. "Quite a mess, evidently." He put his drink on the desk, as if it wouldn't be proper to hold one while saying what he had to.

"Einschuffen was taken by surprise, it seems. Thought he was going to be freed, especially after you were. When they explained he began crying. That didn't stop them, but it went from bad to worse. The noose wasn't tight when they opened the drop and it slipped up his face, catching the tip of his nose and cracking his neck."

"And I asked him to come over."

"It's a risk every spy takes." He ran his finger around the rim of his glass, making a slight musical noise. "You yourself worry about being shot."

"He was hardly a spy. And I worry about accidents, nothing planned."

"Good God, you don't feel bad about it, do you? People die. It's war."

"Yes, but not people I choose."

"The Abwehr chose him, not you. You merely asked that they send someone."

"'Even one hair casts a shadow,'" Claus said. It was one of Bertram's pet phrases from earlier in the war.

"Well, a shadow, yes," Bertram said. "But in the grand scheme of things, with the Nazi cloud, no one's going to notice his shadow."

"I will."

"Don't you Americans have a phrase? That you'll 'get through' it?"

Was that to be it, all sins forgiven because a greater sin lurked above them?

"I'd like to know, what's the point of luring someone like that to his death?" Dieter had been so pleased to see his name in the paper, so disappointed that it had been misspelled. It was like killing a child. "He wasn't a spy. You said yourself he was a fool. Do you think they'd waste a real spy on such a dicey mission? It's nothing short of murder to invite someone like that to come and be killed."

"You do have some of the strangest notions. We've done it throughout the war. A bit hard to develop qualms about it now."

"Not when the war is nearly over. Not when we know they're going to send fools. And why on earth would you put me in the cell with him? Bad enough if he were just a faceless figure, but to have met him?"

"The war is far from over, and it will serve you well with the Abwehr. To make them believe in you, the danger you face. The more real it is to you, the more real it will be to them. Tell your handlers that not only were you caught but that Dieter was caught, and that if they send another, for whatever reason, he should be better prepared."

"Wonderful. We'll have them sending in agents we can't identify. That should help us." Claus stood.

"It will, if we know they're coming to meet you." Bertram sat on the corner of his desk and smoothed his yellow school tie, bright as corn. "And I believe they already have."

Claus looked at him.

"You have no idea what I'm talking about, do you?" Bertram shook his head. "I thought you managed the arrest to give yourself a few days to think things over."

"I'd have told you if I planned to do that. And why would I need to?"

The green scrambler phone rang, but Bertram ignored it. "Spur of the moment. In any case, the Germans have sent someone else, I'm sure of it. Though I can't yet prove it." He moved to the wall and looked at a map of Germany before running his palm over the long crack in the plaster beside it. "Remember when I told you to trust no one? I had someone in mind even then. You know her, you see." He turned to face Claus. "The nurse. Mrs. Zweig."

"Kate?" Claus said, before his body even had time to react. "You're nuts." Then he felt as if he had no legs and sat. The phone was still ringing, Bertram still ignoring it. Claus felt guilty for ever having doubted Kate—the test at the racetrack. Bertram must have planted the seeds of doubt long ago and he'd been foolish enough to water them. "Dreaming," he said. It was a good front, but he wondered now. Worst of all was that he knew Bertram intended him to.

# JULY 25

TWO BUZZ BOMBS HIT almost simultaneously, the sounds of their explosions so close it was hard to tell them apart. The curtains blew in from the first and were sucked out by the second, and Rosalyn called down from the roof that both were in their sector.

Claus sat up on the couch and rubbed his eyes open, relieved that sunlight no longer hurt, more relieved to have something to do. Unable to sleep, he'd tossed and turned on the uncomfortable couch while working over Bertram's claims. His breathing had been shallow, his heart heavy, as if someone had laid a piano on his chest.

"She's too tidy," Bertram had said. "We have to worry most about foreigners. Turks, Spanish Jews, Greeks, Balkan half-castes, every one of them innately perverse and all crossbreeds, men of no particular patriotism or honesty, but she's English, so naturally we're less suspicious of her. And a woman, which the Germans could be smart enough to take advantage of. And a nurse—who would suspect them? Yet one of the Germans' best agents in the last war was a teenage girl cycling around Belgium in a Red Cross uniform."

Claus had asked how she'd looked when she'd arrived. He'd been brought in occasionally to verify a refugee's story or to trip someone up, since he'd spent much time shooting films in Germany between the wars, and the real resistance refugees were haggard, as if they'd stood facing winter winds for months.

Bertram had flicked his hand dismissively. "Terrible. Exhausted, spent, drooping. Real, in other words. And her stories have all checked out. One of our Parisian friends corroborated her account about the dyed dog. Though that doesn't make me trust her. Perhaps the Germans are just getting smarter. Her story is too tight."

Now Herbert came in from the other room, buckling on his belts.

"Duty calls," Myra said.

"Yes," Herbert said. "Would anyone like to answer?" His words were slightly slurred as his false teeth didn't quite fit.

*Hard to find choppers on the black market.*

Rosalyn yelled down again from the roof. "The flats in Chandos Place, I think, and over near Beechum's Furniture, on Craven."

Myra glanced at Claus before turning to Herbert. "You take one and I'll take the other." To Claus she said, "Charles, stay here and man the phones."

"No," Claus said, and then, realizing his voice had been sharp, modulated his tone. "Please. I'm okay, really." He disliked being coddled, and Myra hadn't sent him out since he'd been back. "Herbert's been out twice already."

"Fine with me," Herbert said, as Claus had known he would.

Myra said, "You haven't seemed well. A bit snappish, frankly."

"I'm sorry. But it's the sitting here that's driving me crazy, as if I'm fragile."

"Humpty Dumpty," Herbert said, unhelpfully.

Myra blew out her cheeks. "All right. We're short-staffed today. No sense overworking anyone." She bent over the map. "The flats are mostly abandoned, and Beechum's fire watchers are probably there. Too early in the day for the pubs." After a pause she said, "Take Beechum's. Help the watchers out if you can."

She was still coddling him, but he guessed he didn't have the luxury of a second protest, so he merely nodded and checked the map. He tapped where the other one was supposed to have hit, not far from Winifred's. "Hope everything's all right there."

Beechum's was far enough away that he had to ride the post bike. His balance was poor and he rode slowly through the deserted streets, a commercial district, as empty as on a Sunday. The rare slanting morning sunlight warmed his back, and the bike with its warped wheel squeaked and clanked, the peculiar rhythm oddly soothing.

*And she found you in the hospital too?*

*She saw my name on the admissions list.*

*Do nurses regularly scan admissions lists? Aren't they busy enough as it is?*

*It's the hospital she works at.*

*Perhaps she was honest, then.* Mendacem oportet esse memorem. "A liar has to be good at remembering." *Why not tell the truth, if it won't reveal anything about you?*

From Carting he turned onto Savoy, broader but darker, the half-timbered buildings leaning out over their storefronts; his teeth jarred as the metal wheels struck the cobbles.

*But she said she'd helped fliers escape. Surely that's easy to check up on.*

*Yes. Relatively recently. A good cover, wouldn't you say? A few free airmen, and then an escape through Vichy France, Spain, and Portugal?*

*She was searched, wasn't she?*

*She had nothing. But remember, if her story is true—and like most good spies' the majority of it would be—she's an experienced smuggler. Think of how many borders she's had to cross already in times of war. Don't you see, Claus? It would be just like them to send an incompetent like Dieter to distract us, to make us think we knew what they were up to, while at the same time sending someone far more clever.*

*But even if they have, that doesn't mean it's Kate. Mrs. Zweig.*

*Of course. But we can't chance it, can we?*

*You can't,* Claus thought now, stopping before he pedaled into the bomb's dust cloud. But could he? He wasn't sure. He stood beside his bike, cooler in the shade, waiting for the dust to settle before he continued on. He glanced at the shop window beside him and the hair on his neck rose; someone was watching him. Immediately he felt foolish. A life-size picture in the window, a model displaying wartime fashion. Bertram had him paranoid now, which of course was what he'd desired as it would make Claus wonder about everything Kate had ever said to him, turn over every question she'd asked. *How did you end up at the MOI?* He didn't want that and remounted the bike and pedaled on.

His inspection lasted only a quarter of an hour. No one was dead and the bomb had penetrated far into the ground before exploding. A small corner stationery shop had disappeared but it had been deserted before the bomb came, and except for the dust hanging in the air and the flurries of paper blowing about, nothing might have happened at all. The risk of looting was slim. Had it been food or liquor, he'd have stayed, but the inevitable crowd gathered at the site was tiny, and even if they scooped up the stationery, where was the harm in that? Beechum's fire watchers waved him off and he remounted the bike and pedaled away, bypassing the post since the incident report could wait.

Steering through the streets toward the flats was harder than getting to Beechum's, the damage from the second blast far more extensive. Blocks away, dust glittered in the morning air like mica, and closer it thickened the air like fog. He began to cough. Light posts were down, cars crushed or flipped on their sides and leaking precious fuel, a row of windows had been blown into the street as if for a stage set; the chunks of masonry were bigger than him. If he hadn't been responsible for the bike he'd have abandoned it.

Rosalyn had been off by two blocks and as he worked closer he began repeating the same line over and over like a prayer: *Please let it not be Winifred's block.* It was, though when he got there he didn't realize it right away since the local geography had become unrecognizable. The front walls of buildings were mounded in the street, and the surrounding row of flats looked like a diorama of progressive destruction. The first building had its windows blown out, the second its roof leaning down, the third no front whatsoever and its roof collapsed onto the top floor; the next building had little standing but its two side walls. Between them were long slats of wood from the shattered roof and floors, jumbled about like pickup sticks, and beyond that there might never have been buildings at all; piles of brick rubble looked like they'd been dumped by an enormous truck. Rescuers were digging there.

He leaned his bike against a lamppost and climbed into the rubble. Twenty yards took five minutes, and the sharp debris cut his ankles through his rubber boots. At last he came to an enormous crater, and beside it, impossibly, an undamaged Anderson shelter, soil and plantings blown from its sloping sides. He stood on its rounded roof, and after several minutes decided that though this was Winifred's block, her building hadn't received a direct hit. Still, the one next to it had, and he didn't have much hope for her. Why hadn't the stubborn, silly woman taken his advice and left?

The blue incident flag stood in an alley, the control van there, one tire white as if floured. Heavy Rescue workers were already present in their blue smocks, fitting up a block and tackle, and the muddied gas men stood at the bottom of the watery crater; farther out, men from another post were carrying children over the rubble or helping their mothers navigate it. Two of the women clutched white towels as if to surrender.

Tradesmen's vans with the names sanded off, remnants of the invasion scare of '40 and '41, were serving as hearses and ambulances, and a few trees without leaves made the landscape look wintry. From one hung bits of human flesh; beneath it were dozens of dead blackbirds, killed by the blast. The usual initial depression consumed him, though he knew from experience the only thing for it was to do something: motivation followed action, not the other way around. He asked a pair of Heavy Rescue men where Miss Thornton was.

"Who?"

"The IO," Claus said.

"Gone back to her post," the shorter one said, looping rope around his shoulder and elbow. "No phones, and she had to call it in."

Herbert showed up, overalls open at the throat, and whistled appreciatively. Oddly, he smelled of mutton. "Myra was right. This'll be a long one. Daft to start rigging that up," he said of the Heavy Rescue men beginning to work on a beam. "Won't find anything here."

"Oh, shut up, you bloody bastard," Claus said. "They'll hear you."

"Who?"

"Survivors."

Herbert laughed. "You're dreaming, then," he said. "Do you really think anyone survived this?" His sweeping gesture took in the damaged and destroyed flats, one with its stairway exposed, a bloody handprint pressed at intervals against the plaster wall like a stencil. The print was small, feminine-looking, Mrs. Keever or Miss Styles, and it stopped at the first floor; Claus would have to see if either was at a nearby shelter or hospital. Both worked as volunteers.

"We assume survivors," Claus said. "You know that. Let's have the sheets."

Herbert handed him the clipboard with the list of apartment occupants.

"Who updated it last?" Claus said.

"Me."

Useless, then. Herbert merely filled in the forms after looking at the previous ones. Mrs. Larsen, for instance, Winifred's Swedish tenant, had left for Wales once the V-1s started coming, and Herbert had her listed as apartment-bound.

"Well, we can't go by these." Claus slapped the clipboard on a rickety table, where the dusty wind fluttered through its pages. Two buildings down, the Heavy Rescue workers were letting people with suitcases in, and one of the rescuers sent a message over to let Claus know they'd given the people half an hour. *Not sure the building will hold up beyond that. Anyone thought trapped in it?*

Claus scribbled a quick *No* and sent it back. When the rescuer got the note he waved at Claus and made his way toward him.

"You're in the right spot," he said.

"For what?"

"I swear," he said. "It was right here. We heard something."

"Something," Herbert said. "That's helpful."

"Someone calling out," he said. "Someone's alive, you mark my words."

For a long time the three of them stood listening, Claus growing agitated when men tossing aside rubble yelled; there was just the possibility that their voices would mask sound. Herbert pulled a bag of prunes from a side pocket and ate them, one after the other, without offering any, all the while watching the Salvage Corps girls carting away an armoire, their brass buttons flashing in the sun. It wasn't the girls Herbert was interested in, Claus thought, but the pile of chairs and mattresses and blankets and prams toward which the armoire was heading. He could sell those.

Finally Herbert said, "Anyone heard anything? A voice? Knocking?"

Claus tried to silence him with a chopping motion of his arm.

"You can hardly tell it was a building," Herbert said. "There'll be no one left alive beneath it."

"Well, we certainly won't hear if there is," Claus said. "Not with you going on."

"It wasn't a voice," the short one said. "A moan, rather."

After another few minutes they heard it.

"Could be worse," the Heavy Rescue man said, looking at Claus and smiling. "At least she's still got two walls standing."

"It's six stories on top of her," Herbert said. "No sense wasting our manpower."

Claus pointed, ignoring him. "We'll start digging there."

"Shouldn't Myra make that call?" Herbert said, plainly in no hurry to work. "Otherwise, who'll coordinate?"

"She'll be here soon. And things seem to be going fine on their own. If that changes, we'll worry about it then. You can take over, if necessary."

That seemed to mollify him as it involved less digging.

Early on, Winifred's husband came home and began calling, "Fred! Fred!," his face distorted by grief, but Claus didn't go out to see him. What could he possibly say? He chopped through a bit of wood with his ax, then kept digging, turning up a pile of plaster and a set of keys bound by a bright pink ribbon. Not Winifred's; perhaps Mrs. Dodd's from the apartment above. He scooped it into the basket and handed the full basket to Herbert, who handed it on to someone else and returned Claus an empty one. Later he came across three books, identically bound in cheap imitation leather, and thought of Kate's collection; he had the odd desire to tear them apart.

After two hours they had a three-foot tunnel and Claus called for silence. Winifred's name, tapping on beams that canted farther into the wreckage, whistles; nothing got a response. He squeezed one finger meditatively, watching blood ooze out over the torn, dirty skin, wondering if he'd cut it pulling out ceramic plumbing fixtures or passing up timber and parts of chairs, and looked up at Herbert, standing above him on mounded bricks.

"Won't help, wearing yourself out," Herbert said. "Let someone else have a go."

Genuine concern or just laziness? Claus couldn't make out his face since the sun was now directly overhead, so reading his expression was impossible, but either way he was right; Claus hadn't realized how long he'd been working, how tired he was, how much his back hurt. He took Herbert's extended hand and climbed up from the hole, pulling his shovel after him. A redhead crawled down in his place and Claus stood bent over on the debris, crossed hands resting on the shovel handle, forehead resting on them.

The afternoon heat clouded the air. He caught a whiff of his own sweat and heard an excited buzzing. A rescue? No, a mobile canteen, its arrival marked by the steady stream of men heading toward a cleared patch, Archie among them. Herbert caught Claus's eye and nodded toward it.

"Go," Claus said. "I'm not ready yet."

Herbert made his slow way down the piled rubble and Claus wondered if he'd return. *CDS* had been chalked on some nearby buildings, which meant they'd been searched and found free of casualties. Near the closest one a cluster of Heavy Rescue men stood smoking, three of them shirtless, browned from the dust. A tall one took a pair of glasses sitting on a post, cleaned them on his shirt, and put them on. "That'll do," he said. Though no one had asked, he said, "Lost my own in an explosion."

Then he squatted and began picking things up, slipping them one by one into his pocket. He must have felt watched.

"A potato," he said, removing one and holding it up toward Claus. His tongue was bright pink inside his dusty brown face. "You're not thinking it's somebody's, are you? Could be anyone's, after all. No sense wasting it, the way I see it."

Claus shrugged and took his place in the line of men handing wicker baskets back, one after the other, until they reached a spot they could be safely dumped. That the potatoes might be Winifred's didn't matter; she wouldn't miss them and at least it suggested he was digging in the right place. Half an hour later word was passed back that they'd heard a noise again, and for a while the work seemed to go easier, though that let his mind drift once more to Bertram.

*Did she ever know your whereabouts when you weren't together and hadn't told her you'd been somewhere?*

*No. Well, yes, once. But that made perfect sense. Greta had seen me.*

*Greta?*

*A probationary nurse.*

*Ah yes,* he'd said. *The German.*

*You're wrong there,* he'd said. *She was here before the war started.*

*Yes, and Mrs. Zweig arrived after. Are you saying that makes her a spy?*

After another three hours the man in front of Claus, shirtless, his dun-colored back runneled with sweat, straightened and removed his Civil Defense beret to wipe his face, grumbling about the idiocy of their task.

"Bloody wild-goose chase," he said, to no one in particular.

Claus had to keep himself from snapping and decided to break; otherwise, he'd soon be useless. He stood in line for the relief canteen—a completely blacked-out bus that served tea, coffee, and sandwiches from the conductor's platform—and tried to uncurl his fingers; in the first two minutes he straightened three of them. The men in front of him were all coughing up dust, and the site was still swarming with workers. News of the explosion would reach the papers, where it would be recorded as having happened in "southern England." Finally it was his turn and he took the offered sandwich and scalding tea and swallowed half of the tea at once, trying to clear dust from his throat, while standing with his hand on the platform rail.

A female auxiliary firefighter, dressed vaguely like a nurse, lifted his hand.

"Can I fix that up for you?" she said.

Claus pulled his hand away and said, sharply, "I'm fine."

"I was only trying to help." Her voice sounded teary and he looked at her for the first time, a young volunteer, her face reddening from embarrassment.

He mumbled an apology and walked to where the other men squatted in a small cleared space behind the bus, eating their sandwiches or staring silently into their tea.

*The new communication plan from the Abwehr. Had you not worked for the MOI, what would have been the most difficult thing about the whole process?*

*Finding a microscope. To read the microdot photographs.*

*Yes. And as a nurse, Mrs. Zweig has access to microscopes all the time.*

Claus had parried that thrust, but others were harder to turn aside.

*What route did you take to work the day she met you?*

*Through the park, as I often do. The necessary routine, we said. But I don't follow it every day.*

*Not every day, no. But often enough. How do you know she hadn't been there weeks before, hoping to meet you? Perhaps it was just that this time she was successful.*

He'd looked down at his notes, playing up the drama.

*Why didn't you tell me she was German when you first met her?*

*She's English. She married a German.*

*And lived there for more than twenty years.*

*And I grew up speaking German. It doesn't mean we like Hitler.*

But then he'd paused.

*What? Something about her trip you up?*

*Nothing. You're wrong, that's all. I'm convinced of it.*

Bertram observed Claus. *Quite a coincidence that you met her at the park, but let's leave it aside. What about Cupid's Arrow? Had you ever seen her there before?*

*No.*

*She'd been there, several times, and hasn't been back once since meeting you.*

*Why would she go back? She's already met me.*

*Precisely.*

Claus had meant that she liked him and therefore wouldn't be looking to meet anyone else but couldn't think fast enough in the face of Bertram's certainty.

One of the tea drinkers broke the silence. "What's 'e after?"

Their heads swiveled as one. Near the Anderson shelter a man was collecting the dead sparrows, stuffing them in a birdcage.

"Dinner," another man said, to general laughter.

Claus saw black. His activity seemed as pointless as theirs, digging through tons of rubble to find someone they hadn't heard from in hours. Then he was distracted by a buzz bomb, its cranky engine sounding to the south.

"'Ere's one bird 'e won't be after," the first man said.

They all watched its even flight across the skyline, heading a little north of them, until it dipped below a steeple. The ground shook, but not terribly; the edge of their sector. Maybe Beechum's hadn't been so lucky this time. Claus hoped the fire watchers had been able to get down from its roof.

He poured out the tea dregs, splattering his boots, put his mug on the window ledge of the bus, and headed back, Herbert walking beside him. From his numb silence, he must have been working the entire time too, which surprised Claus. They made their way to the front of the line of men clearing the site and tapped others on their shoulders and told them to break for tea, and as the last man came out, blinking in the light, Claus crawled down the tunnel—ten or eleven feet deep now—and began digging. The dust had turned to mud, the beams were wet, they were near the bottom of the cellar where the water would be pooled. If he didn't find her soon, he wouldn't find her at all.

He clawed at the debris, ignoring the pain in his fingers, pushing the mud and splintered lathe and chunks of damp, heavy plaster back over his legs; the work took on a surreal rhythm, him digging out the debris and pushing it back over himself and crawling a few inches forward to start all over again. The things he wanted to do to Kate. Bend her over in only stockings and braces, lean her up against the wall while he knelt before her, face buried in her tap pants, inhaling the mixture of scents: the faintest tang of sweat, lavender, her arousal. Her head, tilted back, would bump against the wall as her fingers worked in his hair. The lavender sachet she stored with her lingerie was the second gift of the German surgeon, the one she'd kept. Who had never touched her, she assured him. He was no longer sure he believed her. Betrayal as an aphrodisiac. It made no sense.

Then he decided it did, that he was seeking release in the physical, as he had sought communion with her almost from the start, she with one knee bent over his shoulder, the other leg wrapped around his back, skin and nerves and breath, the intrusive world locked out. So tantalizing. And he was seeking absolution too, from his own guilt at not having trusted her enough to prevent a single one of Bertram's doubts from entering his own thoughts, where they multiplied and threw vast shadows across his recent past. *How long have you worked there? How do you know about the parachutes? Oh, you'd be surprised at what I'm capable of.*

And he'd told her about passing on information to higher-ups in the ministry. If she was a German spy, would she think that meant he'd been lying to the Germans all along? How many people had he endangered? What a fool. It was like sinking into bed at the end of an exhausting day and finding his pillow stuffed with roofing nails.

The digging continued. After a time he had a mental image of himself as a giant mole, tunneling to nowhere, his reverie broken only when he felt someone tapping the heel of his boot with a hammer, and he shimmied back out to a wider opening to find the short Heavy Rescue man.

"Someone's after you, I think," he said.

Above them a voice called. "Any wardens about?"

"Down the hole," someone else said.

Where had Herbert gone? Claus left off scraping mud from his thighs and looked up when a shadow darkened the opening.

"A post was hit," the man said.

A piano board was holding up part of his tunnel; Claus rested his hand on it. "Which one?" he said.

"Eight," the man said.

Claus's hand started to tremble, as if he were plucking at the piano strings. The Heavy Rescue man watched him without saying anything, and Claus tucked his hand under his armpit to hide it.

"Anyone hurt?"

"One dead."

Myra would be around here somewhere, overseeing the incident, but it was possible Herbert had gone back. Lawford, Williams, Rosalyn. He hoped it wasn't any of them, and he felt peculiar trying to decide who he'd sacrifice—the kind of game he might have played as a child, though now with real consequences—and decided to continue digging as a way to occupy himself.

"Thanks," he said, and turned and squatted and crawled ahead. The debris was cold when he lay down, and he wished he hadn't taken off his shirt. When it was his turn to break, the man was just making his way to the head of the tunnel again.

"Heard the gal's name," he said, "if you're interested."

Rosalyn. Claus felt a pang of sadness. She'd always been a lascivious flirt, eighteen with the freckled innocent face of a thirteen-year-old, enormous feet, and the mouth of a Piccadilly Commando. Early on he'd discovered she liked to pepper her buttered toast and had kidded her about it often.

"Myra Thornton," the man said. "Stupid, too, the way it happened. Just coming out of the post and blown across the street into an open car. Sitting there as if waiting to go."

"For fuck's sake," Claus said. Madge and Myra, perhaps Winifred. Who else were these damn bombs going to get, and why hadn't he changed their landing coordinates? It was inexcusable that he hadn't. Bertram could go to hell.

"Sorry," the man said. "Thought you'd want to know."

Claus turned away.

"Maybe you should quit for a while," the man said. "Have some tea."

"No. Not now. Later." He didn't want to stop. At least while he worked there was the chance that Winifred was alive.

The man tugged at Claus's sleeve and pointed at the sky. "Best wait," he said. "Here comes another. If it hits close enough, the tunnel could collapse."

Claus pulled his arm free and went back to digging.

*Has she had any contact with American military?*

*Of course. You can't avoid it. They've swarmed the city, for God's sake.*

*Yes. But anything closer?*

*He'd shrugged. One that I'm aware of. A major. A medical procedure.*

*You were there for it?*

*No. She told me.*

*Ah, and we should trust that. And by any chance would he be in intelligence?*

*How should I know?*

*You didn't notice his markings?*

*They don't put intelligence badges on their uniforms, and in any case, he approached her first.*

*Yes. But think. Some of your contacts met you, not the other way around. And who has she met so far? This major, the German nurse, exactly the people she'd want to meet if she were a spy.*

*The German nurse? What possible use could Greta be to the Germans?*

*Not her, the family she was a nanny with. The man's RAF general staff. She's not supposed to have any contact with them now, but that doesn't mean she hasn't. He intervened years ago to keep her from being interned. Who knows what she knows? And Mrs. Zweig herself. You said she was bitter at England.*

*Understandably.*

*Agreed. The blockade was not one of our finest hours. Given that, what would prevent her from acting on that bitterness?*

*I haven't acted on my bitterness toward America. Just the contrary. With some prompting.*

That had surprised Claus, the first time Bertram had acknowledged any level of coercion. But his surprise had been short-lived.

*And what's to say she didn't leave something behind that has allowed the Germans to prompt her?* Bertram had said.

*Left what behind? Her husband's dead.*

*So she's told us. But even if he is dead, who knows what else might still have a hold over her? All it would take is some relative she's inordinately fond of. Emotions can lead one to disaster quite easily.*

It turned dark before they were done. Wardens kept saying, "Lights," when they heard V-1s, which was infuriating; dousing their flashlights meant they had to stop digging, and for what? A full moon and the V-1s with no pilots. Claus didn't have the strength to argue and had said "Lights" himself on too many jobs; now he ignored them.

Beneath two crossed beams the digging grew suddenly easier, and Claus and a beefy, bearded Heavy Rescue man crouched side by side. The beams groaned above them, sprinkling them with dust, and Claus was conscious of the man's worry, the overpowering smell of his sweat.

"It's all right," he said, to calm him. "We'll find her soon."

Just then those above them doused their lights, and in the dark the groaning of the beams seemed louder, the sprinkling dust heavier.

"We can't stay here, chum," the man said.

"Please," Claus said. "It's just a few minutes."

When flashlights came on again the man said, "I'm done for," and turned away, tripping over a piece of wood sticking up from a nearby mound. He squatted and said, "Look at that," as he pulled it up. It had pierced an arm, like a convenient handle. He dropped the arm and it raised a small cloud of dust as flies swarmed over it. He picked it up and dropped it again.

"Stop that," Claus said.

"What are you going on about then?" the man said. "She was for a goner before ever you started digging, you knew that. It's others we've been looking for, and if you ask me, no one, just the groaning wood."

"Hold this." Claus handed the man his flashlight and cleared away rubble. The soft give beneath his hand nearly made him sick, the brown stain of dried blood clotted with flies, the apron with its blue parrots. Until the moment her limp arm sprang free and he recognized her apron he'd hoped that she was still alive, had managed, despite all indications to the contrary, to survive. It took minutes to uncover Winifred's chalky face, her hair a mess of plaster and wood and strips of wallpaper, and he found himself crying and saying, "I'm sorry," over and over as he combed her hair with his fingers.

She hadn't even tried to get under a table. Her Morrison shelter was nearby, but she'd never used it. With her radio on, she wouldn't even have heard the bomb. He felt a sudden urge to know what was being broadcast when it fell.

"What time did it hit again?" he asked the beefy man.

"Don't know. I'll ask." He shouted a question back up the tunnel, and the answer echoed back down the line to them. "Eight oh-seven," he said. After a pause he asked, "Knew her, did you?"

Claus nodded, but he was thinking of the radio. What would have been on then? Letters probably, from Canada and the various fronts. She would have been daydreaming about Harry.

"Maybe you'd be better off going on," the man said. "I'll stay with her until the doc comes."

She wouldn't be officially dead until the doctor said so, but Claus was irrationally angry, convinced that the man was a body rifler. "You go," he said. "I'll wait until they take her to the morgue."

"Suit yourself." The other man gathered up his shovel and flashlight. "Got the living to find." He squatted, knelt, and crawled out of the hole, some of the tunnel wall crumbling behind his retreating boots, and Claus was alone with Winifred. His breathing caught in his chest again—the end of sobbing—then slowed. Waiting for the doctor, he occupied himself by keeping the flies away from her face and trying not to breathe in her smell along with the dusty air.

HURRYING THROUGH THE DESERTED, moonlit streets toward Kate's apartment, he checked his watch: 4:00 A.M. No wardens would be out looking for strangers, as it was always the hardest time for them; cards abandoned, awful tea gone, stories told, little to do but sit and stare. Kate would have a story too. He wanted to know what it was.

Her neighborhood seemed dead: deserted flats, shuttered stores, not a single noise to disturb it aside from the occasional buzz bomb flying over and the crackle of ack-ack. Piccadilly Circus had been crowded—sleepy tarts huddled near the warm underground entrance in the chilly air—but even the usual dull rumble of the city was inaudible here.

White Horse Street with its high dark apartment buildings sent his footsteps echoing back to him. He felt unsafe, as he always did in unfamiliar surroundings. In his own sector he knew the strong doorways, where the public and private shelters were, and that someone would start looking for him within the hour should he go missing. Not true here. But more powerful still was the old, unfounded, superstitious belief in the invulnerability of home.

A buzz bomb sounded just above him—had he not been paying attention?—and he lay down in a mucky gutter outside Shepherd Market where the storefronts were still miraculously intact. It passed over, and he stood, less certain of what he'd intended. Perhaps he should turn back. Then he dismissed the thought. He had to reassure himself, to prove Bertram wrong, and he had to tell someone about Winifred and Myra. He stood looking at Kate's windows for a long time, but he didn't know the police routines here. Sooner or later one would be along and he had no explanation for what he was doing.

The front door was open, Kate's rooms unlocked. Breathing heavily, he pushed open the door and called her name. She didn't answer, and he stepped in, shut the door behind him, and stood listening to low voices. Did she have a visitor? Music struck up and he thought of her radio. Had she been deceiving him about her husband and her loneliness, or had she not wanted him to touch the radio, afraid of what he might discover? But no, someone else was awake in the building, playing a Victrola; too late for the radio. He called Kate's name again, louder, in case she was sleeping.

Like a good citizen she'd cracked her windows against blasts, and the noises of the city drifted through them. He closed the kitchen blackout curtains, nearly knocking a glass off the windowsill, which he held to his nose and sniffed. Scotch. What was it doing there, aside from collecting plaster dust each time a bomb exploded nearby? He drank it in a single gulp and gasped. It must have been Herbert's, not the major's; only someone with Herbert's connections could get something so good. He had to refill the glass twice with water before his breath came easily again.

A silver bowl was stuffed with pinecones. Then she'd been to the cemetery again, to clean the graves. Had he missed something there? He hefted a pinecone, and black dust speckled his hand, spices, cinnamon and cloves. All of them were sprinkled with it. Scents mattered to Kate. Long years of going without them, she'd told him, yet spices were expensive. Where was she getting them? Contacts at the hospital, maybe; perhaps the American major was in the picture again.

Her radio was English, but that was meaningless. He picked it up and turned it over, tapped its sides. None of the panels seemed fake or hollow. He removed all of the screws from the bottom and lifted the case, finding wires, tubes, and everything else where they should be, but there was a chance it was a new model, something he was unfamiliar with, so he broke two tubes in their sockets and loosened some of the wiring. At the very least it would take her a bit of effort to repair.

A bowl was on the counter, filled with brown, coarse flour, stockings stretched over the bowl to be used as a sieve. Illegal, but he'd broken dozen of petty regulations himself, he couldn't condemn her for that. On a chair was an outrageously large hat, the style in Paris, he'd heard, but certainly not in London. A gift? Beneath it was a rail ticket to Bristol for the following weekend. Bertram had commented on her occasional weekend trips.

*It's where she's from. But it's also where American convoys arrive. Rather too convenient.*

He fingered the ticket, pricked by a troubling sliver of doubt, longing for certainty. Why should she inform him of every detail of her life? They hadn't known each other that long. Still, it was suspicious. Bertram had mentioned her trip to Hamburg from Paris in 1943. On her passport had been stamped *German Army Interpreter,* a pass she claimed to have received from a German she'd treated in the hospital, and necessary if she was to go to Hamburg. Bertram maintained it proved she'd gone to receive instructions from the Germans. Claus had told him what she'd found there, all that Marie had endured.

*And does any of that prove her innocence? Or just that she's a precise observer?*

Claus unwound a long cantaloupe-colored scarf from the hat brim and filled a bowl with water and dunked the scarf, looking for bleeding ink, but nothing came of it, nor of a box of rolled-up toothpaste tubes on her bureau, where she might have stored small tools. A good girl then, doing as she was bid, saving metal. But not with the stockings. She was like everyone, obeying as many rules as possible, breaking the ones that seemed absurd. Like he did.

He took up one of her journals. Details of a busy surgical day in eastern Prussia—removing teeth from the legs of one man, an eyeball from the back of another; human shrapnel, she called it—then Hamburg in 1923, Kate and Horst, having almost recovered from the blockade, eating dinner in a café and ordering everything at once, including dessert, just so they'd know what they would be charged; otherwise, the prices might go up between the time they sat down and the time they paid.

Beyond that, Claus wasn't sure where to begin. What could he read that would prove Kate's innocence? Dozens of postcards fell out as he riffled the pages, Belgian beaches, Parisian landmarks, Rouen's enormous crumbling cathedral. Bertram had mentioned two that she'd had with her when she'd first arrived.

*Not that there was much to search,* he'd said, *given how quickly she was supposed to have left. A single handbag stuffed with clothes, pictures, a bit of silver. And two peculiar postcards. One of them seemed to be in some kind of code, but we couldn't understand it.* He'd shown Claus pictures. *You'll see they were never sent.*

Claus had studied them, both apparently from Berlin. Of one he'd said, *Those are poetic meter markings.*

*That's what she claimed. But we doubted it. There's no poem, for one thing.*

Puzzling but not alarming; certainly nothing the Germans had ever asked him to do. *Anything else suspicious?*

*Only a map of England in German, which she claimed came from a 1940 newspaper that she'd held on to in ironic protest; the Germans had told them the maps were "to keep track of future developments." She said that when the Germans hadn't invaded, she was glad.*

*And you don't believe her?*

*It's hard to tell. Such maps were printed in newspapers, and hers is of the proper time and typeface. Many other refugees have them. Still, we kept it.*

Impossible to decipher. Like any German refugee, Kate had been brought to Glasgow and underwent a routine examination at the Royal Victorian Patriotic School, ostensibly to see if she knew anything of German troop distributions. Evidently Kate had told them about a few Germans from a certain regiment that they hadn't known about, and other, later immigrants and the French underground confirmed the information; those troops were indeed in northern France, which could be of great importance for the invasion.

Still, they were suspicious, so she'd been sent to Camp 020, Latchmere House, in southwest London, used to turn spies. But she'd not revealed anything, because, she'd maintained, she wasn't a spy, and because her interrogators, unusually, had nothing to use against her—no Abwehr intercepts about her, no information that a spy was coming. They'd let her go, to Bertram's great dissatisfaction.

*So far she's outsmarted us, but she can't do it indefinitely, no woman could.* He was entirely dismissive of women as spies. *Even Edith*

*Cavell was responsible for her own death. She gave her address to those she'd rescued, and the fools wrote to thank her when they reached England! The Germans intercepted the letters, and that was it. No man would ever be so sentimental as to give away his address.*

It was peculiar that he and Kate had also discussed Cavell, but Claus didn't mention this. Defiantly, he'd said, *It's possible that Mrs. Zweig isn't a spy.*

*Possible, but unlikely. And I have to know.*

Bertram had gone on to reveal that they'd told Kate her Paris apartment had been searched by the Gestapo after she'd left—a routine event—and that her response had been what one would expect. *Concern for the person, not the belongings.* He'd consulted his notes again. *She asked about her concierge, a woman named Madame Dufair.*

*In other words, if she's an actor, she's the best yet?* Claus had said.

*Yes. Which is why I don't trust her. Sooner or later, they were bound to find someone who was good at it. Not every German can be a fool.*

*She's not German.*

*But she might be a sympathizer.*

*Yes. Of course. As I was during the last war.*

*Your American accusers were amateurs. We've been doing this a bit longer.*

In her closet, a man's faded flannel shirt had a German label, probably a memento of her husband. And of course there was the threadbare military overcoat. He stood looking at it for a long time— the music in the other apartment switched to another song—and thought about slicing open the lining, but knew he couldn't. She'd link its destruction to him. Who else but he would know about it? He pinched the seam of the lining between finger and thumb and ran down one lapel. A few lumps—they might contain microdots, for all he knew—but he wasn't going to find out. Before it made him too angry, he stopped.

That she had it made sense. She would have sent it on along with everything else back in the thirties: journals, books, a few pieces of furniture, though even those Bertram viewed with suspicion. What better way for a spy to insinuate herself than to have all her resources in place before hostilities actually began? It frustrated Claus. What, exactly, was he looking for? Since she readily admitted to having lived in Germany, nothing from Germany was necessarily incriminating, and nothing in this well-ordered apartment held a clue, or rather it all did, but clues that could be read any number of ways.

On the shelf was the blue builder's chalk they'd used on their cemetery outing, next to her perfume bottles with their decorative stoppers: a nude wrapped in a floral scarf. Hoffman. He grabbed one, pulled the stopper, inhaled. It was comforting and he did it again until the scent lost its power, when he put the bottle on her bedside table to rest his nose. At a noise behind him he turned swiftly, an explanation already forming on his lips, knocking over the bottle with his elbow. It shattered on the floor. No one was behind him—the building had simply settled—but what was he going to do now?

For a long minute he stood looking at the perfume pooling on the floor around the shiny broken ceramic shards, then pushed over a stack of books and sent them tumbling, to make it seem like a robbery. He'd seen enough of those to make it look believable, and as he pulled apart the lavender sachet from her drawer, he found it oddly satisfying to create here some of the disaster, on however small a scale, that he'd spent hours digging through elsewhere, and suddenly he was destroying everything, knocking over and tearing down and ripping indiscriminately, saying, "That's for Winifred and that's for Winifred and that's for Myra," which only fed his fury.

When he was done, his breathing was labored and his nose was running and the air was filled with feathers. Some stuck to his damp hands, and, looking at his feathered fingers, he couldn't believe what he'd done. What had he accomplished? He was no closer to the truth—whatever that might be—and Kate's apartment was in shambles, and now he felt guilty in addition to powerless. What a fool.

He grabbed a handful of clothes and tucked them under his arms along with several of her journals, the earliest, the most recent, and three or four random ones, then hurtled out the door and down the steps into the street, where despite his worry that the police would mistake him for a looter he began to run. A stupid thing to do, committing one crime to cover another, though what that original crime was he couldn't say. Having doubted Kate? Or not having doubted her enough?

THE HEAT AND UNMOVING AIR made the smell of formaldehyde seem stronger. Feet kept tapping by in the busy hallway and now and then Claus lifted his head, but mostly he sat and stared at his script. His long absence had doomed the film, though Max had tried to soften the blow.

"Hold on to it," he'd said, returning a copy. "It's very good. Perhaps after the war you can have it made commercially. It might be even better that way." The time for propaganda films had come and gone, the possibility of funds vanished. "I'm keeping the other copy, just in case that changes. And I'm bringing it to every meeting that might have the remotest mention of funding. I'll have something ready—something *good*—to show them."

Max's kindness had been hard to bear; it smacked of pity, and Claus detected in it a tone of resigned fatherly understanding that Max had used with others from his days at Strand Films, people who'd thought they might be able to work their way back into the business under his auspices at the MOI. Max always had to tell them they couldn't.

Claus shoved the script aside, Kate's journals too. The entries detailing her arrival in England, her time in France, her final years in Hamburg, were written upside down in different-colored ink between earlier entries from years ago. Reading them, especially those covering Horst's decline and death, had drained him. Her hand was slightly changed: a greater slant to the letters, tighter loops; older and wiser, perhaps, certainly sadder. How could she not be? But upside-down writing was hard to follow if you weren't trained to mentally block out the other lines, something the Germans had schooled him in by scissoring out every other line on a sheet of blank paper. If Bertram was right, she'd have learned the same method from the same masters.

In his apartment, he'd laid one page flat on the ironing board, the gentle heat of the iron meant to bring out any organic inks—lemon, most likely, as she'd had so many. After a few passes with the iron he peered closely, found nothing. Next was vaporized iodine, which no hidden writing could withstand, but having neither the requisite tin oven nor the time to purchase one, he'd mixed powdered iodine, water, and a bit of crushed aluminum in his sink and stood back from the explosive reaction, the acrid purple vapor that browned the paper and settled wherever the page had been disturbed. There'd been no secret inks and no hidden messages, no obvious reason to mistrust her, only the visible and now discolored lines.

He'd felt a dupe holding the mess, unsurprisingly; the spy Bertram suspected her of being wouldn't be caught so easily. Then he'd sat and read. His own name was in the final entry, along with Sylvie's. Sylvie had asked her to walk after their shift and Kate had agreed, but soon came to regret it. They seemed to have little to talk about, and soreness pulsed from her ankles to her calves the longer they went. Her face was cold, her eyelids weighted, the silence between them grew and grew; she felt she could almost lean against it. At Park Square, Sylvie steered her onto a curving gravel path where, in a small declivity surrounded by dying elms, a sparse crowd sat listening to an orchestra play some early Delius. *Appalachia.* The calm violin gave way to the rushing Dixieland trumpets, pounding drums superceded the trumpets, and then all yielded to the delicate triangle. Sylvie's touch on her elbow stopped her.

Sylvie had leaned against the back of a wooden bench and began to hum along as a gust of wind stirred up the scent of decaying leaves. Her humming seemed somehow intimate, and Kate felt a surge of warmth for her, almost affection.

The piece ended, the rim of the eastern sky deepened to indigo, and the surrounding granite buildings, pink moments before, faded to a pearlescent gray. Their way back toward the park entrance wound along the path, wet grass brushing their ankles, and they passed a beggar, a mother with three young children. Young herself—her dirty face looked no more than sixteen—she squeezed two of the children between her knees while holding the third upright on her shoulder to stop its crying. Her laddered brown stockings bagged around her ankles, and her collarless coat had no buttons; she held it closed with the same red hand she used to support her colicky baby. Kate had felt so close to Sylvie until she'd made the comment about the beggar being a Jew.

The force of her anger and guilt was the kind of thing she would have shared with Horst, she'd written, and that she wanted to share it with Claus stunned her; she hadn't understood he meant that much to her. It seemed almost a betrayal of Horst, leaving Germany for France, France for England, and there meeting another man, as if layer by layer she'd sloughed off all their years together, move by move their shared past, and now was creating a new communal future with someone else.

If she was a spy the lines had probably been planted on the off chance Claus would read them, but he couldn't help wishing she'd written more. An earlier journal contained a passage from her German postwar years. Horst was alive but turning reclusive, and Kate had written of her peculiar, troubling feelings. Before the war Horst had been glamorous and it had felt noble to sacrifice every bit of her past to join him in exile, and during the war, regardless of the rightness of the German cause, they'd done what they could to save and restore shattered human lives, but in the long years after, nearly all of her family gone, she found herself increasingly isolated in Germany, neither fully German nor completely English. One Christmastime, the blockade long over, the hyperinflation past, a bit of political stability settling on the city, she'd begun frequenting an English store in the fashionable Harvestehude district.

Carols had poured from a Victrola that was wrapped in a plaid ribbon for the holidays and surrounded by cured hams—one was "Good King Wenceslas," Kate's favorite. She'd stood beside it, reminded of the poulterers in London, the fat geese and slimmer ducks hanging from overhead hooks, as she hummed along with the boys' choir, her nose vibrating on the lower notes as the king pushed on through the snow. When he'd completed his mission of mercy, she chose four Bosc pears and half a dozen exotic oranges and moved on to the lemons, where she'd paused, wondering if she should restore the holiday tradition of her childhood, a blue ceramic bowl of them in the kitchen on the coldest, darkest days of the year. For tea, to spice the punch, to put on the Dutch oven spiked with cloves like a pincushion, as an ingredient in her father's favorite cookies. One couldn't control for such things, so why not give in a bit to the past, since it was so insistent? She'd dropped a half a dozen in her bag and moved on.

In line, she'd found herself behind a tall woman with a streak of silver in her hair and a festive green and gold holiday scarf knotted elegantly at her neck. Partridges and pear trees with a running border of holly, the small irregular berries bright as rubies.

Kate touched the woman's arm. "What a beautiful scarf," she'd said in German.

"I'm sorry," the woman said, looking at her blankly. "I don't speak German."

Kate repeated what she'd said in English.

"Oh, this? Thank you." The woman fingered it and smiled. "From my son."

Kate had removed her hand when the woman's glance flicked over it, worried that her touch had been inappropriate; the English were particular about that and after so many years abroad she'd forgotten some of the rules. "He has exquisite taste."

The woman leaned closer and Kate caught a whiff of her perfume, Domaine dePuy, something she herself wore, which gladdened her. Perhaps they were kindred spirits. "I went with him to pick it out. If I didn't, I'd get something orange or purple. You know how sons are. They get their taste from their fathers."

Kate had smiled sympathetically and nodded.

The clerk rang up the woman's last purchase, bagged it, and announced the total, and the woman turned to pay. She waited for her change without resuming their conversation, and Kate reminded herself not to get her hopes up, but then took a chance anyway. It was the holiday season, after all, people tended to be more open, and the store's bright interior made the world seem less grim than it had in her darkened bedroom the night before. The season had awoken a desire for companionship that was hard to suppress, a desire for interaction with others not her family and that went beyond holiday greetings from a grocer and a mere exchange of pleas-antries with the girl who parceled out her medicines or the man who cut her hair.

"Does your son live nearby?"

"Yes." A quick shift of the head though not of the shoulders, which remained turned away, a briefer smile. "About a mile from here."

"Do you see him often, more than just the holidays?"

"No," she'd said, and folded her change and tucked it in her wallet, then dropped the wallet in one of the brown bags and scooped the bags into her arms. "This is my first time here, and probably my last. The truth is, I don't like the Germans." From around one of the bags she'd raised two fingers to Kate as she left. "Ta-ta."

The worst thing about both those scenes, Claus thought, was that they *were* scenes. They'd have been perfect for his movie, showing the returning refugee's loneliness, the things she'd had to overcome, and he'd have filmed them both, to show her life as an exile. He felt an upsurge of bitterness that he couldn't, of anger; for one mad moment he had an image of a vast conspiracy between Kate and Max and Bertram, their wanting him to think he could make a film and then crushing his dream.

Footsteps came closer, and an unfamiliar, heavyset woman stood in his doorway.

"Mr. Charles?" she said.

He recognized the voice, though it took him a second to place it, during which time she reached up to resettle her brown hat.

"Greta!" *The German,* Bertram had said. *Find out anything you can from her. Or at least* about *her.* He stood, embarrassed that he couldn't recall her last name, though not surprised she couldn't remember his.

"Yes." She smiled. "So you remember me. Good, I hope it is not with badness."

"Not at all." He came around the desk to take her hand. "Please, have a seat."

She sat and smiled, but her face looked troubled.

"I am sorry to say this, but you look the sick," she said. "Are you all right?"

He sat down behind his desk and said he was, though he knew he looked terrible. He didn't remember clearly what he'd done during the last twelve hours. More work as a warden, certainly, as someone had thanked him for helping her change a tire, and Mrs. Dobson had said early this morning that he looked quite the sight leading a goat out of the nearby stables with all the horses following him. She'd sounded insane so he hadn't responded and had gone to his room, where he'd found a doll on his bed that he didn't know if he'd put there as some kind of signal. He'd counted the plates in his sink to see if he'd had supper—he hadn't—and tried to take a bath, once again filling the tub beyond the black line. He'd known Mrs. Dobson was listening because the floor creaked as she shifted her feet outside the door, but he'd ignored her, though in the end she had her victory, as the water was tepid.

"I have heard that there is here something you might be able to help me with," Greta said. "A record. I'd like to want to make one."

"Oh. You sing? I didn't know."

Her cheeks reddened and she shifted her handbag on her knees. "To make one, yes, but not the singing."

She gazed at his desk, at Kate's journals, and he wondered if she recognized them. Unlikely, but he couldn't cover them right away or she'd notice. She turned her attention back to him and he was glad. "For my family?" She slipped into German—"*Meine Eltern?*"—then switched back to English. "They still to live there, you see. I was hoping to hear them my voice."

He was surprised to find himself flustered at her childish smile, so desperate and full of hope. As a warden he was used to helping people, sending them to the local salvage department to recover goods or to the city council for housing vouchers, but in the ministry he was never asked to do so. It made him feel out of place. He knew of people making wax recordings, a few simple words they could send abroad, to friends in Sweden, perhaps, who might send them on to Germany. "We don't do that here, I'm afraid. That would have to be a sound studio." Where they must have some controls, he thought, especially for those making records in German.

"Not here?" She was obviously trying to keep up her smile.

"No." He took out paper, letting the extra sheets fall and cover the journals, and scribbled an address of another MOI office that put out records.

Her lips moved as she sounded out the unfamiliar English words.

"Try them. It's in White City," he said, and watched her reaction. She didn't flinch or flush.

She read it again and smiled. "I know where it is," she said. "Near my church."

"Ah, you're religious," Claus said.

Without leaving her seat she turned and looked behind her. It was almost a parody of caution, something from the beginnings of the silent-film era. If Griffith had seen it, he'd have fainted.

She leaned toward him and whispered. "No," she said. "It's about the kaiser."

He shook his head, not understanding.

"Mrs. Zweig has told me you're part German. *Ja?*"

He nodded.

"I pray for him. The anniversary of his birth." Then she colored and put a hand to her mouth. "I should not to say anything. Please don't to tell. I could be in the trouble."

He tried to reassure her. No use scaring her off. She was either a genuine fool or a brilliant actor, as good as Kate if Bertram was right. And Kate's telling Greta of his ancestry fit either scenario. He couldn't keep her here any longer, so he stood and walked her to the door.

She held up the address before tucking it in her bag. "I can to say you told me?"

"Of course." He said goodbye to her. Max stood in the hallway, watching her go. Claus didn't want any more avuncular advice. He turned back, picked up the journals, and left, shutting the door behind him, walking by the smiling Max without stopping or speaking a word, unwilling to give Max the pleasure of being magnanimous.

'M AFRAID I HAVE plans for a picnic," Kate said. She stood in her doorway, looking displeased. He'd asked her to drive with him to the country but she'd still barely opened the door. He thought he could better clarify things somewhere they had no history. London had become theirs, them.

"Please," he said. "You must."

She raised one eyebrow. "Must?"

He rocked back on his heels and closed his eyes. Too forceful. He breathed out heavily and started again.

"I'm sorry. I need your help. That's all I mean."

"You do look terrible," she said. Her pause gave him hope. Then she said, "But as I told you, I have plans. A kind of picnic that we've arranged for the patients."

He smelled cooking, a baked pie crust. It made him wish for home. He stepped back. "I should go."

"Wait." She opened the door a fraction more. "Why did you disappear?"

"I was digging. My sector was hit hard. Our post too." He held up his hands to show his dirty fingernails. No matter how he scrubbed he couldn't get them clean.

"But Greta saw you, at the MOI. She told me."

"Yes. This morning." Is that why Greta had come? As a pilot fish for Kate?

"And before then?" Kate said. "Before you were digging? It can't have been five days straight. You never even called."

"I was arrested."

"Whatever for?"

"They thought I was a spy."

She laughed and tilted her head against the door. "I thought you worked for people 'higher up.'"

"I do. This wasn't them. This was the police."

She grew serious when she saw his expression. "They thought *you* were a spy?"

He shrugged. "It's not important. I was at a bomb site and they found me suspicious. When I realized that, I ran, and that made them certain."

"How awful." Outside, the air-raid sirens started up and he shifted from one foot to the other at the claxon's shrill call. She was watching him. "But even if I weren't already leaving, I have other things to do. Look at this." She pushed the door open and waved at her apartment, which was only partially reassembled.

"My God." He knew he sounded incredulous; he hadn't realized he'd been so thorough. "What happened?"

"Robbery, I think, though a peculiar one. A scarf, a jacket, and some shoes. Whoever it was seems to have been more interested in making a mess than anything else. He left big footprints everywhere, which seemed intentional, that blue builder's chalk. One was on my bed."

Had he done that? He didn't remember.

"And he was a cheeky bastard," Kate said. "Drank my scotch too."

"I'm sorry," he said.

"Why? It wasn't you, was it?"

He shook his head, unable to meet her eye though he knew she meant it rhetorically. "No, just that you have to go through it. I wish you didn't have to clean up. I wish you'd come with me."

She looked at him and sighed. "So your post was hit."

He fished a pack of cigarettes from his jacket pocket and gave her one. When he tried to light it, his hand shook so much the match went out. "Some friends died."

"Myra?" she said.

He nodded. "And Winifred."

She touched his arm. "Now it's my turn to be sorry. Uselessly, probably."

"Why uselessly?"

"One can't be sorry enough to bring back the dead."

She lit both their cigarettes, let him in, and walked to a window, where she stood looking down on the street, but she was going to go with him; she'd invited him into the apartment, after all. His trembling hand, perhaps, her nurse's training. But he had to be silent. If he pushed, she might pull back. He watched people on the street lining up for their public baths, women with rolled towels curled around their necks, hatless men.

Something in their movements seemed to decide her. "I have to make a phone call," she said, and reached for the phone. It was to Sylvie. After a bit of small talk she asked if Sylvie could cover her afternoon shift. "Yes," she said, "something's come up." Sylvie's voice was indistinctly loud on the other end. Kate laughed and said, "Yes, Claus."

So she'd told Sylvie about him. That could mean anything, but Bertram had sketched out Sylvie's history, White Russian parents living in Paris, friends of the Germans since the Germans were Soviet enemies. Kate had mentioned Sylvie's name in the hospital too, though Claus hadn't caught it then, drowsy from his concussion. Why were they still friends if Sylvie had so offended her?

Kate hung up and stood with her fingers resting on the heavy black receiver. Finally she said, "All right. I don't suppose this mess will miss me, and the patients will have others to bring them food."

Then she was bustling, packing pies and green bottles of wine and blue ones of cider and two entire bananas in a wicker hamper on the table. "I'm going to bring everything edible," she said. "Otherwise some bugger's likely to come back and steal it."

"My, this is ancient," she said, patting the car. In the hazy sunlight its black paint looked even duller. "Where did you unearth it?"

"The Old Muller," he said, reflexively, and wished he hadn't. He used to use the car without a second thought to its origins; that had become impossible after Dieter. Now he'd have to explain. "At the MOI. Someone left it to them in their will. Muller, whoever that was." A lie, but one he was used to telling, one that didn't pain him. Muller had been a spy in the last war, caught early on and executed, though the British had continued to send news from him and collect his money until the Germans decided his information was no longer good. The funds had purchased the car, and Claus had borrowed it today without explaining what he needed it for. Bertram's new girl was rather easy, with none of Madge's spunk. She wouldn't last long, Claus thought; Bertram would eat her up.

He nodded at the spare tire mounted on the faded black door. "I'm not very high status, you can see," he said.

"Higher than me," she said, sliding in. "And that you have petrol at all means you're very high indeed."

They passed over the Vauxhall Bridge and drove behind a windowless bus through Lambeth and Dulwich, which appeared oddly undamaged by bombs. But as they passed the bus and weaved through the double-decker tram traffic in Croydon, they saw that the devastation was total, entire blocks gone, others marked only by jagged foundations, and talking became impossible. Leaving Croydon, the car backfired twice, causing pedestrians to jump, and the farther they went the more the silence began to feel cumbersome, but after they passed through a wood and fields of sheep to reach Purley, where the organ was playing "God Save the King" at the ABC cinema, Kate said, "Let's hope *someone* saves him. If this goes on much longer, he'll need to be."

The countryside was beginning to roll. Claus turned southeast on the Godstone Road, and Kate shifted her feet, pushing aside a series of maps. "Going someplace special?" she said. "I suppose I should have asked sooner. A girl likes to know."

They rose up a hill toward a group of barrage balloons, sleek and silver in the summer sun, and Claus stopped beside their thicket of cables whistling in the wind.

"Past this," he said. "I want to get away from London, from the war, for a bit."

"I don't think we'll be able to do that in a car."

He laughed, a single bark. "No, I'm afraid not. Certainly not this one. But at least from its most obvious effects, somewhere that I won't have to see it."

A mile past Purley, farms spread out over the rolling hills and he began to relax. They reminded him of the Pennsylvania he'd grown up in, at least until Kenley, where the population grew heavy again; these dense towns in the middle of farmland, that was the main difference. She shifted beside him.

"I like your hat," he said.

She touched its purple felt rim. "Do you really? My first new one since 1939."

"It looks expensive."

"It is." She frowned. "We all got a bonus this week. One of the girls I work with took me to her milliner. My hat cost twice as much, because I'd never been to her before. On the other hand, she said that if I wasn't killed, she'd reduce the cost of the next one."

He wished she hadn't joked about it and fell quiet.

"Don't be sour, Claus. She's right."

"That doesn't mean I have to like it."

A marker said they were on the old Roman road, which led to the coast, and Kate clapped her hands. "Are we going to the beach?"

"Sorry, no." Claus turned off the car as they rose up to the edge of a steep scarf and let it coast down the hill. "Off-limits, I'm afraid, and we haven't the fuel for that."

"Listen to you," she said. "'Haven't the fuel.' You sound so English. Next you'll be playing cricket." Normally he liked their banter, but now it felt forced, a cover for something they both knew was amiss, so he didn't respond.

The road wound down to the valley, where trees sprung up on one side and a field of yellow rape bloomed on the other. Ahead was Whyteleafe, and from its dark, squat church came the sound of bells striking the hour.

"How different from France," she said, letting the wind push through her open fingers outside the window. He sensed she was searching for safe subjects. "All the bells there have been bundled off or buried. The Germans wanted to melt them down, and the French, naturally enough, didn't want them taken. If they acted quickly, they were able to bury them. If not, kaput."

"Let's listen to them, then," he said, coasting into town and pulling to a stop in the square. He set the parking brake with a savage yank.

Kate got out to stretch her back. The bells had already stopped. "I wouldn't want to travel too far in old Muller. He's not too kind to old bones."

"Not old," Claus said. From the glove compartment he took the driver's booklet. "Just not used to sitting in ancient cars."

Kate watched him fill out the booklet. "You didn't prepare," she said.

"I didn't think you'd come."

"Very good," she said, looking pleased. "But here I am. So what are you putting as the object of our trip?"

"Scouting locations for my film."

"And its necessity?"

"Very high." He snapped the book closed, put it back, and joined her outside the car, where she leaned against the warm hood. "The film needs to be done within weeks." He had decided not to tell her that his film had been canceled. She would be sad for him, or at least feign sadness, and that wasn't what he wanted. He wanted her to talk.

A young girl pedaled past on her bicycle, a dog in the basket, the noise of its barking barely audible over the racket the wooden wheels made on the cobbles, and beyond her two middle-aged men in sea green overalls were remounting Whytclcafc's road sign, which had been taken down in 1940 when the Germans were expected to invade.

"See?" Kate said. "Another reason to be happy. The war might end after all."

He leaned toward her and her lips parted slightly, as if expecting a kiss.

"Why did you let me walk you back to your place?" he said. "That night after the dance?"

"What?" she said, and pushed herself upright with her hip. "What a peculiar question." Her cheeks turned red.

He was glad he'd thrown her, a bit surprised, but he wasn't going to be sidetracked. "That night just keeps coming back to me," he said. Now he tried to put her at ease. "It's meant so much to me. It led to everything. I was thinking about it while in jail, and it just amazed me."

"You made me laugh again," she said. "That first meeting. Hyde Park."

"You didn't laugh."

"Not then. It had been so long. After. Some of the things you said, I found myself going over them all day at work. I didn't show it, but I was hoping to meet you again."

"I'm glad you did," he said.

"Me too."

Her smile was genuine, or so it seemed. It wouldn't do to show too much doubt. He leaned forward and kissed her, touched her jaw. As he pulled away he saw thick parallel bruises, low, on each side of her neck.

"My God," he said, spreading her collar with his fingers. "What are those?"

She put her hand to them. "A patient," she said. "Evacuated from Normandy. He woke as I was checking his temperature and grabbed me by the throat. Another patient had to whack his ribs to fully wake him."

"How horrible."

"Worse for him. The poor boy."

"He looks like he can take care of himself."

She shook her head, averted her eyes. "No. Couldn't. Jumped off the hospital roof the next day."

"I'm sorry," Claus said, knowing she'd be thinking of Horst. But as he held the door open for her and she got back in the car, he wondered. Was any of what she'd just said true? Or had all that information been planted specifically for him, to make her entire story plausible? Had all of her touching emotional moments been manufactured earlier, to be produced at the proper time, or, worse, was she merely a wonderfully intuitive actress who understood what was necessary in every scene and could unearth it? The giddiness when he supplied a word, the glimpses into a once-perfect life crumbling under the weight of uncontrollable events so neatly parallel to his own. Wouldn't Bertram be thrilled to know the despairing depths of his doubts.

Claus had turned off the engine again on the down slope, and when they rounded the corner past a stand of oaks they seemed to catch the Home Guard by surprise. One quickly stepped into the middle of the road and raised his right hand, palm out. Over his shoulder an older man was leaning against a tree, smoking a pipe. Briarwood, Claus thought. They looked like father and son, the father in his early fifties and the boy a teen, a younger and less puffy version of the older man, the same prominent Adam's apple, the same red ears, though the boy's uniform was too big for him, and his father had on a privately tailored one. The father was also wearing shoes rather than boots and anklets, which had been disallowed years before. He took his time inhaling on his pipe before covering the bowl with his thumb, at last tucking it into his breast pocket and walking slowly toward the driver's side, where he touched his cap and bade them both good afternoon.

"A routine check." He leaned on the door frame and smoothed his long white mustache, smelling of real cherry tobacco, which Claus hadn't come across since before the war. "Sorry to bother you."

"Keeping up regular patrols, are you?" Claus asked.

"Certainly. Now's the last time to let our guard down."

"Has Hitler got a secret plan to invade us while we're in Normandy?" Kate said.

"That's fine," Claus said, not wanting any difficulties. He cranked his window down farther. "I perfectly understand."

They chatted about the weather and local conditions, seemingly innocuous, but Claus knew the questions were designed to nose out information; he'd had the same training. Everything went fine until he asked Claus his name.

"Murphy."

"Irish, are you?"

"Yes."

Kate was too self-possessed to dart her eyes in his direction, but her hands tightened on her hat.

The colonel turned over Claus's identity card. "What's the *C* stand for? Conan? Colin? Colleen?"

His son laughed. "That's funny!"

Claus waited before responding, to show he wasn't amused, then said, "Charles."

"And what's yours?" the boy asked Kate.

"Zweig," she said, leaning forward to speak to the father.

"Zweig?" he said.

"*Zweig*." She pronounced it this time so that it sounded especially German and he dropped his foot from the running board and stood straighter. "German, is it?"

"Yes. My husband was German."

"And how about you, miss? Are you German?"

"I was born in Surrey." The man seemed to relax until Kate went on. "Though I did serve with him in a German field hospital during the last war."

"I see." His voice was clipped now. "And what's brought you our way?"

"An outing," Claus said, interrupting, still hoping they'd be let go without further trouble. "I work for the Ministry of Information. Official business."

"Get their book, will you, Brian?" the father said, and went to the back of the car to open the boot. Kate handed out the driver's booklet and the boy flipped through it while the father came forward with their hamper. "And where did you get all this?" he asked, bringing out the bottles of wine and cider. "Not black-market supplies, are they?"

"If they were," Kate said, "we wouldn't be bringing them *to* the country, would we?"

He pawed around the hamper a bit more, put the bottles back. "That's a nice hat."

Kate smiled and touched it. "Thank you."

"New, is it?"

"Just this week."

"They're quite expensive, aren't they?"

Kate leaned toward him. "Is there a reason for these questions? A hat-smuggling ring at work hereabouts, perhaps?"

He lowered the hamper to the roadway, the bottles clinking, and asked his son for the booklet. "You'd be surprised how clever these black-marketers can be," he said, and paged through it. "Bound for Godstone, are you?"

"Yes. I have to find what kind of damage the V-1s are doing, for a movie."

The young one bent down. "That'd be much worse in London, I should think."

"No doubt. But I was still asked to check."

The older man stood and waved the driver's booklet over the roof of the car. "That's what it says here," he said. "We can let them go, I think."

Claus started to open his door to return their things to the boot, but the colonel stopped him. "No need to get out," he said. "I'll put the hamper back."

His sudden about-face puzzled Claus, but he wasn't going to ask the reason behind it. Kate said, very loudly, "Come, Claus. Let's be off."

The father didn't seem to hear, but the boy cocked his head. "Claus?"

"Her nickname for me."

"All right," he said, and tapped the roof twice.

As they drove off through fields of rape, Kate said, "Nickname?"

"I didn't want more trouble."

He braced himself to go on, but she responded before he could. "I know. I'm sorry. I do have a tart tongue. But he wasn't the type to do anything."

"Oh?"

"Yes. I ran into many of them in France. If you'll pardon me saying so, they bring out the bitch in me."

"Run-ins with the law?"

"Stupid ones, and my own fault, really. Twice I was nearly arrested because I insisted on speaking English."

"To the police?"

"Hospital administrators. Don't worry," she said when he looked at her. "I wasn't aiming to get shot. French administrators, not German. They had framed letters over their desks saying they'd been fired by Germans for being unsupportive, but with both it was a question of timing. They'd been collaborating all along and then got out just early enough to prove that they were against the Germans."

"Late patriotism is better than none."

"It has nothing to do with patriotism. If the Allies win, after the war such a letter proves they were good. It's a license to print money. And people like that are no less prominent here. Those two aren't the first. I ran into quite a few when I came over."

"Oh? You were interrogated?" At Latchmere House, suspected spies were stripped naked and confronted by a screaming officer while their clothes were gone through, their stories repeated and checked, repeated and checked. He'd helped with a few such interrogations.

284

"What's terrible is that you're certain they don't believe you."

"They must have. They let you go."

"Yes. But I still have the sense I'm being watched at times."

"Followed around? Spies hiding behind newspapers at the cafés?"

"It's all very well to joke, Claus, but I have my suspicions. That robbery. I'm not at all sure it was a real one. He drank my scotch, but if he liked scotch, there were two entire bottles. Why didn't he take them? Thieves don't have scruples."

"Perhaps he wanted to leave you something to drown your sorrows with."

"Or perhaps he wasn't after items, but information."

"Ah. And does the nurse have any?"

"None that I can imagine interesting anyone. Though, of course, who knows what that lot might find interesting."

"But Kate," he said. "You have to think how it looks to them."

"Do I? Why?"

"You do seem to have an attraction to trouble. Those men back there, or that time you came to my rooms. If my landlady had found out . . ."

"She didn't, did she? And if I were nefarious, I'd hardly be looking for trouble, would I?"

He didn't answer. The real question he wanted to ask was why she'd shown up at his apartment so soon after he'd been to White City. Checking to see if he was transmitting to Germany? But of course he couldn't. And before he could formulate another question, Kate turned in the seat to face him.

"Don't you see how it is?" she said. "With the Germans suspecting I work for the English, and the English suspecting I work for the Germans? I don't want to live my life worried what will happen. I did that for far too long, so now, who cares? Arrest me, if it makes them happier. Otherwise leave me alone."

A very convincing performance. Time to push, he thought. "It's natural, Kate. It happened to me at the beginning of the war, and for them, this is the beginning of the war with you."

"Who's *them?*" she said.

He shrugged. "Whoever you think is looking for information. The Hamburg trip," he said. Bertram had brought it up, and here his doubts had stuck. If Kate was a spy, what better way to ensure Claus's loyalty to Germany than to prey on his feelings for his mother's family?

"Yes?" she said.

"Was it hard to arrange?"

She was gazing at the passing fields of rape. Her reflection in the window looked yellow, haggard. "Define *hard*."

"Did you need passes? Special ones, since it had been destroyed?"

"Of course. One can't just travel about Germany. Especially a foreigner. Especially to high-security zones."

"Yet you were able to."

"I had family there."

"And friends who were German."

She shifted away from him. "Yes. Are these questions from your 'higher-ups'?"

"No," he said. It wouldn't do to have her wary. "If people suspect you, that's exactly the kind of thing they'd look for. But my questions are for my movie."

"But how?" she said. "Your character is moving around France, not Germany."

"True. Though in the immediate aftermath of liberation, it will perhaps not be much different. People suspicious of every new person."

"That's not restricted to war zones, believe me."

He lifted one hand off the wheel and stared at the speedometer and gas gauge, seeing neither, contemplating his next move.

"Sylvie," he said, after a small silence.

"What about her?"

"Nice of her to take your shift. But I thought you were angry with her."

"I can't like everyone I work with, Claus. You don't either. Herbert." She sighed and moved her purse between them. "There are times it comes in handy, when it means I'm free to do other things. Like today."

He suspected she was beginning to regret having done so; her voice was flat. For a mile or two they were silent. A cloud shadow raced beside them up a hill; more clouds were coming from the south. When the shadow reached the top, Kate said, "Do you know what's worst of all? That you doubt me."

Part of him was glad he hadn't fooled her. "I don't doubt you, Kate."

She laughed and said, "Of course not. You didn't do that to my apartment, did you?"

He recognized the move, one he'd made in difficult situations. If you feared the answer, you couched the question as a joke. The wrong reply could be passed off as unimportant, to the other, if not to yourself.

"Kate," he said. "My God." He was going to say more but stopped. The first rule of good acting: know when enough is enough. He saw himself from the director's chair, adjusted his body language, stiffened his jaw but didn't shake his head. Kept his eyes straight ahead, feigning anger, rather than checking to see if she believed him, and he got the result he wanted.

"Sorry," she said, and rested her hand on his forearm. "I'm just so sick of it."

After an appropriate pause, he said, "It's all right."

She seemed immeasurably sad. He wanted to believe that she was. On a distant hill the Caterham spires stood out, houses and stores hard up against the church, and abruptly he turned on a side road.

"What's this?" she said, her hand on the dashboard for balance.

"Our destination." The car bumped up the dirt track, the tall humped grass in the middle sweeping against the undercarriage. "Time to enjoy ourselves."

They passed an old mill with the millrace still running though the wheel had long since fallen apart; four stone houses and a stone church; a farm with a few horses, three dirty sheep, and a single gaunt cow. The unused road ran on. When the farm was out of sight, Claus pulled aside in the longer grass, bumped over a hidden rock, then turned off the engine.

"Why did you close your eyes?" she said.

"Prayer," he said. "Never sure it'll work again. And relief. Don't you hear it?"

"Hear what?"

"The countryside."

She opened the squeaking door and listened. The wind pushing through the tall trees like a river, crickets, a dog barking in the distance. She sat looking out over the blue oats bending in the wind, the green mass of the woods. "Yes," she said at last. "You were right to bring us here."

They walked toward the brow of the hill, Claus holding the hamper, Kate a blanket. They didn't talk. A squadron of fighters passed low overhead, rattling the plates in the hamper, and Claus began spreading out the blanket. "Can't that wait?" she said.

"I'm in no rush," he said. "I just like to set things up beforehand."

"All right." She opened the hamper and swore. "The dirty bugger!"

"Someone shortchange you?"

"The bastard Home Guard. He took our cider!"

Claus laughed.

"What's so funny?"

"The brave and loyal Home Guard."

"Given the shortages, a little stealing is all right," Kate said. "My landlord pinches a slice of bread every other day. But this is too much. He didn't have to take both bottles. I've a mind to report him."

Claus reached into the hamper. "Let's see. Bananas, cucumber salad, cream cheese–stuffed tomatoes, Scotch eggs, and some cheese. Looks like Hereford. Am I right?"

She nodded and sat.

"And what's this?" He pushed aside the cloth cover to reveal three pigeon feet poking from a pie crust. "Pigeon pie, is it? He didn't take that much."

"I suppose you're right. If he'd been a true bastard he'd have confiscated the lot."

"And it's a lot to confiscate. I got you at just the right time. And to think you almost didn't come."

"No," she said, plucking the warm grass beside her. "I was going to from the moment you asked. You'll think me foolish when I tell you why, but I had this odd fancy. Whoever broke in took some of my journals too. I found myself rereading remaining ones from the last war, passages about the soldiers and doctors I served with, some of my patients. And except for Horst, when I tried to recall their faces, I couldn't. They'd blurred into nothingness, as if I were looking at them under moving water, and since I wanted to see a face, I closed my eyes and concentrated and they floated to the surface and were borne away, just as I was about to see them clearly." She stopped and raised a hand, palm up, letting the grass fall out, as a sign of her difficulty.

"And what?" Claus said, leaning closer.

"And at last I did see a face, attached to name after name, but each time it was yours." She laughed. "You see, it's absurd! But since it was you I kept seeing, I supposed that it was you I *should* see. And so here I am."

The plates clattered in his hands. Kate looked at him.

"You'll need to take another break from your duties," she said. "It'll only get worse if you don't. I've seen it happen. A surgeon on the ward killed someone that way last week. His scalpel nicked a subclavian artery. The poor boy bled to death before we could stop it."

"Good thing I'm not operating then, isn't it?"

"Claus." She grabbed his wrist. "It doesn't matter what you're doing, you need to stop."

"I wish I could," he said.

She lay with her head in his lap, face turned to the sky, which was beginning to cloud up. In the distance a train whistle sounded, the engine smoke a jagged black smudge against the blue horizon. In this position, the bruises on her neck were just visible. He slid his fingers under her collar and pressed lightly.

"Ouch," she said.

"Sorry. Forgot."

He moved his hands a bit lower, kept them there. The truth was he'd wanted to see if they were real. He felt guilty for doubting her, yet even so doubted her about other things, if not the bruises.

"I've been thinking about your movie," she said.

"The train scene?"

"The woman's dilemma. You know, it's rather easy to turn your back on a German military band marching down the Champs Élysées, but what if it's some small German boys' choir singing at Notre Dame, or the Lyon symphony playing Bach, or a book on imperial

German gardens? Is paying for any of those collaboration? Have her struggle with that. The French will understand.

"And the war hasn't been bad for everyone." She recrossed her ankles. "You should see what's become of farmhouses. Indoor plumbing, pianos, fur coats, stained-glass windows, and even then they can't spend all they've made from their black-market successes. You'll want to work some of that in too."

"Now you sound pro-German."

"No. The farmers don't have it easy either. The Germans have already begun on them, burning their beehives, confiscating their seeds. And when boys write anti-German slogans on stone walls with tar, the local dairy farmers have all their milk requisitioned and the boys are made to churn it into butter. Then they clean the walls with it. Intentionally galling, you see, all that butter, all that labor, all that waste."

"Anti-German, too," he said, and shook his head. "You're a mess."

He'd meant it as a joke but she said, "Yes, I think so. Nationality means nothing, less than nothing. It's a disaster, if you ask me."

He smoothed her hair. Was she simply trying to disarm him? "What's brought this on?"

"This," she said. She sat up and faced him. "This picnic."

"You don't like it?"

"No. Yes. I love it." She shook her head. "I'm happy, but that's just it, you see. I can't stop thinking of France." She tore up stems of clover and rubbed them between her fingers, discarding them only to start over again. A car drove over a distant ridge, dust trailing up behind it. Its straining engine note reached them. "I hated watching what the Germans did to the Jews. Rounding them up, shipping them off, the rumors of their murders. But it started before that, immediately after the Germans came to France. The very next day the Jews were forced to clean the German soldiers' toilets and sweep the streets. The daily humiliation was horrifying, sickening to watch, and yet I did nothing."

He touched her wrist. "I know, Kate. I saw it in Germany. People tried to cover their Stars of David with newspapers on trams, and with their briefcases or purses when they walked. Looking at them made me feel as if I'd decreed they wear them myself, so I turned away, but of course that probably just made them think I despised them."

"Yes, but you didn't have to see it done to nurses you worked with, and then to realize that your having said nothing earlier meant that their being arrested later was easier. It didn't matter that I'd remained quiet because I'd feared making their lives worse. That I hadn't protested in the first place meant that I couldn't in the end."

"But I don't see the connection."

She laughed without humor. "It's that that wasn't what made me leave."

He shook his head, puzzled.

"Before I left, I kept noticing the German boots. New and noisy. Real leather. And all the parcels their soldiers carried. I knew what was coming, the deprivation. Not for the Germans, but for the rest of us. I'd seen it before. I'd started to live through it again this time and I knew it was only going to get worse. I'm sure it has. In preparation for the invasion, the French had started to rebel, minor things mostly, like burning fields of rape, but of course that didn't do anything to the Germans. What did they care? They had butter and they simply cut back on the margarine rations, which hit hardest those who could least afford the blows —the old, the young.

"The senseless deaths, the horrible hunger, the messages written on hotel walls for lost family members, those were all ahead of me. I'm afraid I didn't have sufficient courage to face that again. That decided me." She laughed again, more quietly. "So here I am, enjoying my picnic with you. If the wages of sin are death, the rewards of cowardice are much better."

She couldn't be acting. It seemed impossible. He looked away. "It's common sense, Kate, not cowardice. No one would go through it willingly."

"Perhaps not, but not everyone would have run away either. I wouldn't have, younger."

"Younger, you didn't know all you'd have to endure." It was a comfort to try and comfort her, to steer her through her doubts. It made his less forceful. But as soon as he thought that, she seemed the mirror of his own deception, and his thoughts turned black.

She shook her head. "I'm just tired of it."

"As am I."

"Are you, Claus? Really?"

"Of course."

She twirled the long grass around her forefinger, pulled some free and let it loose on the wind. "It's just that there's so much about you I can't figure out. Your secret code at the dog track and your refusal to tell Max the truth. It feels as if you're hiding things."

"What kind of things?"

"Like the radio. You were going to tell me about it. What did you mean?"

He shrugged to mask his surprise. "It's German. I've been suspected because of it. I wanted you to know the things I've been through, why I collect that information and pass it on. I've felt coerced into it for a long time."

"I can imagine."

"Can you?"

"Yes, of course. I lived under it in France, after all."

"And did you report to the Germans?"

"God, no. Or not in that sense. I worked for them, in hospitals, so yes, but I never told them anything."

"So how can you say you understand? It's not the same."

"Because nothing is ever simple, and because each of us makes deals with our own consciences. Yours must have made sense to you at one point, even if it no longer does."

He felt judged, and unfairly so, since she didn't know everything, but of course that was his fault. And he'd been guilty of judging her. It was a brilliant move, to cast doubt on him, a neat reversal, one that would take much time to undo. A flight of planes came from the south, shaking the ground, the same ones that had flown earlier toward France it seemed, probably a raid on Calais. Was it his imagination or were there fewer this time?

He was about to speak when she stood and slapped grass from her skirt.

"How about a little exploration?" she said.

"Oh?" he said, and raised an eyebrow. "What did you have in mind?"

She laughed. "Not that."

"I'd rather not," Claus said. "I like it here."

"Oh, please," she said, and held out her hand. "Don't be a stick-in-the-mud. You brought me all the way out here, after all. Don't you think you should indulge me?"

He laughed and shook his head.

"Fine." She turned. "You'll have to catch me then if you want to bring me back."

She was halfway up the hill when he started after her, and he'd just about caught up when she stopped abruptly below an old stone wall nearly hidden in the tall grass.

"Oh, Claus, look. We'll pretend it's Hadrian's Wall and everything beyond it is unknown land. Wild. We'll make it our own."

Kate ran her hand over the stones as they walked. Beyond the wall, fields of wildflowers stretched toward a creek-fed pond, two worn wooden benches to one side. Buttercups and dwarf daisies spilling down the far bank, purple myrtle nearer, the scent of wild onions on the wind.

"The barbarians are gardeners," Claus said.

"Yes. Quite the landscapers, aren't they? Well, let's see how it looks up close." She climbed up on the wall.

"No." Claus tried to tug her back. "Let's not. Let's stay here." He was standing shin-deep in a drift of leaves, thick as in the fall but healthy and green. From a buzz-bomb blast, which couldn't have been far off. He needed to ask her more questions, though he hadn't decided which ones.

"Oh, do come," she said, pulling her hand free. "Let's not let a few benches stop our adventure. Please, Claus?"

Before he could respond she jumped down on the far side and began splitting the tall grass like a ship the sea. A hundred yards distant was a farmhouse with green shutters and a red roof. "It looks like something from a fairy tale," Kate said. "It's deserted. Let's go look at it, shall we?"

It wasn't deserted; it had animals. "If you think it's deserted, you don't know farms," Claus said.

"And if you think we can just wander about without their permission, then you don't know the English. They'll think we're after chickens and you're liable to get a backside full of buckshot if we don't."

"But I don't want to wander about. I want to go back. We have to leave before long." Her shift at the hospital, his as a warden, another scheduled broadcast. And he hadn't figured her out yet.

"Please? It's the only thing I've asked."

He blew out a heavy breath. "All right. You go in. I'll wait at the gate."

But the gate was open, an old woman standing by it with two stoneware bottles in her hands, as if she'd expected them.

She had, it turned out; the dogs had been barking, and Peter was snorting up a storm.

"Peter?" Kate said.

"He's in the garden, that one." She turned to lead the way. "Mind him. Sometimes he doesn't take to strangers. My name's Helen." She said the dogs were safe inside the house.

The garden turned out to be a small graveled patch bordered by boxwood, Peter a pig who looked about to charge when he saw Claus. Helen bent and cupped his shoulder with one hand. "Now, Peter. That's enough." When he sat on his hind legs she produced a withered apple from her apron pocket, after which he climbed onto a small deck chair.

"Likes to sun himself," Helen said. "He'll be fine now." She turned to them. "Now what about you two? Tell me all about yourselves and what you're doing here."

"A picnic," Claus said. "We just wanted to be sure you didn't mind."

"Mind? It's nice to have people about. In fact, I was going to bring you these." The bottles clinked together when she held them out. "But Peter wouldn't let me go on my own and I was afraid he'd bite your ankles. Here," she said, and handed them each one. "My own ginger beer. Enjoy."

Kate unwired the cork and opened it. The fizzing soda tickled her nose and she sneezed and giggled, and Claus caught a glimpse of the happy child she must have been. They both tasted it.

"Rhubarb!" Kate said. "Just as our cook used to make it! Are you Welsh?"

"No, dear. Born and bred on this very farm. Is it how the Welsh do?"

"Ours did," Kate said, and drank some more before giving a contented sigh. "My, how delicious. And look at your tomatoes. I have to stand in queues for hours to get any, and when I do, they don't look like that. Write down this location," she said, and winked at Claus. "We'll have to come back and pinch some."

"No need for that," Helen said. "I'll give you some before you go."

Her curiosity wasn't easily slaked, though she seemed most interested in Kate's affairs, her time in France. She wanted to know what it was like to live under the Germans. "I was sure they were going to come, you see."

Kate told her a few small details—that tram seats next to Germans were always unoccupied, and that the French had become adept at letting lit cigarettes fall on German laps. "So adept that by the end of '42 smoking was no longer allowed on trains."

They sat on a bench, and Peter watched them talk, his head bobbing back and forth as if the conversation were an especially fascinating tennis match, and Claus noticed the displaced gutter, the hanging shutter, the crumbling garden wall that meant there was work to be done on the farm and no man to do it. It made him want to leave all the more quickly, but Kate seemed settled in for a long talk.

He watched Helen's pleasure as Kate told her about a recipe with lingonberries she'd loved in Germany years before, and the thought came to him: What would an elderly woman in the country do for Kate if Kate *was* a spy? Nothing, he realized, not a thing. Bertram was wrong, it was as simple as that. Her kindness was entirely unfeigned.

He felt as if he was able to breathe again, as if a too tight wrap had been removed from around his ribs. Kate seemed to sense it too, reaching out and taking his hand.

Helen suggested she get her Victrola. "We could have some music. I'd turn on the wireless but it's stopped working."

"Could you fix it, Charles? You're good with mechanical things, aren't you?"

Was she alluding to her radio, which he'd so skillfully ruined? Did she suspect him of that? Impossible; her look was entirely ingenuous. It infuriated him how Bertram lurked in every corner, but he couldn't let on. "Cameras I can do. But I'm worthless with radios."

"Yes," Kate said, dropping Claus's hand as she stood. "And even if he could, I'm afraid I shouldn't have suggested it. We can't linger. It's time we were off. Past time, really. I have work tonight, in London."

"That far off," Helen said, as if it were hundreds of miles. "Can't you miss it, dear?" The depth of her loneliness was apparent in her suddenly moist eyes. She reminded him of Winifred. "I've got stew almost ready. A bit small for the three of us, but with a salad I think we could make do."

She removed the lid from a small wooden box nearby, revealing two clay pots nested in hay.

Kate picked up the overstuffed pillow that had been beneath the lid. "What's this?" she said.

"A hay box," Claus said, involuntarily. "My mother used one for porridge and stew. The food cooks in the hay and needs only a bit of warming in the oven to finish it."

"How smart you are!" Kate said. "I'd never have guessed it."

He recognized Helen's smile, the same one his mother had offered whenever astonished city people commented on farmers' surprising intelligence.

Kate stood. "Well, Helen. I'm afraid we can't stay. But I would like to come back. Your place is absolutely restorative."

"All right, dear," Helen said, and turned away to dab an eye. "But please make it soon. And when you do come, make enough noise for me to hear you too. Even though he knows you now, I can't guarantee Peter's reception."

Most of the ride back to the city they were quiet, Kate palming Helen's tomatoes, Claus speeding to make time. The sky had turned quickly gray, and thunder began to sound the closer they came to the city, over which clouds hung low like a pall, like the smoke from fires during the Blitz. At last Kate shifted the tomatoes from one hand to the other. "I'll cook you something with these you'll like," she said. "Tomato soup. It needs yogurt."

"I can get that," he said.

"Yes?"

"Herbert."

She looked out the window at the remains of a windmill. "You should probably stay away from him, don't you think? His lot only ever bring trouble."

He felt judged again but he didn't have a ready reply, so they rode in silence the rest of the way. He wanted to tell her what he'd felt when he was watching her talk with Helen, but he couldn't figure out how to bring it up. The car seemed the wrong place for it. They joined the London road near Norbury, where two girls were playing ping pong against an alley wall, and passed under a windowsill with a pair of red boxing gloves beaded with rain hanging from it. Water spumed up from the damp shiny pavement behind cars, and Piccadilly with its streaming traffic was slower going. White Horse Street was packed with pedestrians: mothers with their prams hurrying from the closing stores and soldiers looking for bargains in the side alleys before the rain turned hard. He pulled in front of her building just as it did, and they sat in the car listening to it drum on the roof, watching it blur the outlines of people and buildings as if melting them. Kate was looking at her building.

"Trust me to make it on my own?" she said.

He laughed. "Yes."

She turned to him. "Trust me?"

*Clever woman.* No wonder Bertram suspected her—a woman with brains always terrified him. Madge had played the fool around him, and Bertram had never seemed to realize it was an act.

"Of course."

"Then what was all that about earlier? Those questions."

"I was trying to figure out some things."

"About me?"

"No. Me."

"You?" She paused. "And did you?"

"I did."

She waited. Thunder sounded again, louder, and lightning flashed above them. "My," she said. "Talkative. So I'll ask. What did you figure out?"

He touched her thigh. "Sorry." How to say it? He should have trusted his instincts about her from the start. Bertram had told him that a good spy had a sixth sense about such things, but he wasn't a spy, really, he was simply a man who'd twice been caught up in times when the forms of his ancestors cast a suspicious shadow over his life, a man who'd been trapped in that shadow by those who seemed to have the power to move both the steady sun and the inconstant moon. He wanted to come out from under that shadow, and this seemed to be all that Kate wanted too.

The clock struck the hour, interrupting his thoughts. She turned up her wrist to look at her watch.

"Oh, dear," she said. "I was hoping you'd be able to come up."

"Too rushed?"

"I'm afraid so." She shook her head. "Sylvie's shift, I have to take it. I promised."

He held up both hands, as if in surrender. "I understand."

"You're not angry?"

"No. I've work tonight too. Warden duties. I'll be busy with them a few days."

"You need to rest, Claus. From either the MOI or as a warden. You're exhausted."

"Everyone is."

"All right. I warned you." She brightened. "I'll be busy too. But Sunday morning, bright and early, you can stop by. I'll make tea. And your favorite pancakes."

"I'd like that," he said. He'd have to get more potatoes from somewhere, but this was a good sign. And it would give him a chance to think over how he was going to tell her.

"Wheat with lemon juice," she said, and opened the door to step out. The rain had lessened.

"You!" he said. But he was happy. Teasing was the ultimate forgiveness.

The air had a peculiar smoky scent, almost charred, like roasting chestnuts, and they both said at the same time, "Christmas." It made them smile. He handed her the wicker hamper from the boot. "Do you want me to wait? Drive you?"

"No. Thank you, though. I'll bathe first. It'll be a while."

"I don't mind. I could sit by the tub."

She laughed and leaned in to kiss him. "Sweet, how you're always thinking of me."

As she ran into her open doorway he called out again, "Sunday!"

She smiled and waved and disappeared up the dark stairs.

Crouched over his radio, Claus forced himself to concentrate, ratcheting the dial back and forth, zeroing in on the frequency. With the lightning and thunder it was harder than normal to pick up Hamburg, almost impossible to hear them at the usual volume. He turned it up ever so slightly and began keying his message. Weather first, a few rumors about Plymouth, and then the real material, times and locations of V-1 landings. It had taken him the better part of half an hour to decide how much to alter them—a little or a lot. Mr. Morgan was already done with his bath by the time Claus had settled on the latter, since small changes were probably meaningless, especially after this long, and if he could convince them that their telemetry had been thrown startlingly off they might adjust accordingly. A big leap, but it would put many more of the V-1s in the country. Helen. Well, the odds were long that any would land near her, odds he was willing to take. At last. All his sparkling reasons for not having done it before couldn't hide the fact that he'd been scared of the consequences.

When he switched to receive he got a request to repeat the last part of his message. The coordinates hadn't gone through evidently, or they were decoding as he tapped out the message and someone in Germany was stunned by how far off the landings were. Normally he wouldn't repeat during a broadcast, but he decided in this case it was worth the risk.

The floor creaked outside his door. Mrs. Dobson, spying on him? He wasn't worried. He closed his eyes and concentrated, keying in the last of the information in exactly the same fashion one more time. He wasn't going to make too many more broadcasts anyway, and if Bertram found out and it meant jail, that prospect wasn't as terrifying as it once had been. They wouldn't shoot him—not even Bertram was capable of that—and they couldn't lock him up forever. The war was bound to end soon, now that the Allied troops had broken loose from Normandy. Herbert was betting that it would all be over by Christmas.

# AUGUST 4

WHEN THE MATRON CALLED HER, Kate was on the
ward, dressing the burned hands of an elderly woman. Each
finger took several minutes, as they had to be done separately.

"You have a visitor," the matron said. "A man." The matron's
admonishing look didn't get a rise from Kate; she wasn't about to
apologize for someone coming to see her that she hadn't asked to. Or
perhaps it was the V-1s that made the matron snap; they seemed to
be hitting now with greater frequency and that had everyone on
edge. Kate continued to wrap the gauze as the matron turned on her
white heels. "At the main entrance."

It had been a week since she'd seen Claus. He hadn't returned
her calls, though she'd left messages for him at the MOI, or if he had,
it hadn't been while she was home. She let him wait a few minutes
while she checked her patient's heels and hips for bedsores, wanting to do a thorough job and happy to hold, however briefly, the upper hand.

"All set, Mrs. Bellers," she said, and rolled her onto her back.

Mrs. Bellers held up her bandaged hands. "Will they ever heal?"

"They will," she said, and squeezed her shin through the sheets.
"Not as good as new, but you'll be able to use them." She didn't like
to lie to patients.

In the hallway were two men, one younger and taller, the other short,
bow-tied, florid-faced, and jowly; he looked like someone she might
see on the ward in a few years after he had a heart attack. They stood

before a large, ornately framed mirror, a gift of some lord long ago, which Kate had tried several times to have moved—the burn ward was nearby, for God's sake—but she'd been told it had been there forever and so it would remain. The younger man, almost boyish, was eyeing his reflection unobtrusively, and as she got closer he faced her completely and raised his hat, showing that the unfortunate orange coloring of some Celts, the freckled face and hands, extended to his hair, yet her eyes went to the other man. She'd lived through these interrogations before. He was making an effort to appear nonchalant, studying the upturned toe of one worn shoe as if he'd just noticed a spot on it, which only reinforced the notion that he was a big noise, and she had no doubt that he was the one in control. One of Horst's favorite lines from Seneca sprang to mind. *Et sceleratis sol oritur;* "the sun shines even on the wicked."

"Mrs. Zweig?"

"Yes?"

"I'm Bertram Swales. I have something of yours." From a leather satchel he took a bundle. She recognized immediately the pomegranate-colored calf-leather-bound journals.

"You found them! Where?"

He paused. "This is a bit difficult. Do you know a Charles Murphy?"

"Claus? Yes."

"And his relationship to you?"

"He's . . ." She paused.

"Nothing?"

"No. Not at all. A friend. A good friend."

"Yes, you left a message for him at the MOI, didn't you?"

"Then you know I know him."

"He's dead, I'm afraid."

"What, how?" Her devastation was such that at first she didn't feel it. She seemed to have no body at all, to not be present in any corporeal sense, and then her legs grew enormously heavy and began to tremble. They were liquid, made of water, how did they hold her up? She felt like a building that somehow managed to stand though its foundation buckled.

The intuition that Swales had planned this public announcement in order to gauge her response helped her gather herself; she made an effort not to show more. She decided not to sit, determined not to give him that satisfaction.

"And those?" she said of the journals. She couldn't stop herself from reaching for them. "What do they have to do with that?"

He put them back in his satchel. "That's the tricky part, I'm afraid. We think he was a spy. Do you mind if we ask you a few questions?"

Her heart was beating rapidly, her face coloring, but she would not betray herself. Or Claus. She was careful not to speak until she was sure she could control her voice. "A spy? You're mistaken. But ask away," she said.

"Do you recognize this?"

It was a display case, filled with pipes.

"Not exactly."

"Could you explain that?"

"Yes. I've not seen them, but Claus told me about them. His collection, that is. Nothing about the box they were in. The pipes, how he found them, why he kept them."

"Claus? You've called him that twice. Did you know a lot about him?"

"Yes. Shouldn't I have?"

"Did you know he had a radio?"

"Many of us do."

"Not one for broadcasting, I presume."

"Broadcasting?"

"To Germany. He was shot while doing so."

"Shot?"

Swales had already moved on. "Did he give you anything?"

"No." Her voice was barely a croak but she looked directly at him.

"And this, is this familiar?"

"Certainly." It was the wax rubbing Claus had made of the gravestone on their visit to clean her family's grave. Had they taken it from her rooms? It was horrible to think of this man pawing through her things, through Claus's. She read the Latin aloud. "'*Est unusquisque faber ipsae suae fortunae,*'" then translated it. "'Every man is the artisan of his own fortune.'"

"You know Latin?"

"Claus did."

"Really?" Bertram studied it.

"Did he get it wrong?" she asked.

"No. That's a fine translation. It's just that he wasn't known to understand Latin. No matter." He rolled it up and turned to go, then abruptly faced her again and held out a scrap of paper. "Do you know what this is?"

She did. It was torn from the dog-track betting sheet, Cursed Woman's line. She decided swiftly that she wouldn't tell him. He wouldn't sully that day too.

"No," she said, turning it over as if checking for clues before handing it back. "I'm afraid I can't help you."

"Don't apologize," he said, and lifted his hat. "You've been far more helpful than you can imagine." He made to go.

"Please," she said, stopping him. "Will there be a funeral?"

"No."

"Nor a service? But there must be."

"Who would come?"

"I would. Coworkers, perhaps, from the MOI. I should think they'd want to."

"Not if he was a spy."

"I've told you he wasn't."

Swales smiled at her, indulgently. She wanted to slap him.

"And my things?" she said. "May I have them back?"

"I'm afraid we must hold on to them for now."

Hours later she emerged from the hospital to thin clouds and crisp air. Swales and his assistant Taylor were sitting in a screened gazebo in Green Park, where Swales had guessed she'd walk. She tracked down the elderly park attendant and rented a chair, settled against its cool wooden slats and closed her eyes, breathed in the smell of the crushed grass. She might have dozed, but across the gravel path some American servicemen were playing a game of catch and their shouts echoed, their easy laughter, the smack of the ball in their leather gloves. They had patches sewn onto their shoulders, red number ones. She hadn't seen that before; they were a new unit, though she'd heard of them. Weren't they already in Normandy? Replacements, then; the death tolls were appalling, though still nothing compared to the last war.

She shuddered, thinking of Swales molding that baby-faced orange boy. He was an odious man, the kind of man who traded in doubt, leaving bits of it behind like weeds because it pleased him. She wouldn't believe a single thing he said, even if he told her the world was at war.

He would have been the one Claus reported to, the higher-up Claus had referred to. He'd have had a hold on Claus from the start. She could imagine the story's outlines, Claus with vague nationality at a time when borders were supposed to be impermeable, the pressure points obvious to all, but what had caused Claus to ransack her apartment? The moment Swales held out the journals to her, she suspected him. Had it been Claus? If so, why had he doubted her? And what had driven him to such fury? She was at least certain that her face had shown none of that, to Swales's great displeasure. He'd wanted to see her doubt Claus.

Claus. Charles. Claus within, Charles without, and behind both apparently someone else, someone secret. Peel, pith, and some inner, unknown fruit. Which was seed, which soil? Immaterial, really. The soil had worn out, the seed rotted. Though he had seemed different, calmer, sitting in that car. Hadn't he been about to tell her something?

The pale disk of the sun through the clouds wasn't warming, and she sat upright and pulled her cloak more tightly around herself. A matron passed with a line of dozens of children, all about two years old, their left wrists tied together with string, as if she were a kite and they her long ragged tail. Not a school, as school was out of session, and no one family would have so many. Orphans, she decided. She'd been pregnant once and lost the baby, far along. The lingering effects of malnutrition from the blockade, the doctor had told her, confirming her suspicions. Horst must have known too but said nothing. Then regular miscarriages for several years, black years. Life gives you a message and eventually you come to accept it. Though she was able now to take joy in the presence of boisterous children, the old bruises began to ache, and she stood and walked toward the tube.

"Should we have her followed?" Taylor said.

"The German woman?" Bertram said.

"Yes. She could disappear, blend in. She's English, after all."

"Not thoroughly," Bertram said.

It had been the same with Murphy, the Irish in him made him impossible to trust. He'd understood Latin, for God's sake. And if the tapes from the car had revealed nothing about the German woman, aside from the unpleasant surprise that she'd visited Murphy's apartment, they'd told plenty about Murphy. Along with the broadcasts they'd been monitoring, on which he'd begun to alter the times and coordinates of V-1 strikes, they showed that he was utterly compromised. He'd been about to tell the German woman of his double role, Bertram was sure of it, which would have been disastrous. He'd already told her much that he shouldn't have—there was the comment about the "higher-ups" for one thing—but something had changed on that outing. Murphy's tone was different on the ride back, the doubts he'd expressed on the way out gone. At some point he was going to have to ask the Zweig woman about that. Luckily they'd stopped him in time, but she'd not have been able to work her insidious magic if Murphy hadn't been bent from the start.

"*Facilis est descensus Averni*," he said to Taylor. "'Easy is the descent to Hell,' for the Murphys and the Zweigs of the world. No," he added. "No reason to stop her. After all, where would she go?"

"Bristol."

"Where her people are from? We'd find her soon enough."

"Before she could do any damage?"

"The breakout from Caen is accomplished. Even if the Germans move the mechanized units now, they'll be too late."

"Then we don't have to watch her at all?"

"Of course we do. Simply none too closely. She'll stay here, try to find out what she can."

It was evident the boy wanted to go on. "Yes?" Bertram said.

"It's just, well." Taylor breathed in, gathering his courage. "Won't she be even more cautious, now that she thinks we believed Murphy a spy?"

"That's what we want. She'd have been vigilant, but now she'll pass on to them our certainty, which will increase the Germans'. In their minds, we wouldn't have killed him if he weren't a spy. We planted a few surprises through him near the end, and those will flower in due time. Events on the Continent will unfold quickly, and they'll be desperate. Sooner or later she'll reveal herself. She hasn't a transmitter, we know that. But she might have been given the name of someone who has. All we need is for her to lead us to him."

"I suppose it's better that Murphy died, then."

"Unfortunately, yes. He may save thousands by his death, something he was no longer able to do for us alive. I suspected something like this would happen once the Germans sent Einschuffen. He was meant to provide cover for the German woman, and it indicated they wanted to bypass Murphy, that they no longer trusted him. And now that he's gone, the German woman becomes even more valuable to them, more necessary."

"And you don't think we should bring her in then? She seems awfully competent."

"Yes. Appeared to shrink within her skin when we told her Murphy was dead. But did you notice? Pulled herself together very quickly. A cool customer. Not a surprise, really. She must have known it meant Murphy had destroyed her rooms, but she didn't react at all. And she certainly recognized this." He smoothed the dog-track line flat on the gazebo railing. "Did you see her eyes widen?" He ran his fingers over the numbers slowly from one end to the other, as if reading Braille. "We'll have to hold on to it until we figure out exactly what it is."

*Cursed Woman.* How apt. Further proof that Murphy had been a fool. Not that Swales had needed it. He'd never seen a woman more in control of herself. She was almost to the subway entrance. He didn't have to watch her, not yet. He had the journals. There might be clues in them, or in the script that Murphy had been writing. Max had given it to him. Though incomplete, it was good, Max said. Very. He seemed pained at having misled Murphy, had absolutely refused to continue the charade once Murphy had been wounded by the V-1, which Bertram hadn't anticipated. His truculence would have to be watched. He hadn't anticipated Murphy falling for the German woman either, though he couldn't blame him for that. She was quite striking, and obviously very smart, as manipulative women often were; he would have to look through the script to see if she might have influenced him. Something might have slipped through that she hadn't intended.

Taylor was leaning forward. He seemed as eager as a hound to spring after her. Bertram rested a hand on his shoulder.

"Don't worry," he said. "She'll make a mistake, they always do. Murphy did. Then she'll be ours." He took his pipe and pouch from a jacket pocket and began stuffing the bowl full of tobacco with his thumb.

Near the subway entrance she passed long ornamental grasses that lay limp and bent, like seaweed after a retreating tide, like the starbursts of fireworks made palpable and frozen. The warm air rushed up past her as she entered the tube. Halfway down the stairs she stopped, contemplated doubling back to see if anyone was following her, then decided against it and continued her descent. There had been the accusation of spying at the end of the last war too. It would never end.

On the platform she passed the pale souls waiting for a train and kept moving, past others, paler still, who'd come to live here. The smells of urine and unwashed skin. Bunk beds, chests, blankets. They had bothered Claus for some reason; she wished she'd asked why. She stood near a small three-legged dog and watched an extremely short man shave himself in a kind of mirror he'd rigged up. It wasn't one mirror, really, but dozens, made from the shards of others fitted into a warped frame. They returned to her gaze a nearly infinite number of her own reflections.

Swales. The war was almost over. Peace would come. Perhaps it was better that Claus hadn't survived. If under Swales's influence the war had made Claus into the man that could distrust her, what would the peace have done to him?

In a way it didn't matter. Though his death was another unbearable loss, it wasn't just the past Swales had been holding out to her when he'd produced the journals. That gesture had trapped her like an insect in amber, had swung shut her future too, the past not only prologue but epilogue. He'd known she'd reach for the journals, but really, what would she want them for? To write in them again?

She didn't need to. Innocent communion with the familiar was no longer possible. What would she write that she hadn't before? Desolation and disaster? She knew all that; she'd simply forgotten. She wouldn't again. It scared her how easily she could slip back into that line of thinking. She needed only to scrape off a bit of rust in order to reveal the long-established life beneath.

The train would be coming soon, and she found herself leaning down the tracks, waiting for it to clatter into the station, trying to spy out its lone headlamp far down the dark sloping tunnel as the train bawled toward her. She could almost feel her skin hardening as she waited, the carapace forming. It wasn't there yet. It would come. She leaned forward farther still, waiting, eyes closed, expecting a warm wind to push her back. Horst, Claus. Twice men had lured her into the light and twice the light had not been strong enough to keep her. She would not be lured out again, not by hope, not by Swales, not by the rumble of the subway train whose speeding approach she felt now, about to envelop her entire trembling body.